THE OTHER MRS. SMITH

a novel by
Bonnie Burstow

inanna poetry & fiction series

INANNA PUBLICATIONS AND EDUCATION INC.
TORONTO, CANADA

ALSO BY BONNIE BURSTOW

FICTION
The House on Lippincott

NON-FICTION
Psychiatry and the Business of Madness
Radical Feminist Therapy

*This novel is dedicated to my cherished old friends
Don Weitz, Carla McKague, Wendy Funk,
Sue Clark-Wittenberg, Mel Starkman, Connie Neil,
Shirley Johnson, and Leonard Roy Frank
—heroic warriors, all of you.*

*It is dedicated likewise to my long deceased father,
Sam Grower, and my paternal grandmother, Molly Grower.*

A LITTLE MATTER OF SOME BINDERS

A T APPROXIMATELY TEN A.M. on the first Saturday of November 1977, Gerald Smith began ascending the main stairway of a large two-storey house, a bucket of slightly murky water in one hand, a raggedy mop in the other, the end of a grey dusting cloth peeking out of his back pocket. It was not his house. He was not being paid to clean it. But who could not see that Nomi still needed help? Perhaps always would? And if he had let her down initially, let her down with all the consequences that this entailed, sure as shit is a cat, he never would again. Yup, Miu was on his case about how much time he spent here, and yes he adored Miu—adored her to distraction—and yes he owed Miu for continuing to be his own sweet honey, but there were other considerations. Had he not originally dragged everyone from Winnipeg to Toronto just so that he and Miu could be together? So the least she could do was cut a guy some slack. Besides, Nomi was his friend, was as loyal to him as he was to her. And doing for Nomi, why by now that was simply who he was. Had been since he first began getting an inkling of the extent of her tragedy. And this was family. Also—and how could he possibly hope to explain this?—being around those binders felt important because there was more to this whole business than meets the eye.

In truth, there was more to Gerald Smith himself than meets the eye, "or less," his wife Miu would jest, "depending on how you think about it, right?" He was a decent soul who would lend a hand to anyone in distress. "Tender-hearted to a fault," Miu called it. And everyone could see that, but unbeknownst to most people, coupled with this decency was a dim view of the world. While he didn't believe in evil, deep in his bones Gerald was convinced that the forces of destruction had progressed so far that those with vision had to work tirelessly. "Not to improve the world exactly," he would tell Miu, "though heck, I'm all for that. Just to maintain the status quo, though, you know, of course," he would add, a twinkle in his eye, "yours truly's not exactly what folk would call 'status quo.'"

Indeed, he was not. Nonetheless, even most conventional people instinctively liked Gerald; and he counted on that. While there were long months when he would not dream of doing so, time and again, he would approach perfect strangers, this inviting smile on his face, as if to say, "Who have we here? I'm Gerald Smith; and, hey, you and me, we're gonna be buds." And likely as not, they would smile back. These days, of course, he would observe people first—try to get a sense of who they were. And fortunately, he had a good eye. Good but fallible. And so, of course, Miu worried.

Gerald was nearing forty, but a casual onlooker could easily have mistaken him for a man just starting out in life. Why but a week last Sunday, a young engineer whom he had stumbled upon at a party had jumped to precisely this conclusion. "Guys our age, we need the freedom to do our own thing, right?" the man had asserted, raising his beer mug and giving Gerald a knowing look. "Wouldn't do to get saddled with kids and a mortgage." Recollecting the exchange, Gerald chuckled to himself, then mounted the last stair, set down the bucket, and began cleaning the floor—first the black-and-white tiles in the washroom, then the long stretch of gold linoleum in the hall.

On the short side—a fact he seldom lost sight of—Gerald was five feet, five and a half inches. "Five *and a half*," he made a point of telling his friends, puffing out his chest and hooking his thumbs into the top edges of his trouser pockets. "Not just five, eh?" He had a round face, a dimple on his chin, and skin as smooth as a baby's bottom. He had short cropped hair—no sign of thinning—but people seldom noticed the thick hair, for his head was generally covered by a Panama hat.

Gerald was a meticulous dresser. Old style. Everything tailored, polished, ornamented. Today was different. Jeans for cleaning, his Panama hat tilted slightly to one side.

Still chucking over the exchange with the young man, Gerald finished mopping the hall, then eyed it carefully. *Yes, yes. It'll do. But no. Just a minute. A spot over there.*

He leaned forward and scrubbed the offending stretch of linoleum, humming to himself. Coming upon a smaller spot seconds later, he shrugged his shoulders. Then he laid the mop against the wall, removed the dust cloth from his pocket, and entered the master bedroom.

The problem hit him almost instantly. One of the black binders was lying in the middle of the floor. And if *one* of the binders was out of place, some of the others might also be. Now a speck of dirt on the floor, Nomi could care less about, but as he knew only to well, simple though this might be for anyone else, on a bad day, binders out of place could cause her no end of misery.

Gerald approached the bookcase and immediately began surveying the top shelf. The rest of the binders, yup, they were all present and accounted for: the other two black ones, the three red ones, the two green ones, the two yellow ones, the orange one. And yup, the labels were still sticking. But just look at that! Hopelessly out of order. And even with the labels intact, why it could take her from now till the ships come home to know what's what. *Les, damn it! Had to be Les.*

"Lester, Lester Reginald, get your motherfuckin' ass up here this second. This second," he bellowed.

"*This* second. Geez!" Can't I at least have *two* seconds," came a child's voice.

"Les, *now.*"

"But...."

"No buts. No ifs. No maybes. Right now!"

At this, a nine-year-old boy with long curly brown locks came bounding up the stairs. He hesitated for a second on the top stair, then plunked his right foot down on the wet linoleum and scurried over to Gerald, leaving a trail of footprints behind him.

Taking in the footprints, Gerald uttered, "Sorry to make you trudge through that." Then he laid his hand on the boy's shoulder and pointed toward the binder on the floor. "Les, see the binder over there."

"Ye-e-e-e-s," answered Les. "Hey, I don't have trouble seeing."

"Just drop the smart ass. The binder, it shouldn't be on the floor."

"No."

"And the binders in here," he added, pointing to the bookshelf, "totally out of order. You were into the binders again, weren't you?"

"Sort of."

"And what did I tell you about Nomi's binders?"

"That I'm s'pposed to stay away from them."

"Look. I don't want to come down on you like a sledgehammer or anything, but I need to wrap my noggin' around this. You were playing with the binders, and somehow, well, you got them in a jumble, that it? Some sort of accident, was it?"

Les begins smirking, but says nothing.

Gerald takes in the smirk and presses on. "Accident or on purpose?"

Again, no answer.

"Les?"

"What?"

"Come on. Help me out here, son. Accidental or on purpose?"

Les shrugs his shoulders.

"I'm waiting."

"Kinda both."

Gerald's eyes narrow. "Accidental at first, *then* on purpose?"

"Well, yeah."

Gerald crouches down and looks his son straight in the eye. "Why did you do it, boy?" he asks.

Once again, Les shrugs.

"Okay. Okay. There's two things here. Number one. You're never never never to play with the binders. They're Nomi's. They're personal; and they're just too important. And number two, whatever you may think, purposely confusing her like this, c'mon now, fella, it's not funny. It's not even clever. How can something this easy to pull off be clever? But more than that, it's cruel. Now I know you're a good kid. You're my beautiful brilliant little boy. And I know you didn't mean any harm. But this, it won't do."

Les was silent, and the smirk had vanished from his face. Gerald took in the change and realized that for the time being anyway, Les was sorry, but he also knew that Les was not about to say so. Now why most boys find apologizing demeaning was beyond him, but he respected his son's sensitivity and did not press the point, though he knew that the matter was hardly settled. Then this worry began niggling away at Gerald. He glanced nervously at the wall near the dresser, then focused back on Les. He hesitated for a second, as if unsure. "The notes," he finally asked, "Les boy, you didn't by any chance start messing with the notes again too, did you?"

What Gerald was referring to were the index cards. In addition to an extensive collection of photographs, index cards graced the walls of this otherwise conventional looking house—lined index cards, writing scribbled all over them. Index cards on every solitary wall in the master bedroom. Index cards on three of the four kitchen walls. Index cards in the washroom, just above the towels.

Les assured Gerald that he had not touched the cards, that he would not dream of touching them. Relieved, Gerald rose and urged Les to go outside and play, promising to join him in about an hour. "Hold your horses," he added just as Les reached the door. "Your shoes. Off with the wet shoes, and when you get downstairs, grab a rag and…"

Les turned and faced Gerald. "How am I s'pposed to know where the rags are?" he objected. "Geez!"

"You're here every weekend. How can you not know? No. No. Scratch that. You can hardly be expected to know the ins and outs of two households. Grab a rag from…"

"From under the sink," announced Les causally. He paused, took in the bewildered expression on Gerald's face, and giggled. "Gotchya."

"Why so you have," admitted Gerald, grinning good-naturedly and giving his son the thumbs-up. "Had me totally buffaloed. Anyways, grab a rag from under the sink, and wipe the bottom of your shoes. Be a pal and wipe them real good, okay? Now scat."

Losing not a second, Les kicked off his shoes, picked them up, hopped his way down the hallway on one foot, then charged down the stairs in a gallop, yelling, "The cavalry's coming; the cavalry's coming." Alone once again with the binders, Gerald adjusted his collar, then began arranging them in order. Black Binder Number One on the far left. Then Black Binder Two. Then a space for Black Binder Three, then the three red binders, then the yellow binders, then the green, then the orange. Good, he told himself. Mission accomplished. No. Mission not yet accomplished. He turned around, approached Black Binder Number Three, picked it up, and stared at it sadly.

Taped to the front cover was an index card which read "Memories/Thoughts: October 2, 1971 to January 29, 1973." Gerald nodded with recognition as he took in those words, then began flipping through the pages. While it was a four-inch binder that could have easily accommodated over two hundred pages, he didn't have long to flip, for precious few had been inserted. Realizing how unlikely it was that anything new had been added, he closed the binder and started to slip it back into place. Something, however, drew him back. Despite the fact that he knew everything inside that binder more or less by heart—he had typed a fair part of it for Nomi and poured over it with her many a Sunday morning over crumpets and tea—something always drew him back to Black Binder Number Three. And so it is, Gerald took a break from his labour, pulled out the binder again, sat down on a chair, and began to read. While the binder held almost a year and a half of Nomi's memories and so might be reasonably expected to cover many items great and small, this, only this, is what Gerald found:

Pound. Pound. Pound. Adonoi, Mary Mother of God, Buddha, Ishtar, Inanna, Allah, anyone with ears that receive and a heart that quickens, make it stop. Pound. Pound. Pound. I swear on the holy Torah, I swear on the blessed cross, I swear on the winds that lift up and the rivers that tumble from the Creator's bountiful lips, I will do anything. Do this, and lo, I will walk through the rest of my days humbly revering thy name. I will set up a table for thee in the presence of mine enemies. Night and day, will I sing hallelujah, my knees flat against the earth, my eyes lowered, my hands brought together in prayer. I will press the horn of a ram to my grateful lips and issue a call to all corners of the earth; and the sweet young children, innocence dripping from their milky breath, will come running, running, running toward the sea; and we will all join hands and ascend to the glorious orchard. Then we will gather together in the New Jerusalem and sing hymns in thy praise. But please, I beseech thee: Make it stop. Make it stop.

Pound. Pound. Pound. Where is that room where pain is born?
*   A glimmer of someone hovering. Like a head shot, taken from below. Could it mean…? No. No. Don't want it. Don't do it! Please! Not another one!*

Pound. Pound. Pound. Ham … ham … hammer. Now I'm getting somewhere. That's what I'm feeling. The relentless blow of a hammer. A hammer is smashing my head into smithereens. But not from the outside. I remember. There were these lights, sizzling lights. Then there was a three count, or was it a ten count? Then later, possibly centuries later, this hammer began striking again and again and again....

Into the room, the wheels go. Squeak, squeak, squeak. Lightly. Lightly. Lights. Lights. Action.

An eerie smell in the air, as if a tin plate had been accidentally left on a red hot burner. Bloated bodies dressed in white floating over me. Something cold and sticky on my temples. Something rubbery in my mouth. A band pressing in around my head. Uncomfortable. Uncomfortable. Straps wrapped about my legs, shoulders, torso. "Just relax. This won't hurt a bit," says a voice, as a needle punctures my arm. "Come on now. Stop fighting us. There's nothing to be scared of. Count backward from ten, and you'll be fine." Ten. Nine. Eight. Oh my God! Can't move a muscle. No way to breathe. How could they not know?

A chilly morning somewhere in a distant galaxy. Freezing toes peeping out of a meagre gown, inching their way down the bare concrete floor. The sound of a fork clinking against a plate. The unmistakable scent of freshly brewed coffee. "Hey, no breakfast for you today, Naomi, and don't forget to take your hair clips out." How come I'm getting nothing? Yes. Yes. I've been here before. Who knows in what year, lifetime, incarnation? They'll be prepping me again soon. And soon, mind, body, that mysterious thing they call a soul will get sucked into this vacuum. And I'll be back in the fog.

Pound. Pound. Pound. After this jackass of a schoolmaster picked on me, after I was caught trying to return the Underwood typewriter I had foolishly stolen, after four hundred blows and more, I escaped from the reformatory and ran for miles, my boyish arms swinging nimbly at my side, just like a professional athlete, faster, faster, faster. Till I found myself at the sea and stood there staring silently out into the waters, my head lowered, realizing that there was nowhere to go.

My eyes are swollen. I am flat on my back. I glance to the side, hoping to get my bearings. I can't make out much, but it is clear that I am lying on something that resembles a stretcher. To one side, through a doorway with no door, is a room with a scattering of people milling about. I can hear someone or some thing crying in that other room. Can make out giggling. A tale fit for winter is being told in a lisping mellow voice.

There is a wall on the other side of me. Nothing on the wall indicates where I am. What country, city, town is this? And what manner of people are meeting in that other room?

Eyes peer at me, then quickly look away. Because they are afraid. Because they sense the humiliation. Because they know not what else to do. Stretchers in front of me. Stretchers behind me. Some poor soul being dragged where none of us want to go.

Who would have thought that a single shriek could fill the universe?

Everyone has a name, an identity, a past. And if everyone else has, so must I. What am I called? And why is everything always such a blur? And where is she? Where? One touch. Two touches. Where?

Pound, pound, pound. I am a teenaged boy who stole a typewriter. Maybe. Maybe not. But if I am not a teenaged boy who stole a typewriter, who am I? Perhaps the silent Mrs. Vogler? But if I am the silent Mrs. Vogler, where is sister Alma? And why are there so many people milling about when sister Alma and I are supposed to be cloistered together at a cabin for the summer, just the two of us? If I could just catch a break, maybe I could.... If I could just stop that infernal....

Pound. Pound. Pound. What am I? I am a totally blank wall.

All the while that Gerald was reading, his face was calm, his gaze steady. Now the time was when he would have shaken his head in dismay. When he would have objected that the woman had never been crazy and cried out, "So why?" But not today. He simply took each passage one by one, scrutinizing them, repeating the odd word aloud, pausing to consider. Once he came to the end, he pulled a corn pipe from his side pocket, then a tobacco pouch. The sweet odour of overripe apple instantly greeted his nostrils as he lifted the flap. He sniffed it, nodded, filled the pipe, tapped down on the tobacco, added some more. Then he just sat there, sucking on the unlit pipe, his eyes keen, his heart determined.

He was proud of what Nomi had achieved and was intent on doing whatever he could to help her accomplish more. But it wasn't this that made Gerald's eyes sharpen. There was something of monumental importance in this binder. Not on the surface so much as tucked away. Something *in* the words or *underneath* the words. Something beyond the obvious. Beyond the anguish, the damage, the terror, the sheer stupidity of it all. And maybe not today, maybe not tomorrow, but sure as his name was Gerald Smith, sooner or later he was going to find it.

NAOMI'S MEMOIR

BOOK ONE
1944–1973

BUT

NOT

NECESSARILY

IN

THAT

ORDER

1. NAOMI

MY NAME IS NAOMI, Nomi for short. Not two years ago I was at a public meeting in Toronto where an aged woman looked everyone straight in the eye and asked, "After all our years of service, is this what we have to look forward to?" Two months later, a far younger woman who is ever so precious to me called with an urgent request. "Write about everything," she pleaded. "Do it for whoever—yourself, me, others at risk. Just do it." Hence this curious journey on which we are embarking.

Now in the sweep of literature, there have been many unusual, one might even say "oddball" narrators—corpses, the cross on which Jesus Christ hung, even—and I kid you not—a fish. By these standards, I am a fairly everyday narrator, for as best I can make out, I am neither the holy rood nor any kind of fish—well, leastways not since I last checked. What I am now is a sixty-five-year-old activist with holes in my head and a whopper of a memory problem. And that is the crux of the matter. But enough said.

This is one of those stories, you see, best left to unfold on its own. Like a surprise autumn sunset. Like a murder at dawn. I would only point out that there are depths here to plumb, truths to probe. Step into my world, additionally, and you will quickly find yourself rubbing shoulders with a vast array of some of the most endearing and fascinating souls that a person could hope to meet—some housed like

Gerald, some from the streets like my buddy Jack who could always roll the meanest cigarette in Turtle Island. Ah, but all in good time.

Now I could begin almost anywhere—when I discovered the films of Ingmar Bergman, when I fuckin' *re*discovered the films of Ingmar Bergman—but if I am to trust in that old Spenser formula, "where it most concerneth me," there is really only one place to begin: When I first started crawling out of the void. When those glimmers of consciousness first came upon me in the opening days of March 1973.

Something was fading in and out of consciousness. Something was hurting. But I did not know that I was a person or even quite that I was the subject of this pain. Only that there was this pounding sensation, this nausea, this heaviness that made some*one* or some *thing* want to sink to the floor and never move again. There came this time, however, when I faded in with some sense of personhood. I could tell that I had legs, that those legs were moving, that I was walking somewhere. I needed something desperately. To lie down. I was trying to get to that place where "lying down" happens. The word "lost" slowly took shape in my mind. I am lost, I told myself. Who comes to the rescue of people who are lost?, I asked, and for some reason that is not totally clear to me, my answer was "police officers." I wanted to find a police officer and explain who I was and that I had somehow lost my way. *But how to locate a police officer and how to explain…? How? How?* Then something most peculiar struck me. I could not explain who I was because I did not know. For a split second, I felt this giddy rush of freedom. After the freedom came panic. After the panic came confusion. And in the midst to the confusion came a voice. It said something like, "Naomi, take my hand."

Trembling, I looked up, half expecting God to be there, parting the waters. What I see instead is a stretch of corridor and a blur of a figure—definitely a human-sized figure—which appears to be a man.

I strain my eyes to try to take in a feature, an expression, anything that can help me identify him. What little I can make out—the bulk, the heft of the shoulders, the beardless face—I do not recognize. Must be a stranger, I tell myself. It slowly dawns on me that he has probably been talking to somebody else, and a disappointment comes over me. Then I feel this hand in mine. So, he has been addressing me after all. What did he call me? Naomi.

Next thing I know, I am stretched out on what must be a bed, my head propped up on what feels like an under-stuffed pillow. I am in a cubbyhole of a room, a dresser and mirror directly in front of me. The man is sitting in a chair to the side, something or other attached to his head—a hat, I suspected. Now I must have commented on the pounding, for he is nodding in agreement. "Yes, they tell me that's *some* headache," he observes.

"Headache, is that what this is?"

He chuckles, then reaches over and takes my hand again. "Sorry. It's just that you always ask that. Yeah, that pounding you're feeling, it's a headache—a doozy of a headache; but it'll pass. So try not to worry about it. Don't worry about the confusion either. Shit! Everyone's always in a muddle after shock."

"Shock?"

"Electroshock Therapy. EST. ECT. The big zap. I hear from the grapevine you've had at least one other series. That's the bad news, kiddo. The good news? This is probably the last treatment for a while anyway. Doc H., he always gives eleven per series."

Something of singular importance was being conveyed. I was trying very hard to follow, but I couldn't make head or tail of it. Therapy for what? What does electricity have to do with therapy? And why would I need therapy anyway? Then I started to feel myself slipping, slipping, slipping into the fog.

And so ended day one of my return to the land of the living if such it could be called.

"Naomi, pass the fuckin' butter already," a voice was bellowing. "Jesus! Some people!"

If you can imagine suddenly coming to in the middle of a busy intersection, cars piled up behind you, all of them blasting their horns, you are on your way to understanding my predicament. There was a clinking of dishes all around me, loud chewing in my ear, and voices everywhere, one on top of another—declaring, demanding, objecting. "The butter, you're holding onto the butter," a high-pitched voice insisted.

"Are we just gonna hafta sit here forever?" complained someone else.

While I kept hoping that some other Naomi was being addressed, I had a sinking feeling that those words were being directed at me. Now I must have been looking down, for I gradually became aware that I was staring at a hand that might be mine, also at this blur of an object in it. Hoping that the hand was indeed mine and that the object was nothing less than the much-sought-after butter, I decided to try passing the blurry object. I flexed some muscles, and sure enough, the hand began to move. But oh! Something wasn't right. When had that twitching started? I tried to assert control. Couldn't. Nervous what else might be amiss, I began to take stock of the rest of my body. Absolutely nothing felt right. Everything was in a jitter. My mouth was strangely parched, as if I hadn't drunk for days. And my legs, it's as if whole armies of ants were crawling up and down them.

"The other way. Pass it the other way," came another voice, the words badly slurred.

My eyelids felt heavy. If only I could sleep and forget all about the dry mouth, the butter, that noise that kept assaulting my ears! But then I heard a more promising sound.

"Shit!" boomed a loud deep voice. "Give the lady a break.

You know she's been zoned out. And you know she can't exactly see."

I lifted my head and peered about. A crowd of blurry faces were hovering in the air before me. Among them one I seemed to recognize, but from where?

"Kiddo," he said, his voice now gentle, "don't worry about the butter. I've got it. Say, want me to fetch your glasses?"

I was about to say "yes," when that moment of stillness came upon me. That moment when the world freezes, just before the lights begin to flicker, and just like that, I am gone.

When I faded back in, I was still at the table. For a second there, I did not know what had happened. I was about to call out for my sister but realized that my sister was not in this universe. Now this man had gone to get my glasses. Or at least I hoped he had.

Glasses, I thought. Yes. I wear glasses. Have ever since the first grade. Yes, yes, everything's clearer now. My name is Naomi Cohan. I live on Inkster Boulevard. My sister is Rose. My parents are Moshe and Ida. I'm a Jew. I'm a long-time member of the Winnipeg Film Society. And my life ambition is to follow in the footsteps of revolutionary filmmakers like ... like.... And here I came to a full stop. To my surprise, I could not think of the name of single director. Maybe if I shut my eyes and concentrate.

As I wracked my brain, I could hear the buzz of conversation about me. Someone was saying something about being sorry for being impatient earlier. Someone was complaining that he was tired. I could make out the meanings more or less. But many of the people were slurring their words, which made it difficult. Why were they slurring so?

As I pondered this question, once again I heard that familiar voice. "Kiddo, your glasses," it said, and I realized that this was the same man who had helped me to my bed, who knows in what distant century? And there and then, I knew that I had a friend.

I took hold of the glasses, eager to get a better look at this friend, but I had trouble making my fingers work properly.

"Catch you later, Naomi. Gotta go right now," he said.

"Please, just give me a second," I urged.

"Sorry, but I'll be back. Promise."

I could hear footsteps trailing off in the distance as I struggled with the glasses. Eventually I managed to slip them on. Once again I found myself staring at my hand. My hand still had fuzzy edges, like a photo taken from a moving vehicle, but my sight was significantly clearer than before. I took a deep breath. Then I lowered my hand, pushed my chair back from the table, and at long last dared to look around.

I was in a huge room, about thirty-five feet by twenty feet. I was seated at a long narrow table, second from the end. There were seventeen, eighteen people at the table. A number were visibly twitching, one drooling. A black man with a pot belly was slouched over the table, barely able to keep his eyes open. A white woman was snoring, her head to one side. Now while earlier I'd had the impression that everyone was talking, I had clearly been mistaken. Most were quiet, some utterly still, but not like people lost in thought, more like people who just could not be bothered.

Ours was one of three tables in the room—the one closest to the door. At the farthest table was some sort of commotion. Bending over, seemingly trying to re-establish order, was a woman in a nurse's uniform.

I rubbed my eyes, then began searching for details—clues to some mystery which I could not name. About a third of the people in the room were clad in what appeared to be blue hospital gowns, in some cases ones that demonstrably did not fit. Except for the nurse, the rest were sporting everyday clothes—jeans, trousers, the odd skirt. I instinctively checked my own duds. Oy! Hospital gown. Probably not a good sign.

I was clearly in a hospital. The million dollar question is: Which?

I pulled my chair back in, grabbed the edge of the table, and turned to the old woman on my left. "Excuse me," I said. "What hospital is this?"

I could hear it—hear it only too clearly. When had I begun slurring my words?

Giggling to herself, the old woman picked up a piece of toast and started chomping away, as if she had not heard me.

"Excuse me," I begin again, "but..."

"Ahem," comes this other voice, somewhere from the other side of the table.

"Excuse me," I try once more.

"Ahem! Ahem! Ahem!"

I look over. Seated immediately across from me is a plump middle-aged woman in a filthy yellow T-shirt, a tie-died cloak draped over her shoulders. Crumbs are dribbling out of her mouth. She is looking directly at me, I think smiling at me, though it is hard to tell as her face is strangely contorted.

"That there's Annie," the plump woman clarifies. "Pointless asking Annie a thing. Why the poor lamb hasn't spoke in years! But I can help you out. Let me introduce myself. I'm Zelda."

"Nice to meet you," I try.

"Oh sure, sure! That's what we all long for! To open our eyes and find ourselves being introduced to a bunch of loonies. Anyway, we've met before, but to answer your question, this here bastion of loveliness, this gourmet capital of the world is St. Patrick-St. Andrew's Mental Health Centre, but us old-timers, we like to call it St. Pukes. Eat them eggs on your plate, honey, and you'll quickly discover why."

I glance down, take in how runny the eggs are, chuckle despite my discomfort, then focus back on Zelda. "St. Patrick-St. Alfreds..." I begin.

"No. St. Patrick-St. *Andrew's*."

"St. Patrick-St. Andrew's Mental Health Centre. So I'm..."

"Committed, oh yeah. Certified and certifiable, if you know

what I mean. Lock, stock, and ever lovin' barrel. Want me to introduce you to some of the other esteemed patrons of this here commodious abode?"

Without further ado, Zelda rises from her chair and points to a scraggly-haired young woman in a hospital gown who is sitting half way down the table. "Dora," she calls.

"What?"

"I'd like you to meet Naomi."

"But I already know Naomi."

Zelda scowls at Dora. "Look, your highness. If you want me to keep slipping you my bennies…"

Dora immediately says hello, yawns, then asks if I have any bennies to spare.

"Don't think so," I answer.

"Bennies," Zelda explains, "that's benzodiazepines. Your everyday minor tranq. Now moving right along, this here is Emily."

Zelda seems to be indicating a young emaciated-looking woman on her left. Upon hearing her name, Emily casts her eyes about nervously. "The sperm, it's everywhere," she insists. "On the walls, under the carpet. They're planting it. Dr. Gordon says they aren't, but they are."

"Its okay, dear heart," says Zelda. "We can find ways around them sperm people."

"Hey, baby," pipes up someone from another table, "if you wanna see sperm, I can show you sperm."

"James Limon, shut that filthy mouth of yours," calls out a nineteen or twenty-year-old man seated to Emily's left.

"And this here is Brad," Zelda explains.

Brad takes a sip of coffee, lets out a belch, then stares at me. "They call me schizophrenic," he states point blank. "I call them assholes. Don't call me schizophrenic, and you and me, we'll get along fine." Then he glares at the man on the other side of him—a Chinese fellow with granny glasses. "You hear that, Bob?"

Bob eyes him with contempt. "You *are* schizophrenic. Dr. Hopper say so."

Brad whirls around and faces Bob. "Bob Sook, you're a damn toady. And as far as I'm concerned, you can blow it up your ass. Or, I know. Call your imaginary stockbroker. Eh?" he asks, his tone mocking. "Isn't it time to call your stockbroker?"

I am starting to feel dizzy. I take a bite of toast. Tastes like chemicals. I gulp down a tumbler of water. Inexplicably, my mouth remains dry. If only that man would return!

"Zel ... Zel," I stammer.

"Zelda. Rhymes with Helga," Zelda offers graciously.

"Zelga, could you tell me the name of the guy who brought me my glasses?" I ask. "And you any idea how long he'll be?"

"Zel-*da*" she reiterates pointedly. "Rhymes with..." Zelda stops abruptly. "Oh, I see, honey. Not the most fortuitous rhyme, is it?" Wiping some crumbs off her face, she proceeds to explain that Jack—that's what she calls him—has probably slipped out to the washroom. "Even the indomitable Jackman has shitty days," she adds, grinning mischievously. She quickly clarifies that 'the indomitable Jackman' is Jack's nickname, then launches into a vivid description of digestive problems—Jack's, hers, Brad's.

"Now when I say long bouts of constipation," she points out, "I don't mean ten or eleven days. Pssh! That's nothin'. Mere child's play. I'm talking five, six weeks here."

"Sometimes twelve," offers Brad.

"Right you are," Zelda concurs. "And that's when they have to dig you out."

Now much as I feel for their plight, what I really want to know is: Why haven't I heard of this hospital? And how on earth did I end up here?...And wasn't I just thinking something? Thoughts, do thoughts go where the westerly winds blow?

Zelda is still going on about digestion conundrums when Jack re-enters the room. He momentarily places his hand on my shoulder, then without uttering a word, slips into the chair to my right, and begins wolfing down his now cold eggs.

I take a good long look at him. A large burly man, somewhere in his late thirties, he has long raven black hair and
keen welcoming eyes. He is clad in jeans and a t-shirt. Now
earlier, I thought he was wearing a hat. But no. While it does
not appear to be on, curiously, there is a yellow transistor radio
pressed up against his left ear.

Jack speedily polishes off the rest of his breakfast. Then he
puts down the radio and removes a tobacco pouch and a pack
of rolling papers from his shirt pocket. Soon half the patients
are watching him with rapt anticipation. Making the most of
the moment, Jack dramatically plunks his elbows on the table,
then begins to roll, his eyes sharp, his hands steady. In mere
minutes a perfectly proportioned cigarette emerges—one he
is clearly proud of. "How bout this?" he asks, raising it high
over his head and looking about.

Brad grins from ear to ear. "Man, no one can roll like you!
No one, nowhere, no how."

"Sheer perfection, Jackman!" concurs Zelda.

Jack generously offers me the cigarette. When I explain that
I do not smoke, he pops it into his mouth, lights it, then just
sits there puffing. Now he is holding my eyes at this point,
almost as if he were waiting for something.

"Jack," I say, "this is St. Patrick-St. Andrew's Mental Health
Centre, right?"

"Right."

"But there's only two mental hospitals in Manitoba. And
neither of them are called St. Patrick-St. Andrew's. And neither
of them is in Winnipeg."

Jack takes a drag from the cigarette. "That may well be,
Naomi," he answers, the smoke slowly drifting out his nostrils,
"but we're not *in* Winnipeg."

"In Brandon, then?"

"Nope."

"Selkirk?"

"Not Selkirk neither."

"So where?"

"Toronto, home of the Maple Leafs. More importantly," he adds, "land of the Mississaugas. I'm Aboriginal, you know."

Barely noticing that somewhere to my side, someone is muttering, "damn Injun," I stare at Jack in disbelief. Part of me wants to stop right here, but before I know it, my lips have formed the most frightening question of all: "What's the date?"

Jack downs the rest of his coffee in a single gulp. Then he looks at me, his eyes filled with compassion.

"Jack?"

He does not respond, leastways, not with words. Just holds still, his face soft, his eyes melting.

"Zelda?" I hazard, turning toward her.

"March 13," she responds.

"March 13, 19..., what?"

"Oh, honey, 1973."

What was I to do? 1973 was a good nine years later than it should be. I had never been in Toronto. Never been in a nuthouse. I needed to get out of here. Get out right now. Or perhaps call my folks. Or better yet, hit the sack, fall asleep, wake up, and discover that it was all a dream. I took a deep breath, pushed down on my feet and rose. I took a couple of wobbly steps, fully intending to return to my room. Then I realized that I hadn't a clue where it was. And the nausea was rising up again.

While nothing was as confusing as those first few days, the days and weeks that followed were a muddle to say the least. Time passed, with me largely shuffling down the corridor aimlessly, slipping in and out of the fog. Not exactly an act to take on the road, if you get my drift. Fortunately, there were moments when I had the wherewithal to make an effort, though my recall even of them is spotty. This, however, I do remember: Trying to get my bearings was rather like trying to assemble a puzzle with missing pieces only to find the ones already in place vanishing. Now Jack and Zelda were a blessing. They kept showing me the ropes, taking me to the washroom, telling me where to line up for meds, repeating the simplest information over and over. And for all of that help, which so many never receive, I am eternally grateful. Oh Jack, Zelda, when I think of it now! But there were times—terrifying times—when one or both could not manage. Whole days when Zelda was mortified by her facial contortions and found no comfort in our assurances that we loved her. Yes, and those ominous mornings when Jack would just sit expressionless in the dayroom, his nose dripping, his radio pressed up to his ear. "What's he doing?" I would ask.

"Trying to drown out the voices," Zelda would answer.

And while she would say nothing further, for Jack was far too private to have revealed much, I quickly came to understand that this man who seemed on top of everything was struggling with demons that I could only barely intuit.

Intermittently, other patients would come to my aid when Jack or Zelda could not. Nonetheless, many is the time I found myself stranded. Moreover, whether I was lent a helping hand or not, I was in a terrible predicament; and I knew it. A huge chunk of my life was gone—vanished, as if it had never been. And something was seriously wrong with my mind.

At first, I could make little sense of it. Why did I forget some things and remember others in intricate detail? Was I really forgetting or was this someone's idea of a practical joke? Depressed, exhausted, and not having a clue what I was dealing with, naturally, I did not have even the most rudimentary idea of how to proceed.

One evening, as I lay alone in bed, a possible solution came to me: finding my way back into the fog permanently. There were people on the ward who appeared to have done just that. Annie, for example. Why not me? If I just closed my eyes, who knows? Maybe I could pull it off. Alternatively, maybe

I would wake up with my faculties intact. A win-win, either way. Too tired to really care which one, I did indeed close my eyes and drift off. And for the first time, I was visited by this most unusual dream:

I am tearing down a long dark hallway, frantically searching for the secret exit. After hours of hunting in vain, something penetrates the stillness. A barely perceptible hum. I scrunch up my eyes to get a better look. A machine appears in the distance. Mounted on four wheels, it is rolling relentlessly toward me. At first, the features are unclear, but eventually, I can see that it is metallic and perfectly rectangular. It is equipped with hundreds of dials, and protruding from it and running in every direction are thick black wires. Closer and closer it comes. And the hum becomes a buzz. And the buzz becomes a roar. As it closes in, the wires begin to glow. "Not another one. Not another," I scream.

I awoke shrieking. Minutes later, in rushed a nurse, needle in hand. Without a word, she lifted my gown. Something sharp nipped into my skin. Then she shot me a faint smile and murmured, "It's okay, Naomi. First thing tomorrow, I'll talk to the doc about increasing your meds."

"Please," I asked, "when am I gonna be able to remember stuff again?"

"Stop worrying. Four, five days, you'll be right as rain."

"*Believe the woman in white. Don't believe the woman in white,*" chimed in a voice from everywhere and nowhere. But of course, I wanted to believe her, right?

"Jack, can't find my room," I cry out for the umpteenth time. I am stranded in the middle of what feels like an alien corridor, confused and miserable. Jack is facing me, his trusty radio pressed to his ear. While I expect him to reach for my hand, thankfully, he does not. Rather, keeping his wits about him—another Jackman talent—he takes his time, leans against the nearest wall, turns up his radio, listens to some disco. Then he slips it into his pocket and stands there, his hands on his hips, his eyes deep in thought. "Okay, kiddo," he finally answers. "Let's you and me try something. See that steel door there at the end? Well, if you set out from there, your room, it's fourth on the right. I'll just stand here. Now go to the steel door, turn yourself around, and start walking toward me. When you reach the fourth door, just go on in. Know how you can remember it's the fourth?" he asks, his eyes lighting up. "The nursery rhyme. Three, four, shut the door."

Not confident, but eager to give it a try, I approach the steel door and turn about. I glance at Jack, see the reassuring glint in his eye, murmur, "three, four," and begin to walk. When I come to the fourth door, I whirl around and stare at the door directly opposite. Then I stand there, stymied.

"Know how you can remember which way to turn?" calls out Jack. "That steel door, it's never left open. Get it. *Never left.*"

"Never left," I tell myself. And my body aquiver, and totally without conviction, I entered "my room."

Ever after, I was able to find my room, though only if I proceeded from the steel door. "Naomi, three, four, shut the door; Naomi, never left," I whispered endlessly.

Learning the location of key rooms was one thing; learning the logic of the hospital was quite another. Staff told me that I could wear my own clothes if I earned the privilege. Patient after patient told me that I should not get emotional or my meds would be increased. Now I understood that all right. But not the distinctions.

"No. No. You can cry," Jack clarified. "Just not when staff's around."

"But Brad was in tears in group therapy," I pointed out. "This, I remember."

Jack nodded. "True enough, Naomi, but that's different. In group, it's appropriate."

The time came when I felt utterly discouraged. While I knew

where my room was and had held onto trivial bits of information here and there, I was keenly aware that I had forgotten more than I had retained. Moreover, I had learnt little that specifically pertained to me. I knew that I had received new modified electroshock—that's what the nurses called it, wasn't it?—but not what that meant. Years of my life were still missing. And I knew nothing of the personal circumstances that had led to this predicament.

As I sat in the cafeteria mulling it all over one afternoon, I also started to feel just a little peeved, for clearly memory loss was not the only problem. If I did not understand about the shock, it is not because I had forgotten. I could tell because whenever I asked for clarification, staff dodged the question. "It's just something that works," said Nurse Beth. "It's Dr. H you should be asking," insisted Jim the orderly. Nor did they cast any light on how I ended up here. Not even Jack, though I kept getting the feeling that he knew a thing or two. Nor did a one of them lift a finger to help me contact my family. Oh, I had tried. I had waited a good hour for the patients' phone while Bob yammered on to his "stockbroker," only to discover that the phone was not hooked up for long distance. I had asked this one nurse to take me to a pay phone so that I could call my folks, but from the expression on her face, you'd have thunk I was asking directions to Mars.

"Damn St. Pukes!" I muttered to myself. I smiled, then repeated the words louder. It felt downright exhilarating. And that is when I remembered a curious life detail. While I didn't do it often, when the circumstances were right, I had always enjoyed a good bout of swearing.

For the next half hour, I strutted about the ward, cussing away, always being careful to tone it down if I detected staff nearby. Ignoring the people like Bob that stared at me in amazement, and smiling at the many more who gave me the thumbs-up, I literally waltzed over to the washroom—one two three, one two three—twirling as I went. I stopped at exactly the right place. Damn the washroom!" I declared. I whirled around and danced down the hall, past OT, through the dayroom doorway, coming to a full stop at the bulletin board on the far right. I pointed to the list smack in the middle of the board—the one specifying who did and didn't have bingo privileges. "Damn the frigging list," I thundered. I felt strangely powerful, as if the world were at my fingertips.

Moments later, in rushed Nurse Ann, her cap slightly askew, a serious look on her face. "Naomi," she said, grabbing me by both shoulders, "you're upsetting the other patients. If you don't pipe down, we're going to have to inject you."

Immediately, I apologized. Now I figured that this was the end of the issue, but no. Suddenly, four orderlies were in my face. I started to run, but before I knew it, I was down on the ground, someone or some thing tugging on my leg.

"But I stopped swearing," I screamed. "Someone please tell them I stopped."

It was morning, and I was in bed, more exhausted than usual. Was it my imagination or had my head been stuffed with cotton batten? Remember you are in St. Pukes, I reminded myself. Zelga. Rhymes with Helga. I pulled myself up, stumbled down the hall, entered the cafeteria.

After what seemed like an eternity, Jack turned up, sidled in next to me. He shot me one of his broad Jack grins, said something about me being dragged to my room and injected, then whispered in my ear, "Gotta be more careful around Bob and Janet; they always tell, right?" What's he talking about?, I wondered. Then I recalled the dancing. The look on Bob's face. And suddenly, I knew.

Now I was shaken, and my faith in humanity was at an all-time-low, but I had learned a lesson that I was intent on remembering. Just to be on the safe side, Jack wrote it out in huge black letters on what appeared to be an index card: Number One: Not safe to show feeling. Number Two: Dangerous to act inappropriately. Number Three: Some people will squeal on you every time.

There it was—Lunatic Self-Management 101. And given the consequences, clearly, failing was not an option. Hey, I was certifiably crazy—not certifiably stupid.

Just before lights out, Nurse Ann entered my room, drew a chair up to my bed, and sat next to me, a clipboard in her lap. I was bracing myself for a lecture about swearing. Wrong again. Compassion in her eyes, she inquired how I was making out. Then she placed her hand on my shoulder and informed me that I had an appointment with Dr. Higgins tomorrow. I wondered if my recent behaviour was the reason, but she assured me that it was not, that the appointment had been scheduled weeks ago. "He's your personal psychiatrist," she explained. "He's an international authority on ECT, and you've met with him numerous times. Remember?"

Of course, I did not. At the same time, befuddled though I was, how the prospect of this appointment excited me! I was about to meet with the head honcho, yes? And finally, I was going to get some answers.

While the desk was immense—gobbled up a good half the room—to my relief, the man behind it did not seem especially intimidating. Dressed in an unassuming grey suit, he was short, middle-aged, with a deep receding hairline, and he had an odd habit of looking away, then glancing at you from the corner of his eye. When I first entered, he had given me a shy sort of smile, murmured, "I'm Dr. Higgins," and gestured toward the empty chair. Then for the next five, ten minutes, he'd plied me with questions, now and then scribbling something in a chart. His voice was gentle—a distinctly promising sign. But I could not exactly relate to his questions: "Have you ever married?" "Why have you never married?" "Was your sibling—well, sister—ever diagnosed with schizophrenia?"

Finally, he began talking about St. Patrick-St. Andrew's.

"And we're known internationally for our leading research into electroshock therapy," he observed.

Although I was having trouble following, I saw the opportunity and grabbed it. And it was then that I first heard the official line on electroshock.

"Exactly what is electroshock?" I asked.

"A form of therapy that works by electricity."

"But *how* does it work?"

Dr. Higgins wet his lips, looked slightly to one side, and smiled. "Oh, don't worry about *how* it works. What's important here is *that* it works."

A solitary folder laid open on the desk. He stopped, rifled through the papers in the folder, then looked up abruptly. "Now I understand you have complaints about memory loss," he went on. "Every ECT recipient suffers some manner of memory loss, but let me assure you, the loss is temporary. The memory, it comes back. The thing to keep in mind about electroconvulsive therapy—really the only thing that you need to know—is that it is safe and effective. No appreciable long-term side effects. You understand?"

"But my memory hasn't come back."

Dr. H. nodded. "Patients differ. With some, it takes a bit longer. Also sometimes worrying about memory loss creates the very problem that you're worrying about. Memory isn't an isolated phenomenon, you see. You worry, you get depressed, and that affects your memory. Also, you know, Naomi, sometimes patients don't let on that their memory has come back—not even to themselves. That's because forgetting serves them somehow. They're getting something we call 'secondary benefits.'"

"Can you tell me something?" I asked. "What am I being treated for?"

He looked off into the distance, then glanced at me from the corner of his eye. "I'll be frank with you. The original diagnosis was 'reactive depression,' and there is no question but that your depression's at least partially reactive, but you are also schizoaffective. Easy now," he added, sensing my alarm, and raising his hands as if to calm me. "These terms, you'll get accustomed to them in time."

"But everything sounds so serious. Please tell me that I can be cured."

"I'm afraid I can't. You'll have the illness the rest of your life, but the good news is, between electroshock, neuroleptics, and antidepressants, we can keep it under control."

Horrified, but intent on finding out more, I proceeded to ask several follow-up questions. I learned that a neuroleptic was also called an "antipsychotic"; that "schizoaffective" was a "mood disorder" that resembled schizophrenia. More importantly, I found out that this was my second hospitalization and that I'd been given electroshock both times.

Now I was hoping to learn more about my hospitalization. I was especially interested in learning about the involvement—or lack of involvement—of my family, but before I knew it, Dr. Higgins was talking about drug dosages. Then somehow—I'm not sure how—the issue of dosage turned into a warning about what he called "the incident."

"Swearing, yelling, jumping about—we can't allow you to do things like that," Dr. Higgins asserted, tapping his pen on the table. "You understand why I'm saying this?"

I nodded. "And it won't happen again."

"It's disruptive," he continued. "It is also unseemly. Unseemly no matter who does it, but especially for a woman. You get my drift?"

Now I was shocked by the distinction, but I was not about to rock the boat. So I said, "Yes, of course." At this, he began searching through that folder again. Guessing that it was mine, I asked, "Any chance I could see my file?"

Dr. Higgins shook his head. "It's not recommended." Then he closed the folder slowly, as if lost in thought. "Well, there *is* something here that I would like you to see," he finally uttered. And to my surprise, he passed me the folder, adding, "Now please don't be frightened, but I'd like you to get a good look at the name on top."

My heart pounding, I took hold of the folder and stared at the caption. And with this simple act, my life was to take an about-turn. While for a second there, I had trouble making out the letters, the name was unmistakable—"Smith, Naomi."

"There's been some sort of slipup," I exclaim. "This isn't right. My last name is Cohan—not Smith."

"But I'm afraid it *is* right."

"No, this is *meshugah*. My file must have gotten mixed up with someone else's. Honest, that's not my name. I'm a Jew, right? A Cohan. Naomi Cohan."

Dr. Higgins leans forward once again, takes back the file, and for the first time looks me squarely in the eyes. "Naomi, try to calm yourself. I know that what I am telling you is huge, but you've got to try to take this in. You remember my asking just now if you ever married?"

"Sure. My memory is bad. But, hey, not *that* bad."

"Why do you think I asked that?"

"Cause you wanted to know," I answer, feeling increasingly uneasy.

"Try again."

Feeling the blow coming, I cover my head with my hands. "Oh no. Don't tell me…"

"Precisely. You are married. Your married name is Naomi Smith."

I lower my hands and grip the arms of the chair. "But how is that possible? I don't even believe in marriage. And to someone named 'Smith!' Please!"

A grimace ripples across Dr. Higgins' face. He leans back, crosses his legs. "Not believing in marriage," he states, "well, that's not exactly a healthy attitude for a wife, and you want to start being a better wife, don't you? I mean, surely you want to get well and get out of here some day."

My impulse is to run, but recalling the events of the other day,

I refrain. "I don't know," I respond, "but tell me something: Who is this man I'm supposed to have married?"

"A teacher, and as far as we can make out, an extremely kind man. You're a very lucky woman, Mrs. Smith."

"Look, I'm not trying to make trouble here, but if this man really is, well, my husband, why hasn't he ever visited?"

"Oh, but he has. You've just forgotten. Tell me. Do you know what month it is?"

"March or April."

"It's late June," he points out. "Your last ECT treatment was in early March, and your husband's been here a few times since then. Now it's perfectly normal that you don't remember. Up until a few weeks ago, you were forgetting most things, and he's not visited since then."

"Late June," I mutter, trying to grasp this new reality. "Husband been here.... Um, um, so why didn't anyone say anything about him? And why hasn't he come recently?"

"You kept getting so upset that we figured it best to let everything be for awhile. Anyway, we're expecting him around two p.m. tomorrow. Perhaps some other members of the family also. That's why I arranged this appointment—to help prepare you."

"So my parents, they'll be coming? And my sister?" I asked, getting excited for the first time. "I'm dying to see them, and..."

"You're forgetting," he interjected. "They don't live here. You are a twenty-nine-year-old woman and you live in Toronto with..." At this point, inexplicably, he paused and began tapping his pen. "You know, your parents and you..." he finally resumed. Once again, he paused. At long last, he smiled and said, "You know something? It's not so good just being told things. Anyway, it's probably best if your husband fills you in. In cases like this, we find it helps with the bonding."

Now I was appalled by the idea of my life being turned over to some man that I did not know, however nice someone else thought he was, and I was on the verge of asking if it were all right if I put off meeting with him at least until my memory returned. Suddenly, however, I found myself moved at the thought of this poor *schmuck* who had waited God knows how long for a wife who actually recognized him. And to my surprise, I heard myself saying, "I'd rather not meet him like this. Please, can I wear my own clothes?"

Dr. Higgins nodded and wished me luck. Reeling from the craziness of it all, I headed for the door. Just as I was turning the handle, I realized that I had failed to find out a pertinent fact. "Excuse me, Dr. Higgins," I asked, "but this Mr. Smith, what's his first name?" Once again, Dr. Higgins hunched over and peered into the folder. Now I am reasonably confident that he responded. By the time that I had arrived back in my room, however, I did not remember his answer.

That evening over supper, Jack and I had our first argument. "You must have known," I protested. "And hey, you could've at least warned me."

"Shit! Since when is that my responsibility?" roared Jack. "And you think I don't know what's going to happen now? You're gonna hightail it out of here with that consummate asshole."

Later, as I was sitting in my room, I heard someone approach. "Please God, let it be Jack wanting to talk further," I prayed, but no, it was Nurse Ann, a plastic bag filled with clothes in her hands. She placed the bag on the bed, muttering, "Naomi, these are yours. I recommend the dress." Then she wished me luck and left.

I picked up every piece of apparel one by one, eyed each intently. Oy! I didn't recognize a single item, but the dress, that was downright bizarre. Why I had stopped wearing dresses when I was seventeen!

I put it to one side and tried to wriggle into this one pair of pants. Didn't come close to fitting. Reluctantly, I pulled on the dress. On the tight side, but a distinct possibility. I hesitated. I really did not want to know what I looked like, but eventually I did it. For the very first time, or at least as far as I was aware, I peered into the mirror on the wall, and a fat woman with jowls and love handles peered back at me. Humiliated, I tore off the dress, piled all the clothes on the top of the dresser, and crawled into bed.

I slept little that night. For some time, I just lay there wondering about the elusive Mr. Smith. Just what was he like? I imagined him a Chaplin look-alike, complete with moustache and walking stick. I imagined him a man so skinny that the only way that he could lose weight is if he fell on the sidewalk and chipped. Then I began worrying. I worried about meeting this strange new husband. I worried about Jack. I worried about worrying, having just discovered that it causes memory loss. And hour after hour, I struggled with that terrible question of who I am: Naomi Cohan or Naomi Smith? A budding young filmmaker or the schizoaffective patient in room B?

Intent on finding a resting place, eventually, I fluffed up the pillow, laid down, and let myself drift back to the early days. Before the memory loss, before University of Manitoba, before even St. John's High. And images of a happier time began filling my mind: The white stucco house where I was born. The grass-filled boulevard that ran down the middle of our street. My sister Rose and I, mere toddlers, rushing out the front door and hitting the boulevard, hand-in-hand, the thrill of anticipation coursing through our limbs. His *tallis* draped over his shoulder, my father reaching across the table to light the *havdalah* candle. My mother setting aside the broom, muttering, "Yeh-yeh," then holding forth on the significance of the politician J. S. Woodsworth, her head high.Like the photograph of a friend long deceased, the images comforted me, and within a short while, they lulled me to sleep. Some hours later, that nightmare returned. I bolted upright, screaming for my sister, then drifted off again.

Next morning, I awoke with a curious sensation that I'd not had since childhood. As if Rose were somehow with me. I got up and put on the dress, unsure where I was, terrified at what the day might bring, but determined to meet it with the dignity of a Cohan.

2. NAOMI

HOW VIVIDLY I RECALL the place of my childhood! I was born and raised in north-end Winnipeg. That's Winnipeg Manitoba, doorway to the west, home of the *schmata* factories, but most importantly of all, leastwise for us Jewish or Ukrainian north-enders, site of the Winnipeg General Strike, where beleaguered workers took on the owners, scared the b'Jezzus out of Ottawa, and brought the city to a standstill.

"What did your gramps do in the strike?" us kids would ask each other.

"My *zeda* Saul was one was of the organizers," I would announce proudly.

"Wow!" some boy or other would exclaim, his eyes popping. "Jeez! Did he get thrown in the slammer and everything?"

"Ya' better believe it. Just like J. S. Woodsworth."

Everyone knew, of course, that I was referring to none other than the first leader of the Canadian Commonwealth Federation—a man greatly esteemed in our neck of the woods. On the anti-Semitic and racist side, to be sure, what with this worrisome mission to civilize and Christianize, but, hey, a socialist nonetheless and one willing to do time for his principles to boot. And so we forgave him for the rest, perhaps overly generously, perhaps because we too had holes in our analyses.

North-end Winnipeg was this fascinating mix of first, second, and third-generation Eastern European immigrants—Jews, Ukrainians, Poles, almost all of us working class, most with a profound sense of history and our place in it. Socialism was our passion, the Winnipeg 1919 strike, our collective inheritance. Mention anything about Winnipeg history to north-enders of my parents' generation, and likely as not their eyes would light up, and within minutes, off they would be searching for their photo albums.

As a child, I saw many such photographs; and from my earliest years, they never failed to astound me, although, curiously, more than anything else, it was the medium itself which most spoke to me.

"What are they doing?" I asked my mother. I was four years old; and we were sitting at the kitchen table, hunched over an open album, me and my sister Rose on one end, my mother on the other. Mom had just pointed to a most curious photograph, in the middle of which was a very long car, with a gigantic crowd surrounding it. The car was tipping to one side as if about to topple.

"Naomi, this may seem strange to you," my mother explained, "but they're pushing over the tramcar. "You see this?" she asked, pointing. "That's called a tramcar, yeh?"

"But why would they do something like that?"

"You remember Daddy telling you about the strike?"

"Uh huh."

"Well, in strikes, people do things like that."

"But why, Mom?"

Mom glanced at Rose, took in how bored she was. "Just a sec," she urged. Then she opened a drawer, pulled out a deck of cards, and began playing crazy eights with her. As Rose bit her lip, trying to figure out what to discard—it always took her so long that a person could pee their pants waiting—Mom glanced toward the ceiling, and her eyes got clearer. "Now to get back to your question, Naomi," Mom continued, focusing on me again, "pushing over a tramcar is a way of saying 'no.' Sometimes, it's good to say no, don't you think? Like when things aren't fair."

"Aren't fair?"

"Say if you are punished but you've done nothing wrong."

I look up into her eyes. "So did all those thousands of mommies and daddies get together to say no?"

"All those thousands of *workers*, yes," she asserts, confirming and correcting at the same time, as was her way.

I sat there staring at the photograph and marvelling. Thousands of daddies and mommies called "workers" said "no" a long time ago, and there it is on this piece of paper. And I am able to look at it!

With this began my fascination with photography. In the days that followed, I checked out all the photo albums at our house. When at anyone else's house, I made a point of asking to see their pictures. "You're interested in photos, Rose?" some grownup or other would inquire. I wouldn't even bother letting them know they had me confused with my sister; I was that avid to get my hands on another album.

Now my interest in photography never disappeared, not even after that silly-dilly Jake Pepinski teased me, but for good or for ill, it was soon eclipsed by a discovery I made in my sixth year. We had all bundled ourselves into our galoshes and heavy coats and trundled off to something that Mom called "the cinema" to see *Bambi*. I grinned with delight as Bambi sprinted through the clearing. I fretted as the winter progressed. I sighed with relief as the music lightened and the first patch of grass appeared. "Bang," went the rifle. And Rose and I were in each other's arms, wailing.

"How could they kill Bambi's mother?" I protested.

"Yeah, how?" echoed Rose.

That evening our house was in turmoil. "*Oy!* No way we're doing this again!" my father exclaimed. And Rose and I sobbed for hours.

Neither my sister nor my father was inclined to go to the cinema again, but the screen beckoned me and I kept pleading. And so it was that Mom took me to see Bob Hope in *Fancy Pants*. And that's when I put it together. Movies were a special photograph where people moved, talked, even made jokes. As I lay in bed that night, I conjured up movie-like images of the tramcar incident: The crowd yelling in unison, "let's turn it over." A look of determination in a young woman's eyes. A close-up of hands reaching toward the tramcar and pushing. And from that night on, movies became a preoccupation—more than that—an identity.

"What grade the two of you in?" an adult would ask.

"Grade one, and I watch movies," I would answer.

Identity was a complex issue for us north-end Winnipeggers. No one was simply a north-ender. We were first and foremost Jews like my family, or Ukrainians like the Schreyers down the way. Being Jewish meant embracing our own history, holidays, language, even schools. It meant a universalistic commitment to fight for the rights of all people while thinking, eating, marrying Jewish. Almost invariably, it meant socialism, or Communism, or anarchism, with Yiddish and Jewish issues like Israel an integral part of the politic. Of course, the particular flavour of politics would depend on the specific region of Europe from which your family hailed, which complicated everything considerably. And people in my parents' and grandparents' generation frequently confused the CCF, or the Co-operative Commonwealth Federation, with the further left parties that they knew in Europe, complicating matters still more.

Beyond that, we were *north-end* Winnipeg Jews, which meant that we were poor and were regarded with a degree of disdain by south-end Winnipeg Jews, who were quieter, more affluent, and voted liberal. Still, we were *Winnipeggers*, which meant that we were not from Toronto the Good—a fact in which we took tremendous pride. "*Chaverim*, let's sing so loud that they can hear it all the way over in that *farshtunkener* city called 'Toronto' that I think some of you may have heard of," our music teacher Mr. Mendelson would shout as he stepped onto the platform to lead us in song.

We also identified as Canadians—well, western Canadians—and had a sophisticated analysis of the power that the capitalist east exercised over the farming, labouring west, though tragically, almost no sense whatever of the power which we ourselves were exercising over Aboriginal peoples. Finally, we dwelt on a specific street, and while we took delight in knowing the ins and outs of most north-end streets, indeed, of most Winnipeg streets, we had a special affinity with our own. Now the street where my family lived, celebrated Shabbes, and quoted from the Regina Manifesto—which we did at the drop of a hat—was called "Inkster Boulevard."

As a wee child, I loved living on Inkster and was convinced that either Inkster or Odessa was the capital of the world—I just wasn't sure which. Now Inkster was almost as far north as you could go and still qualify as north-end Winnipeg. It stretched for what seemed like miles; and down the centre of the street ran the boulevard—a glistening green paradise that beckoned the local children, promising hours of fun. Come summer, day and night, there us kids would be, smack in the middle of the road, regaling each other with ghost stories, turning ourselves into human cannon balls and rolling about the grassy way, then lifting ourselves up and giving chase. And how I would run—faster, faster, faster—my arms swinging at my side! "Gotchya! You're it!" our friend Morton would squeal. Feeling a slight tap on the back of my shoulder, I would whirl about just to check, only to find myself exactly where I expected—yards from anyone else. Inevitably, my sister Rose would be standing in the distance, pouting, while inches from her, Morton was glowing with that unmistakable grin of victory. "Damn! Nomi, did he really get us?" she would call out. Albeit knowing full well that he had only tagged *her,* had come absolutely nowhere near *me,* "think so," I would answer. A curious exchange for the uninformed ear perhaps, but one which the local children intuitively understood and accepted. Then darkness would settle in, and we would sink onto the ground and just lie there, our eyes half shut, aware that the moment would inevitably come when some parent or other would disturb the dreamy stillness and call out "bedtime."

Nor was the boulevard the only local site that stirred our youthful hearts. Our house was but a block and a half from the famous Peretz school—the brick building on Aikins where Jewish elementary students poured over Yiddish literature and dreamt of a better world. How often I passed that building and yearned! It was likewise a short walk to the Deluxe Theatre, where the curtain would rise and you could take in the magic of the movies. "Look, I can't take you as often as you'd like," Mom would say. "Better we do something Rose likes too, yeh?" Still, the first Thursday of the every month, the two of us would set off for the theatre, even if it was one of those freezing winter days where your nose went white and the howling Winnipeg wind bit straight through your overcoat.

Having poor blood circulation, Rose and I had trouble with the Winnipeg winters, by the way. Now while Ro tended to keep indoors, I would brave the elements anyway, especially for something as vital as the cinema, though making it back home could be daunting. So what a relief when the white stucco frame of our house came into view!

Our house was one and a half storeys, with the kitchen, dining room, and living room opening up into each other. With the exception of one beige chair and Ottoman—my father's seat—none of the furniture matched. Everything was second-hand, and arrived bit by bit, as my father *schlepped* one stick of furniture after another from his second-hand shop at Selkirk and Main. By the time I was six, to my great delight, my father made the find of his career, and as a result, a piano came to stand in the centre of our living room. There my father would sit for hours at a stretch, his daughters at his side. "No. No. No. Listen, Rose," he would say, moving those large hands of his gracefully over the keys. "See. That's C sharp—not C. Now *you* try."

Upstairs were two bedrooms and a washroom. My parents had the master bedroom. The other bedroom initially went to Rose and me, though eventually, to a series of different tenants, starting with a square-faced Mennonite woman named Leah, whom my folks took in when I was three. "*Kinderlekh*, we're okay, but we could use the rent money, yeh?" is how Mom put it. Rose and I shared a single bed in the tiny sunroom, which could be accessed only via Leah's room—an arrangement that we found fun for the first two, three years, but which the respective tenants found a trifle disconcerting, especially when faced with those unscheduled trips to the washroom in the middle of the night. "Now girls, if you have to *pish* in the middle of the night, you'll be quiet as a mouse, yeh?" my mother would instruct, lifting her finger to her lips. And quiet as a mouse, I would tiptoe through Leah's room, then tiptoe back again. Minutes later, Rose would awake, and quiet as a mouse, she would set off on her own journey. "Oh no! Not again!" the current tenant would groan. Hence a rapid turnover in tenants was the norm.

Now for the first few years, whenever a tenant left, I would be beside myself a good part of that first day, touching barely a morsel at supper, only vaguely aware of my mother calling out, "C'mon girls, no more pouting." Come night, I would bury my head under the covers and wonder if I would ever see her again. How could the world be so unfair as to take her away? And why was no one going on strike to change it? At some point, though, I would feel this head nudge mine, lightly, repetitively, like it was butting me, and then I would hear these jags of crying. For a few minutes there, I would be far more upset, almost as if I were holding the grief of two. Then I would reach over to take her hand. To comfort *her*, or was it *us*? And that is when it would happen. I could feel it. She was beginning the message. The first squeeze ever so gentle, the second, somewhat firmer. I would delay. Then I would squeeze back. One quick light squeeze, one quick firmer one. Then together we would drop our hands and hold our breath, waiting for the right moment. Without looking at one another, without a sound uttered, we would know when our moment had come, and simultaneously, we would reach for the other's hand again, each giving and receiving one long squeeze. Then there we would be—touching elbows, holding each other, wiggling our noses in unison, giggling. We are two but we are one, we were telling each other. This was our joke, this our triumph over the turmoil of the world.

No one was closer to me than my twin sister Rose. She had been there from the beginning, lying next to me, squeezing my hand, cuddling up to me in the stroller as those gigantic faces bent over us, oohing and ahhing. For hours on end, we would speak without words, using squeezes, head bunts, hand signals. Once we were talking, time and again we would find ourselves finishing each other's sentences. Oh, and what kisses we would give each other! Direct kisses on the mouth. Indirect kisses we called "bumba kisses," through that wondrous object next to our bed that Dad called a "mirror."

"See. That's us," I would say, pointing at those round faces—at those special friends with dimples and hazel eyes that were grinning back at us.

"Us," Rose would echo.

And we would bring our hands to our lips and blow kisses to the faces, giggling as we received kisses back without even having to wait.

In those earliest years, being twins was the centre of our

universe. It was as if being two but being one was the secret meaning of life. We would chase each other about the house, anticipating that precious moment when we would fall down and tumble into one another's arms. We would bound down the boulevard, squealing in ecstasy. We would play hide-and-seek, and upon finding each other in minutes, would be as pleased with ourselves as if we had discovered the Holy Grail. Putting our heads together, we would take special delight in bamboozling cranky old Mr. Schwartz next door, who was always on our case about stepping on his grass. "You incorrigible little brat, didn't I tell you just yesterday to stay away from my yard?" he would snarl, his hands on his hips. "Must have been Naomi," I would answer. And how we would laugh at these jokes that no one else understood—not even Mom. And we almost never felt alone, for right at our side was the dearest friend of all—the kind everyone else longs for—someone who knows you from the inside out, someone who knows every bone, muscle, and sinew of you.

Not that being an identical twin was without its hazards even then. I would never feel quite right if Rose was not there. As if part of me was missing, and I needed to get that part back just as quick as I could.

"But where is she?" I would ask.

"Easy now," my father would answer. "She's just down the street with your mother and she'll be right back."

"But I'm here. How come *she* isn't?" I would persist, horrified that such a thing were possible.

Nor was that the only difficulty. Once in a while, once every long long while, I was dying to have Mom to myself. I wanted to leaf through the photograph albums with her. I wanted just to sit on her lap, sniffing in her perfume, nuzzling into her arms. But there Rose would be, hanging onto Mom.

And then there were those people whom our mother called "the clueless *klutzes*." They were a twin's nightmare. "Not because they're trying to be mean," Mom explained. "Just because they don't know any better." It was easy to land yourself in trouble if the clueless klutzes were around.

"Okay, *now* lettuce," Mom instructed, her arm extended, her finger pointing.

The three of us were shopping at Safeways, Mom in her turquoise dress, Rose and me in matching orange shorts. We were taking turns finding the items on Mom's list. As Rose lifted a pale head of lettuce in the air, Mom shook her head. Then Rose chose the greener, leafier variety, and Mom nodded.

Once we arrived in the canned vegetable aisle, Mom caught my eye and called out, "Okay, corn, you know, the mushy kind that you like." Now I was busy finding the cream style corn and placing it in the shopping cart. So I did not see it coming. When I looked up, to my dismay, a handful of people were milling about, pointing at Rose and me.

"Freaky, isn't it?" a plump woman said.

A middle-aged man at her side smiled. "Oh, I think they're cute.... Twins, they're so adorable, you could just gobble them up, couldn't you?" he added, turning to my mother.

Mom nods good-naturedly, says something innocuous—I can't remember what—and grabs our hands as if about to move on. But then these two bigger kids begin snickering—the very boys who pinched me just a few days ago earlier to see if pinching *me* would make *Rose* yell "ouch." Now they don't actually touch us this time round—they wouldn't dare with grownups present—but Rose and I freeze anyway. Then a boisterous woman who has just entered the aisle begins pointing us out to the brood of children accompanying her. "See. See. They're twins," she bellows. Suddenly, dozens more eyes are gawking at us. I can feel Rose's heart flutter, and I instinctively reach for her hand. Mom notices, shakes her head, spits out, "They're twins, yeh? Not the Taj Mahal! Get over it!;" and the woman turns away. And with this, Rose's heart goes quiet, and with only the odd grumble here and there, the crowd disperses.

We finish shopping without further incident and proceed to the cashier. Rose and I both light up when we spot Olga on duty. Olga is a sweetie and always gives us caramels as a special treat. We hold our breath in anticipation, and sure enough, out come the big squares of caramel, two for me, two for Rose. And now it is time to pay for the groceries. Proud that Mom has gone one step further this time, actually letting one of us pay, I hand Olga a piece of paper called "ten dollars" that Mom pinned to the inside of my pocket but an hour ago, saying, "Now don't touch this until it's time." Olga takes one look at it, winks at Mom, then reaches over and pats my head. "Paying the bills at this young age, are you?" she says. "Good for you, little monkey. You're Naomi, aren't you? *The smart one.*" Then she turns to my sister and adds, "Now don't anyone tell me.... You're R ... R ... Rose." And suddenly, Rose is in tears.

Eager to spring to Rose's defence and, in that moment, forgetting our entire history with Olga, I spat on the counter. Instantly, Rose stopped crying and spat on the counter as well. Of course, Mom yelled and reminded us how kind Olga had always been, which made us feel so guilty that we apologized before being asked. Mom also made us give the caramels back. "It's okay, Ro," I whispered quietly.

Once home, Mom sat us down on the couch and explained, "You know, Naomi, there are all sorts of ways of dealing with the problem, but this isn't one of them."

"But what do I do?" I asked, honestly confused.

Mom sighed, then looked me in the eye. "Well, you can always tell people about the special things that Rose does, like weeding the garden. I don't know. Anything but spitting. Now I'm not saying it's wrong to want to defend your sister, but you don't take your closeness out on other people. Okay?"

"Okay."

"And you," she added, turning to Rose. "You've got to grow a thicker skin, yes?"

"Yeah, Mom, but it's..." Rose started.

"Awfully hard," I continued.

"You little *pishers*," said Mom, "you think life's supposed to be easy?"

At this, Dad entered the room, sat down in his chair, and asked, "So what's new?"

Mom took a deep breath but did not answer.

"I can tell something's up," he asserted.

"So what do you want, Moshe? A medal for clairvoyance?"

Dad shrugged his shoulders. "C'mon, Ida. Whatever's going on, I'm not the bad guy here. So out with it."

Mom nodded and explained.

"Tell you what I think," he began at long last. "I have a brilliant wife. Also two beautiful little girls. Know what else I think? If my little girls end up half as smart as their mother over there, I will consider myself a blessed man. As for the rest of the world, they're complete idiots!"

Rose and I grinned. Mom looked at him quizzically and caught his eye.

"Moshe, what a thing to say in front of the girls! And what kind of attitude is that for a revolutionary?"

"Look. I care about all of God's creatures, and I want everyone to have a fair shake, but I'll tell you, if I've learned anything in four decades, it's that most people are *meshugah*. And if I had to choose between *meshugah* human beings and the rest of God's creatures—birds, say..."

Exasperation flitted across Mom's face. "Forget about the birds for once. What are we going to do about the situation?"

"The situation?"

"The girls have been bad and have to be punished."

Dad lit a cigar. Then he turned to the two of us and said, "Your mother's right, girls. You've been bad—not as bad as the *meshugah* people you came across in that idiotic supermarket, but bad—and as king of this house, I hereby decree that you hafta go to bed without supper, and..."

"And you're grounded for one week," Mom added.

"*Two* weeks," my father corrected. "What kind of punishment is one week? They could do that standing on their head."

I caught Mom's eye, knowing that she was fully capable of commuting the sentence if she wanted to. "You heard your father," she warned. "So whatchya waiting for? An announcement over the radio?"

As we lay in bed that night, I kept touching Rose's arms, legs, face. Is her skin getting thicker yet? I wondered. And if she grows a thicker skin, will we still look alike? And is there really a solution to the problem of the clueless *klutzes* or is that just one of those things mommies are supposed to say?

My mother was a tiny woman—five foot one inch in stocking feet. Of darkish complexion, she was frequently mistaken for Sephardic, though to the best of our knowledge, her family was Ashkenazi. Her folks had emigrated from Galicia in 1911. She had met my father at a demonstration in 1938 and a year later, they married. More particularly, they wed on September 1, 1939. No kidding. The day that Germany invaded Poland. Speaking of being upstaged," my father would say, rolling his cigar about in his fingers and putting his feet up on the ottoman. "Now was that Hitler a party-pooper or what?"

Further left than my father, she was a great believer in strikes and demonstrations. She was also passionate about women's health. "Ann Ross, she'll do something about it some day," Mom would say. She was referring to information about birth control, and to a nurse at Mount Carmel Clinic who actually did end up disseminating it long before that was legal, though at the time, the reference meant *bupkes* to me.

My mother was good-hearted and would frequently run to the aid of neighbours in distress. What perplexed me, though, every so often, even while helping some poor *schmuck* clean her house or sell her silverware to make ends meet, she would deliver this eerie warning. "Happy to be of help," she would say, "and if you find yourself in need again, just give me a call. That's what we should be doing, helping each other, yeh?" Then her eyes would narrow, and she would tilt her head to one side and add, "Don't ever cross me though. Me, I'll help anyone, but let someone cross me, or worse yet, cross Moshe or the kids, and mark my words, I'll just walk away and never look back."

The time came when the three of us would exchange looks and roll our eyes whenever she astounded some poor neighbour with this out-of-the-blue pronouncement. Mostly, however, I just saw it as this strange thing she had to do now and again, rather like a hiccup, though I occasionally wondered whether this threat had anything to do with the fact that there were many relatives who we never saw or spoke of. Unlikely, I concluded. She never speaks this way to family.

Now my mother was nothing if not outspoken, far more so than my father; and as a result, she frequently bickered with him over what to wear, who discarded what in the last bridge hand, whether or not to say anything to Rena—the Jewish teenager two doors down who kept dating non-Jews—though nothing raised her dander quite so much as much as politics. Actually, my father's either for that matter.

"You're voting for Joe Zukin!' my father would exclaim. "How can you vote for Joe Zukin? That *linker!*"

"Big shot!" my mother would retort. "Who made you the expert? So what if he's a Communist? He's a good man. Anyway, what's so great about your guy, I'd like to know!"

The bickering notwithstanding, one thing was clear. She adored my father. She never ceased telling Rose and me what a fine man he was. And she would go out of her way to please him. On a regular basis, she would make his favourite dishes. And even though she herself could have cared less about such things, she kept a kosher kitchen.

Unlike my mother, my father cared deeply about Judaism,

you see. First thing every morning, he got up and prayed, his blue-on-blue tallis draped over his shoulder, a matching blue yarmulke on his head. Every evening, once supper had been served, the family would sit at the dining room table, utterly still, awaiting the moment. Nodding ever so slightly, he would begin chanting the ancient blessing over the bread, his voice strong, his eyes glistening: "*Baruch ata Adonai Eloheynu Melech ha-olam, hamotzi lechem min ha'aretz.*" As he came to the end, I would join in and utter "amen," aching to enter into this mystery, though I could not totally manage it, and sometimes, it was utterly impossible, for I had already snuck a piece of bread when no one was watching—well, no one except for my mother, who had shaken her head, a look of vague bemusement on her face, but said nothing.

Shabbes was particularly dear to him. And who could forget those early years, where he would start to sing a *niggun*, and one by one, we would all join in!

"Know what's special about Judaism?" he would ask. "It's built on time—not space. Shabbes, this is our temple, this our Holy Mount. It can be found on no map, nor anywhere else. And so it can never be destroyed."

My father was a stocky man and a bit on the short side, five foot nine, if I recall correctly. He had deep hazel eyes, a beard, and a full head of black hair that was so curly that his yarmulke could never quite sit flat; and so he was forever adjusting it.

Like my mother, he was born in Winnipeg. His folks had come from Odessa, lured by the promise of the new land where everyone had food on the table. Imagine their surprise at finding themselves hungry! After graduating from St. John's Tech, Dad started working full-time with Zeda at a second-hand store on Selkirk and Main, and after Zeda's death, he took over the shop, eking out just enough to support a small family.

Now originally he had been an atheist who had simply celebrated Jewish holidays pro forma. According to my mother, though, he came down with a particularly serious case of scarlet fever as a teenager, and after that had never quite been the same, though exactly how that brought him closer to Judaism, she never did say.

My father's major passions were birds, Judaism, and socialism—in that order. "Naomi, Ro, time to feed the birds," he would call out.

When we arrived in the backyard, there dad would be, shirtless, a pail brimming over with bread crumbs in hand. Generally, his back would be toward us and he would be working his way toward the fence, reaching into the pail and flinging the crumbs into the air. And the sparrows would be everywhere—in the maple trees, throughout the grass, next to the rhubarb—perching, pecking, hopping. Our mouths agape, we watched in amazement as bird after bird winged its way into the yard.

"C'mon girls," he would urge, stopping to pop a cigar in his mouth. "Give your old dad a hand."

For this early introduction to wildlife, I remain eternally grateful. I can only hope that somehow he knows that once a year, a candle burns for him.

If you're looking for some dire mental illness lurking about my childhood—something that would come bite me in the ass in later years—you may be getting frustrated around now. And hey, if this is your primary interest, I am likely to continue to frustrate you. I did not foam at the mouth. I did not get lost in my own private world. Nor was my family "dysfunctional," as professionals are so fond of putting it. For sure, we had our quirks, also our share of problems, but the truth is that despite the evitable ups and downs, I had a relatively happy childhood. Even a relatively secure one. I knew who I was. I knew where I belonged. I had a family who loved me. And I had a sense of history and my place in it. That said, let me admit that while my childhood was blessed for first seven years, after that, things did begin to complicate, though I was not the one who found myself adrift.

It was a June afternoon—one day after Rose and I received our first pair of glasses—and recess was over. The blackboard that ran across the front of our classroom had been erased, but not washed. So you could see powdery smudges everywhere. All of the students were back at their desks. Some had their arms crossed in front of them and were resting their heads. Lenny Cherniak was sticking his tongue out at Jill Bloomfield. Scrawny Becky Balek was biting her fingernails. Just one seat over from me, my sister was holding her new glasses in her hand, carefully examining them. Delighted to be able to see better at long last, I was sitting upright, casting my eyes about the room, but I eventually came to focus on the woman facing us—our beautiful teacher Miss Sampson, whose blonde hair always fascinated me.

Miss Sampson tossed back her head, and a ray of light caught some of the strands, making them glow. Then picking up a package, she rose from her chair and went through the class, row by row, placing a sheet of paper on each desk. Once she was back at her desk, everyone was sitting up straight, and all eyes were on her.

"Boys and girls," she announced, "we're going to do something really fun right now. You see that sheet of paper on your desk?"

"Yes, Miss Sampson," we all called out.

"Good. Now take out your crayons and draw the most important thing that has ever happened to you. And Becky, try not to worry about anything," she hastened to add, glancing at scrawny Becky Balek. "There's no right and wrong here."

Ignoring the barrage of questions that instantly ensued and checking only once to see what Rose was up to, I started to draw the tramcar story. I began by creating a general outline of a tramcar. Then I added windows. Then wheels. Asking myself what to put in next, I decided, the Mounted Police with their horses charging. I began to draw a Mountie all right, but barely had I commenced colouring in his jacket than I found myself staring at the crayon and pondering a hypothetical that many a child comes to ponder at some point or other—what it would feel like having a crayon in one's nose? Why not find out? Without giving it a second thought—I was that curious—I stuck the crayon up my left nostril, fully confident that it was extractable. Instinctively, I sniffed in. Just like that, the crayon was gone. Frantic, I plunged my index finger up my nostril searching for the missing crayon. Nothing. And how strange my nose was feeling! Like when you have a bad cold and are all plugged up, but ever so much worse. And something way up high was throbbing. Trembling and realizing I had just made a whopper of a mistake, I raised my hand. To my dismay, at that very moment, up went Rose's hand.

As it happened, Miss Sampson was standing in the aisle to Rose's left, bent over Becky's notebook. So she didn't see either of us. Rose's arm kept waving back and forth and stretching higher and higher. Finally, beside herself, Rose could wait no longer. Tears trickling down her cheeks, she sprung up and yelled, "Miss Sampson, something's wrong with our nose."

Turning pale, Miss Sampson dropped Becky's notebook, and before I knew it, there she was, hovering over Rose.

"Sweetie, what's happened to your nose?" she asks.

"Dunno," Rose answers.

"Well, Rose, what does it feel like?" she persists.

"Can't breathe."

I see Miss Sampson place her hand on Rose's forehead. I see her pick up Rose and start walking toward the door. And I just can't believe what's happening. How can Rose confuse people at a time like this? Doesn't she know I'm in trouble? I rise from my desk and screech something the like of which I've never said before. "Miss Sampson," I shout, "it's not her. It's me. It's me."

Miss Sampson turns around, gently lowers Rose to the floor, and stares at me. Rose stares at me too, but as if I have just wounded her.

"Nomi, you know it's *us*," she insists.

I pause for a second, but ultimately, it is not the shock on Rose's face that compels me. It is the uncertainty on Miss Sampson's.

"It's me, Miss Sampson. Honest," I reiterate.

Miss Sampson's eyes begin darting back and forth between the two of us. Maybe if I explain.

"Oh Miss Sampson, I made a booboo," I blubber. "I stuck a crayon up my nose, and when I tried to get it back, it wouldn't come."

Her eyes settling down, Miss Sampson reaches for my hand and rushes Rose and me to the principal's office. Once the two of us are seated, she takes Mrs. Esherwood aside, whispers something in her ear, then leaves. The second that Miss Sampson is gone, Mrs. Esherwood smiles at us tenderly. Then she pulls two tissues from the box of Kleenex on her desk and hands one to each of us, saying, "Now don't be scared, girls, but I'd like you to blow. Blow real hard, okay?" Relieved that something is finally happening, I do as she instructs. On the first blow, nothing much does happen. I blow another five times, adding as much force as I can muster. The tissue is soaked in blood. I glance over at Rose's tissue. No sign of blood.

I feel as if I am going to faint. I see Rose checking out the two tissues. I take in the confusion on her face.

"Oh Nomi," she asks, looking at me uneasily, "are we bleeding?"

"*I'm* bleeding," I shout. "*You're* not bleeding."

While Rose says nothing further, she places her hand in mine and starts initiating the message. One squeeze. A second squeeze. Wishing that she'd go away, I continue blowing my nose. If I just keep blowing, maybe the crayon will come out. But no. It doesn't.

Mrs. Esherwood assures me that everything is going to be fine, that lots of people go through life breathing through a single nostril—which, somehow, does not make me feel one iota better. Before long, Mom and Dad show up. Now where Rose and Dad disappear to, I am not sure, but Mom takes me to the doctor, who sticks this strange instrument up my nostril and, thankfully, removes the crayon. "Here, Naomi," he says, offering me the crayon. "A souvenir, eh?"

That night, as we lay next to each other in bed, Rose kept her distance and said nothing for the longest while. Eventually, she turned toward me and asked, "Nomi, our nose is feeling better, isn't it?"

I knew that I had hurt her; and this terrible realization came over me—that despite how much we loved one another, I was going to hurt her again and again. Overwrought, I started to weep. I could hear her crying too. "Yeah, our nose is feeling better," I said.

This was the very last time I ever referred to "our" nose or "our" feelings, and this was the beginning of a shift which was nothing short of titanic. From now on, whenever Rose asked, "are *we* it?" I would answer, "I don't know if *you're* it." And when Rose gave my hand two squeezes, I would continue to hold her hand, at times even quite tenderly, but I would not give the mandatory response, though I can't count the times that Rose would initiate.

It is not that I was trying to be mean. But I kept finding myself bothered by things that had once been dear to me—bothered more and more with every passing day. I would grit my teeth when Rose would look at me knowingly and I could tell that she was in my head again. I even began hating it when teachers called me "Rose." "I'm not Rose, right?" I would snap, glaring at Miss Shkwarok. "My name is Naomi. Doesn't even sound like Rose." What I most resented, though, was being stopped from doing things that were important to me just because they didn't interest her. Sure, I got to go the cinema, but only once a month. And it looked as if I was going to be stuck at Champlain Elementary forever. As for talking to Mom or Dad about it—totally pointless. How many times had I asked to go to the cinema more often only to have them mutter something about Rose, then shake their heads!

What made matters worse, Rose was clingier than ever. "Wait for me," she would call out as I headed for the washroom.

"Leave me alone," I would answer.

The impasse continued for over a month. The time came when I was grasping at straws. I so wanted to be more individual, separate, private, that I would use any strategy, however impractical. When I was happy, I would purposely give myself sad thoughts just to throw off her inbuilt radar. And I would eat food that both of us found yucky because I knew that Rose would never touch it.

"How come you suddenly like kasha?" my father asked, his eyebrow raised. "Thought I was the only Yid in this family that liked kasha."

"Kasha's yummy," I answered.

Fortunately, I was more transparent than I realized. And so it is that one evening, my mother called me into the living room.

"Want me to fetch Rose?" I asked.

"No. We'll talk to Rose some other time. Right now, we wanna talk to *you*," Mom answered.

When I arrived in the room, Dad was in his favourite chair, puffing away on a cigar, and Mom was on the couch. Two coffee mugs sat on the end table, and Mom was reaching for one.

"Baby, come sit beside me," Mom invited.

After I nestled in, she looked at me earnestly. "Naomi," she said, "you know, sometimes, when you get older, it's not so much fun being a twin. You maybe wish you weren't one. You ever have feelings like this?"

"I love Rose," I answered, instantly panicking. "Please don't take her from me."

"No. No. That's not what we're talking about. But maybe you'd like something different?"

"Different?"

"You know. Like how you go to the movies and she doesn't. Well, maybe there are other things you'd like, yeh? Things, Rose doesn't like."

Touched by how kind Mom was being, and figuring that it was now or never, I went for it. "Mom," I began, "do we always have to wear the same clothes?"

She took a sip of her coffee and looked at me tenderly. "No," she answered.

"You don't like it when people confuse the two of you, do you?" asked Dad.

I shook my head.

"Yeah, I was getting that feeling. Makes perfect sense," he added, a mischievous grin coming over his face. "You know, that's why I make sure to wear different clothes than your mother over there. Otherwise, how are people going to be able to tell us apart?"

At this, we all burst out laughing.

"Moshe, you're impossible!" Mom exclaimed. "Okay, Naomi," she continued, focusing back on me. "Anything else?"

"The movies. I'd like go to the movies once a week."

"And just when do you think you'd be going to those movies of yours?" my father asked.

"Well, my friend Kenneth goes on Saturday afternoons."

Dad rose from his chair and began pacing back and forth. "On Shabbes, the girl wants to go? No way any member of this family is going to desecrate Shabbes."

"Well, how about Thursday night?" my mother suggested.

"A seven-year-old going out every Thursday night? Who has ever heard such *meshugahs*!"

Mom glared at my father. "Moshe, for God's sake, sit down. What's wrong with you anyway? We agreed we were gonna hear the girl out. So we'll hear the girl out, yeh?"

"What's wrong with *me*? What's wrong with *you*? She's seven years old. That's seven. Not eight. Not nine. Not ten. Seven."

"Moshe enough. We'll just listen to what she wants, and we'll make a decision later."

Dad continued to object, but eventually he did sit down. Also, he placed his feet up on the Ottoman—a fairly reliable indicator that he was intending to stay put.

"Okay," he grumbled, taking another puff on his cigar. "What in blazes else?"

"I, uh, uh, I'd like to go to Peretz school," I stammered.

"You wanna what?"

My mother shrugged her shoulders. "What's the big deal? Lots of kids go."

"Do you have any idea how much that costs? And you know how much religion they teach? Zippo. Socialism, yeah, but not religion. Still, I'll give you this. Getting a good Yiddish education, it never hurts. And as long as we're just talking..."

For the next little while, Mom and Dad discussed the pros and cons. Then they asked me to leave, promising to give everything serious thought. "Sweetie," Mom added, just as I reached the door.

"Yeah?"

"You'll be nice to you sister, yeh? You know, this isn't her fault, and none of this is easy on her."

"Yes, Mom. Promise."

It felt absolutely wonderful cuddling up to Rose that night. For the first time in weeks we touched heads, squeezed hands, held one another. Though I could not help but feel that I had betrayed her. Would she ever be able to forgive me? I wondered.

Next day, the verdict was in: I could start going to the movies weekly as long as it was only to the Deluxe. And they would look into getting me into Peretz school next year.

The die was cast. And the world that I so longed for was at my fingertips.

3. NAOMI

HOW DOES ONE PREPARE to meet a loved one whom one *ought to* know, that rhyme and reason suggests one *does* know, but whose entire being alludes? When almost nothing adds up, how does one navigate—so to speak—the world of the "sane"?

In the closing weeks of June 1973 I met a handful of people from that mysterious world beyond the hospital walls—people, it would seem, who knew a great deal about me, had literally known me for years, in some cases intimately, but whom I oddly did not know. Now those meetings, for sure, were technically "memorable." However, even when I did recall those forays into another dimension—those moments when I was treated to a sneak preview of the strange new existence awaiting me—as often as not, I would want to crawl back to the safety of "everyday life"—e.g., lining up for meds, *kibitzing* with the other patients, discussing the ins and outs of digestive problems. When the craziness of the sane world met the craziness of mine, moreover, utter confusion could rein—though it was not without its tender moments.

It was one p.m., and with lunch over, several of us patients were hanging in the dayroom. The indomitable Jackman was leaning against the south wall, rolling a cigarette. His glasses inching down his nose, Bob was standing in the middle of the room, alternately proclaiming the superiority of the English language and earnestly imploring us economically challenged peons, "Buy low, sell high." Her hands probing behind the cushions, Emily appeared to be checking the couch for sperm. Just your typical Sunday afternoon, all of it alluringly comforting, the way the familiar is, yes?

This notwithstanding, there was a heaviness in the air. Not ten minutes ago, you see, an older patient who'd been taciturn for days had broken his silence. "Young people," he'd observed plaintively, "you do not know what it is like to suddenly realize that you will never play in a world-class philharmonic because in the final analysis, you haven't the talent." And while his regrets might strike some as privileged, a good half the patients nodded. Shattered dreams, is that what we're all doing here?, I wondered. I glanced at Jack, then at each of the sensitive souls who'd found it in their heart to care, and I felt pride at who we were. Little did I suspect that I was destined to find that moment again. Shortly afterward, I checked the clock. Then I turned my mind to the task at hand—the imminent arrival of "my husband."

Thankfully, I recollected most of my visit with Dr. H., was as prepared as one could be under the circumstances—had slipped on my dress, even turned up early. Determined to give this my best, I was sitting on my favourite chair, trying to recall this putative husband when Zelda slipped in next to me. "Take a gander at how I looked before this here venerable institution got its hands on me," she urged, passing me a photograph. "A knock-out, wasn't I?" I lowered my head, squinted. To my surprise, the image before me was of a slim young woman, her eyes clear, not a hint of a tic anywhere. Dear Zelda, and to think! I looked up, about to comment. And that's when I spotted him. Crossing the threshold, his step bold, his head high, was an astonishingly over-dressed stranger.

Five-foot-five at most, the visitor was wearing a pin-stripped suit, a black silk shirt, a midnight blue cravat. Oxfords were on his feet, cuff links on his shirt cuffs, and what appeared to be a South American hat on his head. He was also carrying some kind of container—a briefcase, I think—and he kept dipping into it.

My first reaction was disappointment, even a kind of embarrassment, for I had been expecting someone taller, yes, and more virile, though I'm not at all convinced that this is the right word. However, I quickly took in how everyone else was responding. Jack and Bob excitedly rushed over and slapped him on the back, which rather surprised me since I could swear that Jack had referred to him as "a consummate asshole" just yesterday. Zelda grinned from ear-to-ear. Even Emily lit up. Not a bad endorsement all and all, given that Emily was suspicious of most men.

"You're right, Zelda," I murmured half apologetically. "You really were gorgeous." Then I took another long look at the man.

He was not what you would call "conventionally handsome," but in addition to a swagger that was strangely pleasing, he had engaging dark eyes. As people greeted him, he would reach into his briefcase and hand them a cinnamon bun, those large eyes of his twinkling. Before long, he was distributing these icing-coated goodies to everyone, even staff, most of whom seemed to be as delighted to see him as the patients, though Eliza—a part-time nurse—kept her distance. The moment came when he looked my way, the most endearing smile on his face. And instantly, my disappointment vanished.

Catching my eye, he raised his hand as if urging me to wait. Once a good two dozen buns had been eagerly grabbed by the excited throng around him, he gallantly pulled out a box of chocolates and began advancing toward me. "Why look at you, sitting up and everything," he gushed, stopping inches away. "Great to see you, Naomi girl." Then as if it were the most natural thing in the world, he leaned forward and planted a kiss on my cheek. Not one of those hasty pecks, but lingering and full-lipped.

While Jack and Zelda held my hand now and then, while I

had been jabbed, dragged, strapped down, prodded—indeed, had every manner of thing done to my body—no one had touched me that way for a long long time. Not sexual, but intimate in its own way, as if we were flesh of each other's flesh. And I felt strangely grateful.

"Thanks. You're uh, well, Mr. Smith, aren't you?" I stammered.

Curiously, he continued to smile as if nothing in the least out-of-the-ordinary had happened. Now I was hoping he'd say, "Call me Bill," or "Call me Jeff." No such luck. He simply nodded, then graciously tipped his hat. Obviously, a gentleman.

"These for me?" I ask, taking hold of the chocolates.

"Surely are, love."

As he sits down, I put aside the chocolates and begin nibbling on one of the buns, praying that his first name will come to me.

Picking up something's amiss, his eyes soften. "Naomi, girl," he begins once more, "I was giddy as a recently kissed schoolboy to learn you were doing better. Now please don't get your knickers in a knot if you don't actually remember me. Whatever you've been told, it's fine. And you and me, we'll just take it from there."

"I'm so sorry that I don't know you—I can't imagine how that feels."

"Oh, sweetie, nothing to worry about," he murmurs. "You're the one in trouble, and we're gonna do our damnedest to make sure everything works out this time."

"Kind of you. Also good of you to bring buns for everyone."

He proudly announces that they're his own.

"Bake in your spare time, do you?" I ask in all innocence.

"Nope. A professional."

"Sorry. My mistake. I could have sworn someone said you were a teacher."

At this, he startles, then leans toward me, takes both my hands in his. "Oh Naomi," he utters, his eyes holding mine, "I should have realized and explained right away. You see, I'm not Earl, and Earl, he's not coming for another hour or two."

"Earl?"

"I see. I see.... Okay, buddy. Let's start from the beginning. Your husband's name is Earl—Earl Smith. Me, I'm Gerald—Gerald Smith."

"You're a relative then?"

"Well, in a manner of speaking."

"I thought..."

"Yup, of course, you did. What else would you think? Now am I a total clodhopper or what? What a muddle, eh?"

Feeling doomed to keep making mistake after mistake, I am on the verge of tears. However, Gerald begins to grin, and in seconds we are both chortling.

He explains that he is a relative by marriage. Then he excuses himself to call his son Les. When he returns, he clarifies that while his son is a big boy now—all of five, he puts it—he sometimes needs check-ins. Then, again he gallantly tips his hat.

"Well, he's one lucky little boy," I gush. "To be honest, I was a little disappointed when you said you weren't my husband. I may be crazy, but, hey, not so crazy that I can't see you're a very sweet man."

"Hell, Naomi, I've never thought of you as crazy. Hard times, is one thing. Crazy is another. As for your sentiments about yours truly, I'm flattered. Truly flattered. Though I should tell you, Earl, he's a real good chap too."

"So I've been told. You're sure of that, are you?"

"And then some," he declares mysteriously. "But hey, hows about I explain?"

Murmuring something about privacy—hardly St. Pukes' strong suit—he takes my hand, and moments later, we are in my room. No sooner are we seated than he gives me an encouraging smile, assures me that we've had this little chat before, that he knows it'll be okay.

"Earl, he's not exactly a prize, that it?" I check. "And that's how I ended up here."

"Oh Naomi, we all have our faults, but rest assured, Earl, he's decent. And here's the thing," he adds, eyeing me intently. "I should know. I was his first wife."

"You were his what?" I ask dumbfounded.

"His first wife. I'll explain in a sec. Right now, suffice it to say that we both of us found other partners that were, well, better suited, and you can believe me when I assure you that you've nothing to worry about on my account."

This was too much. "Look," I interjected. "I'm not meaning to be a bigot, and I'm sorry if this hurts your feelings, but I really wasn't prepared for a gay husband."

"In this case," said he, an unmistakable twinkle in his eye, "you're not gonna be disappointed. That chap of yours—straight as a fuckin' arrow."

Perplexed, I eyed Gerald from head to foot, as if his body would magically clarify what his words did not. And that's when I notice. The way he was positioning his legs. Closer together than before. A bit like...

"You're a woman?" I finally asked, the charm of the situation beginning to hit me.

"Well, that's kind of a matter of definition, isn't it?" he pointed out good naturedly, "and if you'll excuse the pun, it's not straightforward. But if you're inquiring about the status of my genitals, yup. Sure as shit is a cat. Vagina, clitoris, uterus, the whole nine yards." Then he winked at me and smiled.

"And so Les is..."

"He's my own sweet little boy—mine and Earl's. Now he's at your place weekends and can get under foot, but he's a fine lad, and I'm sure you'll come to love him."

The family dynamics were getting far too complicated, though I could not but be drawn to Gerald. Man, woman, or ministering angel, there was something wonderful about him. And, hey, I had been in the loony bin long enough to know that the whole idea of "normal" was a bit of a crock. Anyway, I was comfortable with him and was getting the distinct impression that we had something in common beyond the obvious. Now I was so given to doubting myself that I was about to dismiss this feeling as foolishness when I called to mind that look on nurse Eliza's face. Leaning against the south wall in the day-room, she had been staring at him as if he were from another planet. Not unlike how the clueless *klutzes* used to gawk at Rose and me. Had I been a clueless *klutz* a moment ago? Just who was this Gerald Smith? And how was I to think of him?

As I struggled with these questions, he whipped a corn pipe from his trouser pocket; and for the next little while, he puffed away, casually relaying one highly personal story after another as if we were bosom buddies who'd simply lost touch. He spoke of initially meeting his partner Miu in Toronto. "A dyke also but hardly butch," he clarified. He spoke about divorcing Earl. About moving to Toronto to be near Miu. While I was not sure why, he made a particular point of specifying that the only reason that Earl came to Toronto was to be near his son. Then he began talking about how supportive Earl was.

"And y'know, were Earl a jerk," Gerald pointed out, his eyes narrowing, "he could have gotten sole custody just like that. I mean, look at how the courts would see it: Two dyke perverts—one who struts around like a man! And trust me, I've heard the stories. Most fellas would've. So I know what I'm talking about when I say he's a good guy."

Now while he said not a word about how I fit in, he genuinely seemed to care about me. He asked about my digestion. He inquired about my memory, showing far more interest than anyone else to date except Jack.

"I'm aware I didn't help much last time round," he acknowledged, "but I'm eager to help now. Those memory problems, love, any way I can give you a hand with them?"

"Not sure. But telling me things, that works. Though I'm afraid you might have to keep repeating yourself."

"In that case," he answered, "we should be a great match you and me, cause I'm forever repeating myself. Can't tell you how embarrassing it is to be in the middle of a perfectly good yarn only to see folk rolling their eyes. That ever happen to you, Nomi?"

Now "Nomi" was Rose's name for me. So his using it took me by surprise.

"Sorry. You rather I not call you that?" he asked.

"No, actually, I like it....I...I mean I *think* I like it."

"Oh Nomi girl," he exclaimed, "not being sure of anything, that must be hard. You know," he went on, catching my eye, "I can't pretend to understand the hell you're in, but my guess is that it takes the courage of a tiger just to get up in the morning."

I nodded gratefully. "Gerald," I observed, "you say that like someone who knows. It like that for you too?"

"Well, I've been lucky—real lucky—but for sure, I have my days."

Oh yes, I wanted this man in my life, wanted him no matter what ended up happening between me and the mysterious Earl Smith.

At Gerald's insistence, I opened the chocolates at long last. Then we set aside the picture map, which I couldn't make out anyway, and took turns guessing what was inside each piece. One of us would guess. The other would take a bite. And then the two of us would giggle like teenagers upon discovering that we were way off base.

"Let me ask you something," I finally hazard, setting down the box. "Gerald, no one's been able to tell me how I ended up here. Just what happened?"

"Sorry, love. Been asked not to talk about that, but this, I can assure you—you've nothing to be ashamed of."

I breathe a sigh of relief. Then I begin fingering another chocolate. "Well then, let me ask you something completely different, but likewise important," I say, chomping into my eighth piece with renewed gusto. "This is *klutzy* of me, I know. So pardon my ignorance, but how am I refer to you? 'She' or 'he?'"

"'He' generally," he tosses out without a moment's hesitation. "'She' on those increasingly rare occasions when I don a dress. No 'he-she's.' And for the love of God, never never never 'it.'"

"Got it. And what would you like me to call you?"

Gerald leans back in his chair, takes a puff on his pipe, and considers. "Now, Miu, she calls me 'Ger,' which would be just fine. On occasion, some folk in the know call me 'the other Mrs. Smith'. While not my favourite name, that'd also be fine, but it could get a tad confusing since some call *you* that too."

"Do they really?" I ask, amused at the turnabout.

"Well, just those who knew me and the mister back when.... Now most folk, they just call me 'Gerald.'" Suddenly, he smiles to himself. Then he reaches into his back pocket, pulls out his wallet, and removes a picture. "Well," he qualifies, handing me the picture, "except for Les boy here."

I look at the picture, take in the family resemblance, nod. "And Les boy, what does he call you?"

"'Dad' when necessary. And, of course, 'mom' when necessary."

"And when it's not necessary?"

"Momma Gerald."

How fortunate that Momma Gerald was part of this family! No criticism of anyone else intended, I have no idea how I would have navigated this life of mine otherwise.

Over the next couple of visits, I was to learn much about the man. In his thirties, he was something of a history buff. He lived on a street called "Church" with his wife and son. As was readily apparent, he was an exceptional parent, with the patience of Job. His favourite Sunday activity was pounding the b'Jessus out of a full-sized punching bag that dangled from his bedroom ceiling—his "ace in the hole," he called it. Oh yes, and his remarkably deep voice generally allowed him to pass.

In all likelihood, additional details came out during that first visit also. The thing is, however, while we yakked on for another half hour at the bare minimum, the rest of the visit is a total blank. What is far more problematic, neither do I remember the ensuing visit with Earl. Not any of it. Not now. Not one hour after Earl left. Although I understand from staff, fellow patients—everyone—that meet we most surely did.

"You absolutely certain he was here?" I asked Jack.

As irked as ever by the thought of this all too real husband, Jack angrily plunked his elbows on the dayroom table and began rolling another cigarette.

"Jack?"

"Oh yeah, the consummate asshole was here chatting you up all right," he snorted, continuing to stare at the cigarette. "Couldn't be more than a hour ago."

"Any chance you could stop calling him that?" I checked.

"Nope."

Now preparing to meet a husband of God-knows-how-many years for the first time, that was one thing. Going through it all a second time and having to admit that I'd again forgotten, I couldn't imagine it. And as I tried to wrap my mind around it, willy-nilly, I again found myself sinking into hopelessness.

That night, I hit the sack early. The following night also. Of course, much as we might want to, no one gets to hide forever.

"C'mon, sleeping beauty. Phone call," called out Zelda, barging into my room.

It was early evening—and I was hiding out in bed. Last thing I wanted was to budge. However, Zelda insisted. Reluctantly, I advanced into the corridor and picked up the receiver. Now barely had I said hello, than a totally unfamiliar baritone voice came blasting at me.

"How's she cutting?" it demanded to know.

I wrack my brain for a possible answer. "Must have the wrong person," I finally respond. "Now I'm really really tired and so..."

"C'mon, Nomi," he objects. "Don't be telling me you don't

recognize my voice. No. No. Not this again. Darling, I was just there."

"Just where?"

"At the hospital. The fuckin' hospital!"

"When?"

"You know, just after you visited with Geraldine."

"Geraldine?"

"Gerald, Momma Gerald, or whatever fool thing she's now calling herself," he continues, mounting annoyance in his voice.

And that's when it hits me. "Earl?" I ask.

We are off to a dismal start, and we both know it. I quickly fess up to not remembering. And the two of us proceed to go in circles, growing more frustrated by the second.

"Look," he says at long last, "I'm coming in two days time for a visit, and I'm bringing Ruth with me. That's what I phoned to tell you, is all. You've outside privileges. How about we grab a table at a nearby restaurant, just hang out?"

For a moment, neither of us utters a word. "Oh, no! Don't be telling me you don't remember my explaining about Ruthie either!" he exclaims.

"What do you want from me?" I shout. "I don't know you. I don't know this Ruth. I greatly regret that you've been saddled with a wife who is *meshugah,* but maybe you should just cut your losses and get on with your life."

Earl's voice instantly becomes gentler. He assures me that he is in for the long haul. He points out that this is hard on him too. Then again he goes quiet.

"It's just that I needs my wife back," he suddenly announces, "and Ruthie," he adds, "she needs her mother."

"Her mother?"

"Yeah. Nomi, we have a baby girl."

Stunned, I feel the breath leave my body in one big whoosh. "I have a daughter?"

"You surely do. A beeuudeeful little girl. She's going to be two in a few weeks. Now woman, I'm not wanting to be rushing you, but Dr. Higgins says that you could be discharged in a couple of weeks, and it would be good if her mom were back home by her birthday."

"You mean you've been raising her by yourself for two years! And ... and I have a daughter!" I repeat.

"That's what I'm after telling you, Missus."

For the longest while, I stood there, the receiver pressed up against my ear, taking in nothing, feeling nothing. Suddenly, the receiver slipped from my fingers, and I was weeping. Weeping for myself, who could not function. Weeping for this helpless little creature who had no mother to speak of and perhaps never would. Weeping for this irritating but guiltless man who was trapped like a bird in a cage.

Naomi, you're on the phone. Pick up the phone, I told myself.

Inauspicious though it was, this was the beginning of my exodus from hospitalization number two. To say that the authorities had not properly prepared us would be a gross understatement. Nor did some all-pervasive maternal instinct sweep over me, guiding my hand, tutoring my heart, though Ruthie, for your sake, how I wish I could say otherwise! All I was sure of was that I could not function, that I did not want such pressure, and yet somehow I had to make this obtuse brain of mine turn over—for everything had changed. Suddenly. Fundamentally. Irreversibly.

For hours after that call, I paced the corridor, trembling at the sheer magnitude of it all. Eventually, I calmed down. And little by little, I found myself wondering about this tiny being called "my daughter." What did she look like? When had she started to walk? Had she ever called out "momma?"

As images of babies appeared and disappeared, Earl's voice began filling my head. At first, I worried that my schizoaffective disorder had developed into full-blown schizophrenia. But no. The voice wasn't outside. Inside. All of a sudden, sweat was pouring off my brow, and my entire body was trembling.

Something about that accent, those expressions. What had he said? "That's what I'm after telling you, Missus," and "how's she cutting?" What was it? Irish. No. Irish but not Irish. A Newfoundland brogue, I was sure of it. Yes. Did I recognize it from some east-coast film? Possibly, but there was something *beyond* the accent, *beyond* the expressions. Something in the timbre of the voice. I'd heard that voice before. Was it coming back? Was my memory coming back just as Dr. Higgins promised? And was everything going to fall into place after all?

I lay back down, cautiously optimistic.

4. NAOMI

Progress appeared to have been made, and it was with a giddy excitement that I drifted to sleep. Next morning, Earl phoned repeatedly. Initially, I held my breath, so sure was I that memories would start coming hard and fast. It seems that I was in a greatly altered universe, however, where the old rules no longer applied. Where one memory did not lead to another. Where associations stopped dead in their tracks.

Now I was determined to be positive regardless. I accepted all Earl's phone calls. I asked about Ruthie. Additionally, I availed myself of the opportunity to inquire about my family of origin. Many a salient fact came to light—Ruthie adored her half brother Les. We lived on a street called "Palmerston." Still, I learned sweet bugger all about my family of origin. Earl routinely responded, "Come on, Nomi. You aren't supposed to be thinking about your folks yet. Doctor's orders." What I couldn't wrap my mind around is: How could thinking about loved ones jeopardize one's recovery? What was likewise disconcerting, with every call, the plans for our family outing would mysteriously alter—and I could not keep up. Fortunately for the lot of us, "the other Mrs. Smith" kept running interference. Generous to a fault, at one point, Ger hightailed it over to the hospital, and with the aid of the most elegant pen that ever I'd laid eyes on—"the silver Montblanc" he called it—he printed out "the agenda" in extra large letters. Shortly after he departed, much to my surprise, I dissolved into tears, whether from gratitude or fear, I couldn't for the life of me tell.

Strange. When I fanaticize travelling back in time and be-friending a younger version of myself, as to this very day, I occasionally do, this is one of the moments I think of visiting. I imagine myself wrapping my arms around this bewildered young woman, drying her tears, and guiding her step by step. *Iz gut*. Even in fantasy, though, I can't do what she wants—can't alter the course of her journey.

"Naomi, how's she cutting?" boomed a gargantuan voice. The big day was upon us. And this time, there was no question who this had to be. I looked up, my heart in a flutter.

The man approaching was tall as a mountain, on the hus-ky side, and at least ten years my senior. He had dark bushy eyebrows, a ruddy complexion, and thick angled lips. He was wearing jeans. With his hair prematurely grey and hanging well below his shoulders, he looked rather like a cross between a hippie and an Old Testament prophet.

Earl was clearly a man of action, for in short order, he had slipped a sweater over me. Then he gave me a quick peck on the cheek, placed his arm around me, and within minutes, we were outside the institution.

We took one step off the grounds, and I instinctively turned around. Interesting. While I had been imagining something along the lines of a medieval dungeon—people in lockup do—before us stood an utterly unremarkable building, one of those modern cement monstrosities that jut high into the skyline. So this's where us St. Pukers wile away our days. I began counting, trying to locate our ward, as if that innocuous site were the alpha and omega—the still point in a shifting universe.

"This way, Missus," called out Earl.

After that, everything becomes rushed, loud, dizzying. With Earl holding me tightly, we step off the curb, begin hurrying across what appears to be a major intersection. We are not even half way when horns begin to honk. The honking horns, they feel like so many hammers hitting. *Dear God, they're penetrating my skull! If I just turn around, I can get back to my bed in no time,* I tell myself. Then the noise lightens, and to my relief, we are on the other side of the street.

Now I am still trying to keep tabs on the hospital—if necessary, I can always beat a hasty retreat—when suddenly, we are into an abrupt turn, and what little sense of direction I have evaporates. Terrified at finding myself lost again, I call out "Earl," fully intending to beg him to take me back, when we approach a four-door Chevy.

"It's okay, Nomi. Here we are," says Earl.

Aware of the gravity of the moment, I take a deep breath, Then I peer into the back seat. A slender young Chinese woman is sitting there, a toddler on her lap.

"This is Mui—Gerald's partner. And Missus," he adds, opening the door and picking up the toddler, "bet you can guess who this is."

Now I greet Miu, but it is my daughter that grabs my attention. She is a chubby little being with alert hazel eyes. A big smile on her face, she is gazing at her father dreamily as if he were the prince of heaven. My heart suddenly aching for her, I open my arms and reach out. "Ruthie, this is your mommy," murmurs Earl, passing her carefully to me. Now for a second, she seems relatively content in my arms. Then, the babe is shaking her head and screaming "no." Whereupon, Earl hands her back to Miu.

And for all intents and purposes, so ended our first mother-daughter encounter.

What I remember next is finding myself in a dimly lit restaurant with a large oak bar at the back. We were seated at a table next to the window, Earl and I on one side, Miu on the other, the baby in a high chair next to Earl. A menu was in my hand. Aware that I could no more make it out than run a marathon, I let Earl order. Now initially, Miu talked nonstop with Earl, assiduously avoiding my eyes. Within short order, though, Gerald appeared, a little boy with an impish look at his side, and what tension there was lifted.

"Why hi there, laddio," called out Earl, smiling at his son. "How's she cutting?"

"Like a knife," the little boy answered.

It quickly became apparent that this gregarious little group knew a thing or two about having a good time. As we waited for dinner, Earl chugalugged an entire bottle of beer, the whole family watching as his Adam's apple bobbed up and down, the whole family cheering as the last drop of liquor vanished. Then half describing it, half acting it out, Gerald began providing a lowdown on his day.

"And you know what Sammy in delivery said today?" he asked at one point. "That he thinks Sadat's gonna go to war with Israel."

"Ger, he's not likely to attack Israel," Mui insisted. "In '67, he saw clearly enough what that militarized state could do."

Gerald reached for his pipe, lit it, and considered. "I kind of think Sammy's right. I mean, the tide is turning. And Sadat has guts."

Ruth was beginning to fuss. Noticing, Earl lifted her out of the high chair, placed her on his lap. "So the man has guts, you say," Earl observed, looking over at Gerald. "Now this could be interesting. He attacks Israel, and the whole Middle East blows up. Come to think of it, that has all the makings of an excellent film, especially in the hands of a good lefty. How about Godard, darlin'?" he asked, turning toward me, a conspiratorial expression on his face. "Think the chauvinist could handle it?"

Having understood little of the conversation and recollecting only snippets of a Godard film, I said, "Sure." Now I was scrambling to think of something at least vaguely intelligent to add—trust me, no easy feat when you're running on empty—when something caught my eye. Seated at the bar was a heavy-set woman looking my way. As I sat there wondering about her, mercifully, our dinner arrived.

After the waitress had deposited the last dish on the table, Earl returned his daughter to the highchair, and what appeared to be a family ritual commenced. A solemn look on his face, he announced, "Prayers everyone," and a hush came over the gathering.

Recalling my father's mealtime observances, I assumed that I had ended up in a religious family—Catholic perhaps? Now as it happened, Earl crossed himself all right. And he lowered his head. Then he looked up, winked at Les, and trumpeted, "Holy Mary, full of grace. Keep your son outta my face."

"Outta my face. Outta my face," little Les gleefully echoed.

As I was beginning to discover, Earl was what religious Christians call "a blasphemer." Not mean-minded, let me be clear, but someone who loved to poke fun at anything sacred. And as long as it was his own religion, why not? And, hey, no question, the man was a hoot.

Now I was finding them all likeable enough. However, by the time dessert rolled around, I could barely keep my eyes open. Trying to put my finger on the word for "hospital," I was about to suggest that we call it a day when the woman at the bar began to make her way over. I instinctively braced myself.

"Naomi," she exclaimed, bending down and kissing me on the cheek, "why I haven't seen you in years! You wicked girl, you! Why haven't you called?"

"You'll have to forgive me," I answered. "I haven't been well."

"Yeah, you do look, well, peaked," she acknowledged. She proceeded to press me for an update on a film that I'd apparently once intermittently been working on.

"Actually, I know nothing about the film," I finally said. "Now I mean no offence but I don't even remember you."

"That's just not possible," she objected, shaking her head

vigorously. "We used to get together daily. C'mon. It's Clara—Clara Merkowitz from film class."

"Sorry. You see, I've had uh, this procedure, and it's affected my memory."

"What kind of procedure?"

"Well...uh," I stammered, "electroshock."

"So you must have been in..."

"A mental hospital, yes. Still am. Just out for the day."

Clara startles, takes two steps back. I instinctively reached for Rose's hand only to remember that there was no Rose.

"Well, dear," she resumed, "maybe it'll all come back to you." Then she rejoined her friends at the bar but only after telling Earl how very sorry she is for him.

Only one thing that I wanted at that moment—to get back to hospital as quickly as I could. What had made me think that I could manage on the outside?

Now as I sat there mortified, I felt a hand on my shoulder. I looked up to find Gerald standing at my side. "Nomi," he cooed, "don't let the fuckers get you down."

"Be fair," Earl objected. "The woman's heart's in the right place."

Gerald glared at him. "Easy for you to say, idiot! You, she was actually nice to!"

"Hey! When we gonna play I-Spy?" hollered Les.

One hour and six I-Spy games later, I was back on the ward. Once again, I had a night of tossing and turning. I thought of Ruth screaming blue murder as I held her in my arms. I thought of a world filled with Claras lying in wait.

I would like to think that I chose to go home, that I chose to be with my child and husband. What mother and wife wouldn't? And for sure, Ruth and Earl deserved someone capable of making such a choice. In all honesty, however, that's not what happened. In the universe in which I found myself, words like "choice" were forever on everyone's lips; yet choice as the world defines it was strangely elusive. What did I have? Like Zelda and countless others, I had expectations and clearly prescribed roles. I took my meds because I was supposed to take my meds, because there was a line-up for meds, because day after day Nurse Ann announced, "time for meds," and into the line-up we all dragged ourselves. I called these people my family because everyone else called them my family, because they had been waiting for me as if they were family, although they bore oh so little resemblance to the family that I remembered and loved.

Now don't get me wrong. I was going home to them all right. Had not Nurse Ann said, "Naomi, you keep getting better, you might not need another course of ECT"? And had not Dr. H. made it crystal clear that doing better meant acting like a good wife and mother? Moreover, my imminent return to the bosom of my family was celebrated in group, discussed ad nauseam at meetings, marked down in the case file. So it had all the earmarks of a fact. But "choice?" That was a completely different kettle of fish. Additionally, while I liked the Smith family, was touched by their trying so hard, I was far from easy about this development.

What, after all, had I in common with them compared to the family I had lived with and loved these many years? And then there was Jack—that remarkable man who had been there from the beginning, who had almost single-handedly plucked me out of the fog. As had become abundantly clear, the mere presence of Earl was driving the two of us apart. Why, at this point, my best buddy was not even speaking to me.

Not the brightest career move, becoming a mental patient, eh? No options. No information. No end of complications. Few fringe benefits. 24/7 hours. As for retirement, don't even ask.

It was the day before my release. Everything had been arranged. Earl and I had even met with Dr. Higgins and had received something officially called "suggestions," but which had all the markings of instructions. Suggestion number one: I was not to worry about the memory problems, for they would resolve themselves shortly. Suggestion number two: Earl was to supervise the pill-taking until my memory kicked in. Suggestion number three: we weren't to talk about my family of origin until I was doing better.

Now I was sitting in the dayroom trying to recall the third "suggestion" when in walked Jack. To my surprise, he walked straight over to me and sat down on the tubular chair across from mine. "Hi there, kiddo," he said.

"You talking to me again?"

"I wasn't exactly *not* talking to you. I was *thinking.*"

Whereupon, he opened his cigarette case and popped a cigarette into his mouth. And an oddly reassuring ritual set in. Just as he had dozens of times before, he offered me a cigarette. And just I had dozens of times before, I replied, "Thanks, but I don't smoke."

"Really?" responded Jack unexpectedly.

"Yeah, really."

"Okay, kiddo, but it's one thing to jump to the conclusion that you don't smoke. Quite another to conclude that this family that you don't remember is safe for you."

"So, what kind of reason is that to act like a jerk?" I asked, starting to rankle.

He immediately apologized for his recent behaviour. He'd been scared that he wouldn't see me again. Now I tried to reassure him, but he was hardly convinced.

"Maybe you'll end up visiting. Maybe you won't," he retorted. "As for my being a welcome guest at your place..." he went on, the smoke slowly drifting out of his nostrils, "shit! Just cause you feel that way doesn't mean Earl does."

Once again, I had the distinct impression that he knew something that I didn't. Be that as it may, he suddenly went quiet—just sat there, the cigarette dangling from his lips, and when he did start speaking again, his tone had changed dramatically. "Naomi, please be careful," he urged plaintively. "This new family of yours, it really is new, and where are any of us without our roots?"

"Jack, forgive the presumption, but it's, well, yourself you're talking about, is it?" I hazarded.

There was a moment's hesitation. Then he cleared his throat, and as one second gave way to another, perceptibly, his face clouded over. "What happened to me," he murmured at long last, "it's called a residential school. Now those years, they're not something I go into. The thing is though, I was taken from *my* people and nothing's been right since."

I nodded sadly. "Jack, I'm so sorry. And the voices?"

"Started in long ago. Now contrary to what the goofball staff here think, there's damn well nothing wrong with most of my voices. Since when is it a sign of an imbalance to be in touch with spirits? But Principal Plank's voice, when that comes to me, I need to get rid of it, right? Also certain other voices. People say things, see. Hell, even here, even now—and what they say, it sticks in my head."

For a frightening moment—and God forbid anyone should land here often—a desperation came over Jack. His eyes wide, he began looking about anxiously. Then he grabbed his radio, turned it up high, and with it blaring like there was no tomorrow, held it tight to his ear. Moments later, he re-pocketed it, smiled as if to reassure me. "You know that orderly with the tattoo?" he asked. "Calls me Chief Bow-and-Arrow, right? Now Brad, he calls me stuff too."

"But Brad adores you."

"Only some days."

He went on to elaborate on the various shortcomings of St. Pukes. Now I cannot recall how the subject of meds arose. At one point, however, he threw up his hands and exclaimed, "As for those happy pills, worse than useless."

"They don't help with the voices?"

"They wipe out *all* of the voices, and thank-you very much,

I've had quite enough of me wiped out courtesy of the Canadian state."

"Yeah, I can see that," I said, laying my hand on his shoulder.

Then I found myself staring at Jack's face, hands, legs. And that is when I first took in a very interesting curious detail: There was a monumental difference between Jack and most of the other patients. To all appearances, except for the odd digestive problem, he was physically intact. No tremours. No tics. Why, he did not even look tired!

"You got the doc to cut back on your meds, didn't you?" I asked. "How on earth did you pull that off?"

Jack eyed me intently, but he did not answer. Eventually, he fished out his tobacco and ever the artist, he rolled three more cigarettes, each of them perfect. And we sat in silence as he puffed away.

As Jack started in on the second cigarette, Zelda pulled up a chair. Moments later, we were joined by Bob and Dora. "Say, anyone know 'Pack Up Your Troubles?'" asked Dora. She puckered her lips, whistled a few bars, then looked at the rest of us invitingly.

For the next couple of hours, most of us woefully off key, Jack periodically raising the radio to his ear, and Zelda slobbering throughout, we proceeded to lift our voices together, cheerfully mangling one golden oldie after another. Now and then staff poked their heads into the room, but they slipped away like moisture in the sun.

"Naomi," said Jack as I got up to leave, "how about standing next to me in the meds line tomorrow? Something I wanna show you. Who knows? Just may come in handy."

"You've got it," I answered.

I am told that I called Earl later that evening. Of this, I have no memory. What I do recall is getting up early next morning, at once excited and fearful. I bid farewell to the nurses on duty, then started to search for Emily. "Don't you remember? She was discharged yesterday," pointed out Brad. "Broads, they have all the luck."

I muttered an explicative under my breath, then hurried over to Zelda's room. Zelda was standing in the middle of the floor, trying in vain to zip up her jeans. After lending a hand, I threw my arms around her and held on for dear life. "You'll visit this here establishment once in a while, won't you?" she asked, her eyes tearing, "but dear heart, don't become a regular patron, if you know what I mean."

"Oh Zelda, you're an angel," I exclaim. "And don't think I don't know what you've done for me." Not yet ready to part with this incredible woman, I place my hands on either side of that dear twitching face and plant a kiss on each cheek. Then at long last, I head over to the nurses' station and cut in behind Jack in the meds line. And with this simple act, a new vista opens up, even choice.

Jack does not notice at first for he is listening to Bob hold forth on the significance of "the three eatables." I tap him on the shoulder. He gestures for me to move ahead of him. Now Brad is at the head of the line this morning, so receives his pills first. Finishing, he looks back at Bob, blurts out, "Your turn, Chink." "Schizophrenic just like I always said," jibes Bob, stepping forward. Bob done, I am next. I approach the counter, dutifully take my pills, and wash the lot of them down with water. Jack's turn. He deposits the pills in his mouth just like the rest of us—in his case, four pink ones—and downs the entire cup of water in a single gulp. Then he nods at Nurse Ann and begins strolling down the corridor, seemingly aimlessly, while I follow. Once out of view, he reaches into his pocket for a hanky, brings it to his lips, then slips it under my eyes, and there are the pills—all four of them. Here it was. Patient Self-Management Graduate Level.

"Called tonguing, right?" explains Jack, quickly re-pocketing his hanky. "You conceal the meds under your tongue, spit'em out first chance you get."

"And that's what *you* do?"

"What *a number of us* do. A couple of us pretty regularly, right? Now I'm not recommending anything here, but I wanted you to know how."

It has never so much as occurred to me to try to fake it, and my initial reaction is terror. I shake my head. "No way, Jack," I say. "Yes, a lot of what they do here is idiotic, but not taking my meds? I mean, I wanna get better."

"Fair enough," says Jack. "Just try to remember, is all."

I nod, fully aware that Jack's only trying to help. Then I excuse myself and begin racing toward my room, hoping that if I lie down, I will be able to still the pounding of my heart.

"Naomi," I hear Jack call out as I pick up my pace. I turn around to find Jack approaching me, his eyes tender.

"Sorry, kiddo," he says. "That was piss poor timing, wasn't it?"

"You can say that again."

We both smile. Then I reach for his hand, and we just stand there. "Oh Jack, how can I possibly leave you?" I murmur.

Well might I ask!

It was one hour later, and already, I was on my way. The car was on College St. directly in front of St. Pukes. Earl and I were standing next to it, and he had just popped my one and only suitcase into the trunk. I glanced up at the seventh floor, wondering if group had started yet. Almost instantly, I heard the trunk door slam, followed by Earl calling out, "C'mon, Missus."

I peered into the back seat, where Gerald and Ruth were engrossed in an adult-child game. Ruth reached up, grabbed Gerald's hat, then threw it on the floor. Gerald exclaimed, "Now where could my hat be?" while Ruth giggled. I smiled, pleased that little Ruthie was enjoying herself. I opened the back door, poked in my head, called out, "Hi there, sweetie." Ruth glanced at me nervously. As I inched closer, she grew progressively alarmed, and so I stopped. I simply told her that her mommy was happy to see her, then closed the door, climbed into the passenger's seat, and hoped for the best.

Seconds later, Earl was in the driver's seat, his key in the ignition, but for some reason, the car would not start. As he struggled with the engine, I turned to the side and caught sight of Gerald butting his head against Ruth's. Just the way Rose and I used to butt heads. For the first time, I could see something of Rose in Ruth. Something about the expression of the eyes, the way her head moved. I felt my heart leap. Yes. Yes. This surely was my daughter. Then I found myself wondering about Rose. What was she doing now? How could I have allowed that distance to build up between us? And what if anything had this to do with how I ended up at St. Pukes?

As I ponder this question, Earl exclaims, "Damn. Not dis again." Then he throws back his head, and begins to laugh. Minutes later, he turns the key again, and purr, goes the engine. It is the laugh, however, not the engine which grabs my attention, for with that laugh, something from those lost years, a tiny island of memory comes floating into view:

I remember that scene in Godard's *Sympathy for the Devil* where a group of terrified women are being raped at gunpoint. I remember coming out of the Winnipeg Film Society's special showing of it so appalled that I could not stop myself from muttering "that sexist jerk!" I remember this stranger noticing, tossing back his head and laughing, then sauntering over to me, his arms crossed, announcing, "Hi. I'm Earl. Now I don't mean to be rude, but that man's a solid supporter of women's rights." I remember throwing up my hands, exclaiming, "Sure. Sure. Celebrating the raping of white women, what a great way to support women's rights!" Then he begged me to join him for dinner, ignoring every solitary "no." Finally, I broke down and agreed. Where did we go? Kelekis. Yeah, the Greek burger joint at Aberdeen and Main, where I introduced him to the yummiest shoe-string fries in town. And there I sat, listening as this male chauvinist pig droned on and on about what a great director Godard was, totally missing the point that in the name of anti-racism, violence against women was being celebrated. Eager to change the subject, I asked him where he was from. He named several Newfoundland towns, villages, outports—Witless Bay, Harbour Grace, Brigus Junction. "And how do you find Winnipeg?" I inquired. Understandably, he shuddered as he spoke of our gruelling winters. Then he began critiquing various parts of our community, at one point referring to those "snot-nosed Winnipeg Jews," and it was all I could do not to walk out on him. Now how did the date end? Can't find it. Can't find it. Oh yes. I thanked him for the evening, but assured him that it was strictly a one-time deal. Then I hopped on a bus, happy to be free of him at last. When I arrived home—or was that someone else's apartment?—I immersed myself in a long hot bath, as if trying to scrub away the very feel of the man. The second I was out of the tub, I phoned my friend Alice, told her what had happened. "Pity the poor woman that ends up with that *schmuck*," I jested. Then I made myself some cocoa. And then.... No. That's it! That's all I can remember.

I wrack my brain, hunting for another island of memory or even a telling detail. Now I wrest a few more exchanges out of this electroshocked brain of mine, but no further meeting, no additional scene of any sort with or without him, and nothing that would in the least endear him to me. Had I made the blunder of the century for God knows what reason and married a man whom I could not stand? An anti-Semite even! Panicking, I reach for the door handle and begin to turn it when a few salient points come to mind. While he may be sadly lacking in some respects and while he may well not be my type, Earl did have some absolutely sterling qualities: He supported Ger when he could have thrown him to the wolves. He is clearly a wonderful father. And in his own way, is he not standing by his nutso wife? His nutso *Jewish* wife even? And do I not owe him? Owe all of them? Anyway, who knows? A more promising memory might yet surface.

I removed my hand from the door and chuckled at how ludicrous the situation was. I saw Earl glance at me nervously from the corner of his eye. I immediately quieted down, realizing how a madwoman laughing out-of-the-blue would strike him, indeed would strike most anyone in this eerily sane world that I was entering. Then ever a pragmatist, I took the only sensible course of action: I leaned back in my seat and dreamed of the Winnipeg years, while allowing myself to be driven away from my dear friends to a home which I did not know, in a city which was alien to me, to live with daughter that I could not remember and a husband that I had dated *once*— and found insufferable.

5. NAOMI

How do you know but every Bird that cuts the airy way
Is an immense world of delight, closed by your senses
five? —William Blake

DESPITE SOME REAL CHALLENGES, my early life continued to be one of riches. The animal world beckoning us, twice a week at the bare minimum, Dad, Rose, and I would rush outside to feed the sparrows. A year seldom passed without some new tenant taking possession of the room adjoining ours, and while that meant facing new expressions of exasperation whenever we tiptoed through the room to go to the bathroom, it also meant whole new worlds of experience waiting to be tapped. Of all the magical times together, however, it was Shabbes I most adored.

Starting in my eighth year, early Friday morning the whole family would rise from our slumbers. Breakfast quickly behind us, Mom would say, "Okay girls, one and half hour of cleaning." And together we would take on the *mitzvah* of putting the house in order, "'Scratches,' you know what they are?" Dad would ask whenever he noticed a new mark on some stick of furniture. "God's way of assuring you that someone's been here before you." Come evening, we would sit around the dining room table, pleased by what we had made together, in awe of what had been graciously allowed. "Girls," Dad would murmur, his eyes aglow, "remember this—Shabbes is our temple, Shabbes, our holy tabernacle. And you know something else? Our enemies, they can never destroy it because it is built on time."

Now Dad had been expressing that sentiment as long as I could remember, but it was not until my eighth year that I started actively grappling with it.

"Dad, you always say that," I pointed out one Shabbes, "but I don't get it. Being built on time, what's that mean? And just why can't you destroy something built on time?"

Dad pushed his chair back from the table and stopped to consider.

"Well," he said, "you can't put your hands on time, now can you?"

"But why not?"

"Well, cause ... cause ... Ida, help me out here," pleaded Dad.

Mom's eyebrow arched as she turned the question over. "Naomi, look around you," she eventually answered. "Shabbes, just where is it?"

"Well, there's the candlesticks," I offered.

"Fine," said Mom. "Now, watch." And without further adieu, she removed the candlesticks from the room. "Don't worry. I'll bring them back," she assured us, sitting back down and eyeing us intently. "But tell me, it still Shabbes?"

"Uh huh," Rose and I answered in unison.

"And what if we were in jail instead of at home? It still Shabbes?"

"Jail!" I exclaimed, surprised by the question. "Mom," I teased, "tell me you aren't thinking of taking up bank-robbing."

Mom giggled, then scrunched up her face. "Good one, but answer the question."

"Well, I guess so."

"And Shabbes, it would still happen Friday at sundown, yeh?"

"Uh huh."

"Very good. So, Naomi, you thought the candlesticks were Shabbes. Anything else you think is Shabbes?"

At this, a mischievous look came over Dad. "Please, not the food. Don't anyone say it's the food," he begged, holding onto his plate tenaciously.

While we all cracked up, Mom had made her point. Of course, I still did not fully understand the concept. Nonetheless, I had a burgeoning sense of this mysterious dimension so powerful that once something were wrapped up in it, no one could touch it, hurt it, make it vanish. Time, it was called. And it was not that thing that my teacher Miss Bokofsky saw when she glanced at the clock. Not that thing that Dad wasted or Mom ran out of. Something steady that came back to you again and again, no matter where you might be. Something shared, yet tucked away, hidden so deeply in the recesses of your soul that those bent on harm could not find it, could only search in vain. And from that day hence, I harboured a special respect for time.

Now my eighth year was something of a turning point in our family, for our folks began creating more family outings. Did our resources allow us to tackle anything ambitious? Hardly. However, like so many other working-class parents of that era, mine had a knack for making even the most modest excursion seem special.

We would be sitting in Kelekis—the legendary Greek hamburger joint at Aberdeen and Main. Inevitably, Dad would lean back in his chair and say, "So, let's see what's new." And dutifully, we would pour over that well-fingered menu. "Okay, girls," he would ask after a respectable amount of time had elapsed, "what's it to be today?"

"Burgers," I would announce.

"Oy! I was thinking just a soda. A hamburger yet the girl wants? Made with unkosher meat too. Impossible! Mind you," he would eventually hedge, "we're instructed only to keep a kosher home. And I ask you—is this our home?"

I would adamantly shake my head. Then he would turn to Rose.

"Now *aroisgevofeneh gelt* number two—I suppose you want a hamburger also?" he'd ask.

"With shoe-string fries."

"Hamburgers and fries both! Just don't know. Ida, whatchya think?"

"Well, if we top it off with a soda," she would suggest, a glint in her eye.

At which point Dad would turn to the waitress and announce, "Miss—large cokes for everyone...and...and...and..."

"Fries and burgers with the works," Rose and I would eagerly add.

Now it was in my eighth year as well that our jaunts to Winnipeg Beach began. I remember the entire family swimming together and everyone trying to get as far from Dad as possible because he had this worrisome habit of sneaking up and dunking you. My most poignant memory, however, is of something that surely would have been an utter bore, were it not for Mom's ingenuity.

Of course I was already convinced that Mom could solve everything. This only confirmed it.

It was two weeks after that momentous meeting in the living room. While my folks had seemed agreeable to everything, to my chagrin, not a single change had yet materialized—this despite their having spoken with Rose. Apparently, they'd asked her if she too would like something special, and she'd kept insisting, "what Nomi's getting." Eventually, though, she'd set her sights on trips to Winnipeg Beach. And so here were Rose and I, sweltering in the back seat of the family Buick, twiddling our thumbs, on this stuffy drive that seemed endless.

Every ten, fifteen minutes, one of us would pipe up, "Dad, almost there?"

"What do you think? I'm Merlin the Magician?" he'd reply.

Just as Rose was inquiring for the fifth time, Dad slammed

down the break pedal because he'd come perilously close to this two-toned Chevy.

Mom leaned forward. She stared at the Chevy disapprovingly. Then she looked over at Rose, her eyebrow arched. "Girls," she suddenly said, "see that good-for-nothing car up ahead? Think we should pass it?"

With all due diligence, Rose and I scrutinized the offending vehicle. Then we took one look at each other and trumpeted, "Let's pass the Chevy."

"Let's pass the Chevy," echoed Mom. And to our surprise, first chance he got, Dad graciously obliged.

"Too slow or just right?" checked Mom, pointing to a Volkswagen minutes later.

We had stumbled upon a new game, yes? And for the rest of that trip and every trip thereafter, moment by moment, the family collectively worked out which car to pass, which to let be. And the outing to Winnipeg Beach was a smashing success.

"Hey, Mom," I called out as we pulled up in front of our house that evening, "had a nifty time, but going to the beach, that's Rose's thing. How 'bout what I want?"

"Trust me," said Mom, astute as always. "We had to do this first."

My family remained a bastion of care, celebration, learning. As the years passed, nonetheless, and as children are wont, I stepped further and further into the outside world. And truth to tell, the world outside the family became a veritable oasis of discovery, thanks to that meeting in the living room those many years ago.

My parents—bless their hearts—were as good as their word. Tackling first the problem of people confusing Rose and me, the day after the trip to the beach, Mom took the two of us out on what she called "a shopping spree," and bought us each a couple of distinctive outfits—I can't remember what. Then she dragged us to Hymie the barber and pointed directly at me, announcing, "Okay now, make sure that *this one's* hair is a lot shorter." Did that solve the recognition problem? Hardly! Though how it thrilled me days later when pudgy Morton Nells strutted over, puffed out his chest, and bragged, "Big surprise, Naomi—I've started being able to tell you and Rose apart. Guess I've just got a knack for junk like that, huh?" Having done their best with this relatively insoluble problem, Mom and Dad proceeded to the other items on the to-do list. About two weeks later, my Thursday evening movies started up, with Mom initially accompanying me; and a couple of weeks after that, I was actually signed up for Peretz School.

Now Peretz school, that was a budding young Yiddishist's dream! Our heads high, at assembly after assembly, we belted out the school anthem. "Marsh, marsh," we sang, half willing into existence the life committed to social justice that stretched out before us. And once every long while—and with what indignation we protested its disappearance from our midst—us kids would exchange looks, take a deep breath, and trumpet out this even more stirring Yiddish song. One which challenged kings, tyrants, despots just as surely as the heroes of the Winnipeg General Strike had said no to the lords of industry. It called upon slaves, upon the wretched of the earth, upon the starving, it called upon prisoners and soldiers; it called upon workers everywhere to arise and to build *Gan Eiden*. The Garden of Eden, no less. The Yiddish version of the Internationale, yes? Do they really sing this song in every country through the world? I would ask, my jaw dropped, my eyes beaming with pride.

North-end schools of that era being what they were, in subsequent schools as well, I was to be exposed to songs that mattered, and I would let them spirit me away to distant places—real and imagined. Although St. John's High was just a regular high school, its deftly chosen anthem similarly uplifted me; and again and again, it got me dipping into poetry that was not remotely part of the curriculum. "*Bring me my bow of burning gold. Bring me my arrows of desire,*" I sang, my voice coming alive. Who penned these remarkable words? I wondered. I talked to my homeroom teacher Miss Ironside, took myself to the Salter St. library, and before long was scurrying home, text in hand, every so often stopping to lean against a pole and drink in verse after verse, my eyes ablaze, my heart, a pounding drum.

"His name is Blake—William Blake," I eagerly explained to my parents, rushing into the kitchen, "and he's a romantic."

Dad was seated at the kitchen table surveying a newspaper, while Mom swept the floor. "Mushy sort of guy, was he?" Dad asked, peering at me over the top of the paper.

"No, not romantic like mushy. Romantic like William Wordsworth. Anyway, just look at this." My hands trembling from the sheer magnificence of the work, I opened the text to the *Songs of Innocence* and handed it to my father. And already knowing a good part of the verse by heart—for my memory was close to picture perfect—I began reciting, "*Little lamb, who made thee? Dost thou know who made thee?*"

Dad flipped through the pages, read snippets here and there, then handed the book back, an uneasy look on his face. "You like anti-religious Christian poetry, Naomi?" he asked.

Now despite Dad's misgivings, the songs and poems were an inspiration, the daily debates at school, a *mitzvah*. However, of all that the treasures which the various houses of learning offered up, it was the stories of radical Jewish writers like I. L. Peretz that touched me most deeply. I saw the passing away of Bontshe Shvayg, a lowly labourer whose untimely death went barely noticed either on earth or in heaven. And I swore that this must not be. I saw Reb Shloymele shake his head in protest, adamantly refusing to utter the *havdalah*—that last Shabbes prayer which returns us one and all to the every day working world. There is far too much human suffering. So God must change the world now! insisted the *rebbe*.

"Forcing God to do your bidding, that what they teach you nowadays?" Dad would ask, wherever he noticed that I was caught up in that particular story again. "For this, we pay good money to send you to Peretz schul?"

"Let the girl be," Mom would insist. "It's a metaphor, right?"

"A metaphor for the secular Jew? Fine. Fine," he would spit out, raising his feet onto the ottoman, and popping a cigar in his mouth. "You know, Naomi, God built the world from metaphor. They teach you that in that *farshtunkener* school of yours by any chance?" And gradually, his frown would turn into a smile and he would motion me closer, then wrap his arms around me and ply me with kisses. And in that moment, my heart would go still and the universe would fall into place.

Being distinguishable from Ro remained important to me. Schools and the magical universe onto which they opened was important. But one realm, one institution continued to loom larger than anything else—the movies. And with what fervour I embraced it! Without fail, off I would trot to the cinema every Thursday evening. And virtually lifting out of my body—so eager was I to enter the mystery—I would sit there in the dark, all eyes, as Gene Kelly tap-danced his way into my heart in *Singing in the Rain,* as Marlon Brando gave us a lesson in courage in *On the Waterfront,* as mysterious Marlene Dietrich threw us all for a loop in *Witness for the Prosecution.* Significantly, though, while I adored the movie stars, unlike other kids, I never dreamt of becoming one. Nor did I ask myself what these august personages were like in real life or whether I would ever meet them. I would ask: By what stroke of genius, what clever maneuver did the director of *Witness for the Prosecution* pull off that image of Sir Wilfrid's monocle sending out shafts of light? How did he know when to pull back and when to fill the entire screen with Dietrich's luminous head? And how do I harness this power to body forth the Winnipeg General Strike or the lowly labourer Bontshe Shvayg?

"Cripes. Not this again!" Rose responded when I posed that last question aloud. "C'mon, give it a break. Hey Nomi, how about you and me head over to the Donans and shoot hoops?"

"Later, alligator," I answered. "Well ... unless I could interest you in a flick."

"In your dreams!"

"Naomi, play with your sister," piped up Mom.

There it was—the proverbial fly in the ointment. Rose and I were supposed to be friends—bosom buddies—and while we continued finishing each other's sentences and occasionally still took delight in tricking people, we were clearly not what we had once been to one another.

It was less than a week after my eleventh birthday and something was decidedly bugging Mom. For the last two days, she'd been storming about the house—slamming doors, picking quarrels. Me, I was doing what I could to give her a wide berth. Having taken refuge in music and eager to give the "Moonlight Sonata" another go, I sat down at the piano, faltered through the first few chords, then quickly found my stride. "Naomi, can you come here a moment?" came Mom's voice suddenly. "I mean *now*," she added but seconds later.

Reluctantly, I joined Mom and Rose around the kitchen table. "What's up?" I asked.

Mom hesitated, glanced downward and took a sip of coffee, then gradually looked up again. "I might as well just spit it out. Girls, you know our neighbour Dana Fenster. Well, here's the thing. She's not our neighbour any more."

I could tell that Mom did not mean that Mrs. Fenster had moved. Clearly, so could Rose, for she cast me a knowing smile, then centred in on Mom.

"She do something wrong, Mom?" asked Rose.

"You can say that again. Insulted your father. Made him look like an absolute idiot. At this community meeting, right? Now she didn't have to. Could have made her point some other way. But did she? No. Preferred to humiliate the man before everyone. So the family, we just aren't talking to her any more."

"Mom," I exclaimed, utterly perplexed, "what could she have said that's so terrible?"

"It honestly doesn't bear repeating—just stay away from the woman, yeh?

"I love Dad, but please don't make me do this," I persisted. "And like, what if she's willing to say she's sorry?"

Whereupon, Mom shook her head and shot me a feeble smile. She explained that unfortunately, some things can't be fixed. "Now Naomi, I know that you're fond of the woman," she went on, "but this is family and it can't be helped. So no talking to her. No anything. You understand, girls, yeh?"

To my surprise, Rose nodded. How could she just go along with Mom without the slightest protest?, I asked myself. It was not primarily Rose, however, that was getting to me. Disloyal though this felt, I knew that Mom was making a mountain out of a mole hill. And for the first time I found myself seriously grappling with that peculiar warning of hers: "Cross Moshe or the kids, and I'll just walk away and never look back."

I lay in bed that night unable to put her warning out of my mind. Is she going to keep on exiling people?, I wondered. And if so, who's next? Cranky old man Schwartz next door who's always on Dad's case about feeding the birds? The Dziadecki sisters on Polson?

Now Mrs. Fenster was a remarkable woman who had lived six doors down as long as I could remember. She advocated for prisoners. As most everyone in north-end Winnipeg was aware, she was a fearless fighter for workers' rights, made speeches all over the world, had even rubbed shoulders with the great revolutionary Emma Goldman. And on top of everything, this chubby tender-hearted old woman had always been kind to me—made a point of remembering which twin I was, would come smiling toward me, her freshly baked chocolate chip cookies in hand, saying, "Naomi, you'll maybe have a few?"

Nonetheless, Mom had spoken, and so I followed her instructions to the letter. No greeting. Not even a nod of recognition. But it was only a matter of time....

I was standing in the middle of the boulevard, in tears because of something Rose had said to me—I can't for the life of me remember what. Mrs. Fenster must have been watching from her living room window, for suddenly, there she was on her front porch, shoeless, her tiny gold-rimmed glasses creeping down her nose. To my surprise, she walked straight over, put her hand on my shoulder, offered me a Kleenex. "Naomi," she murmured, "life can be hard, specially at your age.... No, no, sweetie pie, you don't have to stop crying; go ahead and get it out of your system. Feels kinda good, don't it?"

"Mrs. Fenster, sorry I've been so rude lately," I blubbered at long last, barely able to face her. "You see, I...I..." I stammered.

"Sha," said Mrs. Fenster, lifting her fingers to her lips. "Sweetie pie, you and me, we're old friends, aren't we?"

"Uh huh."

"Well then, no explanation's necessary."

Now I was well aware that there was a hidden premise here that could simply not be relied on, but I was moved nonetheless. And from that day forth, whenever our paths crossed, I would greet Mrs. Fenster. And many is the time I would perch on her steps—all ears—as she spoke of revolutionary leaders she'd known, actions she'd taken part in, though I would always look around carefully. Was there anyone nearby that might tell? On their porch a few doors down?

Time ticked by, and to my relief, Mom had no more fallings-out, albeit seemingly as a matter of course, she continued to issue those peculiar pronouncements of hers. Obviously, I'd been taking them too seriously, I concluded. And who knows? Maybe she just has this thing about Mrs. Fenster. And this concern put to rest, my life continued on as before. I took in movie after movie. I went to school. I celebrated Shabbes with the family. I had weekly—sometimes biweekly—schmoozes with Mrs. Fenster. And from time to time, I fretted about Rose.

6. NAOMI

Naturally, having my old flawless memory back would be ideal. I do not need flawless, however. I need passable—a toehold. Something—anything—to get the ball rolling.—Excerpt from Red Binder One

EARL'S OLD CHEVY continued to barrel down the streets of the strange metropolis in which I had somehow landed. Now daydreaming about Winnipeg had been a welcome distraction. Barely had I replayed a few scenes from childhood, however, than Earl announced, "Almost there." Seconds later, with an abrupt turn of the steering wheel, he pulled up behind a silver station-wagon. "Okay, people, everyone out," he announced.

As I climbed out of that car, I took a deep breath. Hoping to recognize something—as a starter even the shape of the building would do—eventually, I raised my eyes and dared to look about. Before us stood a stately two-storey brick house, a knotty pine porch at the front. It was an impressive abode by normal standards, but not a thing about it was familiar.

Earl clearly had his own doubts, for he kept glancing at Gerald nervously. As for me, I was struggling to reserve judgment. This, however, I recall. While I prayed for a miracle, one failed memory rapidly followed another.

Entering that house, I stepped into an oak-trimmed hall. While I had apparently lived here for years, I recognized not the trim, not the shape, not even the white swirls on the ceiling. Gerald quickly picked up on my agitation. "How about letting yours truly give you the grand tour?" he suggested, his eyes meeting mine. "Getting one's bearings, it can be hard." I nodded. Then ever the gentleman, he gallantly tipped his hat, hooked his arm under mine, and walked me through one area after another. I could not catch a break. The kitchen, the living room, the dining room, it was as if I were indeed touring somebody else's home. Same with the upstairs.

Now initially, I was loath to touch a thing. I kept feeling as if I were intruding on someone else's space. When we arrived at the master bedroom, however, Gerald opened the top drawer of a tall maple dresser, then looked at me invitingly. "It really is okay?" I asked.

"Sure is, love," answered Gerald.

Moments later I was rummaging through the drawers, frantically trying to lay my hands on something I could not name. Now I was about to give up when suddenly I spotted it—a landscape style photo of Rose at age twelve, her basketball sailing through the air! I looked at Gerald pleadingly.

"It's okay, Naomi girl," he assured me. "It's yours, and you've every right to it."

Scrutinizing it more closely, my spirits soared. Oh yes, I knew this picture all right. Recognizing it—that had to be a good sign. I picked it up, trailed my fingers the length and breadth of it as if it were a sacred relic, the mere touch of which would bring back those lost years. Then it dawned on me. The photo, it was from pre-amnesia days. Recognizing it means *bupkes*. But so what? I countered. This is a piece of Rose. Something to hold onto. Thanking Gerald, I pressed the picture to my lips, then carefully slipped it back in place. Whereupon the two of us joined the family in the living room.

As Earl fetched the coffee, I surveyed the room more fully. Palatial, with oak trim and a bay window, it held a vast array of furniture, all of it comparatively new, most of it matching—

three burgundy chairs, a large stuffed couch, a Ferguson TV
a framed mirror on the south wall, a baby grand with not a
scratch on it luxuriating in the corner.

On the wall facing the window was an item that Dad would
have appreciated: a magnificent silk screen of what appeared to
be a Canadian landscape, a lone evergreen in the centre. Has
to be of Northern Manitoba. Maybe around the Pas.

"Well, how about that! Congrats on recognizing the Varley,"
offers Earl, re-entering the room. "Nothing like a Group of
Seven painting, right?" he adds, his face beaming.

"Group ... group of..." I stammer.

"Best thing you and Rhoda ever wheedled me into buying.
Now don't be getting me wrong. I'm no fan of Ontario land-
scapes. But in the hands of masters like the Group of Seven,
that's a whole different kettle of fish. Incidentally, Rhoda,
she'll be dropping by Monday to give you a hand while I'm
at work and so..."

"Who's Rhoda?" I ask.

"But... Oh sorry, darlin'," he quickly recovers.

Unable to wrap my mind around a single part of the exchange,
I slowly sip my coffee, try to stay calm. I tell myself that at
least I came upon something important upstairs. For the life
of me, however, I cannot recall what. I tell myself that many
things can be counted on—objects staying put, one second
following the next. As if this had ever been the case in the
post-ECT universe!

Before long, the moment that we all dread is upon us. Gerald places his hand on my shoulder. "Got to go now, guys,"
he announces. "Sorry, but Miu's expecting me." It is all that
I can do not to drop at his feet and beg him to stay. Judging
from the fear in his eyes, Earl also is worried. Clearly, the two
of us have to find a way.

I instinctively dive into the deep end, let Earl know that
I'm aware of how we met. "But tell, me," I continued, "what
attracted us to each other?"

"People often wonder about that," he replied good-naturedly, "cause we're so different and all, but we've one monumental thing in common—we live and breathe foreign films. You know, in the early days," he went on, "we'd take in four, five films a week, and with each and every one, we'd be up to all hours analyzing"

"Yeah—I get that.... And you and Gerald, how did you originally meet?"

It seems that Gerald's mother Nora originally hailed from Brigus Junction, Newfoundland, that Nora had been an old friend of Earl's folks. She had married one James Bennett from northern Manitoba. And when Earl took a job in Manitoba, he made a special point of looking up the Bennetts.

"And your family, they still in Newfoundland?" I asked.

"Actually, I'm an only child, and yes, from a Catholic family," he explains with an ironic smile. "My folks died a few years back, and the inheritance became the down payment on this house. Not the brightest move," he makes a point of stipulating, "well, in light of my less than impressive salary."

"And just what is it you do?"

"Teach."

Having forgotten that I'd been told this, I could barely hide my surprise.

To Ruth's obvious delight, Earl suddenly picks her up, begins bobbing her up and down. "Actually at this point in the local junior high," he clarifies. "Now I sees you're having a hard time pegging me as a teacher," he observes, shooting me a knowing look, "maybe because of my outports manner of talking or maybe it has something to do with the other night." He goes on to explain that he had been horsing around more than usual to ease the tension. "Though Nomi," he quips, "hang in there with me, and you'll find I can be as tedious as the next academic."

I smile, grateful for the explanation. "So what's your subject?"

"Mathematics.... Surprised you again there, didn't I?"

"Guilty as charged. And mathematics, you like teaching it?"

"Well, to be frank, I'd rather be teaching about the environment, and I sneak that in most every chance I get, though no question, it's a great time to be teaching math."

Clearly pleased by the interest, Earl proceeds to launch into a spirited if confusing account of something called "the new math." As words like "octal" and "set theory" fill the air, a look of utter boredom comes over Ruthie. Then she lights up, tugs on her father's sleeve, enthusiastically squeals, "Daddy! Pat-A-Cake."

Now it is around the time the two of them start in on the third round of Pat-A-Cake that I rise to go the washroom. I open what I take to be the washroom door and find myself facing a crib and a tiny chair. Ruthie's room, I realize. I close the door, turn about, try again. This time, I walk straight into a room with a queen-sized bed. *Okay, don't panic.* Never left, never left, I murmur. I hang a sharp right, exit the master bedroom, continue down the hall. I take a deep breath and swing open the door directly in front of me. Inexplicably, once again I am facing a crib.

I feel a scream building and am on the verge of collapsing when to my surprise, Earl appears. Smiling nervously, he opens the washroom door, points to the toilet, then discreetly leaves. In the washroom at long last, I breathe a sigh of relief. I lower the seat, pull down my panties, and sit down. Earl and Ruth, what room are they in? I suddenly ask myself, back in a muddle again. And how do I find it? Half an hour later, I am still on the toilet seat, my underwear around my ankles, too frightened to budge.

"Missus, you all right in there?" calls out Earl.

Stepping into that house, seeing it elude me at every turn—this was more than I could bear. And within six hours, the homecoming came to an abrupt end.

"This is a mistake. Take me back to hospital. Please, Earl," I hear myself begging.

"Easy there, darlin'. Maybe if you took another pill? You remember what Dr. Higgins said about..."

Next thing I know, I am in the day room at St. Pukes, tears trickling down my face.

I remained in a slump for the next several days and largely kept to myself. Now what unfolded after that was deemed progress by the staff, but I respectfully disagree. So intimidated was I by the outside world that I started to revel in the daily goings-on on the ward. Telling myself that St. Pukes was as good a place as any to hang one's hat, I took particular delight in the old routines. I'd cheer as Jack rolled one of his perfect cigarettes. I'd exchange looks with Zelda whenever Brad launched into a rant about "you women." And I watched with fascination as a whole new side of Bob came to light.

"Freud was right," insisted Bob, eyeing Zelda with great seriousness. "Females envy the penis. How could they not? Such an exquisite instrument! It comes equipped with a shaft, a sulcus, a frenulum, a corona, not to mention a urinary meatus."

"Someone, throw this gent into a cold shower," exclaimed Zelda, rolling her eyes.

"What?" I quipped, eagerly joining in the banter. "And risk shrinking his urinary meatus?"

Strange. Over the years I have known many a beleaguered soul who regards the hospital as home. When you cannot function, what could be more seductive? However, I suspect that on some level, we all of us sense the terrible tradeoff, yes? Additionally, for those of us who are lucky, there comes a moment when we can see plain as day that the hospital is not our friend. Perhaps the tip-off is something subtle. Perhaps not so subtle.

It was early morning of my sixth day back. Two patients were in the process of tossing their cookies. Feet away, precariously balanced on the upper rung of a ladder, a lone workman in overalls was repairing a damaged fixture. The door for some reason open, meanwhile, Jack and I were loitering in the alcove just outside the ward.

I had been giving him a blow-by-blow on my homecoming. Now I had just begun describing the living room furniture when I realized that the details surrounding the silk screen remained a mystery.

"So, Jack," I asked, "you ever hear of an art community called the Group of Seven?"

Jack leaned up against the wall. "Actually yeah," he answered, nodding. "A bunch of white men who actually liked Mother Nature. Shit! Can you believe it? A few white guys paint a small patch of Turtle Island tolerably well and the whole fuckin' world thinks that they invented it."

"But who are they?"

"Let me see now. There's Harris, that's one," he began, raising the first of his fingers. "Varley, that's two, oh yeah and…"

And that's when I saw them. "Oh my God! Jack," I exclaimed. "Look over there!"

Exactly when they had appeared I was not sure. However, not more than a couple of yards away were three hapless souls stretched out on gurneys. The eldest was in her seventies; another, around fifty, the youngest, a mere teenager. Pale was their complexion, their eyes vacant. Straps thick as car seat belts hemmed in the legs and arms of the seventy-year-old, despite the fact that she was barely conscious. Suddenly, like Lazarus rising from his tomb, the old woman sprang to life, began to shriek, "Let me go."

"Jack," I urge, "surely something can be done for them."

"Easy there, kiddo," cautions Jack.

I cast my eyes about, praying for a miracle. A steady stream of folk are drifting, shuffling, marching through the halls—some staff, some patients. To my dismay, however, they continue about their business as if this were the most natural scene in the world. And the one patient who does take note appears helpless. A grown woman, she has her hands over her head and is crouched in a corner, cowering.

My heart breaking, I make my way over to the cowering woman, gently help her to her feet. Then slowly, inevitably, my eyes return to the wretched beings on the stretchers. The woman shouting earlier is now lying there expressionless, the odd moan slipping from her lips. There is something hauntingly familiar about this scene. What? As I continue staring at this ghostly vision, without so much as a warning, my entire universe shifts. I can feel a sheet bunching up my legs. A bright light overhead assaulting me. People in front of me. People behind me. No way to escape. Not able to breathe. Not able to breathe. Naomi. Naomi.

"Naomi, listen to me," I can hear Jack yelling.

"Jack?"

"Kiddo, this isn't something you of all people should be gawking at. C'mon. We're going to the dayroom."

I can feel Jack tugging at my arm. I turn to leave, then hear a rumbling, followed by an oddly familiar squeak. I turn back around. The gurney with the teenager is being maneuvered into an open elevator. And still the other two lie there, seeing and not seeing, waiting and not waiting, held in the grip of something inevitable.

"Naomi, the dayroom!" insists Jack.

We sat in the dayroom hunched over a table, and for the longest while, neither of us uttered a word. "That's the line-up for shock, isn't it?" I asked at long last.

Jack lit a cigarette, took a long hard drag. "Uh huh. Now you've seen them lined up before, but you sort of blanked out, you know, the way you do."

Once again silence fell upon us, and I found myself searching Jack's eyes as if those ever alert orbs held answers to a question that I dare not put into words. "Jack," I finally spit out, every fiber of my being trembling, "they're human beings, for God's sake! In the name of everything holy, how can they do that to them?"

Jack's eyes darted quickly to the right and back again. I glanced in the direction indicated, caught a glimpse of Nurse Ann hovering a few yards away, and nodded. "And how can they just leave them there?" I persisted, my voice duly hushed. "I mean, they're so vulnerable."

Still, he did not answer.

"And why in the open where the rest of us can see?"

"Now there's the million-dollar question," whispered Jack.

That night I turned a corner. I still didn't know whether or not my memories would return. Nor was I about to "pull a Jack" and sabotage my meds—not this camper, not with the threat of full-blown schizophrenia hanging over me. This, however, I was sure of: Even if they had a perfectly sound reason for what they were doing, even if their rationales were technically unassailable, I had witnessed something at odds with our better natures. And whether this family and I were right for each other or not—and how I wanted us to be—I had to get as far away from St. Pukes as my legs could carry me.

Next day, Ger, Jack, and I talked. Forthwith, I became co-operation personified. I shared "appropriately" during group, liberally sprinkling in such popular get-out-of-jail-free terms as "symptoms," "limitations," and "insight into my condition." I made a point of weeping at all the right times. Hey, if times got tough, I could always rent myself out as an extra at funerals. Nor did I raise a peep when Dr. H. increased my medication, just nodded approvingly and looked demure—the picture of womanhood, so to speak. The upshot? Five days later Dr. H. declared me stabilized on a higher dose.

"A marked improvement," observed Dr. H., leaning back in his chair and glancing at my chart. "Just what the doctor ordered, if you get my drift. So, Mrs. Smith, are we ready to go home?"

And blotto though I was, I looked that fucker squarely in the eyes and said, "Yes."

7. NAOMI

THE DAY BEFORE I was to be discharged, Gerald literally spent hours at the hospital, briefing me, answering legions of questions, brewing one pot of tea after another. Except for the glaring issue staring us in the face—the circumstance that brought me here—we *schmoozed* about every little thing, and I learned much, although I could not but wonder: What was so unsettling that I couldn't be told?

The family that I was preparing to join, it seemed, was its own special amalgam of two families, with adults and children flowing back and forth between the Palmerston house and Gerald's apartment near Church and Wellesley, and with numerous phone calls between the two a standard feature of life. Les was the ostensible reason that the households needed to be close. Miu originally accèpted the arrangement for Gerald's sake, perhaps also because she felt guilty about forcing the whole family to move. "But Nomi," Gerald hastened to point out, "make no mistake about it. We all love each other."

Ruthie's favourite food was cake, her favourite word, "Daddy"—wouldn't you know it? Family meetings, when they occurred, tended to be on weekends. Now during my prolonged absence quite a number of decisions were made communally, but there were a few hitches. If something primarily affected either Ruthie or me, Earl would be sure to get the last word, the first word, and all too often—God help us—most of the words in between. Additionally—and this, I was to eventually admire—he saw it as beholden on him to veto any family decision that hurt the environment. Let some family direction be injurious to the planet, and he would lean back in his chair, take a good long look at everyone, then ask, "You thinks you can just kill off the planet? You thinks that's your democratic right? Your *God-given* right?" And yet another product would be tossed. As a result, the cupboards under the kitchen sinks in our respective domiciles were missing a good many products standard in most households, but nonetheless were filled to capacity with items that do no harm.

Now according to Gerald, most of the time that I was in hospital, life at the Palmerston house revolved around school, daycare, and a cleaning woman who turned up every second week. What is not surprising, given our expenses and the realities of a teacher's salary, the family eventually found itself in financial distress. So Earl had done what he had to—clawed back on daycare, limited the use of the cleaning woman, and prevailed on friends and relatives to baby-sit in exchange for car repairs and small amounts of cash. "Just until the Missus gets back on her feet," he would explain.

"Things *that* tight?" I checked, after I had wheedled this last bit of info out of Gerald.

"Love, nothing to worry about," answered Ger.

We all made a colossal effort, and I would have to say that my second entry into the Palmerston house went comparatively smoothly. In fact, throughout the entire trip over, Earl and Gerald went out of their way to reassure me.

"Missus," said Earl, as we approached Bloor, "just tell us what you needs."

"You're feeling lost," added Gerald. "Say something."

The instant that I set foot in the house, I took a deep breath, reminded everyone that some things were best tackled alone. Then slowly, I made my way upstairs, knowing that I needed to face that elusive washroom just as surely as the thrown equestrian needs to get back on the horse. "Toward one end but not an end room," I whispered to myself, peering about the hall. "Toward one end but not an end room." Now while it certainly could have played out differently, and did on subsequent occasions, the strangest thing happened when I swung open that door. Before my eyes in all their pristine glory stood a slightly stained sink, a claw foot bathtub, an utterly functional Standard American toilet.

"Hallelujah," I declared.

Determined that I would receive the assistance that I needed, generous as always, Gerald stayed over the entire first night, rushing to my side whenever I awoke screaming. And calling in for a "sub," Earl took two weeks off work to help me orient myself. "Now see, here's the toaster," he explained once, twice, three times, "and over here, that's where we keep the bread."

The rub is—and there was no way around this—it is one thing being functional in hospital, quite another, in the real world. I rapidly found myself in an impossible tangle of new routines, most of them utterly confusing, including ones specifically designed to help. And then there was Les. Every Saturday morning without fail, Les would turn up and go galloping though the house. How my blood would rush in anticipation, for that little boy was a non-ending fount of jokes! "Hey Nomi," he would ask, "know what the smallest room in the world is? A mushroom." I could swear, though, that by the time Sunday came a good half of the lists that I'd so laboriously constructed would have magically disappeared.

"Probably just mislaid 'em, Nomi," said Earl. "Oh, look. Here's one," he'd utter, finding an index card lurking inside the toaster or some other equally illogical place.

Memory Thursday, now that was a special routine that we instigated that very first week: an hour once a week when Earl, Ger, and I would hang out together on the couch and they'd help me fill in gaps in my memory. Not with respect to my family of origin—for that topic remained "verboten"—but flics I'd seen, Torontonians I'd palled with, that kind of stuff.

"Missus, just think of me as your auxiliary memory," Earl would say.

Other noteworthy routines included laundry, closing the child's gate at the top of the stairs. Oh, and something that it would seem no self-respecting Torontonian could forgo—or so I thought for the first few months—ruminating over the weather in Brigus Junction. Hey, come from Winnipeg and have your brains fried to boot, when it comes to the big T.O., you can believe almost anything.

Now sometimes, even with the best of intentions, routines change. And sometimes they don't, though how I wish they would!

"Fuck! Easily another ten pounds," I muttered to myself.

It was my first night "home", and I'd just slipped into the frilly black negligee that Earl had picked up. Feeling like a beached whale, I was peering anxiously at my reflection in the mirror. Gradually, I tore myself away from the unflattering image, sat down at the foot of the bed, tried to wipe the weight gain from my mind.

Now strange though this may sound, I had still not put together that we would be sharing and so as I cast my eyes about, I started reveling at the prospect of having such a huge bed to myself. Just the sort of sentiment every virile young husband longs for in a wife, eh? Then I noticed a telling detail. Two pillows placed neatly side by side.

Even as the reality of the situation was sinking in, the door sprung open and in walked Earl, clad in a black dressing gown, three little bottles and a large glass of water in his hands, concern etched in his brow.

"Sorry, Naomi," he murmured. "You maybe aren't ready just yet?"

"No, it's fine…. Um, this is awkward," I stammered, "but

Earl, please give me time. I mean, I know we're married and all, but I couldn't, just couldn't..."

"Look, I have my faults, but darling, I'm no animal," he responded firmly. Then he carefully deposited two of the bottles on the night table, began opening the third.

Now it is at that moment that I focused in for the very first time on the bottles. Probably pills, I conjectured. Could the man be ill?

"Pills, you sure do take a lot," I observed. "There some problem?"

Amused, Earl threw his head back and laughed. "Well, not quite, Missus. 'Fraid you're the addict in family. But, hell, I can always work on it."

I giggled nervously. "So the pills, they're mine?"

"Bingo."

After thanking him for getting everything ready, I suggested the obvious—"So how about letting me take it from here?"—but he adamantly shook his head. "'Fraid I'm supposed to supervise," he replied. "Doctor's orders, remember?" Then he dispensed the pills one by one, watching me like a hawk as I swallowed. Just like Nurse Ann.

Now in all honesty, for the first week, I was relieved that he was taking charge. Hey, it was a dirty job, but somebody had to do it. As time ticked on, though, the whole surveillance *shtick* started to rankle. "Earl," I would urge, "how about just reminding me, then letting me manage on my own?" And he would cock his head slightly to the side and answer, "Darlin', maybe when you're yourself again."

A duration with no end point, I was beginning to suspect.

Even in those first weeks when I had tons of help and negligible responsibility, there were times when I doubted that the centre would hold. With Earl holding down the fort, however, and Gerald here every chance he got, we muddled through. Then came a monumental shift—no, not the kind that you read about in the Saturday papers, the everyday kind that slips in under the radar. At the end of the first two weeks, Earl returned to work, as for sure, he had to, and Gerald started coming over less, despite the fact that by now every last one of us could see that information leaked out of my brain as quickly as it went in. Now Ger took this in his stride. Earl, however, seemed to be losing heart. And little by little, he stopped turning up for Memory Thursday. He has a meeting at school, he would say. He has work to do. Sorry, he'd forgotten. And how often he would look at me and shake his head in dismay!

It was not that he was giving up exactly. More like he was of two minds. On bad days, he seemed to regard his "new wife" as a lost cause. On good days—if I dare call them that—I could swear that he was telling himself that if only I made an effort, the real Mrs. Smith would materialize. Now as it happened, part of me did indeed materialize, though not exactly the part that we'd been banking on.

I was drying my hands when I noticed something I had not taken in before. There was a yellow discolouration at the tips of two of my fingers.

Interesting, I mused, taking in the telltale stain. So that's why Jack kept offering me cigarettes. Thrilled that I'd captured something of the other Mrs. Smith, I finished drying my hands, then flew downstairs, eager to check out my hunch. At the bottom of the staircase was Earl, seemingly waiting for me.

"Earl," I asked, barely able to contain my excitement, "I'm a smoker, aren't I?"

The man downright beamed. "Sure are. An honest-to-God planet-polluter. An adorable planet polluter, though," he added. "But darlin'," he went on, his eyebrow arching, "you saying what I think you're saying?"

"No. Sorry, Earl. I didn't *remember* about the smoking. Just sort of figured it out."

"Well, that's good too…. Say, I've a thought. Now, Nomi, as you know, I'm not partial to polluting, but doing familiar things, it just might help. So, can I interest you in a cigarette? … I see I can," he went on, picking up on my grin.

Without further adieu, he hoisted Ruthie onto his shoulders. And environmentalist though he was, the two of them trotted off to the corner store in search of smokes.

"Your brand," said Earl, gallantly handing me a pack of Marlborough Light some twenty minutes later.

Thanking the two of them profusely, right there and then, I opened the pack and lifted a cigarette to my lips. I inhaled deeply, caught Earl's eye, inhaled again. Now I cannot say that it gave rise to memories exactly. Nonetheless, something about the way the smoke tickled the nasal membranes felt right.

Shortly thereafter, that hour having rolled around, Gerald dropped Les off for the weekend. Ruth doodling away in her colouring book, and Les charging up and down the stairs, Earl and I immediately began rustling up breakfast. Now everything seemed to be going swimmingly. Suddenly, however, Earl glowered. He hesitated, perhaps hoping that I would catch on. Then he reached over, switched off a burner, let out a deep sigh, then turned on another.

"Sorry. Obviously, I've fucked up again," I exclaimed.

Earl shook his head, then looked me squarely in the eyes. "It's not just the burner. Now Nomi, I'm not meaning to be critical, but in the middle of the night, you must've gone downstairs to watch TV or something. Anyway, I come down this morning, and the child's gate is open. Missus, you really really need to be more careful."

Of course, he was right. As a parent, it was my duty to remember. But how? Nor, as it happened, did the need for change end here.

Later that morning, after Earl had engaged the kids in a spirited game of Blind Man's Bluff, the two of us sat down in the living room over a cup of coffee, and out it came—the eminently reasonable request that I had been dreading for over a week now.

"Darlin'," he asked, handing me a Loblaw's flier, "how about the four of us hit the supermarket? Give the kids a chance to pick up some treats and for you to see where everything is. And well, maybe after you sees how everything's done, you can take on more chores around here. You know, like when I'm at work…. Please, Nomi," he added, catching my eye.

And so it was that I assumed more responsibilities, started venturing forth into the world. Another turning point, though in all honesty, more like a moment of truth.

Despite some good times, the weeks and months that followed were brutal. I kept running into people that I had apparently talked with mere days ago, and I would not know what we'd said, who they were, or what I was to do about that utter shock on their face. And ever more frequently, Earl would shake his head in dismay. And knowing that I could ill afford for him to lose faith—that he was the anchor that kept me from going adrift—my heart would fill with fear.

Indeed, progressively, fear—that was the common thread that wove its way through my days, making them what they were. I feared the growing frustration in Earl's voice. I feared that I would not be able to find my way into Ruthie's heart. I feared that my brain, my memory, my life were lying in tatters somewhere in a St. Pukes' garbage bin. I feared that I would never again be in the loving arms of the sister and parents that I so adored. I feared that all those years of hope and study had come to naught, for no celluloid world would ever issue forth from my shattered shipwreck of a mind. I feared the faces that I met—the ones that looked away embarrassed, the ones that snickered, the ones that whispered to their children as I walked by. I feared myself for I knew not who I was, nor what terrible thing I had done to deserve such a punishment. But most of all, I feared existence itself—my very being in the world—for the unvarnished truth is, I did not have the wherewithal to be, to cope, to muddle through.

Poor Earl expected a wife and mother, the family, indeed, needed a wife and mother; and me, I simply could not function. At night, I would tuck in my child and see her cringe and turn away, holding onto her doll for dear life. If her daddy was not right there, she would scream blue murder. And there I would stand—useless—knowing full well that a mother with her faculties intact would have found a way in. How come I am just fine with the most vulnerable people on the ward and absolutely clueless when it comes to my baby daughter?, I would ask. And Ruthie, if you are reading this, be assured that not a day went by when I did not ask, when I did not long to be the mother that you deserved. Then, my heart heavy, I would crawl into bed with this stranger, even have sex with him, though neither of us was under any illusion about my feeling what he so desperately wanted me to feel. The Mrs. Smith that I used to be, I wondered, did she hunger for this man? Was she able to lift the pain from his heart?

It was a weekday morning, not unlike the ones that came before, not unlike the ones to follow. *Brnng, brnng*, went the alarm.

"Time to get up," announced Earl, reaching over and turning it off.

I rose, quickly closed the child's gate, praying that Earl had not noticed. I prepared breakfast, saw Earl hovering over me. *Gotenyu! Had I left a burner on?*

"Darling, don't forget to mail the letters," he called out minutes later. Then with a hurried peck on my cheek, he rushed out the front door.

Dreading the inevitable, I put off the chore a good half hour. Then I gritted my teeth, lifted up Ruthie, started scouring the streets in search of the mailbox. Where could it have gone? It was here yesterday. At long last, I passed a little green house, a white picket fence at front. Shortly thereafter, I happened upon a rectangular box. I dropped the letters into what appeared to be a slot. Fine and good. But how does one get home? I whirled about, intent on retracing my steps. On my right was the little green house with the white picket fence. I passed it, scrupulously turned whenever the street turned—but back I find myself in front of the little green house.

"Sir," I call out to an older man in Bermuda shorts ambling by, "could you give me directions to 532 Palmerston?"

"No 532 here. You must be looking for Palmerston *Avenue*. This's Palmerston *Square*."

"So there's two Palmerstons?"

"*Three*," he corrects, chuckling. Then a curious look comes over him. "Excuse me, but aren't you the young woman who asked me this yesterday?" he queries, eyeing me ever more keenly. "If this is a joke, young lady, it isn't funny."

I apologize, back away mortified, eventually find my way home. With Ruthie hollering that she is hungry again, and the word "vacuum" mysteriously coming to mind, I pull out what appears to be a Hoover. Then suddenly, suddenly, I remember. *Groceries—God help me—I'm supposed to buy groceries.* Also, my daughter is hungry.

I instantly stash the vacuum in the hall closet, hoping that's where it came from, then feed Ruthie. Then once again the two of us set out into the wilderness that is Toronto. And once again, I search and search. I pass a Victorian house. Vaguely familiar. I come to a corner. A tall burly man in a police uniform is positioned in the middle of the street directing traffic. Now somehow, his hand signals—if that's what they are—do not compute, but this time, I know better than to draw attention to myself. I stand at the very edge of the sidewalk, doing absolutely nothing as the policeman gazes my way. Who could get in trouble just by doing nothing? Suddenly, a horn begins honking. Then another, and another. The policeman stares right at me, while waving his hands progressively more quickly. And now he approaches, his expression very like Earl's.

"Lady, just what do you expect me to do?" he asks. "Turn green?"

Eventually, I catch sight of the local Dominion's, usher Ruthie safely through the door. And while I cannot make head or tail of my grocery list, I recall that we are out of peas. As luck will have it, I spot the right row, the right section of the right row. With trepidation, I position myself smack in the middle of the peas section. I reach out my hand. Then I stand in front of those hundreds of tins of peas utterly stymied. So many sizes, so many kinds—Libby's, Aylmer's—how is a person to choose? Beads of perspiration forming on my brow, I take a deep breath, grab a tin at random, then hightail out of there as quickly as my legs will carry me.

Now I am half way out the door when it dawns on me that I have not paid. Also, that there is one other item that I simply have to pick up. Hoping that security is not on the way, I reenter, make my way to the meat counter—and brace myself.

You see, pig, that turned out to be a staple in the Smith household, and it utterly flummoxed me. Pork chops, ham, sausages, bacon, Newfoundland steak—hell, being Jewish and electroshocked to boot—they all seemed the same to me. Now Earl would answer all my questions about pork, would keep rattling off the different types, but try to hold onto them though I did, every name, every description would almost immediately leak out of my brain.

"So lady, what's it today?" asks the man in white behind the counter.

"A few pounds ... a few pounds ... a few pounds of ... of ... *that*," I stammer, pointing at something reddish.

Meat in hand, I head over to the cashier, give the woman every ounce of lucre in my possession. Her eyebrow raised, she hands me back most of my bills and several coins, together with what must be an itemized receipt. I glance at it. Another blur. Then I pick up my daughter because she is clearly tiring, and scurry home.

"This's just fine," says Earl, hours later, gobbling up a poor imitation of a dinner. But I can tell from his eyes that all of the *meshugas* is wearing him down.

At eight-thirty p.m., I tuck in Ruthie, hear her scream for her father. Then Earl and I sit and sit and sit in that living room. He tells me about his day, and I pretend to be following. I tell him about mine, and he pretends to be listening. "Missus, it's about that time again," he eventually announces. I breathe a sigh of relief, take the pills, observe him watching me.

At long last, the moment that I have been waiting for arrives: I get to crawl into bed—that nice, warm, comfortable bed—and call it a day. I bury myself in the safety of the blankets, eager to fade into nothingness, eager to forget. But now Earl, he's crawling on top of me. I instantly spread my legs. Oh let him come quickly!, I pray.

Finally, finally, I close my eyes. I drift off, glimpse a better place, a better time. It is our fourth birthday, and attired in our new black tunics, Rose and I are blowing out the candles. Now all four candles are out and the two of us are smiling at each other, nestling into the recesses of each other's souls as only we can. "*Mazel tov*," chimes in my mother's voice. "Never mind with the *mazel tov*; Ida, give the girls cake," pipes up dad. Even as I savour the first tantalizing mouthful, a shrill sound shatters the stillness, and I awake with a start. Frantic, I cast my eyes about. I spot an alarm clock. I see a bump in the covers next to me. No! No! It can't be! Not here again!

And so the days went. How can we possibly keep this up?, I wondered.

It was early evening, and Earl was seated at the head of the table, Ruth in the high chair next to him, waving her spoon in the air. I had just finished arranging the cutlery. I proceeded to place the meat in front of Earl. Then I sat down across from him and braced myself, sensing something amiss. He nodded, rolled up the sleeves of his good denim shirt, started eyeing the meat before him. "Christ, woman!" he suddenly thundered, grimacing and pointing at the offending meat. "This's liverwurst. It's not even close to pork chops. Now I'm trying to be patient here, but I'm a grown man, and damn it, I need what I need."

"I ... I..." I stammer.

"You're sorry. I knows that. But darlin', sorry doesn't put food on the table. Sorry doesn't bathe your child properly. Look at her," he insists, gesturing toward Ruth. "Muck all over her neck. And tell you something else," he continues, his voice getting progressively louder. "Sorry doesn't stop us from losing friends who aren't used to people forgetting every friggin' thing."

I try to stay calm. "Earl, can ... can I ask you something?" I manage to spit out.

His face reddening, Earl rises from the table. He whisks Ruth into his arms, then starts storming out of the room. One foot out the door, he whirls around and glares at me. "Don't you be asking me anything," he bellows. "Not anything ever again. Christ! What do you think I am? A walking talking memory bank?" Then to my horror, he blurts out something which calls to mind my one memory of him. "And Jesus!" he goes on, "I saw the receipt for the cake that you bought this afternoon. How can you let someone Jew you like dat?"

"How can I let someone what?" I ask aghast.

Ruth is crying at this point and calling out "Daddy" over and over. Taking in the magnitude of what has happened, Earl stares at me, then at his quivering daughter, then back at me. "Mary, Mother of God!" he exclaims. Then lets out a sigh, and begins caressing Ruth's cheek. "Everything's just fine, princess," he coos. "Your Da, he sometimes says stupid things he doesn't mean. You understand, pumpkin?"

"No more yell," insists Ruth, pouting but already calmer.

"No more yell, Ruthie," vows Earl. "Awfully awfully sorry, Missus," he utters, taking several steps toward me. "Me, I'm the joke in this family—not you. But believe me, darlin', I loves you."

"I know. I really do know," I answer, "but Earl, promise me you'll never use that expression again."

He looks at me apologetically and nods. Then he reaches over, gently places his huge hand at the side of my face. Seconds later he fetches a loaf of bread from the cupboard, sits down, positions his daughter on his lap, and begins making liverwurst sandwiches—one after another, after another.

How to understand what had just happened, I was not sure. But this much was clear. The man was stretched—stretched to the limit. And fearing for the lot of us, I shuddered.

There were times those first few months when I was on the verge of crying uncle. The thing is, though, I had cast my lot with these people, and as best he could, Earl was hanging in. Yes, and for good or for ill, every so often there came a moment....

"C'mon, Nomi," urged Gerald, tugging on my arm. "Your old man's agreed to hold down the fort. Time for us to have fun for a change. Just us two whippersnappers, eh?"

It was a week after the incident, and I was still shaken. I had been on the couch watching TV when unexpectedly, Gerald showed up, knapsack in hand.

"He's really giving me the day off?" I asked, somewhat incredulous. So ... so ... what you have in mind?" I asked.

"How about we toddle over to Kensington?" suggested Gerald, giving my hand an encouraging squeeze. "Take in the sights. Maybe buy you some clothes that actually fit? Some for yours truly too."

Not having a clue what Kensington was, but not about to pass up alone-time with Gerald—that crazy, I never was—I shut off the television, thanked Earl, and off Ger and I sped, as I now understood it, east on Bloor, then south on Spadina. Ignoring the slight drizzle, and stopping now and then to peer into store windows, all the way to College we trekked. Then via a route I could not follow, we stepped into an amazing world—street after street of it.

At the edge of the road itself, chickens strutted about in cages. Tiny shops were wedged in everywhere, their entrances wide open, inviting all and sundry to come in and enjoy—some with all the goods inside, far more with the produce spilling into the centre of street. And what an array of fruits, vegetables, spices greeted the visitor! And that wasn't the half of it. Four different cheese emporiums, their pungent odours gracing the air. Store after store decked out in vintage clothing from yesteryear. Fish markets where even such rarities as shark steak were standard fare. Surrounded by bright colours we were— fire engine reds, succulent orange, vivid yellows. Oh and how those streets rang with the accents of the world—Portuguese, Mandarin—though two more than any other, friendly Italian, and oh yes, that accent that I had been yearning to hear since first coming to in the corridor at St. Pukes—sweet Yiddish. "So darlink, you vant somthink maybe?" asked a bright-eyed vendor as we stepped into our first clothing shop. And to think that all along Kensington had been within spitting distance of St. Pukes!

By the time we arrived at Leather It Up, Gerald had amassed nine different types of cheese, I had picked up a brick of marble halvah, and we'd both purchased two tops.

"Whatchya think? I asked, trying on a used leather jacket, fringes on the arm. "Am I ready to go cruising or what?"

Gerald looked at me, tipped his hat, and winked. "We'll take it," he said to the saleswoman. Then we trotted off to a particularly chic store with clothes circa 1950.

"This one, this one, and this one," Gerald instructed the salesman, indicating one midnight blue silk tie and two brown vests. Now for the first and only time that day, I felt uneasy, for the salesman distinctly looked at Gerald askance, but he otherwise posed no problem.

Nonetheless, later that afternoon as we were sinking our teeth into a pizza deluxe in a glitzy Italian restaurant, I raised the issue. "Gerald," I asked, taking a sip of Espresso, "I don't mean to make you uncomfortable, but that clerk, you saw how he looked at you, didn't you?"

Gerald nodded. "Yeah, and I saw you notice. Thanks for looking out for yours truly."

"But Ger, it didn't scare you?"

"Oh, it scared me all right. Know something though, love? Not safe to let on. Also, I decided long ago, that scared or not, I have to be out there just like I am. I guess we both kinda have to do that, eh?"

"Yeah, though it burns me to think of you having to go through that."

"One day at a time, and—pardon my French—one mother-fucker at a time, sometimes that's all a person can do." Gerald suddenly stopped, and his eyes began to twinkle. "Well how about that?" he exclaimed. "Here I am blathering on about *my* stuff when I wanted to check in on you. Love, everything okay at home?"

"Not exactly," I answered. Then I availed myself of the opportunity to ask him if he had ever heard Earl say anything anti-Semitic.

Gerald looked at me knowingly, and anger flickered across his face. "Damn!" he muttered. "He hasn't been using one of those lame-brained expressions of his, has he?"

"Just once."

"Nomi, don't let him get away with that shit. I know that when he started in on me with the he-she crap, I called him on it straight away."

"Ger, I'm so sorry. He really called you that?"

"*One* time," said Gerald pointedly. "Just once. Now I wouldn't say he ever totally got what was wrong with the expression, but enough to clean up his act. And that's one of the great things about Earl, right? The guy can be stubborn as a mule, but if he gets that he's acting like a cretin, he changes. So be clear with him." Gerald took another bite of his pizza, then stopped to consider. "Easier for me than you though, isn't it? Tell me, Nomi. He still supervising your meds?"

"You'd better believe it."

"And the shrink really ordered this?"

"I think so."

Gerald rolled his eyes. "Idiots—both of them," he proclaimed.

"Morons," I spat out, eager to get in on the act.

"Bonkers," offered Gerald.

"Bats in their belfry."

"One card short of a full deck."

"Whacko."

"Lights on but nobody's home."

"A fried chicken short of a church picnic."

"A fried chicken short of a church picnic!" exclaimed Gerald. "Why, I'm the Christian here and I never heard that one. Nomi girl, what else you got?"

For the next half hour, we sat in that restaurant, gleefully tossing out one synonym after another and laughing with abandon.

"Folk like us, we kinda get the hang of one another, wouldn't you say?" pointed out Gerald, growing serious again.

I nodded enthusiastically. Then a curious look came over Ger. "Love, one more place I'd like to take you," he announced suddenly, hoisting up his knapsack.

Our next stop was in an entirely different part of town—more particularly, a happening little pub called the Brown Derby, where we were joined by a pal of Gerald's: six-foot-three Lena, who had her own take on the people she called "normals." "Darlings, it's not their fault. Poor dears, they were just born that way," she jested, tossing her ample auburn hair over her shoulders. "'Mentis Mediocratum,' I believe it's called. Not enough grey matter, if you get my drift—and not nearly enough pussy." Not surprisingly, when Ger and I arrived home a couple of hours later, it was in astonishingly good spirits.

"Good to see my two favourite wives looking so chipper," announced Earl, as we entered the house. "I take it you had a good time. Come across anything interesting?"

"You'd be surprised," offered Gerald, exchanging looks with me.

Now no sooner had Ger departed than Earl informed me that Ruthie had a cold and was in bed miserable. "You might want to check in on her," he suggested.

Touched that despite everything, he still thought I could be of help, I nodded. Then I tiptoed to Ruth's room. And there the poor babe was, sitting upright in her crib, her Bugs Bunny pajama bottoms on, mucous dribbling out of her nose, tears streaming down her face.

"Oh sweetie," I sighed, seeing how wretched she was. "So sorry about that big bad cold of yours. Here, blow," I urged, bringing a Kleenex to her nose.

Ruth snorted into the Kleenex, but as I was cleaning up her face, she turned away from me as per usual. I proceeded to offer all the standard reassurances. It was no good.

"Wanna crawl into bed with Daddy and me?" I finally asked.

Ruthie hesitated for a second, then uttered a distinct no. Nor did she change her mind when I coaxed.

What happened next never ceases to astonish me. All of a sudden—no conscious intent on my part—my lips open and out comes the lullaby "Hush Little Baby." Small comfort it gives, for now she is wailing. Nonetheless, she is decidedly looking my way. I sing two other lullabies and the wailing continues, and once again, Ruthie turns aside. Then curiously, the old Peretz school anthem comes flowing out of me. "*Marsh, marsh,*" I sing. A Yiddish marching song, yes? Not something likely to comfort a soul. To my delight, however, Ruth turns, faces me. And a calm comes over her. Her tears dry up. And the gentlest of smiles begins playing about her cheeks. "Oh Ruthie, if that's what you want, I can sing," I murmur. She gurgles, reaches out to me, her tiny hands yearning. I pick her up, and Ruthie in my arms, over and over, I sing that tune from yesteryear. For a while, she clings to me tightly, but the sounds, they soothe her, and soft becomes her touch. And slowly, she drifts off.

That night I could not catch a wink, what with my ear alerted to the sound of sniffling, my mind alive with dreams of Ruthie and me. Next morning, immediately upon rising, I crept over to her room. "Sweetie, you doing any better?" I asked, my heart aflutter.

"No," she answered.

Some time later, to her chagrin, I fed her a Contact C and baby's aspirin. Then I started to sing that old anthem again. She looked at me blankly, as if nothing were happening. I sat with her most of that day, and as light began to fade and as creatures everywhere returned to their lairs, I turned to that anthem again. Nothing—except perhaps minor annoyance.

What happened last night?, I wondered. And would it happen again?

8. NAOMI

IT IS NOT EASY growing up as identical twins, especially not when friction sets in—not for the sibling who feels deserted, not for the one who feels responsible. Sometimes, I wonder what would have happened had Rose and I *really* taken the time to reflect. Not that we remotely banished the problem from our minds. And not that in our own way we did not repeatedly make overtures to one another. Strange. To this day, as I linger in bed drifting between sleep and wake, at times I find myself pondering the fate of the lonely atom indelibly split in two. Initially, a chain reaction sets in. This much science tells us. But how about on a different level, and how about years later? Whirling about in the great expanse of space, would the parts not become steadily more distinct? When old and grey, if they came across their other half, how would they recognize one another? Yet surely there are moments when they yearn for one another, when they would give up everything just to return to that ineffable wholeness out of which they sprang. Be that as it may, at this juncture, Rose and I were off on our own individual trajectories, and given the excitement of youth, how decisively our respective journeys were taking off.

Twenty-one days to our twelfth birthday, and already Rose and I were actively lobbying—me for a movie camera, Rose for a trip to Toronto to see the legendary Harlem Globe Trotters.

"What?" Dad exclaimed, pacing back and forth, his eyes darting at me. "You think you're Otto Preminger maybe? And the two of you," he added, glancing at Rose, "maybe you think your mother and I are the Rothchilds with money to burn?"

Come the big day, the dining room table was overflowing with all our favourite dishes—pickled herring for me, stuffed cabbage rolls for Rose, roast chicken stewed with apricots that the entire family adored. Rose and I excitedly blew out the candles. And with bated breath, I started unwrapping my present. Of course, I knew that there wasn't a snowball's chance in hell of it being a movie camera. Nonetheless, I was fully prepared to be dazzled. And dazzled I surely was, for before my eyes emerged the next best thing. The Cadillac of still cameras—the coveted Leica IIF Red Dial.

"Oh Dad, it's wonderful, but the cost!" I exclaimed.

"Let *me* worry about that," insisted Dad.

My practical experience with film began here. I read and reread the manual, took in the mystery of aperture and shutter speeds. And I shot with these in mind, making every picture a kind of experiment. I snapped one of Ro readying herself for the jump, her eye riveted on the basket ball hoop, shutter speed 1/1000. Itching to catch hold of motion itself, I tried one at a lower speed, as Rose released the ball. To my delight, there it was in the photo—a magnificent streak of light shooting through the air.

Rose's present was a regulation-sized hoop—hence the ease with which I captured those moments. She also received a Harlem Globe Trotter jersey. Now the first few months, Rose kept shooting wide of the net, and oh so often the ball would get away from her as she dribbled. She would throw up her hands and bolt out of the yard, discouraged. Generally, though, trooper that she was, within an hour, back she would be practicing. "Get a life," she would shout at the small coterie of neighbourhood kids who happened by to snicker. They sometimes took off at this point. Usually, however, even when they did, they would return later on to taunt her. "Just ignore them," I would urge. One beseeching look from my sister, though, and no way could I leave it at that. I'd amble past her adversaries, seemingly unconcerned. Then I'd turn around tentatively as if having an afterthought, then let fly a zinger. "Just curious," I once remarked, "but were you fine upstanding citizens born like this or did you go out of your way to become jackasses?" The victories, such as they were, were generally short-lived. Nonetheless, they predictably bought time. To the delight of the family, the time came when Rose's detractors were forced to eat their words for her aim was so keen that she was actually winning one-on-ones against Amy Sacks—one of the finest players on our block—this despite being nowhere near so fleet of foot.

"The thing about your sister," said Mom, as we watched her from the kitchen window, "when she puts her mind to something, she generally makes it happen."

Now Rose was my favourite photographic subject, and time and again, I'd approach her, camera in hand. "Nomi, can't you shoot hoops with me instead?" she would ask, shaking her head in frustration. "And like, what's so great about a picture of basketball when you can actually play? You know, Miss Smartypants, if you ate a picture of food instead of real food, you'd die of malnutrition. Ever think of that?"

And there we would be, staring at a mirror image of ourselves, close as our own skin, far as a distant galaxy. Now at such times, to Mom's chagrin, I would turn to her.

"Hey, Mom," I called out, moseying into the kitchen, trying to sound as Rhett-Butler casual as possible, "any idea why Ro and me care about completely different junk?"

I was twelve and a half years old; and Rose and I had just butted heads for the kazillionth time. Her faded yellow apron on, Mom was at the sink tackling a load of dirty dishes. She picked up an emerald green glass, rinsed it, placed it gingerly on the half-filled rack. Then she turned toward me, utter exasperation on her face. "Look, Naomi," she observed at long last, "I've always supported you being your own person, yeh?"

"Well, yeah."

"But you've taken it too far. I asked you to be careful, and have you? This *meshugas* between the two of you, I didn't start it. And really, there's *bupkes* I can do about it."

"Mom, couldn't...couldn't you just...?" I stammer.

Mom rolls her eyes. "Whatchya think?" she snaps. "That I have a manual in my back pocket on how to fix twins? Okay, okay," she resumes seconds later. "Listen, Naomi, you girls, you're something precious called 'twins'. Something that shouldn't be squandered. And that's the point, see? You're the only ones that can squander it."

"Squander? So you think that we..."

"What's with the *we*? *You're* the one who insists on going your own way. Want a relationship with your sister? Then do stuff with her whether you enjoy it or not. Marching to your own beat's more important to you? Fine, but live with the consequences. Just *pish* or get off the pot. You understand what I'm saying here, yeh?"

"Yeah, but Mom, we never used to have this problem."

Mom nods and proceeds to pick away at the crud on the roasting pan. Then she begins eyeing me again, this time downright suspiciously. I can feel it. There's something else that I'm doing wrong—and she's onto it. True to form, for a split second, she looks away, and unmistakably, her nostrils begin to flare. Then she steadies her gaze. And out it comes.

"Incidentally, I saw you *schmoozing* with Dana Fenster yesterday," she begins. "You don't remember?"

I try to steady my wobbly legs. "Um, remember what?" I hear myself utter.

"A year ago that pseudo-anarchist of a woman insulted Daddy at a community meeting. Really hurt his feelings."

"She did?"

"Yeah. Said if it was up to him to lead us out of Egypt, he'd have frittered away so much time feeding his precious sparrows that Pharaoh would have easily caught up."

"And that's all she said?" I blurt out foolishly.

"I'd have thought that was quite enough," answers Mom, placing her hands on her hips. "Anyway, the family, we've had nothing to do with her ever since. But how could you have forgotten something so important? You know, Rose never forgets," she adds, a knowing look on her face, "and you, you're the one with the picture perfect memory."

I glanced at Mom from the corner of my eye, saw her brow crease, got this fleeting image of being led before the firing squad. Then little by little, her brow unfurled. She was going along with the fiction, I realized, but she was counting on me to fall in line.

"You'll remember now, yeh?" persisted Mom.

I nodded, kissed mom, and resigned myself to complying. Then I conjured up an image of poor Mrs. Fenster's stunned face and shuddered.

Now it never got easy acting as if Mrs. Fenster didn't exist. For better or for worse, on the other hand, my worries about Rose were soon to subside.

I was thirteen and a half years old, and it was a blustering Winnipeg day in the middle of an unrelenting winter. The house had been distinctly chilly when I arose that morning; so I did what I could. I rummaged up a thick turtleneck, begged Dad for a pair of his long johns, pulled on my knee-high socks. "Not to worry. Just takes time for the furnace to catch up," Dad assured me as I sat down for breakfast. A plausible explanation at the time, but it was well nigh evening now, and the house had not gotten an iota warmer. I could hear the wind building up outside, working itself into a wildcat frenzy. *Brshhh. Brshhh. Tsssss.* It whistled through the chimney, darted about the roof, tearing at every vaguely loose shingle, creating holes where none had been before. It grabbed at the windows, shook them again and again, rattling the triple glass panes so mercilessly that I feared that they would shatter.

A Yiddish book unopened on my lap, I was in my bedroom. That's that tiny bedroom over the veranda—the one Rose and I used to share before she took over the tenants' old room some two years back. The south wall of the room being lined with one window after another, the wind kept nipping in. And oh how the rattling shot through that tiny space! *Crack. Crack. Crack.* Feeling colder with every passing second and unnerved by what felt like the imminent threat of flying glass, I got up, located my bulky-knit sweater, pulled it over my turtleneck. Then I crept downstairs and made myself as comfortable as possible on the living room sofa. By this point, I was shaking all over, and although Mom and Dad were both home, waves of loneliness were washing over me, pulling me deeper and deeper into I know-not-what. If only I could find an open space—a window onto the world! Frantic, I reached across the coffee table and switched on the radio, much like a drowning man grabs for the lifeboat. Then I lay back and tried to imagine the sun's welcoming rays bearing down on me.

"Thirty below zero," croons a warm baritone. "Winds gusting to fifty miles an hour. Visibility poor. Snow and blowing snow. Long range forecast for Winnipeg, Gimley, and the surrounding…"

"Naomi, for God's sake," a familiar voice suddenly intervenes.

I open my eyes to find Mom crouching next to me, strangely, no outdoors sweater on—just a flimsy cotton blouse—concern flickering on her face.

"Sweetie, *gotenyu!* You're shaking like a leaf."

"Mom, shouldn't you be wearing a sweater?"

Ignoring the question, she begins surveying me all over— my face, my arms, her eyes finally lighting on my fingers. Oh sweetie," she gushes, "you're turning blue, and just look," she adds, lifting up my left hand, "the tips of your fingers. Utterly frozen."

"But Mom, why aren't you wearing a sweater?"

"*Sha, sha.* Just stay put. Mommy will be right back."

Releasing her hold on my hand, Mom bolts out the door and after what seems like hours but is probably mere minutes, she and Dad come dashing into the room, each bearing a wool blanket. Oohing and ahhing as if I were an infant, they kneel in front of me, rub my hands, my feet, my blue-streaked arms. And now they are wrapping the blankets around me, cradling me, cocooning me. But it's no use. The ever cunning wind keeps finding me out, lacing into me. My eyeballs are frozen; and I can feel snow seeping down my sweater, coating my socks, slipping in under my eyelashes.

I try to brush the snow from my eyes. Hopeless. "Mom," I call out, the desperation rising up my throat, "the snow, it's everywhere. I'm lost. Can't see my way."

"Sweetie, I've no idea why you're so cold, but you're not lost, and there's no snow. You're in our nice warm house. Baby, tell me," she asks, peering into my eyes, "you remember where you live, yeh?"

I can feel the sting of cold tears streaming down my face. Mom notices, looks over at Dad, her eyes wide with panic. "Moshe, whatchya waiting for—an invitation from the Queen of England?" she shrieks. "Something's wrong with our daughter. For God's sake, call Dr. Newbaum."

Dad nods and disappears into the hall, but returns almost instantly, his head shaking.

"Well?" asks Mom.

"No good. Newbaum's on holiday, remember?"

"So is he the only doctor on the face of the earth? Call ... call Dr. Allen."

"Dr. Allen?"

"You know, that young *pisher* who came to the house when Rose had scarlet fever."

And with these words, a tiny space opens up; and everything becomes clear. "Rose!" I shout out.

Mom shakes her head. "Baby, Rose isn't here. Had a few things to do today. But I'm sure that just as soon as she learns that you're not well, she..."

"No, you don't understand," I protest. "Mom, it's Rose. She's freezing! She's lost and you've got to find her."

"But how could you...?" she begins, then stops abruptly. "You sure?"

"Mom, she's alone and crying and we gotta hurry."

At this, Mom looks at me knowingly, then glances at Dad. Dad nods, tiptoes over, pats my head gently. "Sorry about your having such *meshugah* parents, they didn't pick up on it, Naomi. Just stay here with Mom, try to keep warm, and leave everything to me." Then he turns around, preparing to leave.

"No, Dad," I plead. "It's *me* she's calling out to. Dad, I've got to come too."

Dad exchanges looks with Mom, then rushes out, muttering something about needing to warm up the engine. Whipping out a thermometer, Mom quickly takes my temperature, then assures me that Dad is fully capable of finding her.

"No. If I'm not going, you've gotta."

I see the uncertainty in Mom's eyes. "Please, Mom," I implore. "I can manage."

I have little knowledge of the next hour or so. Just vague impressions here and there. Mom nodding, then picking up the telephone. A gentle but firm voice commanding me to remain under the covers. The sound of the back door closing, opening, closing. The tip of my nose going numb. Every solitary toe stinging. Waiting. Waiting. Waiting. But gradually growing less panicky, increasingly secure in the knowledge that *my sister's* heard; that *Nomi's* taking care of everything. Then inexplicably feeling warmer. How come I'm getting an overwhelming sense that I'm moving, but not with my own feet? Now the car trip, if that's what it is, feels endless and the whole while there I lie on the living room sofa, beside myself with worry. Then I hear voices and footsteps on the pavement. Suddenly with a whoosh, the front door springs open.

Next thing I know, a shivering Rose comes bursting into the living room, the tip of her nose white, flakes of snow trailing after her, tears streaming down her still frightened face. She casts off her mitts and coat, then bolts toward me, throws her freezing arms around me, and hangs on for dear life. For the longest while we say nothing—just hold one another—while Mom mutters something about getting out of the wet clothes, then retreats to the kitchen to reheat the chicken soup. Rose digs her face into my neck, kisses my yet cold lips, lifts up my hand and blows her warm moist breath onto my icy fingers.

"Naomi, I was..." Rose begins.

"Cold and lost..." I continue, "and the snow was streaming so..."

"I just couldn't make out anything."

Rose draws her head back, looks me directly in the eye, and giggles through her tears. "You're still in there, aren't you?"

I squeeze her hand, feel our pulse quicken.

"And you really know. Knew all along, didn't you?" she exclaims.

"Oh Rose, thank God you're okay. I so wanted to go with them in the car but..."

"Nomi, sorry for everything shitty I've ever said or thought about you. I just get frustrated, is all."

"I love you," we declare in unison.

Later that night we snuggled together on Rose's bed, fell asleep in one another's arms. Waking at the crack of dawn, we whipped out our pillows, launched into such a boisterous pillow fight that we woke the household, though no one shushed us, disturbed the moment. "Nomi," asked Rose, falling into my arms again, "we'll always be able to find each other, won't we?"

The problems between Ro and me did not disappear after that memorable day. However, something had been affirmed, and everyone knew it, none more keenly than the two of us.

Years passed and the family went through good and bad times as families do. Having developed back problems, Dad began working half days only. To help make ends meet, I took a part-time carhopping job at the A&W on Pembina Highway. Rose began washing dishes at the Ponderosa. And Mom started selling real estate. "*Vey iz mir!*" Mom would exclaim. "Moving private property, can you imagine anything more capitalistic!"

In September of 1961, Rose and I began our last year of high school, and what a circus that year was, crammed full of a little bit of everything, including double-dating. Rose's best friend at this point was an ace basketball player, appropriately known as "Joany the Legs". To everyone's surprise, except Rose, for the second year running, mine was Isaac—a "developmentally delayed" teenager with a heart of gold and a fascination with the Bowry Boys. "Nu? You couldn't pick a beau with a little more upstairs?" our irrepressible neighbour Mrs. Schwartz would remark. Early in the school year, thanks to a behind-the-back pass from Rose, Joany scored the winning shot in a game against our archrival—Glenwood High. Toward year's end, I appeared on the local TV show *Bob and the Teens*, where against all odds, the girls' team beat the boys' team four-to-two. A victory which positively thrilled Isaac. It was in that year too that Mom, of all people, started taking what was to prove to be an abiding interest in Pesach. "Girls, listen," she would urge, "Pesach's our defining moment as a people. Also it's what *you* call a metaphor—a cry for freedom—and mark my words: Someday us women will get a fair shake. You understand, girls, yeh?" I felt stirred by her passion, though

Rose and I would exchange looks, wondering what exactly Mom was hoping for.

Now in the fall of 1962, Rose and I entered the University of Manitoba. I remember my first and second year clearly. Hanging out at this hole-in the-wall eatery called "Little Egypt" with my friends. Taking part in demonstrations. Pouring excitedly over Milton's *Paradise Lost*. Receiving the Adele Berenbaum Award for the highest standing in honours English. What stands out most, however, are some very special evenings.

You see, much as I adored the flicks I'd grown up with, with my entry into university, I started to hear tell of a whole different world of film. The Europeans, it seems, had turned film on its head, were actually reinventing the medium. I wanted to see these revolutionary new movies. I *needed* to see them. But this was Winnipeg in the opening years of the sixties. So finding a venue that showed such films was no small feat. I asked several classmates. They were unsure. I turned to my friend Alice. "Sorry, Naomi," she answered. I approached my twentieth century lit prof—Professor Dowley. "Try the Manitoba Film Society," he suggested. I checked the Winnipeg phone book. No such beast listed. And not another soul had even so much as heard of it. It would appear that I was at a dead end, yes? Though dead ends, they can occasionally surprise you.

Having just lunched with Alice, I was ambling down the corridor of the Arts Building, my knapsack slung over my shoulder, when I spotted an oddly shaped poster just above eye-level. Intrigued, I drew closer. To my delight, it read "Emma Goldman's Revolution—Special Lecture by Dana Fenster, Wednesday, 1:00 p.m." Now I had not so much as laid eyes on Mrs. Fenster since high school, for she had moved out of the north end a good three years ago. But here it was—my opportunity to set things right.

Come Wednesday, I entered the lecture theatre, took a seat in the front row. Ten minutes after the hour, and she had still not put in an appearance. Now I was beginning to suspect that something had happened to our august visitor when in breezed a chubby little woman who could only be Mrs. Fenster, dressed in stunning lavender—so help me, beads hanging down to her *kishkes*, her trademark glasses inching down her nose. Good for her!, I thought. Unconventional, as always. Now while she was talking to Dr. Harris from political science, I could see that she noticed me.

"Well, hello there, stranger," she called out at long last. "We on speaking terms?"

"Oh, Mrs. Fenster, if it's all right with you," I responded.

She smiled, then positioned herself behind the lectern and proceeded to deliver an intriguing address on Goldman's approach to revolution, again and again driving home the significance of anarchism. After the lecture, she motioned me toward her. And with what trepidation, I approached!

"Mrs. Fenster," I began, "I owe you an apology and really hope you'll accept it."

Mrs. Fenster nodded sympathetically, commented on how difficult feuds can be on the children. "But you know, Naomi," she went on, looking me squarely in the eyes, "you're an adult now. You make your own decisions, have to pick your battles. For God's sake, don't waste your time getting caught up in useless feuds. There are real injustices out there that need fighting."

Then she suggested that we grab a coffee, and for the next several hours, we sat on the wooden chairs at Little Egypt, catching up.

"And Rose, what's she up to?" she inquired at one point.

"Actually, Rose has become quite the athlete."

"And you, you're still a student of film, I trust? You know, we really do need politically aware artists—revolution or not."

"Yeah, still am, but I've run into a bit of a snag. Can't seem to locate this place called the 'Manitoba Film Society.'"

For a second there, Mrs. Fenster looked confused, but

gradually, her face cleared. "You must mean *Winnipeg* Film Society," she corrected.

I felt my heart race. "It's called 'Winnipeg Film Society?'" I checked. "You sure?"

"A hundred per cent sure," she answered, a twinkle in her eye. "I'm a member."

Just as we were about to part, I reached for Mrs. Fenster's hand, gave it a long squeeze. Then to my surprise, words that I had not planned on came tumbling out of my lips: "My Mom, I love her, but what I did to you, I'll never do again—not to anyone."

To the best of my knowledge, this was the last time I saw Mrs. Fenster. Little did I suspect then how this chance meeting would shape my life!

The Winnipeg Film Society was the first place where film aficionados in the Winnipeg area found a home. It was never what you would term popular. Nonetheless, a broad mix of steady customers reliably turned up—students, artists, politicos. Located in the market area, it was a modest operation—a few dozen rows of seats, a small screen, a tolerably functional projector that would occasionally spew film all over the floor. As far as we enthusiasts were concerned, however, it was made to order.

Now while I would have come no matter what was being shown, my very first evening there, I was treated to a masterpiece that I had heard tell of—Bergman's *The Seventh Seal*. The stark use of contrast amazed me. The parting image of the dance of death made my heart leap. And for days, I could not stop talking about the picture.

"Dad," I gushed, as the family was sitting around the dinner table the following evening, "it asks about the existence of God. It explores good and evil. And the symbolism, it's not just at the periphery. Death is there, stalking the various characters from one moment to the next, actually playing chess with the knight Antonius Block."

"That knight of yours wasn't part of the Crusades, by any chance?" asked Dad, adjusting his yarmulke. "You know how many Jews were killed in the Crusades?"

The Winnipeg Film Society quickly became one of my regular haunts. Sometimes a handful of us would head over to Kelekis after the movie, and when closing time rolled round, there we'd still be, hunched over the table, discussing, analyzing. Eventually, I came across a club near St. Paul's College that also showed "foreign films," as they were then called. And between the two, my cinema education virtually took off. I saw three other Bergman films, took in *The Seven Samurai* by the great Japanese director Akira Kurasawa. I discovered the directors of the new wave: Truffaut, Resnais, Godard, Chabrol. I brushed up on my French, and through nothing less than a Herculean effort, I got my hands on several issues of *Cahiers Du Cinema*. Yes, yes, and with every fibre of my being, I grappled with the bold new approaches to the medium these revolutionary artists were advancing.

I considered the advantage of dispensing with the establishing shot and leaping right into the action as so many of the directors did. I applauded the switch to shooting on location. I thought about how quick cutting could be used to heighten the drama. And given how disorienting it is, couldn't the jump cut be used to body forth the illogicality of oppressive regimes? Perhaps the alienation of everyday life?

"The jump cut, the quick cutting you keep talking about— very interesting," observed Mom. "But don't just sit there on your *tokhes*."

"Mom?" I asked.

"They're tools, yeh?" she explained. "Why not use them?"

Why not indeed? I asked myself. Shortly thereafter, I began drafting the bare bones of a script for a documentary on the Mount Carmel Clinic. Determined to get the straight dope, I got in touch with the legendary Anne Ross. And a borrowed VTR in tow, in the fullness of time, I began shooting.

Now one day I was hunched over the dining room table struggling with a scene that was not coalescing when a most novel idea struck me. What if I could interview some of the leaders of the new wave? At least Truffaut. Better yet, what if I could work for one of them—who cares in what capacity—pick up the craft from the very people reinventing it? Unsure of the logistics, but sensing that the general direction was sound, with my parents' blessing, a week later, I took a job as weekend copyreader at *The Winnipeg Free Press* even though this meant having to burn the candle at both ends. And I started scrimping and saving, living for the day when I could set out for Europe.

Now initially, Rose was uneasy. "You really intending to be gone a whole year?" she asked, her forehead crinkled. "I mean, you and me, we've always been together."

"Ro," I answered, "listen, if it's gonna be too hard on you, I need to know *now*." Catching my eye, she nodded. Then to her credit, she sat with it, and little by little she grew accustomed to the idea, even began to take an active interest in the trip. "Nomi, I can see it's right. Really can," she assured me.

Rose's change of heart meant everything. "Ro, I'll write you every single day," I vowed. And my one and only reservation gone, I doubled my effort. In the hope that it would open doors, I even authored an article on auteur theory, had it published in the Saturday paper. And how exhilarated I felt! At my feet lay the path that my passion, my vision, my entire life had prepared me to tread, and there would be no turning back.

Now the unbridled enthusiasm of youth notwithstanding, even by normal standards, I had arrived at a turning point, a critical moment in my life saga—one of those moments that establish the storyline—a place by which to define oneself and be defined, a place of meaning. It is precisely here, however, that my search for meaning flounders—for here my memory stops.

Without warning, without so much as a word of explanation, here it simply…

END OF BOOK ONE OF NAOMI'S MEMOIR

NAOMI'S MEMOIR

BOOK TWO
1974–1976

9. NAOMI

WHILE I ENDED the last Toronto chapter on an ostensibly high note, that was hardly the main drift. What can I say? That's simply the nature of people's lives who have recently been released from hospital. We place one foot after another, yes? We do as we're told. And we grasp at anything that gives us hope. For some of us, though, there comes a time when we can see so clearly that we're being dead-ended that we would do almost anything to escape. Now paradoxically, the very severity of our situation holds promise, especially if it gets our mind ticking. Nonetheless, as every credible madwoman will tell you, it is precisely here that we are most vulnerable. What is likewise apropos, there are moments in life—possibly everyone's—where the only way up is down.

This blouse, *these* slacks, *this* sweater, I decided. Pooped yet hanging in, I was rummaging through the bedroom closet, a navy blue trunk at my feet. I was determined to keep up my energy long enough to pack up that myriad of clothes that did not fit, that belonged to the *other* Mrs. Smith—to the young quick-witted Naomi that so eluded me.

Ten and a half months had passed since moving into the Palmerston house. While I continued to wonder what mysterious concatenation of circumstances had landed me here, even in the privacy of my own mind, I tended to give such issues wide berth, fearful that in that direction madness lay. As for connubial bliss, while Earl was clearly beside himself now and again, there were no further incidents between the two of us. The solution? A time-honoured formula seized upon by many a starry-eyed couple on the road to marital Nirvana—"expect nothing." I asked fewer questions, and Earl resigned himself to a life riddled with error. And as for Ruthie and me, it would appear that our fleeting moment of togetherness was destined to remain one of those impenetrable mysteries of history—neither understood, nor repeated.

During this time, there had been considerable changes in the people around me. An ever more ardent environmentalist—and no question, this side of him called to mind my father—Earl had begun making notes for a treatise which he hoped to some day pen on the feeding habits of the humpback whale. Having been discharged from hospital in early fall, Jack had initially taken up lodgings in a cockroach-infested rooming house near Ossington. Now he had dropped by our place a handful of times. However, the tension between him and Earl was so thick that no one was eager to give it another try! Then he simply disappeared.

Of course, being the youngest, Ruth was the one who had changed most dramatically. How curious she had become! Why? Where from? How come?--such questions were forever on her lips. Except when Gerald was around—for what parent could hold a candle to Ger?—overwhelmingly, the questions were directed toward Earl. Always Earl. Now he would answer most like the level-headed environmentalist that he was, tell her that tap water came from lakes, add how important it was that we not dirty our lakes—and this too was good—but there were moments when something truly magical would transpire between the two of them.

Rushing up to the bay window, her face pressed against the glass, pointing with glee at the large white flakes wafting downward, Ruthie would ask, "Snow, Daddy! Where from?" "Pumpkin, it's d'old man," he'd reply.

"D'old man?" she'd repeat.

"Yeah. You see all those white feathers?"

"Uh huh."

"Well, d'old man is plucking his goose again."

And her jaw would drop, and her eyes would glisten, and the most gentle "ah" would issue from her lips.

Pausing to savour these memories and saddened that Ruthie and I had no such moments of our own, I imagined introducing her to the wonder of the prairies. Then I turned my attention back to the packing, and deposited yet another pair of slacks into the rapidly filling trunk. Seconds later, I began rummaging through the closet again—for something was not adding up. Despite all the undersized clothes in that closet, curiously, there was not a single *dress* there that would fit a slimmer me. Yet, that day back in the hospital, Nurse Ann had brought me a *dress* to wear. Just when had I taken up traditional female attire? Unsure what to make of the enigma, I glanced back at the trunk. Now I had, of course, totally forgotten that I had searched through these clothes repeatedly over the past year, gleaning from them every fact about my former self that they could possibly offer. And so operating from an incorrect premise, I became alarmed that I had been about to store away these ill-fitting garments without once having tried to cull forth their secrets. And before long, I was frantically lifting every item out of the trunk, scrutinizing it fastidiously, then tossing it aside. "Packing disorder nonspecific variety," I presume it's called.

About half an hour into the operation, I cast my eyes about. *Oy!* The room was an unholy mess—apparel everywhere. Clearly, every last stitch had to be picked up. Giving myself a moment—a glutton for punishment, I wasn't—I hopped onto the bed, reached into my pocket for a cigarette. And once again, I found myself asking: How did I end up in St. Pukes? Something to do with depression, I reminded myself. "Reactive depression," Dr. H. called it. And what could my depression be a reaction to if not the family breakup? Then I lay my head on the pillow and ask the one question the mere thought of which predictably fills me with dread: My family and I, just how did we come to lose one another?

I think of my parents, recall their years of kindness. Inevitably, I think of Rose, and the tension between us seizes my mind. Then an awareness creeps up on me that has visited me often but never with this urgency. I really am alone. I recall Mom's warning, "You girls, you're something precious called 'twins.' Something that shouldn't be squandered." Is that it? Had I squandered the last remnant of our relationship?

Instinctively, I begin retracing our early history. I start with the legendary nosebleed at Champlain Elementary. I arrive at the pivotal moment Mom is assembling my new wardrobe. At the thought of clothes, my eye catches the clutter on the floor. My God!, I realize. My impeccably neat husband, he could come waltzing through that door any second. I drag myself out of bed, reach for the nearest *schmata*, start folding it.

"Missus, hope you're not wearing yourself out trying to make sense of those old duds again," chimes in Earl's voice suddenly.

Now at first, this offhand exhortation baffles me. Slowly but surely, however, the implication sinks in—I've searched this apparel for clues before, so have made this mess for nothing. At this, my spirits plunge. And back into bed I crawl, convinced of the futility of everything.

Now clearly, I had made progress over the last year—and I knew it. I could find my way to the mail box and back; I could tell the difference between a Libby's and an Aylmer tin; and I had gotten the hang of the child's gate. But all things considered, it was not much. Not from the perspective of the one living it! How readily we accept second-class lives for others! Not so when the life is our own.

Now as I lie there half despairing of ever getting a leg-up, a lone tear escapes down my cheek and I start peering about for a box of tissues when, by happenstance, my eye lights on an empty pill bottle. And it is then that an intriguing new question hits me: The confusion, the muddle in my head, who's to say how much comes from electroshock—a factor, admittedly, about which I can do *bupkes*—and how much comes from the pills? It had always been clear that the meds exhausted me. But exhaustion, that was hardly the whole of it. Every time that my dose was increased, I would find myself more befuddled than ever.

Over the next few weeks, that question haunted me. The more I thought about it, however, the clearer it became that I *did not know*, could not even *begin to know* unless I somehow put the whole enchilada on the line.

And with this, the beginnings of a plan began to crystallize.

"Earl, can we talk?" I asked, hovering in the doorway.

It was early evening, and clad in his undershirt and boxer shorts—increasingly, his preferred mode of attire—Earl was stretched out on the sofa, leafing through *The Toronto Star*. He stopped to circle an item, then slowly lowered the paper.

I took the burgundy chair directly across from him. "This is awkward," I began, "but, well, you know the pills I'm on?"

Earl nodded.

"Well, not everyone's of the same mind about stuff like that," I continued. "In fact, several of the patients used to say the pills made them worse."

"I know you're fond of these people," he answered, picking his words carefully, "and I'm sure that many of them are salt of the earth, but face it, Naomi, their judgments may not be the best."

"Your assumption—not mine. Anyway, never mind about that. The thing is, the pills make me feel awful. You live with me. You've seen it. And honestly, Earl, can you really say that you know for certain that none of my confusion arises from the meds?"

He considered for a moment. "Got me there, Missus. I cannot."

"Well, I've a proposition. How bout I take only half the regular dose tonight? If I make out fine, I do the same tomorrow. If not, I won't bug you again. Promise," I added, catching his eye.

His brow furled, Earl threw up his hands. "For Chrissake, woman!' he exclaimed. "You really wanna drag us through all that again?"

"Earl, we've got to do something. Look at me. I'm your wife, and I'm telling you, I can't live like this."

Now to my astonishment, he did indeed look at me, and every muscle in his face melted. For a moment, he seemed to be going along.

"Of course, it's up to Dr. Higgins," he suddenly stipulated.

"I asked Dr. Higgins to cut back on my meds just last month," I pointed out.

"And?"

"He's dead set against it, but..."

"Well, there you go. Now Nomi, I understand about the side effects and all, and no question, they're shitty, but you've a disease. There's medication for the disease, and Dr. H. is the authority—not us. Say," he suddenly added, "how about I tag along on your next visit, see if Dr. Higgins would consider trying a different med?"

Painfully aware that we had been there, done that, I shrugged, and for the next several minutes we sat in silence.

"Well, there *is* something else we might try," Earl uttered at long last, "and it has the advantage of being relatively safe. See this ad I circled?" he said, handing me the newspaper. "They're showing an old Polanski flick at the Roxy next Saturday—one we saw together in the sixties. We go, and who knows? Just might jog your memory."

"But the pills—you won't reconsider? Please, Earl," I beseeched.

"C'mon Missus," he replied, "you knows we can't."

That night I lay in bed, weary as a woman could be at the shell of a life that I was leading. I even began toying with the idea of taking an overdose and letting that be the end of my misery. Then all of a sudden, I remembered something—something Jack had shown me. What did he call it? "Tonguing." "Bless you, Jack Carpman," I muttered beneath my breath. And for all intents and purposes, the fix was in.

It took me all the next day to muster up the courage. The following evening, however, I pulled "a Jackman." Translation: I "tongued" the pills. To my delight, more energy and remaining awake a good part of the night were the only ostensible consequences. And so next morning I did what many a conscientious scientist does with a successful experiment. Replicated it. Once again, I felt fine.

While I cannot be sure of my timing here, late that afternoon, I found myself trembling. Now I shook from the meds at the best of times. So I simply did what I'd done for the last year with the plethora of drug reactions: worked around them, swept the floor, fed my child.

"Missus, you all right?" asked Earl, at supper that night.

"Why you asking?"

"You seem a bit jumpy, is all…. By the by, we still on for the flick tomorrow?"

"Sure."

"Great. I'll call Ger, see if he'll baby-sit. Now don't get your hopes up, but Nomi, if you did end up recalling it—whole new ballgame. Know something, darlin'?" he added unexpectedly, his eyes twinkling. "It's high time that we 'filmaholics' had a night on the town."

And so it is that the two of us formed a pact of sorts, whether consciously or unconsciously is anything but clear.

"Say, kids, did you know that your Da and his main squeeze over there are painting the town red tonight?" Earl asked, advancing into the living room and winking at his son. Then he held my eyes and smiled—I could swear, almost tenderly.

Entering further into the spirit, that evening Earl dressed to the hilt, donning his chocolate-brown jacket, his blue James Wells tie. When I entered the kitchen, he was hovering over the table, polishing his shoes. Could he be seeing this as a *real* date? I wondered. Perhaps hoping to rekindle what once was? Moved, I quickly rushed upstairs, smeared on lipstick, fluffed my hair. Now when Gerald turned up to baby-sit, he took one look at me and shook his head.

"Nomi girl," he cautioned, "you don't look well. You might consider staying home."

"Not to worry, Ger," insisted Earl, "the Missus often overheats these days."

A blatant fabrication. Ergo, the man really had his heart set on stepping out with his wife. As for me, at this point, I was going for broke. And so it is that with all the warning lights blinking, that evening one Mr. and Mrs. Earl Smith of Toronto hopped into their Chevy and headed to the famous ninety-nine cent Roxy.

After parking the car, Earl gallantly opened the door for me. And hand-in-hand, like a couple of giddy teenagers, we stepped into the theatre. We bought a jumbo popcorn and my favourite licorice. "Sweets for the sweet," said Earl, handing me the licorice.

"Ready?" he asked, catching my eye.

"Ready," I replied.

Then our heads high, we entered the Sanctum Sanctorum, navigated the crowded aisle, grabbed seats two rows from the front.

Now as we drank in the ambiance—the mouth-watering aroma of freshly popped corn, the laughter, and friendly chatter—Earl began fidgeting. "Darlin'," he eventually murmured, leaning toward me, "there's something about this film, maybe I should be giving you the heads-up on." Even as he was speaking, the lights began to dim.

"Shush," insisted an irate female voice somewhere to his side.

Trusting that whatever it was would keep, I gave his hand a gentle squeeze, thankful that the two of us were in this together. Then I plunked my feet up on the chair in front of me just like I used to in my youth. And just like in youth, the everyday world disappeared—disappeared utterly— and the magic of the movies was upon me.

A slip of a moon flitted across the screen, only to be replaced by a mysterious abbey. A trailer, I realized. Quick on its heels came another trailer, this one set in the wild west, complete with gunslingers, tumbleweed, neighing horses. Then, my heart pounding with anticipation, the feature began.

Dead in the centre of the screen is a huge eye. In the centre of the iris appears the title "Repulsion." Alas, I have no recall of ever having seen such an opening. How could I forget something so stunning?, I ask myself. And if I can't remember this, what chance have I with the rest of the film? For a split second, I am on the verge of tears, but am quickly drawn in by the brilliance of the execution. What a masterful effect as the camera pulls back into a tight shot of the beautician's expressionless face!

As the story continues to unfold I start feeling queasy. Nonetheless, starved for the old magic, I sit there glued to the screen, thrilled at the artistry, applauding the shock of the imagery—the dripping of the tap, the buzzing of the flies, almost all of it in a diminutive apartment which the director skillfully makes more threatening, more claustrophobic by the second. And now a wall in one of the rooms begins to crack. More scenes take shape, most of them in other parts of the apartment, but back to that ominous crack we keep being pulled. The crack is getting steadily larger. And now it is a hole. And strangely, out of the hole emerges a hand. Its fingers extended, the hand, it is reaching out of the wall. Out of the screen. Into the first row of seats. The second. And now I can feel it on me—on my mouth, my breast, creeping up my leg.

I continue watching, trying to ignore the invasive hand just as I've ignored so many other inconvenient perceptions since coming to in the St. Pukes' corridor. A board is being nailed to the bottom of a door. A freshly minted corpse is being dumped into the bathtub. And still the hand assaults me.

I suddenly hear myself screaming. "Help me! Help me!"

Within seconds, there is a medley of voices all about me. Someone is insisting the racket stop. Someone is explaining that a woman is in trouble. Two hairy hands are on either side of my shoulders, and a man is rushing me out of the theatre—toward what nefarious end, I shudder to think. And now I am in a car, the man's hands holding me up, supporting me.

"Nomi, you okay?" he eventually asks.

"I feel awful," I moan.

"The choice of movie—idiotic of me. You'd been so taken by that opening that I felt certain that seeing it again would bring something back. So sorry. Should have realized. But darlin', something else's wrong here. Were you after taking a few drinks maybe?"

"Earl?"

I can feel Earl's gentle hands turn me around. "Nomi," he implores, "did you take something?"

"That's not it. The pills, I haven't been swallowing them," I confess.

For a moment, he seems unable to register what I'm saying. Then the blood drains from his face, and he beholds me with horror.

"I ... uh, I'm sorry," I utter, hanging my head in shame.

"You're sorry!" he repeats in disbelief. "You're *sorry!*" he repeats once again, his voice rising to a crescendo. For several seconds he continues to stare, his skin from the neck up reddening. Then he clenches his teeth, reaches over, fastens my seat belt, and without another word, starts the car.

"Thank God we're going home!" I exclaim.

"Missus, we're not going home," he responds.

10. NAOMI

BUSTED! I COULD READ IT in the whiteness of Earl's knuck-les as he clasped the steering wheel. I could feel it in the car's single-mindedness as it sped closer and closer to the place of devastation.

"Earl, the electroshock," I suddenly heard myself call out.

"Look, if dat's what's worrying you, Missus, no need. Think I'd really let that happen again?"

For the briefest moment, I was relieved. Next thing I knew, I was screaming, and Earl was cussing. And screams and curses filled the universe.

> *"Noncompliant," they say.*
> *And the word sits there, and the world sits there.*
> *And the word and the world sit.*
> *Who dreamt that freedom passes like a dream?*
> —Excerpt from Black Binder Number Two.

Sometimes I wonder what would have happened had I made different choices, had Earl. Inevitably, however, I always touch base with a simple fact. That one way or another, most everyone who sets foot in these institutions finds themselves a repeat customer. Now generally, even when betrayal rears its head—and to a degree, doesn't it always?—the family stays intact. The power of personal history, yes? And then there are those of us who lack history.

Committal number four was the beginning of a rupture between Earl and me. He blamed me for tricking him. I blamed
him for committing me. And when at long last Earl started
visiting, neither of us had a clue what to say to the other.

"Any point my staying, Nomi?" he would ask.

"What do you want me to say?" I would answer.

Now what Ruth was making of this sudden disappearance,
we can none of us be sure, though everyone else was nonplussed. Not that they hadn't seen it before. And not that any
of us believed that my ever popular disappearance acts were
at an end. What can I say? Like all professional entertainers,
us crazies, we have a responsibility to our audience.

Now being hospitalized again—and let's be blunt about it—
being forcibly hospitalized—was like being dragged back to
square one. Whatever spins one might place on it, the life that
I had worked so hard at piecing together had been wrenched
away. Staff were more in-my-face than ever. "Now open your
mouth wider," Nurse Ann would instruct, bending down and
arching her neck forward. "We can't have you spitting out
your medication now, can we?" In all honesty, though, years
later, it was not this indignity that most haunted me. It is that
secret trauma that us psych survivors seldom breathe a word
about—not even among ourselves—one that I am reluctant to
name even now lest it be misunderstood—the awareness that
I had helped deliver myself to hands such as these.

Mercifully, my summer get-away at Head-Shrink Inn on
the Lake was relatively brief. According to official records,
twenty-nine days precisely. Now for most of my stay, time
hung about my neck like the ancient mariner's albatross.
My mistake, I eventually came to realize was that I had been
avoiding everyone out of embarrassment, when of all people,
my fellow patients would understand.

Now come the middle of the fourth week, with help from
my comrades-in-arms, I once again pulled myself out of my
cocoon—something which proved singularly informative. It

was at this juncture too that I discovered a whole new kind of kinship with other patients.

"Sorry, Nomi, haven't heard from the indomitable Jackman no how, no way," answered Zelda, bits of egg and coffee dribbling out of her mouth. "But back to them pills. You really just kept tonguing them?"

It was breakfast time at the illustrious St. Pukes' cafeteria, and Brad, Zelda, and a medley of others were at the table nearest the door.

"Cold-turkeyed, did you?" asked Alex, a muscular Black man from the Tenderloin. "Actually I cold-turkeyed once," he went on, his face beaming. "Now the coppers turned up, but you can bet your bottom dollar I showed them who's the man."

Three other patients—none of whom I could place—proceeded to recount their cold-turkey sagas, curiously, each and every one ending in an admissions room.

"Anyway," continued Zelda, "though the odd person can pull it off, honestly, honey, that's not the way. You wanna go off," she explained, "you hafta taper."

I nodded. "Zelda, you ever go off?"

"Indeedarooney. In fact, was drug-free for three whole years."

"But if you made it," I asked astonished, "how come you went back on?"

Brad looked at me pointedly and shook his head.

"It's okay," Zelda assured him. "See, my kid died in this car accident, and well, everything pretty much fell apart after that."

"Sorry, Zelda. I didn't know."

"Oh yeah. Died in my arms, she did. And doc said, 'Zeldee— that's what he called me—know you aren't partial to meds, but just to tide you over.' Famous last words, eh?" A tear trickles down Zelda's face. "But Naomi," she goes on, "where in Sam Hill did you get the idea you could just stop taking these here venerable substances?"

"Pssst.... Tell you what I think happened," whispers Emily,

her hands cupping her mouth. "The CIA's behind it. Sent Naomi a subliminal message."

At this, James Limon rolls his eyes. "Sure they did!" he retorts sarcastically. "In their spare time when they weren't busy planting sperms in your skivvies."

"Oh Zelda," I exclaim, looking up again. "I'm not tapering off, cold-turkeying, nothing. Obviously, I need the meds. But I'm so ashamed. Didn't think of the consequences to Earl, Ruth, myself, anyone."

Zelda reaches for my hand. "Child, nothing to beat yourself up over. Honest, honey, we've all of us done stuff like that."

Now it is precisely at this moment that Nurse Ann begins to head for the door. As she nears our table, James' eyes light on the ward key, which, as the fates will have it, is dangling conspicuously from her neck. Now he is staring at it, mesmerized. Noticing, Brad looks at me pointedly, then back at James. "Shit, man, don't," he whispers urgently.

"Is this the key that unlocks the gate to paradise?" James asks, making a grab for the key and giving it a subtle yet all too apparent tug.

As we sit there dreading the inevitable, two orderlies appear. His eyes wide with terror, James releases his hold on the key. Too late. Already they have him by the shoulders and are dragging him off. Once again, I exchange looks with Brad. What's wrong with these people?, I wonder. Us patients, we know exactly why James feels as he does. Why can't staff figure it out?

Frightened for her friend, Emily starts to weep. As Zelda and I endeavour to console her, a couple of our compatriots drift away, their faces pale, their heads lowered. Leaving things with all of us cowed like this, it just doesn't sit right.

Strange. Countless times before, our fellows were hauled off in disgrace. And countless times before, we watched on, powerless. Now this was no Hollywood movie. Clearly, we inmates hadn't a snowball's chance in hell of taking over the institution. One of our own had been snatched from under our very nose, however, and this time we weren't going to take it lying down. Now there are protests and there are protests, yes?

"Hey, Zelda," I call out, raising my voice loud enough for the entire table to hear, "wouldn't you say that staff are a tad *obsessive-compulsive* when it comes to keys?"

Catching on quickly—for the woman was nobody's fool—Zelda's face instantly lights up. "Indubitably," she answers, "and not just with keys. Why they're textbook cases of that there obsessive-compulsiveness. Child, just look at their standard M.O.—habitual note-taking, frenetic checking of files. They're paranoid also, dear heart," she quickly tacks on, a twinkle in her eye. "And we all know what that's a symptom of."

"Oh no! Not the dreaded 'S'!" I exclaim, cowering in mock terror. "Better be careful they don't overhear us," I add. "Wouldn't want to reinforce their delusion that people are talking about them."

"You know," Brad offers, "*they* act out all the time—mouthing off, assault causing bodily harm. Antisocial types with aggressive tendencies, wouldn't you say?"

"Even the women," pipes up Emily unexpectedly, "cause they carry on much like the men. Sperms with perms—that's right, isn't it?"

I stare at Emily in amazement, nod enthusiastically, then cast my eyes about. Face after face is breaking into a grin—waves of gaiety blossoming on a formerly bleak shore. The banter continues, with a few surprisingly knowledgeable patients poking fun at what I could only imagine were some of the more esoteric diagnoses.

"Transient situational disorder," observes Irv wryly, "what's that mean? That your car's on the fritz and you're having a bad day? What geniuses dream up junk like that?"

"All of them. Even put it to a vote," answers Brad authoritatively, "but it seems to me, only when they're constipated."

"Say what?"

"Only stands to reason. When a guy's straining for a shit, any shit'll do."

"Gross," calls out a teenager, putting her finger in her mouth and pretending to hurl.

"Objection! Objection!" protests a naysayer, raising his hand. "They're men of science. They don't invent diagnoses out of thin air."

"The hell they don't," Brad retorts.

"Smartass, you think it's that easy? You try."

A glint enters Brad's eye. And with several newly acquired admirers cheering him on, he rises to his feet, then much to our delight, rises to the occasion.

"*Uno momento*," urges Brad, holding up a single finger. "The name is 'Compulsive Diagnosing,'" he specifies seconds later, assuming an air of mock superiority. "Population most at risk—mental health professionals. The higher up the professional, the more susceptible. It is characterized by a mania for labels, progressive alienation from the Queen's English. Delusions of grandeur. Pathological ignorance of the human condition. Oh yeah, and get this," he adds with a mischievous grin, "an almost irresistible urge to act like an arrogant asshole."

As Brad winds up, we all nod. And barely has he finished when a good half the table begin speculating on which hapless staff member is afflicted with the most dire case of this disorder, several putting forward their own therapist, and not unconvincingly.

"My giddy aunt! To think that on most days Dr. H. looks as normal as the rest of us!" declares Robena—an elderly woman with silver blue hair. "You never know, do you?"

As Brad takes his well-earned bow, peels of laughter ripple through the cafeteria. Shortly thereafter, Nurse Ann returns, and the table goes quiet, and inevitably, once again several of my sisters and brothers begin to drift away—this time, with just a hint of a swagger. Now I am about to take my leave as well when a patient called Nora catches my eye.

An intense woman, with red suspenders and short cropped hair, Nora is an insightful young dyke about five-feet-three with a rare talent for getting hold of razor blades and the scars up and down her arms to prove it. Seen as mouthy and a cutter to boot, she is uniformly disliked by staff, most patients too, though Zelda and I are rather in awe of her, for no one is able to intimidate her—not with threats, not with seclusion.

"Naomi, you know what burns my ass about your story?" she asks, planting her elbows firmly on the table. "Your husband supervising the meds."

"It sucks, I agree, but to be fair, this isn't exactly a picnic for him either."

"Hardly the point. The s.o.b.'s controlling you. Husbands and doctors—between the two of them a straight woman doesn't stand a chance. If you ask me—and like, you'd be a blithering idiot not to—the meds, that's probably not the half of it."

I reach into my pocket for a cigarette, light it, then look up at her inquiringly.

"Well, Naomi, like, you had ECT, right?"

"Guilty as charged."

"I'll tell you something. Everyone I've ever known who's had it is a woman."

At this, Bruce Horkheim and his buddies start to leave.

"You know, lady, you're full of shit," announces Bruce, stopping to glare at Nora. "Lots of guys are shocked. And what's wrong with shock, anyway? I mean if a guy or broad needs it?"

My head spinning, I try to focus in on Nora. Now for some reason, she begins commenting on her partner, but before I can make head or tail of her story, that all-too-familiar sensation comes over me.

When I fade back in, I cast my eyes about. I can see that I am still in the cafeteria, that my coffee cup is back on the table. Also that Nora is still talking.

"Now with dykes, it's altogether different, but a straight friend of Sue's told us how it happened to her," she is explaining, "and the thing is..."

"Sorry. Mind repeating that last bit?" I ask.

To my surprise, without so much as a warning, Nora rises from the table, her face flushed, her hands on her hips. "Like you try to help a person, and they don't even bother paying attention. Screw this! I'm outta here."

Now Nora storms out of the cafeteria all right, overturning four cups of coffee and a plateful of eggs in the process. However, moving faster than any of us thought possible, Zelda takes off in hot pursuit. Not five minutes later, back they both come. A semi-conciliatory expression on her face, Nora sits down directly across from me.

"Listen," she continues, leaning forward and eyeing me intently, "that friend of Sue's that had ECT, well, her ever lovin' hubby signed for it."

"How awful!...Oh I see," I say, catching her drift, "but Earl, he wouldn't do that."

"Suit yourself, but husbands do."

Brad takes a bite of his toast, lets out a huge belch. "Hey, how come you broads are on our case anyway? It's hardly our fault that the institution zaps people."

"The man's got a point," Zelda suggests. "St. Pukes, it could've acted without consent."

For the next several minutes, Zelda goes back and forth on the issue, unable to settle on a position. I thank everyone for their help, hedging my bets by suggesting that there is no real way of knowing. Now I am on the verge of packing it in, in fact, have pocketed my cigarettes and begun to rise when I feel a hand gripping my arm—firmly, urgently. I suck in my breath and look up, unnerved by the prospect of what I may hear next.

"Let me tell you something," states Nora, peering ever more deeply into my eyes. "My aunt's a psychiatric nurse. And, like, one thing I know about funny farms—they like to cover their ass. *He* signed or *you* signed. You really think it's you?"

The next couple of days, I was so exhausted that I could barely keep myself upright—which, at it happened, served me well as it allowed me to keep myself distracted. As I crawled into bed the third night, however, I could no longer keep Nora's question at bay. Had the institution zapped me on their own say-so? And if not—and apparently that was more likely— which of us had signed?

Dreading the idea that it might have been Earl, the father of my child, at first I told myself it had to be me—that I'd fallen into such a funk that I'd been willing to try anything. The more I thought about it, however, the less likely it seemed, for I'd always been leery of medical interventions. I jumped to the conclusion it was my parents, assured myself that this explained the fallout between us. Then it dawned on me: The time frame was wrong. And with this realization, reluctantly, I focused in on Earl.

No question the man was in cahoots with the doctor. Backed up his analysis. Enforced every single medical order. There was something else as well—something recent. Just before dumping me back in the loony bin, Earl had mentioned something about not *letting* them shock me again. "Let"—is that another word for "authorize"?

I had to find out. I pulled the covers over my head, determined to makes inquiries first thing tomorrow.

Little did I suspect...

"Mrs. Smith, we haven't all day. Take your pills and move along," urged Nurse Ann.

It was eight a.m., and I was at the front of the medication line, so depleted that I had to lean into the counter to steady myself. Nurse Ann had just handed me the small paper cup. Two pills only? I lifted the glass of water, obediently swallowed, then stood there bewildered. Had I perhaps taken the rest without realizing?

"Think some of my pills might be missing," I finally suggested.

Nurse Ann shook her head. "You take fewer now; I explained all that Tuesday."

I recall little after that. Just the hum of the institution. The monotonous din of feet shuffling down the corridor. The walls shuddering as only madhouse walls shudder.

Next thing I was aware of, I was in Dr. Higgins' office—not a clue why we were meeting or how I came to be here. I glanced up at the clock overhead. Three-forty-five.

Dr. Higgins's desk was littered with open files. His white cloak on, he was sitting behind it, absent-mindedly clicking his pen. Though it made no sense—no sense at all—he appeared to be in the process of explaining that I was going home tomorrow.

"Tomorrow?" I ask aghast.

"Yes, first thing in the a.m."

I can feel my heart flutter. Then remembering that burning question, I pull myself together, go for it. "But my husband, did he sign for the electroshock?"

"I'm afraid you're confused," he answers. "You see, Mrs. Smith, we're not intending to administer ECT. We're intending to discharge you.... Now about the new medication regimen," he continues, "the dose is a bit higher, but everything's simple now. Nothing to remember. No fuss. No bother."

"Um, what new medication regimen?"

"I see," he says, glancing at me from the corner of his eye. "Well, did you notice that you're taking fewer pills?"

"Sure did."

He nods, gives his pen another click. "Excellent. Well, the beauty of the fluphenazine is that it's long-acting and injectable."

"Fluphenazine? Injectable? I ... I'm not sure..."

"Mrs. Smith, just think of it like this, it gets to stay in your system and keep you well. No chance of forgetting, or, well, spitting it out."

Now I had no intention of ever again sabotaging the meds. Nonetheless, something deep within bristled.

"But I don't want this," I objected.

Dr. Higgins shook his head and assured me that under the circumstances, the change was necessary. "Your husband and I, we're in agreement on this," he informed me, "and in time, you'll see it's for the best. Well, that's all for now. Oh, and Mrs. Smith," he added, "good luck."

Staggering at the magnitude of the tsunami that had just been unleashed, I returned to my room, sank onto the bed. All night long, I tossed about. As I arose the following morning, I laughed what felt like the laugh of the doomed. Earl picked me up at nine a.m. sharp. And in total silence—the hush so loud you could drown in it—back to the Palmerston house we drove.

Looking back on everything, Ruthie, I greatly regret that for the third time in a row, I was in hospital during your birthday. And sweetheart, believe me, there are things that I came to do in weeks following that I regret far more. But over the years, I have witnessed some of those dark lonely places into which people sink. And this much I have learned: Much as all of us would wish it were otherwise, there are times in people's lives—alas, some lives in particular—when there is no place to go but further down.

Still in the descent, hardly able to rub two thoughts together, for the next few weeks, I barely managed. I would drag myself out of bed in the morning, already anticipating the time when I would crawl back in. Trying to keep straight what Earl liked, what Ruthie was allergic to, I would spend a good part of the day starting dinner, tossing it, then starting again. I was so bowled over by the new drug regimen that I simply could not handle a single chore with any clarity, any real intelligence, and holding on to an overview was well nigh impossible. So evening after evening, Earl would arrive home, briefcase in hand, only to have to walk through the entire house, on the lookout for things that urgently needed doing, things that did not feel right. He would pick up one of Ruth's toys that had been lying for God knows how long smack in the middle of the hall. Or he would throw out the disaster that I had whipped up for dinner and start cooking from scratch. And there I would sit, mortified, knowing that I was not remotely pulling my weight. For a while, I tried harder. Eventually, truth be told, I barely tried at all.

Not surprisingly, relations between Earl and me continued to deteriorate. While we were civil to each other, whole days would go by where we exchanged no more than the most perfunctory remarks, and—heaven help us—we would probably have dispensed with those were it not for Ruthie. Where possible, as well, we would keep the bare minimum of a room between us. Come Ruthie's bedtime, invariably, I would flake out on the living room couch, while Earl toiled away in the study, finding solace in some treatise or other on the environment. At night, I would seek refuge in a lonely but secure bed, no sign of a spouse anywhere, and in the morning, I would lift up my eyes, only the crumpled blanket at my side bearing witness that another had been there.

Now for the first few weeks, there were two things that I lived for—visits from Gerald, for Ger remained a dear and trusted friend—and daytime soaps. Come the fourth week, however, as the meaninglessness of my existence sank in, a single preoccupation came to overshadow everything else—the dream of reuniting with my Winnipeg family. At this point, really, what had I to lose?

One morning, after an awkward exchange over breakfast, I decided to take the leap—to actually get a family member on the phone—*any* family member. I waited until Earl set out for work. Then stepping into the hall, I set about the task. Recollecting little about long distance, I began by phoning

Gerald. Now he must have been giving some thought to my predicament for the question came as no surprise.

"Dial 1, then the area code, then the number," he explained. "And love," he added conspiratorially, "if we're talking Manitoba here, well, the area code is 204."

"I love you, Ger," I answered.

Now I dreaded the idea of my folks seeing me as helpless, so I was adamant about dialing direct. So I entered the hall, did a trial run by calling up Kelekis. It worked!

I stopped to fetch Ruthie a glass of water. Then my heart in my mouth, I returned to the hall and dialed my folks. At the sound of the ring, shivers started coursing up and down my spine. The phone, however, kept right on ringing. I waited half an hour, redialed. Still no answer. Perfectly normal, I assured myself.

With the exception of one small stretch when I dozed off, for the rest of the day, more or less every half hour, I called. When Earl set foot in the house, I stopped, but the second that he shut himself up in his study, I resumed. Determined, for three whole days, I soldiered on. Early afternoon of day four, after setting Ruthie up in front of the TV, I picked up the hall phone, then stood there, my spirits beginning to flag.

Something was clearly amiss. Suddenly, the fear that my folks might be in hospital hit me like a thunderbolt. Losing no time, I asked directory assistance for the number for St. Boniface Hospital, then called. "No patient with that name," insisted the receptionist. I tried every other Winnipeg hospital. *Bupkes.*

Relieved but none the wiser, I pursued a different tack, asked directory assistance for a listing for a Rose or R. Cohan. No Rose Cohan. No R. Cohan.

I cycled through a variety of explanations, but one kept returning—the mysterious family fallout. If the family was pissed enough to write me off, it only stood to reason that they would do everything in their power to block my calls. Maybe took out an unlisted number. But *gotenyu!* Just what had I done?

I start replaying what few memories I have of the '64 to '69 years, but my ruminations are interrupted by Ruthie demanding her colouring book. I search high and low for the book, then her crayons, eventually locate both, but not quick enough. When I arrive at the dining room table, Ruthie is sitting in her special orange chair, pouting. She looks up at me askance as I place the colouring book before her.

"Mommy, you're stupid," she says. "Daddy finds things quicker."

"For sure, your dad's a whole lot quicker," I acknowledge. "Know something, though? Slow doesn't mean stupid."

"Mommy's stupid; mommy's stupid, mommy's stupid," she chants. Then she picks up a yellow crayon and breaks it in two. Shortly thereafter, she graduates to a red one.

Curious thing, as Ruthie sits sat there in rapt in concentration, demolishing one crayon after another, I get the strangest feeling that she is destined to be a mover and shaker. I also sense that her life will not be smooth sailing. Saddened for her, I kiss her on the cheek, let her know that when I was I little girl, sometimes I was mad at my mommy too.

"You had a mommy?" she asks.

"Absolutely. And you know what my mommy would be to you?"

"Grandmommies are stupid too," she answers, not missing a beat.

Several broken crayons later, I fetch my daughter some milk and cookies. Then I retire to the living room, put Ruthie as far out of mind as possible—and for that, Ruth, I'm so sorry—and within minutes, back I am, wading through the murky waters of my past.

Clearly, the breakup has nothing to do with my trip to Europe, I reason, for I have a vivid albeit isolated memory of the family seeing me off at the airport. Is it about Earl? The man's not always careful, and it's not hard to imagine someone taking offence. But in that case, why break off communications with *me*? Or had I perhaps broken off communications with *them*? Then I recall Mrs. Fenster's warning, "For God's sake, don't waste your time getting caught up in useless feuds." One of Mom's interminable feuds, is that what's going on? And if so, who did what? And given what we've been to one another, why hasn't Rose at least contacted me surreptitiously?

At the thought of Rose, my loneliness becomes so palpable that I can taste it. Then I grow more confused than ever. As Rose and I know—know as only identical twins could—our bond is too deep for anything on this side of the heavens to sever. It has survived totally different interests, different agendas, different countries. It survived me willfully pulling away for a decade and longer. The second that she was in trouble, the second she was lost in that freezing storm, there it was, in the chill of my bones, in the white tips of my frozen fingers. Communication between the two of us—it does not require good feelings, close proximity, a telephone line—nothing. And yet for some reason, she did not appear when those volts of electricity came surging through my skull. And somehow, I can find her nowhere. As if something deep in my soul—the special duality that makes me "us"—has been snuffed out.

At this, I reach back into early childhood, revisit those precious moments of tumbling into each other's arms, chasing each other down the grassy way. Inevitably, I find myself pondering the crayon incident. Horrified that Rose had confused our teacher at such a critical moment, I did everything in my power to separate from her—even erected a mental barrier. Is that it? Has Rose done something comparable?

Now as I sit there, placing one scene after another under a microscope, once again, a wave of loneliness sweeps over me. Then for the first time in over a year, I recall that picture of Rose—her body soaring, her basketball like a flash of lightning streaking through the air. In some cupboard, was it? No. The closet? No. The dresser. Needing some way to hold onto

Rose—I *schlep* upstairs, open the top drawer of our dresser. It isn't there. I search all the other drawers. Not in any of them. I return to the couch, disheartened, wondering if I could have moved it—worse yet, if Earl might have. Now by chance, from the corner of my eye, I catch a glimpse of the living room mirror. And almost instantly, I call to mind those early years when Rose and I would go scampering up to the mirror, grinning with delight at those identical friends who grinned back at us. The two images, they were the same. If I could see Rose in my own reflection then, if I looked carefully enough, might I not find her there still?

My heart in a flutter, slowly, I make my way over to the mirror and peer in. Nothing that I recognize as Rose looks back. Just this bloated drugged-out mental patient, the lower part of her face twitching. But maybe, maybe.

I stretch out my hand, touch the hand that reaches out for mine. I rub my nose against the nose in the mirror. I kiss the lips. Nothing. If only I could remember what happened, I...

Now I do not recall having a thought after that. Or at least not a thought precisely. More like a feeling. A sense that I needed to pry open my brain, do something—anything—to get inside. Next thing I know I am banging my forehead against the mirror. Again. Again. Again. Crack, goes the glass. And a stream of what feels like *our* blood comes trickling down my face.

"Rose, Rose, find me," I plead.

Now for a split second, I have an eerie sense that we were one. But no. I stare into the shattered mirror, and plain as day appears that shattered creature—Mrs. Smith, mental patient who has just messed up again.

With difficulty, I turn around, intent on stopping the bleeding. Barely able to hold myself erect, I stumble into the hall. And it is then that I see her. Ruthie is crouching in the corner of the dining room, her face pale, her tiny hands hugging her body. Tears in her eyes, she is rocking back and forth.

I can feel my heart sink. "Oh darling," I call out. "Mommy's so sorry. Everything bad is going to stop now. You're safe. Promise."

She starts to whimper, and I draw closer, hoping to comfort her. "Daddy, Ger-Ger," she hollers, her eyes wide with terror.

"Just hold on, Ruthie," I urge. "I'm gonna get Daddy and Ger-Ger right now."

To my shame, for a split second, I hesitate. One look at my daughter's distraught face, however, and I rush to the phone.

"Oh Gerald, something's happened," I scream.

A tidal wave had just been loosed, and like all cosmic events, it was to sweep up every creature in its path in ways that we could not begin to imagine. It began with Ruthie.

Nothing could be clearer but that my presence terrified her. Every time I tried to approach, she would cower, tucking her face further and further into her body. Now as I was backing away for the third time, without warning, my knees gave way and the colour leached out of the universe. I staggered to the washroom, turned on the tap, while continuing to try to reassure her. "Daddy and Ger-Ger are on the way," I called out again and again. No sound came from that room. Not a whimper. Not a sigh. It was as if she were hoping that if she were quiet enough, I would forget that she was there. Oh Ruthie, was that it?

Now as I struggled to control the bleeding, I heard a door open, took in footsteps in the hall. Then I made out Earl saying, "Ruthie, everything's fine now." Thank God!, I murmured. Seconds later, Earl shouted, "Missus, where are you?" My heart pounding, I made my way down the stairs, entered the dining room. Gerald and Earl were standing in the middle of the room, their eyes aghast. Miu was off to one side, Ruthie in her arms. While Ruth did not look at me, she seemed to intuit that I was there, for she abruptly hid her head in Miu's breasts. Earl took one step toward me, then stopped and stared. "Mary, Mother of God, what's been goin' on!" he thundered.

Someone was spiriting Ruthie away—Miu, I was later to discover—and Miu, bless you for that. *Someone* was grabbing me by the shoulders, asking again and again what happened. Words that sounded crazy even to me kept issuing from my lips. "Bumba kisses"! What the fuck are bumba kisses?" somebody yelled. And round and round the words kept going. And round and round the room kept spinning.

"Earl, this isn't the answer," insisted Gerald. "And how come we're never a team when it comes to Nomi's welfare?"

Now how I ended up here, I was not sure, but I became aware that I was sitting on a chair smack in the middle of the kitchen. Gerald was hovering over me, his fingers searching about my head. A few feet away, his nostrils flaring, the top button of his red flannel shirt undone, Earl was pacing back and forth.

Earl came to an abrupt stop in front of Gerald and wagged his finger angrily. "Damn it! The two of them, they're *my* responsibility," he said. "And even Nomi knows that she needs to go back. You do, don't you, Nomi?" he asked, turning toward me, his voice softening.

"Back?" I asked. "Back where?" Suddenly, my head felt as if it were about to split into a thousand pieces, and I saw my poor daughter's face. And only too clearly, I remembered. "Oh Earl, I'm so sorry," I whimpered. "You wanna hospitalize me? You'll get no argument from me."

"See," said Earl, glaring at Gerald.

"She's a mother who's worried sick about her child. What do you expect her to say?"

Now for a moment, the room went quiet. As if the universe and every creature in it were pausing to catch its breath.

"The stinging, it'll stop in a few secs," Gerald assured me, dabbing my wound with alcohol. Then he crouched down next to me and peered deeply into my eyes. "Nomi, just try to stay with me here, okay, love?"

I nodded.

"Now you and me, we've always been frank with each other. And I'm not gonna pretend there's no problem. But sweetie, what's happened here, it's not going to ruin Ruthie's life."

"Not so sure."

"Be that as it may, it's water under the bridge, isn't it? But you set foot in that hospital again, especially with a nasty gash like that on your noggin, who knows what'll happen to you? Now I'm fighting for you, sweetie," said Gerald, taking my head in his hand, "but the thing is, I need you to fight too."

"Just one fuckin' minute," roared Earl.

A heated exchange between the two men followed. Why is Ger so adamant when Earl's transparently in the right?, I wondered. Then the conversation took a most unexpected turn.

Earl had just declined Gerald's offer to let Ruthie stay with them. Whereupon Gerald had made an about-turn, suggested that *I* stay with them.

"And expose the lad to her?" snapped Earl. "Forget it! What you're suggesting, it's just not responsible."

"I know you're upset," Ger offered, laying his hand on Earl's shoulder, "and you've every right to be, but doing the so-called responsible thing, hey, isn't that what...?"

Earl resumed pacing. "So you're after thinking this is my fault?"

"Of course not," answered Gerald, "but be fair. *Nomi* didn't sign those papers. And she never wanted it."

I struggled to make sense of these words. Then I took in the furtive look in Earl's eye. And suddenly, I knew.

"*You* authorized the ECT?" I asked.

Earl stopped in his tracks, eyed me uneasily. "I did. The doc thought it necessary and I did, and maybe that was a mistake. But at this point, Missus, surely you can see, it doesn't change a thing."

I took a deep breath. "Ger, I'm ready to fight," I announced.

A haze having lifted—lifted just enough—Ger and I took one look at each other and proceeded to fight our hearts out, and we indeed made many a salient point. The thing is, though, Earl was adamant. So horrified was he by what he had witnessed, in fact, he was hell bent on having me under lock and key by nightfall.

"Look," he said, relaxing at long last, "let Ruthie stay at Gerald's for the weekend. I'll sleep on it, and the three of us, we'll hammer this out Sunday. But Missus," he added, his eyes sharp as steel, "I needs to be honest here. However distasteful you find hearing this, you're a danger to yourself and others. So the chance of me changing my mind, it's negligible."

The next couple of days offered little hope of reprieve, though seek it, I did. In fact, barely had two hours elapsed when I knocked on the door of Earl's study.

"Missus, something wrong?" he asked, his eyes widening. "You haven't been, well, hurting yourself again?"

"No, but Earl, could we talk? Now maybe I have some kind of illness, but..."

"Please, Nomi, just let me be," he insisted.

Desperate, I picked up the receiver, again hoping to reach my folks when I suddenly realized how livid Earl would be if he caught me in the act. I abruptly hung up. Then I shook my head in dismay, knowing that I now had no plan whatever. Nor did calling up Gerald to inquire about Ruthie bring any solace, for Ger was uncharacteristically vague.

Overwhelmed by the events of the day, I turned in early. In the wee hours, I was visited by a shock dream. I awoke with the word "Rose" on my lips and with Earl hovering over me. "Nomi, it's okay. Just a nightmare," he murmured. I was touched that he cared, but before I could so much as utter a word, he had rolled over.

Next day I again tried to speak with Earl. Pointless. Then

I cracked open a pack of Rothmans, crawled into bed, and smoked one cigarette after another, reeling from the knowledge that there was but one day left.

That night, once again I dreamed of the shock machine. And at the crack of dawn, again I awoke screaming for Rose. My head aching, my mouth so parched that my tongue stuck to the roof of my mouth, I staggered out of bed, downed a glass of water in a single gulp, and began counting off the hours: six o'clock ... seven o'clock ... eight....

11. NAOMI

*N*U? IT WAS A DAY from *"Ma Nishtana"*—an interminable stretch of hours, full of twists and turns. Now
at first, time crept slowly, for Earl had shut himself
up in his study, and it was not until noon that Gerald turned
up. The second that Ger set foot in the house, however, Earl
emerged from his lair, made coffee. Then the three of us hunkered down in the living room. This time, no one shouted or
even raised their voice. Nonetheless, it was quickly apparent
that my putative husband hadn't budged.

"I've already heard it all, said Earl. "Now suit yourself, but
there's really no point."

"You've heard it all!" I exclaimed aghast.

"That's what I'm after telling the two of you."

Unwilling to accept defeat, Ger continued to marshal one
argument after another. "Fella, it's not fair," he said. "Listen,
if you think that Nomi—or for that matter Ruth—will live to
thank you for this, think again," he cautioned, his words sounding eerily prophetic. The thing is, though, he was whistling in
the wind, so sure was Earl that I posed a risk to the children.
As for me, I was seriously considering throwing in the towel
for nothing could be clearer than that Ger was jeopardizing
his relationship with Earl, and I hardly wanted that. Be that
as it may, just as I was mustering up the courage to make one
final observation, all hell broke loose.

"Buddy, you weren't a scrap of help to Nomi after her pregnancy, you know that?" Gerald trotted out, seemingly out of the blue.

"*Her* pregnancy!" exclaimed Earl, throwing up his hands. "Jesus, Mary, and Joseph! As long as we're after dredging up ancient history, how about *your* pregnancy? What kind of a woman messes around with another woman at such a time?"

From the pain on their respective faces, you could read something of the vulnerable history between these two.

"That wasn't fair of me, was it?" admitted Earl suddenly, "but to get back to Nomi..."

Even as he readied himself for his next point, the doorbell rang. The three of us glanced in the direction of the front door, then stared at each other blankly.

"Ding," went the bell a second time.

"Must be the postman," jested Earl, the humour of the situation getting to him.

"Postman?" asked Gerald.

Earl grinned. "You know, as in *The Postman Always Rings Twice.*" Then out of the room he headed.

Seconds later, you could hear his voice barreling through the hallway. "Why now of all times?" he was asking. "And you telling me your folks have had no change of heart?"

"Forget about them! For God's sake, where is she?" a woman screamed, the words rushed, the tone frantic.

I tell this stretch of my story with some hesitancy, for I have spent far too many days plodding my way through the psychiatric survivor scene and indeed though the world at large to mistake it for typical. Still, most of us at some point or other find ourselves inches from where we began. And at that moment, there was no mistaking it—it was my tone, my contralto voice coming from the hallway. I could feel my heart racing. *Oy!* Only one other person in the universe sounded like that. But what had happened? And why couldn't I tell that she was coming?

My limbs shaking, my whole body threatening to give way, I got up to greet her. No sooner had I planted my feet on the floor than into the room stepped this comparatively slim woman, decked in a moss green wrap-around dress, a small cut on her forehead. Unless I was dreaming—and the jury was still out on that—no question it was Rose. And how magnificent she looked—her movements more graceful than ever! Clearly, the years had been good to her, for despite being in uncharted waters, she exuded a confidence that I had not seen before.

Earl followed her part way, then leaned against the doorjamb, muttering under his breath. Ignoring Earl, she eyed Gerald curiously. Then she beheld me, and her jaw dropped. She could see in a glance that I was a poor imitation of the sister she had once tried so hard to emulate. Torn, I stood there, unable to budge, barely able to breathe.

"How could you have called her?" I could hear Earl ask.

"Honestly, I didn't," said Gerald.

I could feel tears coming to my eyes, could see the tears in hers. Now I kept expecting to wake up, that, or for Rose to flee, stating that this was simply too hard. I couldn't be more wrong. Her face filled with longing, she advanced toward me. And without uttering a word, we each took the other's hand, gave it one quick light squeeze, one quick firm one. And now we dropped our hands, and my heart leapt in anticipation of that final simultaneous movement with which this ritual invariably ended. To my surprise, her hand set out before mine. Something had shifted. Something fundamental.

After we'd given each other that final squeeze, Rose threw her arms around me. And with every fiber of my being, I clung to her. When at long last we let go, Rose reached over, carefully wiped what must have been drool off my chin. Then she looked at me sadly. "Oh my poor Nomi," she exclaimed, "what on earth have they done to you?"

"Just one fuckin' moment," objected Earl.

Concern in her eyes, Rose touched my face again—gently, so

gently. And now she was approaching the dressing, but this, she did not touch. Nor did she ask about it. Just cushioned the wound with the soft blanket of her eyes. Then she put her lips to my ear and issued the only explanation of her coming that she was to provide that day. "See, Nomi, I found you," she whispered.

I nodded. "Still need a tad more work on that speed problem," I jested.

She giggled, squeezed my hand again, then whirled about and glared at Earl. And with this simple act, the haze that engulfed us began to dissipate. Also a formidable human being came into view.

"Look, Earl," she stated point blank, her eyes fixed to his, "when you turned me away two years ago, I took no for an answer. Not now."

"You were in touch before?" I ask, astounded.

"Well, just this one phone call," she qualifies, "and only after years of separation. Sorry, Nomi," she adds, "but you know, with Earl, the folks, and, well, the trip and all.... Damn!" she suddenly utters. "Why am I trotting out these lame excuses? The truth is, I let you down."

"But you *did* call."

Rose nods.

I turn to Earl. "And you didn't tell me?"

"Tell you! A reality check, okay? You were in hospital! You didn't know your arse from a hole in the ground. And your own doctor advised against it."

Now I am about to point out that I have been home for most of the last year when a look of extreme concern comes over Rose. "You were in hospital?" she asks. "Oh Nomi, what's wrong?"

"The thing is, I've been in a mental hospital. In fact, awkward though this is, likely to be returning any minute."

Now it quickly becomes apparent that this just might be a whole new ball game, for Earl catches my eye. "Nomi, enjoy the visit with your sister," he urges. "After supper, the four of us, we'll talk."

Gerald having suggested that the men afford us some privacy, minutes later, Ro and I are cozying up to one another on the couch while the guys rustle up dinner. Both of us acutely aware that time is of the essence, we dispense with niceties, and I quickly relay what I can of my recent history. Several times during my story, Rose squeezes my hand, shakes her head. As I launch into the details of the ECT, however, she visibly trembles.

"I knew there was something," she murmurs, her forehead furled, anguish flickering through her eyes. "God help me, I knew."

I pull out a cigarette, light up. "So, Ro, what are you saying here? That all these years, you could hear me when I called out to you?"

"That's not it. Well, for the first year or so, yes, but then everything became quiet. And listen, I'm not talking gradual here. I'm talking sudden. Like, one day, you were there—viscerally there—the next, barely a trace of you. Now I kept thinking you were freezing me out—you know, like when we were kids—but that only made me angrier."

"So that's why I didn't hear from you? You were mad because you thought *I* was blocking *you*?"

"So many reasons—none of them good enough—but yes, I was pissed. Pissed that you were blocking me out, pissed about Earl, pissed about the trip."

"The trip to Europe?"

"Yeah, Nomi. Now I know you only agreed to let me tag along 'cause Mom and I kept bugging you, but then when you reversed on me…. Oh my poor sister," she exclaims, her eyes widening, "you haven't a clue what I'm talking about, do you?"

For the next little while, I go into detail about the amnesia. And Rose talks about the trip—how for months we examined maps together, as if we were both going. Within no time, though, back we were with the compelling question of what she knew of me during our long separation.

"Years ago I started having this dream," Rose begins. To a 't', she proceeds to recount my shock dream—one difference only. *She* is the woman cowering in the corridor. "Still have that dream from time to time," she clarifies, "but at least the pounding has stopped."

I can feel my hair stand on end. "Pounding?" I ask.

"Well, a headache, to put it mildly."

"Rose, these headaches, when did they start?"

"About a year after you and Earl took off. Now I don't get them any longer," she clarifies, looking me squarely in the eyes, "but like, there were days when the pounding was so fierce there was nothing I could do but hold on for dear life."

"So sorry, Rose. Must have scared you shitless."

Rose puffs up her cheeks, then lets the air out with a rush. "You can say that again. Now I went to see Dr. Allen—you remember him, Nomi? But he had no real explanation. 'Probably just a migraine,' he told me, but they hardly seemed like normal migraines. Like every friggin' one was preceded by a kind of sizzling, a sense that something was burning its way through my skull. I kept fearing I had contracted a rare disease. But every so often, I would wonder: Is something happening to Nomi?"

I stare at Rose in amazement. She had felt it or at least an echo of it, and all this time, no one has been intentionally blocking anyone. Whatever my part in the telepathy is, it simply no longer works properly. A minor detail in the history of medical complications, perhaps, but when it comes to identical twins, hardly an insignificant side effect.

"Ro, there never was anything wrong with you," I assure her. "ECT, that's how it feels. Incidentally, that's the good news."

"It's okay, sis," cooed Rose. "The bad news, I've kind of figured that part out."

At this, she again squeezed my hand. Then we both fell silent. Now for a moment, she stared at that empty spot on the wall where the mirror had been. Clearly, she had her own experiences of the other day. To my relief, however, she neither inquired, nor commented—just smiled wistfully and resumed her story.

She had a good life, she assured me. She was an accountant with a passion for challenges and an opportunity to travel. A wonderful thing, she had a doting husband—an optician named Sam. She had two gorgeous children—Larry and Dana—and like us, they frolicked on the boulevard. Despite my pressing, however, all she let slip about our folks is that they had been temporarily at her place.

"So they know you're here? And they don't mind?"

"Sorry. I do the odd stint up north," she clarified, "and, well, I left them with the impression that I'm still in Churchill. Cowardly of me, I agree, but it seemed easier."

"Ro, I have to ask," I hazard, catching her eye. "The family breakup, what happened?"

Rose glanced toward the kitchen, and did not answer. Informative in its own right.

Now well before darkness fell, Gerald called us in for supper. Rose instinctively took the seat next to mine. And cordial to a fault, the lot of us sat around the dining room table, tiptoeing around the proverbial elephant in the room. You could tell from the furtive glances, however, that willy-nilly, that elephant would have its day.

"When you think about it," commented Earl at long last, helping himself to another serving of halibut, "in a way, what happened, it was a whole lot of bother over nothing."

"Nothing!" exclaimed Rose. "You call what you said nothing?"

"For sure not," answered Earl, "but be fair. I apologized for that. But you people…"

"You know, Earl…" Gerald started to say.

Clearly, Earl was implicated in the family feud—potentially, a major player—and it looked as though Ger were on the verge of spilling the beans. Even as Gerald uttered these words, however, he reached for a lump of sugar, and as his arm crossed in front of Rose, she again began eyeing him curiously.

"I can see you're having trouble placing yours truly," Gerald observed. "My fault. Why with all the hullabaloo, I completely neglected to introduce myself. I'm Gerald Smith," he explained, tipping his hat, "but you'd have known me as Geraldine."

Rose visibly startled. "You're Earl's first wife?"

"Hold it right there," Earl intervened. "Treating Gerald with respect, that's not negotiable." To his surprise, however, already she had begun extending her hand to Ger.

"Good to see you again, Gerald," she said. "Look, I'm not narrow-minded," she asserted, turning to Earl. "As an identical twin, I can hardly afford to be. And I can assure you, Gerald's not the person I'm having a problem with."

"That would be me, I take it," said Earl.

"It is. And I'm not just talking the rift in the family—any of that. I'm talking the welfare of my sister. Hardly takes a rocket scientist to see that she's under your thumb. Isolating her like this. And *gevalt*! You have her on enough medication to sink a battleship! Probably signed for the electroshock too."

Gerald and I exchanged looks, both expecting Earl to explode. Oddly, he did not. He leaned back in his chair, began tapping his fork against the table. Then he looked up abruptly. "I've made mistakes—I'll grant you that," he conceded, "but so did your family. As for the rest of it, you weren't here. Don't know how depressed she became."

Rose's face immediately softened. "You're right. That what the shock was for? Depression?"

"That it was. And we were worried that telling her anything would land her back at square one."

Rose's eyes narrowed, and she looked at me sadly. "Nomi, sorry for my part in this. Had I any idea that the separation would have sent you into such a horrid tailspin…. Going along with Mom like that, how could I have been so stupid! For once in my life, I should have stood up to the woman. I mean, to let you get that isolated, that depressed! To put you at risk of..."

"Just a minute, Rose," piped up Gerald. "Honestly, I'm not sure that the separation had a heck of lot to do with anything."

Now Gerald's words took us all by surprise, for no one had ever questioned the centrality of the family breakup before.

"But Dr. Higgins..." Earl insisted.

"C'mon, buddy," urged Gerald, fishing his pipe from pocket. "Forget Dr. Higgins, and think back. Nomi missed her family terribly," he continued, tamping down on the tobacco. "And she always had this hate-on for Toronto. But Earl, remember the timing here. She was sad, yup, but not depressed. Remember when the depression set in? When you called in a panic saying she couldn't even drag herself out of bed?"

"Right you are. She wasn't depressed at first, was she? Now the day I called, just when was that? Not long after Ruthie was born..."

"Seventeen days, to be precise. Now Nomi," Gerald went on, his eyes holding mine, "they say you have this disease, but love, *I* got depressed when Les born."

"Not like Nomi," Earl corrected.

"Sure as shit is a cat, she had it worse, but Earl, Nomi hardly invented the problem. C'mon, fella. Ask any woman who's ever given birth."

At this, Rose lets out a sigh.

Noticing, Earl audibly groans. Then he eyes me nervously, and his face sinks. "Christ, Nomi, if I've made a mistake, if I'm after ruining your life.... But this can't be right. Bashing in your head like that—hardly the actions of a normal person!"

"Oh Earl," says Rose gently, "haven't you ever felt desperate?"

Suddenly, I get an image of Earl stepping into the house to discover a cracked mirror, a terrified daughter, a bloodied wife, and I find myself feeling for him. But then Nora's prophetic words start coursing like an irate river through the pathways of my skull.

"Earl," I ask, "I always swore that if I ever married, I'd

never take my husband's name. So how did I come to be called Mrs. Smith?"

Earl squirms in his seat. "Dr. Higgins' idea. And I guess I went along."

"And just why did you do that?"

"Cause he thought it would help and well, I didn't see the harm."

"It wasn't perhaps also something you wanted? Something you liked?"

"Maybe," he answers, his voice faltering.

"And having me prancing about in dresses," I ask, my voice rising, "letting me think that I'd changed my entire mode of attire—that you and Dr. Higgins again?"

He nods.

"And supervising the meds, did you get off on that too?" I persisted.

"Oh Missus, you can't be thinking that."

Bristling, I rise from the table, steady myself with my hands, lean toward him. You're my fuckin' jailer," I screech. "You lock me away. Control my every move. Treat me like I'm your special project to manage as you wish. Even keep my own sister from me. So tell me, Earl. Just what am I supposed to think?"

Now Earl begins to murmur something. All of a sudden, however, I feel a buzzing in my head; and that moment of stillness steals upon me.

The world, it is fading in. I am on the couch, Gerald on the burgundy chair across from me. I can hear the clinking of glasses in the distance. My sister is snuggled in next to me, concern in her eyes.

"So, Nomi, what do you think?" Rose asks.

Realizing that I am missing a fair chunk of time, I quickly explain about the spells.

"So how about we start over?" she suggests matter-of-factly. "Now Nomi, I need to know what you want, cause clearly, something's got to give. Wanna come back to Winnipeg with me? Now don't worry. I'm not talking forever, but for a while?"

"The folks, they'll accept me?"

"Can't promise that. But *I* want you—sweetie, you have no idea how much."

After all those futile calls, there it is at my finger tips. An escape route, however temporary.

Gerald quickly whispers something in Rose's ear. Then he kneels in front of me, assures me that the best gift anyone could give my little girl is her own mommy healthy and alert.

And at this, I gratefully accept.

"Who's giving what gift to whom?" asked Earl entering the room suddenly.

I held my breath, waiting for the other shoe to drop. However, it quickly became apparent that Earl already knew of the plan.

He sat down, leaned back in his chair. "Missus, I'll tell you what I thinks," he said. "Being in your old stomping grounds—it could be just the ticket to get your memory back. Would give Ruth a chance to recover. It'd get me out of your hair. And you know," he added, "if they can be brought around, it makes a whole lot of sense spending time at your folks. That house, it has to be packed to the rafters with memories."

"And you're really okay with this?" I asked astounded.

Earl shrugged. "Well, under the circumstances....I mean, Missus, we don't exactly have a wealth of options, do we?"

Once again, the man had surprised me. He was acting like a *mentsh*.

Now I was in urgent need of alone-time. So after thanking everyone, I excused myself and headed upstairs. As I mounted the last stair, I could hear Rose suggest that they get down to practicalities. Yes, yes, it was happening. I entered my room, slipped onto the bed, stared up at the ceiling. The family feud—or whatever it was—maybe we'd all get past it. One thing, anyway, was clear. I had a sister. *My* sister! And for the first time in years, tears of joy began trickling down my face.

I opened the drawer of my night table in search of a tissue. Now as I picked up the box of Kleenex, I glimpsed something most unexpected—the picture of Rose, her basketball whirling through the air. So Earl hadn't taken it after all!

Moments later I reentered the living room to find Rose and Earl deep in conversation. As I took my place on the couch, I could see that she had out a notebook and pen. Earl was rattling off the names of my various meds, clarifying what was by pill, what by injection, and she was scrupulously jotting down details.

"Now Rose, she's due for another injection on Wednesday," explained Earl.

"Let's slow down," urged Rose. "As I said before, Nomi's overmedicated."

"You wants her to cut down some, I can live with that as long as it's within reason."

Asking me a couple of questions only—neither about what I wanted—the two of them proceeded to work out what a "reasonable dosage" might look like.

Here it was—the proverbial fly in the ointment—and I knew it.

"Hold everything," I called out, rising from the couch. "Need to think. Need to know if I dare."

Oblivious to how it might appear, I began pacing back and forth. After I had traversed the living room floor a good dozen times, Rose approached me.

"Nomi, terrible things have happened to you," she said, "and you're scared, and I understand that, but my dear dear sister, the Nomi that I know dares. So if you want to cut back, I say: go for it."

"Listen, I don't want to cut back," I asserted. I glanced at Earl, saw his face relax, then turned to my sister. "While I still have a fraction of a brain left, I'm going off these fuckers entirely."

A stunned silence descended upon the room. And a nervous smile etched itself onto Rose's face.

"I can't function on the meds," I explain. "Wasn't able to on a far lower dosage."

"I understand," says Rose, "but going off completely, you think that's wise?"

"Wise?" I ask, throwing my head back. "I think it's fuckin' brilliant. Know why? Cause it's the only chance I have for a real life."

"But Nomi, you really know what you're doing?"

"No, but neither do the shrinks. Listen, Rose. The hospital always treated me as competent when I chose what they wanted, incompetent otherwise. But you can't have it both ways. Either you respect my right to choose or you don't."

Beads of perspiration form on Rose's brow. She hesitates, fidgets with her ring. She begins shaking her head. Then she stops dead in her tracks. "Gotchya," she utters. "Now I don't have a clue what'll happen, but if this is really what you want...."

I catch her eye, see that she is serious, also see her fear. "*Of course* you're scared," I murmur. "Me too. But yes, this is what I want. Hey, Ro," I add, "'member as kids how you used to hold onto me whenever you became frightened. Kind of think we both need to hold onto one another now."

Rose nods, opens her arms, says, "Come here, you." And the two of us embrace. Then we return to the couch. And at long last, I force myself to look at Earl.

Earl is sitting quietly, his hand on his chin, to all appearance, considering it. Then his fist clenches, and his face begins to redden. "No! No! No! No! No!" he protests. "Look, I'm after bending over backward here 'cause I can see that I've screwed up too. But dis is too much. Christ! You any idea what it felt like being in that cinema with you? Every man Jack of them was staring. A stranger—a total stranger, mind—accused me of abducting you."

"It must have been dreadful, and I'm so very sorry, but..."

"You think you can stop and everything will be hunky dory?

Well, it won't. It'll be hallucination city. One nightmare after another."

"But if this really was postpartum depression.... Anyway, I'll do it right this time. Now I know someone who went off safely, and..."

"And this remarkable human being, just where is he now?"

"Well, in hospital, but..."

"Precisely. And you," he asks, beginning to eye Ro with suspicion, "you'd actually go along?"

Rose knits her brow. "I'm uneasy too," she acknowledges, choosing her words with care, "and clearly you've been through a lot I know nothing about—but to just make the decision *for* her!—I can't do that. Her life, after all."

"Well, maybe *you* can't, but *I* can. Tell you another thing. Ruthie and me, we're her family now, and it's our life too. And now that I sees where everything's at, the entire operation, it's a no-go." At this, Earl turns to me and his voice softens. "I'd rather see you back in hospital. And darlin', believe me, it's not 'cause I'm some heartless patriarch. I'm a man who loves you—and no offence to Rose intended—someone who's been around the block enough times to know better. And it's safer, is all."

"And you won't reconsider?"

"Not an easy decision to make, but I've made it," he said.

We had arrived at a moment of truth, and I suspect that on some level everyone knew it. Without uttering a word, I shuffle over to Earl, place my hand on his shoulder. Then I glance over at Gerald.

"Love, this is no time to hesitate," Gerald cautions.

I nod gratefully, and Earl's ultimatum echoing in my ears, I turn to my sister. "Rose, let's go," I say.

For a moment, Earl looks thunderstruck. Then he rises to his feet. "Step one foot out of this house, and I'm calling the police," he threatens.

"The police! What conceivable business do they have here?

Disobeying your husband, that suddenly a crime?"

"Danger to self or others," he points out. "Now I'm not eager to do this, but..."

I take a deep breath. "Rose, right now," I say.

12. NAOMI

ESCAPE—THAT WAS the sole thing on our minds as we bolted out that door. Aware that we could ill afford to dawdle near the house trying to flag down a cab, all the way to Bathurst we ran. "Has to be one," I insisted, peering about as we neared the intersection. Minutes later Rose spotted a Becks in the distance. With cars swerving around her, she boldly advanced into the middle of the street and stuck out her thumb. Alas, the taxi barrelled on. To our relief, however, but a car length ahead, it came to a screeching stop.

As we climbed into the back seat, I could hear my name being called. I peeked out the side window. There was Gerald, a small overnight bag in his hands. He quickly deposited the valise on my lap. "Contains a prescription and few changes of clothes," he stated. "For luck," he suddenly added, reaching into his pocket and handing me his signature pen. "No, Nomi," he insisted seconds later, "don't stop to thank me. Earl's on the phone with the coppers. Just go."

Taking Gerald's warning to heart, we signalled to the driver and took off. Speed, that is what we prayed for. Nor did we do badly, though there was a traffic jam at Islington; and it took seventeen minutes to get the prescription filled at the Shoppers Drug en route. "Almost there," announced the driver as we flew down Dixon Road.

Minutes later, arm in arm, we were entering Terminal One at Toronto Pearson.

It was an immense modern airport, with literally thousands of passengers milling about. No sign of cops.

"Try to stay calm," Rose urged, as I cast my eyes about. "Like how fast are police likely to move on a mental health complaint?"

"You'd be surprised," I replied, "but if we make it into the air, I doubt they'll pursue us."

Luckily, a flight to Winnipeg was departing within the hour and we were able to get side-by-side seats. However, we were hardly out of the woods.

Shortly after arriving in the boarding area, a twenty-five minute delay was called, and when boarding for our flight finally commenced, it felt as if the whole world and their brother were boarding first. I lit a cigarette and watched as a young woman with toddlers started walking toward the plane. A senior with a bad limp boarded next. After he had been helped on, I tried to get a sense of just how many more pre-boarders there were. And that's when I spotted him.

Not three yards away stood an inquisitive looking policeman, leaning against the south wall. His finger was hovering suggestively over the button on his walkie-talkie, and he seemed to be looking our way. When I pointed him out to Rose, those dark eyes of his narrowed. He whispered hurriedly into his walkie-talkie. And now he was advancing toward us. Unwavering in his purpose, directly up to me, he strutted.

"Excuse me, ma'am, but you dropped this," he said, handing me Gerald's pen.

I thanked him, stammered something about the largesse of Toronto's finest, then turned my attention to the boarding.

Everyone else already attended to, the boarding of the regular passengers had finally begun. Six rows at a time they took it, after every call, travellers bundling up their carry-ons and advancing as if we have all the time in the world.

"Rows 18 to 24," the official finally announces. I turn to Rose. She nods. And now we are actually walking toward the plane.

Picking up on my apprehension, Rose becomes increasingly attentive. "Almost out of reach now, Nomi," she assures me as we step into the aircraft.

While there is a short delay because of the throng of people navigating the aisle, eventually, we arrive at our row. A middle-aged man in a grey vest rises to let us in. Then we take our seats—me next to the window, Rose in the middle, the middle-aged man in the aisle seat.

Oblivious to the drama unfolding before him, our fellow traveller inserts a pair of ear plugs into his ears, then whips out a copy of the *Globe* and begins to read. Three little chimes sound. "Seatbelts," Rose reminds me. Seeing me fumbling with the belt, her touch gentle, Rose assists me with it, much as a mother might help a little one. And now the stewardess is explaining the safety features. And now she disappears. Is there yet time for the boys in blue to apprehend me?, I wonder. Suddenly, out of nowhere, a whirring sound assaults my ears. I am on the verge of panic when a glint enters Rose's eye. Offering no explanation, she reaches for my hand, clasps it securely between hers, then curiously, begins reciting a seemingly irrelevant nursery rhyme—one that I vaguely recollect from childhood. "Vintery, mintery cutery corn," she begins, "apple seed and apple thorn."

And now the plane is taxiing down the runway. First slow. Now faster. Ever faster. You can feel your organs rattling about, and you have this eerie sensation as if everything in the universe were about to fly apart. Louder grows the groan of the engine. Suddenly without warning, the groan becomes a high-pitched screech and just holds there—a larger than human wail holding us in its grasp.

"Wire briar and limber lock," continues Rose, her voice soaring over the screech of the engine. "Three geese in a flock/ One flew east/And one flew west."

"And one flew over the cuckoos' nest," the two of us call out triumphantly in unison.

And now the agitation eases. And effortlessly, gloriously, into the air we lift.

My sister Rose Schachter was a remarkable woman. According to family legend, I was the brilliant twin who dazzled, Rose the follower. The truth was far more complex and infinitely more interesting. Rose had her own talents, her own proclivities, and with me out of the way, these had increasingly come to the fore.

Sensitive to others, time and again Ro would pick up on everyone's feelings, and find precisely the right thing to say. She was a warm, intuitive mother with an uncanny sense of when to enter in, when to withdraw. While not political in the traditional sense, she was passionate about human rights. Also, she had inherited Mom's forthrightness. There was something else too—something that knit everything together and made her rather unlike the rest of our family. The woman was in touch with her own body, indeed, delighted in her body.

As I had long realized—hence my eagerness to capture her on film—it had not been the thrill of competition that brought Rose to basketball. It was the racing in her heart, the bounce in her feet, the rush that shot through her arms as she took one last look at that basket, found her centre, then went bounding into the air. It was the unbridled joy of shedding the social veneer and becoming living pulsing flesh.

Now the relationship between Rose and Sam, that was at the core of each of them. How they adored each other! While they could get under each other's skin politically—for Sam was a middle-class kid from the south end who knew *bupkes* about financial hardship—in most respects, they were well-matched. They were both loyal. They shared an uncomplicated delight in others. And as mature human beings who loved with a generous heart and who knew who they were, they had managed to pull off what many a progressive couple talked about in those days but which few tried, and far fewer made work—multiple partners in the context of a rock solid marriage.

"We're not remotely swingers," Rose was to explain to me some time later. "The kids, the family, that comes first. And there are safeguards. Like no one of the opposite sex 'cause that's just too threatening. You know, even at that, we have trouble at times with the jealousy thing. Well, you know me."

"Not surprised you sleep with women," I mused. "Really, I can see that."

"Yeah, and you know, in some ways, I prefer it. It's like making love to your own body, right?"

"Rose, you're perfect. You must know that," I exclaimed, touched by her honesty.

Reuniting with my sister, laying claim to Winnipeg—this was a watershed event. Even as that plane took off, something deep within me settled.

Now at the Palmerston house, I had been so preoccupied with keeping track of minutiae, I had paid little attention to the larger world. It was as if all events on the world stage had come to a screeching halt in 1964. Picking up on this, even as she filled me in on critical family issues, Rose kept a keen eye on the larger picture. Not that sorting out her views from fact was always simple.

It was half an hour into the flight. The stewardess had just brought around coffee. And at long last, I received an account of what went down that fateful day.

"So Rose," I asked, taking a sip of coffee, "Mom ordered Earl out of the house, right? But instead of trying to mediate, I said, 'if he goes, I go.' Now how I could've acted like such a *schlemiel* is beyond me, but if you say I did, then I did."

"Trust me. You were gaga over the man, intending to marry him. Course, who knows what would have happened had you waited for the dust to settle, but you took this occasion to announce it."

"Okay, Ro, so tell me if I've got anything wrong here. Earl rolled his eyes when Dad lit the candles, yes?"

Rose took a sip of coffee. "Yeah. Though actually, that was a month earlier."

"Gotchya. But that's the night that Earl referred to being in 'Jew York,' correct?"

"Uh huh."

"But that's not the straw that broke the camel's back. Something over Israel. I forgot what you said here, but Earl must have brought up the topic and..."

"No," corrected Rose. "Dad did."

"Dad? You serious? Now that's odd! He'd always steered clear of discussions about Israel with non-Jews.... Anyway, that *is* when Earl used the expression 'stolen land?'"

"Uh huh."

"Now here's where I'm lost. Was Earl talking about the whole country or just some part of it?"

Rose's eyes widen, and it is at this moment that she first takes in how little I know of the world. "You don't remember the Six Day War, do you?" she asks, a thoughtful expression on her face. "1967—I should've realized."

Figuring that this was as good a place as any to start, Rose immediately began providing me a lowdown on an area called "the West Bank." Now I listened attentively, followed more or less. Then she asserted something that rather perplexed me—that the land was not stolen, that Israel had simply held onto it for negotiation purposes.

"I see. So when did they finally give it back?" I asked.

After "clarifying" that they still had it, which downright bamboozled me, Rose suggested that we focus on "less contentious issues." And here began the first of a series of much needed current event lessons.

Rose explained that Golda Meir was no longer president of Israel. She launched into a vivid description of "Watergate." Closer to home, she spoke of how our Canadian socialist party—the NDP—had recently received "another" mandate in Manitoba. "Oh and Nomi," she said, looking at me urgently.

"Something you really need to know. The Red River, it flooded a few months back."

"Again?" I asked, for the first time taking in the significance of an event mentioned. Now the flooding of the Red River was the dread of every Manitoban. You see, if Winnipeg is home to the Winnipeg General Strike, every bit as significantly, it is home to flat terrain, coupled with an extensive lake-river-stream network. The downtown core of the city is spitting distance from the fork of two huge rivers—the Red and the Assiniboine. Their watershed extends well over a hundred thousand miles, The result? Massive floods, with a good part of our city periodically under water, and with thousands—fuck, sometimes tens of thousands—of distraught inhabitants forced to flee.

The worst flood in recorded history—and yes, Jack, read worst flood after the European invasion—was the legendary 1826 flood, when the merciless Red River rose 768 feet above sea level and over half of the settlement ended up under water. Now even in my early years, no Winnipegger had been alive long enough to actually witness the 1826 disaster, but we had all heard tell of it. And many had witnessed one almost equally legendary—the devastation of 1950.

That year, precipitation ran high. There was a late frost. While everyone was praying for the warm touch of spring, too late came the thaw, and with it rain, rain, more rain, and higher and higher rose the water. The mighty Red River rose 758 feet above sea level. Well over its banks. Well beyond the meagre protection afforded by the hastily constructed dikes. Ten thousand, five hundred homes were flooded and 60,000 inhabitants were forced to evacuate. And in its wake, like a thief in the night, came influenza, typhus, polio.

Now as I sat in the plane recalling the devastation, something unexpected happened. Little by little, the world beyond my fingertips began to feel real. "My God, Rose," I said, eyeing her with astonishment, "the fallout from the flood, just how bad is it?"

"Not like in 1950," she assured me, "though I'll tell you something. Would have been worse than 1950 were it not for the Red River floodway. Nomi, that's an extensive barrier that was completed a few years back. Quite something. Anyway, while people are hurting in places like Lorette, inside the city, really only St. Vital and St. Norbert were hit bad. No major epidemic, thanks to improved boosters. And Mom, she's been absolutely tireless in her various relief efforts. You'd be proud."

I imagined community leaders like Mom pushing for action, doctors slaving night and day to improve the booster shots, engineers constructing plans, housewives spearheading relief efforts. So everyday people had pulled together, I realized. They hadn't solved the problem, but they had been making progress. And this, this was the stuff of the world. Then the world of floods and community action receded, and into the centre of my mind floated Mom's face, her eyes looking exactly like they had when she forbade us to speak with Mrs. Fenster.

"Rose, couldn't face dealing with the folks tonight, you know that, right?" I checked.

Rose chuckled, then popped a miniature tomato into her mouth. "You any idea what time it is?" she asked.

Late, late, late landed the plane in Winnipeg International Airport. We disembarked without incident. No police to greet us. No loudspeaker announcement calling on one Naomi Smith or Rose Schachter to come to the Air Canada terminal. We quickly secured a cab. Then needing a break from one another, we each of us slipped into our own private world. Now I must have drifted off, for suddenly, I felt someone tugging at my arm, heard Rose whispering, "Sweetie, we're there."

Exiting the cab, we found ourselves in front of a two-storey duplex on the corner of Polson and Aikins. We entered. Then Rose settled me into a chair in a huge living room. "Be back in a jiffy," she said.

Now clearly I'd dosed off again, for next thing I knew, the air was astir with whispers. I opened my eyes. Across from me on what appeared to be a blue divan sat Rose. Rose, what's she doing in Toronto?, I asked myself just for a second there. And that's when I took him in.

Inches from Rose, his arm around her, sat a rake of a man with a nose that took over his face, watery eyes, a boyish smile. He was doing his best to hide it, but something was clearly bothering him.

"See you're awake again. This is my adorable husband," said Rose, giving him an affectionate peck on the cheek. Sam, meet Nomi."

"Welcome to our humble abode, Nomi," Sam offered. "You know, I just can't get over how much you look like your sister. Same nose. Same eyes."

"Oh Sam," I exclaimed playfully, "how ever are you going to tell the two of us apart?"

At this, he broke into a broad grin. "Sister-in-law woman, I think I'm going to like you," he responded.

After fetching coffee for everyone, he graciously inquired about our flight, but a reticent, almost pained look kept creeping over his face.

"Sam," I finally hazarded, "I can see you're uneasy. I don't know what Rose's told you, but I'm dragging you into a God-awful mess and we should probably be thinking about damage control. How about I crash here tonight, find a motel tomorrow?"

Sam's face immediately softened. "Wouldn't hear of it," he assured me. "Nomi, you don't know what it means to Rose to have you here, what it means to both of us." He hesitated, put his hands in his pockets, then glanced nervously at his wife. "But as long as we're talking turkey, yes, there is something. Okay, here's the *schtick*. I've this friend—acquaintance really—who's also schizophrenic and I saw what happened when he stopped taking his medicine."

"Sam, for God's sake!" Rose exclaims.

"Don't get me wrong," continues Sam. "You're my wife's sister, and the two of you say this is what you're going to do, who am I to object? There's children here, though, and so if everything, well, starts to go *meshugah*...."

"I understand," I offer, "but everything *is* likely to go *meshugah,* and I need to know that no one's gonna pull the plug when it does."

Rose looks at her husband pointedly. He notices, nods, and gradually his face relaxes. "I can see I'm outnumbered on this one," he utters, "not to mention outgendered. And actually, if push comes to shove, the little *pishers* can always stay at my aunt's."

"Or Lisa's," offers Rose.

"Or Lisa," he repeats. Then suddenly, unexpectedly, he looks me in the eye and I get a reassuring glimpse into my newly acquired brother-in-law. "Nomi, tell me," he asks, "when I referred to you as schizophrenic, did that, well, bother you?"

"Not important. And the thing about the kids, you have a point."

"I think I have my answer. Anyway, something you should know. While as my wife here tells me, I have the political sensitivity of a gnat, I'm dedicated to family, and that indubitably includes you. And the opinions of my esteemed mother-in-law notwithstanding—and you'll hear those soon enough—I'm decidedly to the left of Attila the Hun. Oh and Nomi," he adds, eyeing me intently, "one other thing: Earl's phoned five times. Say he's been in touch with the police and you'd better call. And apparently, I'm to put you on the next flight to Toronto."

"Fuck! And what did you tell him?"

"That if he stops acting like a world class *schmuck*, he's welcome to check in in a week or so, but short of that, on the advice of my attorney, I'm advising him to stop harassing me and mine."

"Sam, bless you. And your attorney, does he think I'm out of the woods?"

"The *shtick* about calling his attorney," explains Rose, "a standard Schachter bluff. But Sam, do give cousin Roger a ring tomorrow," she urged, reaching for his hand.

Sam having gallantly offered to sleep on the couch, half an hour later, Rose and I were in their room, stretched out on the bed. The two of us snug as a bug in rug.

"You know, I absolutely like your fella," I offer.

"Thought you might. Actually, everyone takes to Sam—especially Mom, though think she'd admit it? You know something, Nomi?" she asked, tossing back her hair. "She rags on him all the time—*cvetches* about his politics, claims that he changes his other partners as often as he changes his underwear—which, incidentally, is only half true—but let Sam and me get into a *kafuffle*, guess whose side she takes?"

Now I was well aware that she was telling me something extraordinary. It was not simply that other partners were part of the picture—that she had already let slip—but they had confided as much in Mom. More to the point, Mom had accepted their lifestyle even if begrudgingly. Was this a new openness on Mom's part?

Now my eyes kept closing—I was that pooped—and I was itching to call it a night, but something was nagging away at the back of my mind. Something I absolutely needed to remember.

"So, wanna cut back on the meds tonight?" Rose suddenly asked.

Bingo. I still had not figured out how to handle the meds. Almost instantly, I found myself trembling.

"Oh Nomi," Rose sighed. "I'm raising this too soon, aren't I? And what with Sam's misgivings, maybe you're not feeling safe."

"Nothing to do with Sam," I assured her. "Anyway, its not *these* meds I should be going off first. It's the Fluphenazine. And that's a problem."

"How so?"

"I'll explain in a sec. The thing is, though, it wouldn't be fair to the folks to initiate anything before they've had a chance to see me. I'm quite enough of a shock without adding withdrawal symptoms to the mix, wouldn't you say?"

A wistful expression on her face, Rose acknowledged that I had a point. Then she fished the pills from her purse, casually handed me the bottles as if doing so were the most natural thing in the world. "The glasses are in the kitchen cupboard to the left of the sink," she pointed out. "Sweetie, that's a left turn, then a right."

"Just like that? You don't need to watch?"

"Watch! And people call *us* swingers!" she quipped. "Nomi, listen," she added, eyeing me keenly, her voice earnest, "whatever mistakes I make—and like, I will make some—honestly, that won't be one of them."

And so it is that for the very first time I took my pills without supervision. And what a rush that was!

Rose smiled encouragingly as I returned. I reached over, kissed her on the cheek. Then once again I brought up the issue of the folks. And we both went silent.

"Think I know how to do this," said Rose at long last. "Mom's expecting me to arrive home tomorrow, and the two of us have a lunch date for Tuesday. When I call to confirm, I'll explain and ask if you can join us.... Now don't get your hopes up, Nomi," she cautioned. "As things stand, Mom can't even abide your name being mentioned."

"I understand. And Dad?"

"*If* she relents—and that's a big "if"— my guess is he will too. Honestly, I could swear that half the time he's looking at me, he's seeing *you*.... Incidentally, something I neglected to mention—Tuesday, like it's the first of the Days of Awe."

"So, Dad still goes to schul on Rosh Hashanah?"

"Religiously," answered Rose with a smirk. "Actually, been granted the *mitzvah* of blowing the *shofar* this year." Rose and

I proceeded to gush about how magnificently he blows that ram's horn. And before long, we were lost in reminiscences.

As Rose began commenting on some Shabbes in '66 which I did not remotely recall, I started to feel my head droop. I was trying to figure out if we could now safely call it a night. Just as I was about to suggest that we do so, however, once again Rose mentioned the meds. And suddenly, I realized—I hadn't yet explained about the Fluphenazine.

"So Rose, remember Earl saying that I was due for a shot?" I asked. "Well for me to actually get that shot, I'd need a doctor to arrange for it and a nurse to administer it. See what this means for coming off an injectable?"

Again, Rose went quiet. "Think we can do this,' she suddenly stated. "The easiest way would be to get it in pill form. And Sam, he just might be able to arrange that."

"How...?"

"Don't ask. Just think of it as professional courtesy."

"But..." I started to say.

"Want a more definitive answer at three o'clock in the morning?" she suddenly retorted, a glint in her eye. "Well, Naomi Brenda Cohan, try this one."

Whereupon, to my surprise, she swung her pillow high over her head and brought it down on my shoulder with a wallop. "Think I've a few answers of my own, Rose Ruth Cohan," I threw out, reaching for the other pillow. And before long, giggling away, we were pelting one another with abandon, wafts of white plumage flying in all directions.

Nu? Some day, the old *meshugas* between us would have to be faced. Not now, we both realized, eagerly taking aim. And light went our hearts. And away melted the decades. And for the briefest of moments—and you grab hold of these when you can—once again, we were in that cozy cot in the wee little room in the white stucco house on Inkster Boulevard. And once again, we were six years old.

AN EVENING IN THE LIFE OF GERALD

THANKFULLY, RUTHIE HAD STOPPED startling at every unexpected sound. She had even perked up some. While it took some coaxing, why at this very moment the little tyke was out front playing hopscotch with Les, Miu supervising. Gerald was glad of this—glad to see a smile return to Ruthie's lips, glad too that Earl had relented. After yelling at him for "aiding and abetting Nomi," after going red in the face and demanding that he bring Ruthie home this instant, Earl had taken in that Ruthie'd had the scare of her little life and that letting her hang out with her older brother a few more days would harm no one. May Earl be of the same mind when he drops by tonight, thought Gerald, already beginning to dread that rapidly approaching encounter. Of course, regardless, how Ruthie would fare in the long run was anyone's guess. Now Gerald had asked Ruthie about that dreadful incident, but something in her eyes told him that the timing was wrong. So he had done what any caring parent would—provided reassurance, let her know she was loved, distracted her with fun events, gave her plenty of hugs, cooked her favourite foods, hoped for the best. He had also found ways to introduce subtle reminders of her mother.

"Hey there, Noodle," he would ask, "if a mommy mouse— let's call her Nomi—is away hunting for cheese for her family and she sends invisible messages of love each day to her adorable daughter mouse—let's call her Ruth—at the end of a week, how many invisible messages of love should Ruth have received?"

"I know. I know," Les would eagerly call out.

"Les, how many?" Ruth would inquire, gazing admiringly into her brother's eyes.

But alas, she had not as yet asked about her mother, had she? And how that worried Gerald! And then there was that more pressing question.

It was seven-thirty p.m. And his tie loose, his shoes off, Gerald was leaning back in his living room easy chair doing what he'd habitually done these last several years—trying to figure out what to say to Earl about Nomi. He lifted his hand to his chin, stroked what felt like whiskers, and his eyes widened. Oh, he understood well enough why Earl was acting like an idiot—sicking the police on Nomi, readying himself to hightail it to Winnipeg next weekend in hot pursuit. Do anything less than continue to create trouble for his beleaguered wife and he'd have to face the terrible truth, wouldn't he? That the whole psychiatric whirligig had been a colossal misadventure from beginning to end.

"You think he knows how royally he's screwed up?" Miu had asked him.

"Yup. Actually, he'd started to acknowledge something," Gerald had informed her, "though he backed right off. Too threatening. Anyway, love, know what I think? On some level, everyone knows everything."

"An intriguing proposition, that. And does that include Nomi?"

"Now there's the tragedy of electroshock," Gerald had answered.

While he was proud of her, of course, Gerald was well aware that Nomi herself had complicated matters. If only she had remained closed-lipped about her intentions with respect to the meds! Though who could expect someone in Nomi's condition to have such presence of mind? Though once upon a time....

Gerald removed his pipe from his back pocket, began filling

it. As he was tamping down on the tobacco, suddenly he called to mind the time he had first warmed to Nomi, and a smile came to his lips. To everyone's irritation—his included—three long months had Nomi kept the family on tenterhooks, again and again changing her mind about relocating to Toronto. At this point, of course, everyone and his cousin knew what all that dillydallying was about. Why the poor child was desperately hoping that her folks would come around. However, at the time, what did they know—except that they kept hearing "yes" from her one day, "no" the next —this with the fate of the whole Smith family in the balance! Now eventually one of her "yes's" stuck, and together with Earl's faithful cocker spaniel Rusty, at long last Nomi and Earl had made the big move. They bedded down in a cheap room over Toronto's oldest tavern—the Wheat Sheaf—on King West. Gerald had just brought the newlyweds some freshly baked bagels when who should step into the room but a total stranger—a speckle-faced old man with a bulbous nose, who was blatantly three sheets to the wind!

An opened bottle of beer in hand, the old gent staggered in, seemingly bewildered. "Blasted! Wrong room," he bellowed. "Now don't get your shorts in a knot, young people," he continued, his eyes lighting up, a coy smile igniting his face. "I'm not the kinda fella that barges into other folk's rooms. Mercy, no. Not Percy Daniels," he insisted, taking a swig of beer. "An accident, an honest-to-God accident, you understand." To Nomi's obvious delight, Percy proceeded to kneel down, pat Rusty on the head, and declaim, "Your dog here knows. Animal instinct, right? You can fool human beings every day of the week and twice on Sunday, but a dog always knows," whereupon the mutt bared his fangs and began to snarl. "Yes siree Bob, a dog always knows," insisted Percy, while all-knowing Rusty continued to growl.

Although Earl mumbled something about calling management, Nomi shook her head, uttered, "Earl, there's no real harm." And Earl having calmed down, Percy proceeded to entertain everyone for the next two hours, regaling them all with chestnuts about the olden days when he had allegedly sung on vaudeville with Bing Crosby. "Old Bingo, ever wonder where he picked up that crooning from?" asked Percy, bending down to pat the dog again, a twinkle in his eyes. "Lord bless you, no one can slur quite that deliciously without taking a tip or two from a man who's kissed the bottle, if you know what I mean." Then his voice cracking, he topped off the evening's entertainment by singing his own version of Joyce Kilmer's poem "Trees." Nomi listened, asked questions, exchanged the odd joke. Why she made the man so comfortable that time and again, when Gerald was visiting, who should stagger in but old Percy, his ever trusty beer bottle in hand! "Just dropping by to apologize for before and to let you know I am not that kind of guy that just barges in," Percy would state. Then he would call out, "Rusty, come here, boy.... A dog always knows. A dog always knows." "Grrr," all-knowing Rusty would invariably respond.

Chuckling at the memory of old Percy, Gerald lit his pipe. He sucked in hard, then harder, and watched as the sweet-smelling strands of tobacco began to glow. Now professional types, he reminded himself, they might well call what Nomi did here aiding and abetting, but not yours truly. The old rascal, why he was who he was, and Nomi had accepted him into her life because he needed to be somebody's family and well, to someone like Nomi, the match seemed as fortuitous as any. And that was Nomi for you. Down deep—deeper even than the filmmaker—was a woman with a passion for folk who didn't fit in. A clear delight in them too. Something else the two Mrs. Smiths had in common, eh? More Nomi's thing, though. But Nomi, she'd never really understood that about herself, had she? Not part of what she would have once termed "her identity." And now that her brains had been scrambled like so many eggs at an Orangeman's reunion, how was she to realize? And poor Ruthie, how was Ruthie ever to know? "Thank God, I knew Nomi back when," Gerald muttered to himself. "Yup. And thank the blessed Virgin—whoever—that I had the foresight to turn to her that day."

What Gerald was referring to was an early, more fragile time when he was struggling with how to broach the issue of gender identity with Earl. A progressive man, Earl had accepted that his ex-wife was a dyke, even that she had left him for a woman. This ongoing foray into a different gender, however, that was another matter altogether. Not that in those days Gerald himself exactly understood what he was about. Nonetheless, sensing the rightness of it, intermittently, for six months behind closed doors he and Miu had conducted themselves as husband and wife. He had even started venturing into certain pubs as a man—not just butch hangouts either. While Gerald did not as yet have a name for what was happening, it was as if a query from long ago were finally being answered—that query that came to him as a child when he would be outside minding his own business and some older urchin would come strutting over and ask, "Hey kid, you a boy or a girl?" That same query that visited him in teenaged years when he would look in the mirror, or gaze at a girl with desire. Then too, there was that time about a year after Confirmation, when as a young lass of eight, he got down on his knees to pray, only to find himself pondering whether or not the Lord Almighty would turn someone into a pillar of salt for ending a prayer with, "Oh, and one more thing, God, if it's not too much trouble, could you give me a penis?"

Now while it took them a while before acting on it—before acknowledging it even—fortunately, Miu had fallen in love with the man in him at least as much as the woman. When Earl had come courting one Geraldine Bennett of the Pas Manitoba, on the other hand, he was distinctly courting a woman. Courted a woman, married a woman, bedded a woman, had a baby with a woman, divorced a woman. Or so Earl thought. And such Gerald had tried to be for him, for everyone. Now no question about it, if Gerald continued on this course, Earl had to be told. Gerald knew that, knew too that time was running out, but with something as monumental as the custody of his darling child at stake, he was not about to risk breathing a word to Earl before first finding himself some help, someone who could act as a sort of champion.

On a hunch that Nomi might fit the bill, he'd invited himself over to the Palmerston house for a private tête-à-tête. For three whole days, he'd gone back and forth on how to broach the topic. Throwing caution to the winds, despite Miu's misgivings, at the last minute, he'd changed clothes, then set out decked in men's attire, complete with trousers, vest, and a wide-brimmed hat. A mistake, he told himself as he stood on their porch. Too late. The door opened, and my oh my, there was Nomi, utter confusion on her face.

While he was scrambling to decide whether or not to pretend that he was on his way to a theme party, she invited him in. Now exactly why he did it, he wasn't sure, but just before sitting down, he tipped his hat and smiled. Nomi looked him squarely in the eye, smiled back, then nodded.

"Geraldine," she asked, a gentleness coming over her, "sorry if this is a stupid question, but this isn't just about being butch, is it?"

"That and not that," answered Gerald. "And love, believe me, your question's hardly stupid."

"Well, some of my others might be, but before I make a complete ass of myself, let me just say this—trusting me with something so intimate, that's a real *mitzvah*, and well, if you're looking for my help with Earl, sweetie, surely you know that you've got it."

Nomi, she really did come through for him too, he recalled, taking another puff. And indeed, she had—talking to Earl for hours, impressing upon him the importance of accepting Gerald as he was, reminding Earl what a sterling parent Gerald was, correcting him in no uncertain terms each and every time he slipped into referring to Gerald's emerging identity as a pathology, as a problem, as "one of those transvestite things," as anything other than a personal awakening to support.

"You think I'm going to celebrate this, you can forget it," said Earl at long last. "But support? Yes, I sees that."

Now Gerald and Nomi did not exactly become fast friends at this point. Their interests were just too divergent. However, over time, a deep and abiding fondness set in. Then came the birth of Ruth, and close on its heals that all-encompassing depression that closed in on Nomi like a mad tornado, leaving her a lifeless remnant of her former self. Gerald remembered Nomi's helplessness. Also his own. "Earl, don't do this," he'd pleaded, but try though he repeatedly had, he could not prevent Earl from hospitalizing Nomi, nor from authorizing those senseless treatments. But it wasn't just Earl. He too had made mistakes, hadn't he? Kept underestimating Nomi's needs. What's more, he'd let himself get drawn into that brainless pact to keep silent about Nomi's family.

Gerald stopped in his tracks, reminded himself how useless regrets were. Then he bestirred himself, went to the kitchen, began baking a fresh batch of ginger snaps. When Earl comes over this evening, he noted, sprinkling in the ginger, as far as feasible, things needed to be set right.

"Guess we have to do this," acknowledged Earl reluctantly, a worn look on his face.

It was nine p.m. Having turned up at Gerald's half an hour early, Earl had just tucked his children in. Now a haggard but surprisingly calm ex-husband was sitting opposite Gerald at the small kitchen table. Coffee and ginger snaps lay in front of them, but neither man had touched a thing. Gerald observed Earl carefully, took in the bloodshot eyes. Not the most promising setup on this side of the Mississippi, but what's a fella to do?

"Love, thanks for letting Ruthie stay," Gerald began.

Earl nodded.

"She's doing better," Gerald assured him, leaning back in his chair, "but if you can find it in your heart to let her, best she remain a mite longer. Well, at least until you've mounted a new mirror."

Earl admitted that Gerald had a point, and they continued discussing Ruthie—the fact that she had always felt at home in this apartment. Then they fell into chatting about Les, despite there being no pressing need to do so.

Gerald sucked in on his pipe. "Think we're both of us kinda pussyfooting around the real issue," he stated at last.

Earl glanced at the wall nervously, then returned Gerald's gaze. "Something on your mind, I'm listening."

"Buddy," Gerald begins, "let me just say something here. Now I know that you've always done what you thought best for Nomi and…"

"It's been a long day, for Chrissake. Spare me the preamble."

"Fair enough. The damage to Nomi, it's gotta stop. At this point, Earl, she's with a sister who knows her in ways neither of us ever will—and face it—she had a right to leave; and there's diddlysquat you can do that won't make things worse. So please, forget about pursuing her. As hard as this is to swallow, doing nothing, it's the only honourable option."

"They're going to make mistakes. Serious ones, I can tell."

"Let them."

Earl's muscles tense. It looks as if he is about to explode. Then his jaw relaxes. "I'll think about it," he states. "That's all I can promise." Now he begins to rise, but then slumps back down, lets out a humongous sigh. "Ger, am I ever going to get my wife back? I mean really?"

"Just don't know, buddy," Gerald acknowledges.

A solitary tear trickles down Earl's cheek. "Don't seem to ever pull off a passing grade in the husband department, do I?" he asks.

Feeling for his former husband, Gerald reaches over, takes

Earl's hands in his. "Love, you haven't exactly had the best of luck. I mean, two wives—one who comes out as a dyke, the other who gets diagnosed as schizoaffective. And this whole partnership thing, well, it's a bit of a mug's game, isn't it?"

The two men looked at each other and smiled, albeit with pain in their hearts. Then Earl shook his head sadly and stepped out of the room. Seconds later, you could heard the front door close.

Earl gone and the kids fast asleep, Gerald sat for a spell, staring absently out the window and musing over the disquieting events of the past few days. Then he roused himself, spent some alone-time with Miu, grateful that they were together, that they were both whole, that along with their children, they were safe in the midst of this turbulent universe—even if only for an instant. They watched TV, cuddled, spoke of some day setting sail for China, even broached the whole question of that operation, though surgery did not strike him as the way.

As Gerald and Miu crawled into bed that night, he took one look at his partner's beautiful form and kissed her tenderly on the nipples, the neck, the lips. Mesmerized by the quickening sound of her breath, he glided down her body, teased open her other lips, flicked his tongue against that place of women's pleasure, blew like there was no tomorrow. Feeling her stir, smelling the ripeness, hearing that half whimper that so thrilled him, he lifted himself back up again, held her tightly, delighted to again feel that reassuring joy. To awaken in the purple hours of an arid evening to this crimson explosion beneath him—surely this was a moment to savour. He heard her moaning start up again and he opened the top drawer of the night table and reached for the strap-on, knowing that the night was yet young.

IDA CONSIDERS

IDA COHAN, WINNIPEG, 1974

IT WAS SEVEN A.M. Tuesday September 17; and dressed in her finest navy skirt, Ida Cohan was sitting on one of the new fiddle-back chairs in her small kitchen. On the sturdy wooden table directly in front of her stood a tiny bottle. In the blue centre at the top of the bottle, you could still see the slight indentation from where the needle had last gone in. Next to the bottle lay the needle, the protective cap still on. Ida had been taking insulin since she was first diagnosed with diabetes some four years ago, though you think she'd gotten used to it? *Vey iz mir!* Pricking herself twice daily. Having to watch how much she drank, how far she walked, every morsel that she ate. Having to monitor blood sugar levels even. "Just what I wanted to be when I grew up," she would jest. "Someone who gets to *pish* daily on a strip of paper. For this, I could have been a dog." Not that diabetes was the worse condition that might befall a person. Might even be the one to pick if you had a choice—at least initially. Of this she was keenly aware, having seen many a person with post-polio syndrome over the years. Not to mention pernicious anemia, Alzheimer's, Parkinson. Still, it irked her. To come down with juvenile diabetes at her age! The upside, of course—and with the best of ailments, there is generally an upside—it gave her *cvetching* rights. "What's the point of having a life-threatening condition if you don't get to *cvetch* about it now and again?" she would ask her husband Moshe.

And *cvetch*, she most certainly did—had from day one, though generally only to Moshe.

"So my having to run to the toilet to *pish* every half hour, know what that's about?" she had exclaimed as she rejoined her husband in the waiting room on the heels of receiving the diagnosis. "Diabetes. Type One, of all things. And Moshe, it's *your* fault."

Moshe had looked at her with vague bemusement. "Sorry about the diabetes. But Ida, tell me, cause I really wanna know. How can you possibly be pinning this on me?"

"You and your sweet tooth! You think I'd have diabetes if you weren't calling for the halvah every few hours?"

"Gotchya this time," he declared triumphantly. "Type One doesn't come from diet."

"So?" Ida had answered, a cagey look on her face. "I said I had diabetes, yeh? I didn't say I was reasonable. You want reasonable, you should have married a *shikseh*."

Now generally, Ida took her morning insulin just before breakfast. Meanwhile, Moshe would busy himself scrambling the eggs. While no doubt being helpful was part of his motivation, he also welcomed the distraction, for something about seeing her jab that needle into her naked thigh made his skin crawl. Of this, Ida was well aware, and after completing the distasteful task, she would quickly cover up, then rise from the table as noisily as possible so as to reassure her squeamish husband that the coast was clear. And a few minutes later, the two of them would sit down to a leisurely breakfast.

Today was different. She would be delaying the injection until just before leaving, for as she had already let him know, she was breakfasting out with Rose. As for Moshe, he would be grabbing a bite at the local deli, then hurrying off to schul. The understanding was that she would drop by schul after breakfast. Not that she generally joined him at schul. But it was day one of Rosh Hashanah—one of those times when Jews who would not otherwise dream of setting foot in schul tend to put in an appearance.

As Moshe entered the kitchen to kiss her goodbye, however, Ida said something that utterly shocked him—that she just might not be able to make it.

"What do you mean 'not make it?'" asked Moshe, adjusting his yarmulke. "C'mon. Once a year, it's gonna hurt you to go to temple?"

"Yeh-yeh," she answered, making a wavy motion with her hand. "You know me. The stuff at home, I like. The *meshugahs* at schul, not so much."

"But Ida, surely you haven't forgotten."

Ida startled, but quickly recovered. "Sorry, Moshe. Yes, of course, I remember you're blowing the *shofar*. Didn't mean I wouldn't show up at all. Just can't tell you exactly when. Enough with the worrying," she urged, giving him an encouraging smile. "At some point, you'll look up into the gallery, and guess who you'll see?"

"You're going to another one of those interminable meetings of yours, aren't you?" Moshe asked suspiciously. "C'mon, Ida. It's important work, but on the high holidays!"

Receiving no answer, Moshe shrugged his shoulders and hurried upstairs to get his *tallis* bag. "Should God happen to ask what to record about you in the Book of Life, I'll be sure to let him know that in Winnipeg 1974 a run-of-the-mill flood trumps the Days of Awe," he quipped, as he exited the house.

Now Moshe had reason to be suspicious, for of late, Ida was frequently preoccupied with flood-related work. Chair of the new Citizens Review Committee, whose job it was to assess the Schreyer government's response to the recent flood, she dutifully attended meeting after meeting. However, the problem at hand was of a different nature altogether, though there was no question that she was keeping something from her husband.

The thing was, how could she tell how long breakfast would last? Or how well it would go? And if it went poorly, as she dreaded that it would, better that her long-suffering husband never know about it. Enough that one of them was on pins and needles.

You see, Rose had phoned last night, and the words that Rose had uttered had ripped the skin from her heart. "Mom," she had said, "I've something very important to tell you.... No, no one's died.... No, no one's been in an accident.... Just listen. Nomi's with me.... Yes, I mean the no-goodnik the family doesn't speak about. And she wants to join us for breakfast tomorrow."

Now this phone call, or a close relative thereof, was something that Ida had been anticipating for years, though every time she imagined it, the drama would come to a screeching stop for she just could not see it. Could not imagine saying yes. Could not imagine saying no. And yet "yes" she'd most definitely said. She'd been about to ply Rose with questions when Rose cautioned her, "Mom, prepare yourself. Nomi's changed. Changed a lot." She'd gotten off the phone forthwith, she was that terrified of what she might hear next. What if she discovered that Naomi had become a bone fide anti-Semite in her own right? But she'd rather shoot herself in the foot for now she had no answers. Just this painful excitement. This anger. Something like regret even though she was hardly the one at fault. No, not at fault. Of this she was certain.

She firmly believed in cutting people slack, in giving that little extra, and all her life she'd done so—especially when it came to Naomi. The family had sent Naomi to Peretz School when they could ill afford it. And again and again, she herself had moved mountains to support Naomi's aspirations. She had even made excuses when Naomi refused to let Rose accompany her to France, heart-broken though her other daughter was. There was a line, though, and in standing with that *farshtunkener* Earl, Naomi had crossed it knowingly, decisively. To think that Naomi would do this—someone who had studied anti-Semitism, someone so perceptive that of course you expect that little extra from her!And indeed, Ida always had expected more from Naomi. This was the child with the genius IQ. This was the child destined for greatness. And so Ida gave more, expected more, blamed more. And feeling guilty about favouring Naomi, when problems would arise between her two daughters, more often than not, she would side with Rose, though exactly who she was siding with was not always crystal clear.

Ida got up, made herself a cup of coffee, then sat back down. She remembered the time when Rose had come crying to her. "Mom," she had objected, "a whole year without her, I just couldn't. And it's not fair. Like, I've had my heart set on the trip for months." Ida had pleaded with Naomi, but Naomi was adamant. Naomi had just sat there on her bed and shot back, "Know what my real mistake was? Letting you guys strong-arm me into letting Rose come in the first place." Ida had slammed the door, refused to speak to Naomi for three whole days, but all she had said to Rose was, "Your sister, she needs this. You'll try looking at it from her point of view, yeh?"

Ida took a sip of her coffee and her mind drifted to later years—to the first time Earl came for supper. She'd been reluctant to invite him. Understandable. What mother would willingly encourage such a relationship? Besides that he was not Jewish—and that, she could live with—why not?—the man was years older, with an ex-wife and child. Nonetheless, he was important to Naomi, so they asked him over for Shabbes. When he turned up an hour late in a pair of tattered jeans and sneakers, she'd kept her peace—simply inquired about his health. Then they'd sat down at the dining room table.

Now to her dismay, as she was lighting the candles, she caught sight of a condescending smirk on Earl's face. The man clearly regarded the tradition as ludicrous. But she had a thick skin. So why make a fuss? But then Moshe began uttering the prayer over the bread, and what did Earl do but roll his eyes! Moshe saw it, depended on her.

"You know, Earl," she pointed out minutes later, "I don't

know what people in your culture do, but in ours we don't roll our eyes at other peoples' religious practices. You understand, yeh?"

He'd said he was sorry, though if the look on his face was one of contrition, she would eat her socks. More like annoyance.

They carried on, got through the evening. Somehow, however, the man could not stop himself from getting in digs about religion.

Later that night, after the last of the dishes had been washed, Naomi pleaded with everyone to give him another chance. And so it was that a week later, back for supper came Earl. No major problems. So he was invited again. This time, smack in the middle of desert, he blurted out, "You know, I was in 'Jew York' once... Oh, sorry. Stupid of me. A slip," he stated seconds later. What did he think? That she was born yesterday? But she'd held her tongue. Then Moshe and Earl began discussing various hot spots around the globe—and with relative equanimity, if one could believe it—and it looked as if the evening were salvageable after all, though the man could hardly be invited back.

Tea being served in the living room, after touching on the Congo, her husband plunked his feet onto the ottoman and asked Earl what he thought about the Middle East.

"Well, frankly, I thinks the Israelis are thieves pure and simple," Earl had answered. Then he'd launched into an anti-Israel diatribe. She was well aware that there were different positions on Israel, but the words he was using! "White colonial state!" "Thief!" She glanced at her husband, saw the tears in his eyes. Then she heard that *momser* utter "thief" again, and she felt the hairs on the back of her neck bristle.

"That's it!" she thundered, rising from her chair. "Get out of our house."

Earl looked at her with amazement and started to rise.

"Mom, you can't do this," insisted Naomi, "and it's not as if his analysis were wrong."

"Don't tell me what I can or can't do in my own house. Anti-Semites aren't welcome here," she stated definitively.

"Jesus H. Christ!" shouted Earl, his face turning red. "You wants me to leave, wants the uncouth Newfie to leave. Fine!" Whereupon he began storming out of the room.

And that's when Nomi had said it. "Just a sec," she called out, rising as well. "Mom, something you need to know. Earl and I are getting married. And if he goes, I go."

That's when Rose got into the act, wasn't it? Ida recalled, fingering the syringe. Accused Nomi of betraying the family. Brought up that blasted trip to France all over again. Then pleaded with her sister to reconsider.

She had watched. Seen the tension between the twins hit a whole new level—the tension she'd struggled most of their lives to temper. But the anti-Semite, he just could not be allowed into the family, could he?

So long ago, mused Ida, taking another sip of coffee. And now this phone call out of the blue. Ida rubbed her forehead, tried to make sense of it all, but couldn't. What did it mean that her *bubeleh* wanted to talk after all these years? And what made Naomi think she could just come waltzing back? Though who knows what befell her after that fateful day. Whether she was safe. Whether she was okay.

Finding no way to settle down, Ida *schlepped* upstairs, located the family albums, then sat down on the bed and began flipping through them. "Gorgeous," she murmured to herself as she stared at a photo of her daughters at three. The two of them—almost identical. Both slim, with dimples on their cheeks. But Naomi, she always had that extra alertness, hadn't she? As if were she were aware even then of that hidden world that a picture held. Was she still taking pictures herself? Maybe made a film? While she had heard that Naomi had left the city, how many times in the last few years had she herself trotted over to the Winnipeg Film Society hoping that someone would rush over and say, "Saw your daughter's latest picture. A real crackerjack director." She would have had to walk away, of course, but at least she would have known. Though no one had, Ida mused sadly. She flipped to a picture of two-year-old Naomi squatting on the grass, staring in awe at a butterfly. So innocent! So precious! Who would have thought that she'd have grown into the type of woman who would side with an anti-Semite over her own father?

Distraught at the realization that despite everything, she yearned for her child, Ida dragged herself downstairs, sat back down at the kitchen table. She glanced at the clock, tears in her eyes. Time, she realized. And without further ado, she inserted the needle into the insulin bottle, drew back the plunger, held the needle close to her eyes, squirted out a little. Then, her gaze steady, her index finger snapping out from her thumb, she began flicking away at the needle, doing her best to collapse each and every air bubble. No matter what happened, even if she chickened out totally and went directly to schul, she reminded herself, it wouldn't do a single member of her family a speck of good—not even the Prodigal Daughter—if she died en route from an air bubble.

13. NAOMI ET AL.

LOOKING BACK ON EVERYTHING, sometimes I wonder what would have become of me, indeed, would have become of the family more generally had my return to Winnipeg gone differently. Now many a time during my hiatus in Toronto, I had envisioned my return. I kid you not—I would see myself rushing up to my folks with open arms. Dad would shrug his shoulders and exclaim, "*Nu?* So what took you so long?" Mom would scrunch up her eyes as if struggling with a dilemma, but would eventually nod. The thing about fantasies, however, is that inevitably the time comes when they fall away and once again you are face to face with real people, real pain, the unfettered longing of real hearts.

"Nervous?" Rose asked. It was the beginning of my second full day back in Winnipeg. Rose and I were in her car on the way to the restaurant to meet Mom. To think that she had actually agreed to my coming! Of course whether or not she'd be able to bring herself to look at me—that was the question.

"Oh Rose, whatever am I going to say to the woman?" I asked. "And what if she…"

"She's a mother," Rose reminded me. "Give her room to be one."

Now tempting though it was to probe further, I must have zoned out, for next thing I knew I was sitting directly across from Rose in what was blatantly a Middle Eastern restaurant, what with pictures of falafels and a map of Tel Aviv on the walls. A young waiter in baggy pants was in the process of bringing a glass of water to the grandfatherly gentleman at the table next to ours.

A thoughtful expression on her face, Rose opened her purse and handed me a bottle. "Your fluphenazine, in pill form. Sam brought it home last night."

I thanked her and quickly pocketed the pills, aware that the woman of the hour might put in an appearance any second.

"Okay, listen," said Rose, leaning in close, "I can't promise Mom'll show. If she does, though, don't take it as game over if she starts to explode. The thing about Mom these days, she…"

Rose stopped in mid-sentence, for she too heard it. A creaking. Could it be…? I turned. There she was, advancing through the door, her head high—punctual, as was her wont.

Except for the obvious signs of aging—a touch of grey, deeper wrinkles—Mom was as I remembered. Tiny, wiry, darker than Rose or me. I recognized that vintage Ida Cohan look of determination, the old navy skirt. I could feel my heart stir, wanted to call out, but I sat, waited. Casting her eyes about, Mom noticed Rose, smiled nervously at her. Then she lighted on me, and the colour drained from her face.

As Mom approached, Rose got up, kissed her on the cheek. "Sorry, if I didn't prepare you," I could hear Rose whisper.

It was now or never. My mind churning, every sinew in my body shaking, I lifted myself up, forced myself to face her. "Mom," I blurted out, "heard I've acted like a jerk, treated the family badly, and I'm so sorry about that. Mom, please, I love you. And I need you—need you desperately."

Mom looked my way but not exactly at me. Her muscles tensed. Then her face softened, and she teared up. "Baby, you're not well," she murmured, holding my gaze.

"I'm so sorry," I repeated.

"Sha. Sha," she urged, reaching over and placing her arms around me.

"Sorry," I uttered again . And within seconds, I was sobbing. I could feel a kiss on my cheek. Then Mom took my face in her hands and stared poignantly into my eyes.

"Naomi, remember that time a thousand and a half years ago when you asked if you could speak to Mrs. Fenster if she apologized?"

"Uh huh. You told me that some things just can't be fixed."

"Maybe I was right, maybe I was wrong, but sometimes, you know, whatever's happened, it's not important any more."

At the realization that it had always been this easy—and how often the seemingly impossible is simple—for a second, I felt like smacking both of us. Then something inside of me settled.

We all sat down, Mom next to Rose. Mom began by commenting on the weather as Winnipeggers do. Not mincing words, in the very next sentence, she informed me that I looked a fright. And before long, she was directing her not inconsiderable intelligence to trying to make sense of this wreck of a daughter of hers.

"Baby, that wound on your head," she asked, her brow furled, "that *his* handiwork?"

"No, Mom, it was me. Honest."

"The *farshtunkener* didn't strike you, that's something. But I'm having trouble understanding here, sweetie. So help me out, please."

"Most of my time in Toronto, I've been in a mental hospital. What happened with my head, well, one day, I got frustrated, is all."

While my explanation was woefully inadequate, Mom nodded graciously. "Frustration, yeh, we all of us do strange things when frustrated. But what's this about a mental hospital?"

As I started to explain, we were interrupted by the waiter asking for our order.

Now I was bracing myself for the standard follow-up questions—about illness, symptoms, how one manages. As Mom quickly demonstrated, however, her gaze was as keen as ever.

"Baby," she asked the second that the waiter disappeared, "you said you *heard* you acted like a jerk. Why did you put it that way? You'll explain, yeh?"

"Nomi has extensive amnesia," Rose clarified. "Except for the past year or so, she remembers almost nothing after second-year university."

Mom scrunches up her eyes. "Let me get this straight," she begins, turning to me. "You don't remember going to France?"

I shake my head.

"Don't remember bringing over Earl?"

"No, nor being with him, marrying him, having a kid with him."

"I have a new grandchild?" she asks, a smile coming to her lips.

"Ruth. Age three."

"Ruth," repeats Mom, nodding as if pleased with the choice of name. She glances at Rose, sees Rose shake her head. Then she leans forward, takes my hand in hers. "Naomi, family, we stick together when there's a problem, yeh?" she assures me, peering deeply into my eyes. "But you're gonna have to tell me what's cookin'. So you have amnesia. You were in some sort of accident, *bubeleh*?"

"No, that's not it."

"Anything to do with you slurring your words? It doesn't take a Mr. Sherlock Holmes to tell you're on drugs."

"Psychiatric drugs yes—and that's a problem too—but we can talk about that in a bit. There's something else.... Okay, listen. You ever hear of electroshock therapy?"

At this, Mom lets out a loud groan, says she'd thought they'd abolished it. Then she begins speaking of an old friend of hers—Eva Kapkinsky, who apparently was given shock decades ago. "The long and short is," Mom continues, "and excuse me for this, sweetie—afterward, Kapinksy was never the same. I'd be talking to her one day, and the next—well, maybe she'd remember, maybe not.... Scared to ask, but...?"

"Mom, yeah."

Mom glances at Rose, then at me, and her eyes widen. "But how could that be? This is 1974. What happened to Eva, it was back in the fifties when they knew from nothing."

As Mom struggles with this anomaly, our food arrives. The two of us quickly fill her in on my last few years, particularly detailing the ins and outs of my memory problems. "So the memory slippage, it really is random," she observes. "Must have trouble getting your bearings." Doing what she can to assist, she proceeds to bring me up to speed on the home front, providing an especially vivid account of her diabetes, also what she calls "your father's various shofar-blowing gigs".

"And you know, dad's blowing the shofar at temple today," she points out. "Hey, I've an idea. Not saying it's a good idea, but hear me out. How about we all go?"

"It'd be okay?" I ask eagerly.

"Better than okay," asserts Mom, a knowing look in her eye. "The poor man, he's not even sure I'll turn up. Imagine his delight at seeing all three of us."

With Mom confident, we quickly agree.

Her eyes on Mom, Rose picks up the last of her French fries. "Incidentally," she asks, "why doesn't Dad know you're coming? You *always* go on Rosh Hashanah."

"Thinks I'm busy attending to flood business. Easily could have been too. Naomi," she checks, turning to me, "your sister get around to telling you what that good-for-nothing Red River of ours has been up to?"

"If she has, I've forgotten," I acknowledge uneasily, "but I can guess. Hope no one close to you got hit."

"Some, plus a whole lot of others. I'm chairing this committee, right? And I've interviewed more victims that I can shake a stick at. Such *tsores!* That husband and wife that work at the university library—the Richardsons—you remember them, Naomi?" she asks, sipping her coffee, "those rare books they've spent a lifetime accumulating, every last one had to be tossed.

Strange thing, the Plouffes just a street over—got off almost
Scot-free. Who can predict? These *meshugener* acts of nature,
they…" Suddenly, her brow furrows. "That…that's what it's
like, isn't it?" she murmurs, her eyes thoughtful.

"Mom?" I ask.

"The electroshock, it's like one of our Winnipeg floods, isn't
it? Oh, the beginning is different, I get that," she states, waving her hand dismissively, "but once they've sent that current
through your head, you don't know where it's going to go,
how much damage it's going to wreak, what it's gonna wash
away, what it's going to leave in its wake. Oh, but *bubeleh*,"
she adds, gazing deep into my eyes, "what happens with the
Red River, that's an act of nature, yeh? And we do everything
in our power to prevent it—build dikes, create diversions, you
know, like a normal person would. *Gotenyu!*" she exclaims,
her nostrils flaring. "We don't call it treatment."

There it was. She had cut through the *meshugas* beautifully,
brilliantly. And it was at that moment that I knew that I was
in the right place. What lay in store was anyone's guess, but if
I could get back on my feet anywhere, it was here.

Its arches as majestic as ever, its gigantic rose windows beckoning, the old Orthodox schul at Mountain and Powers looked
magnificent, the rugged stone edifice a testament to all those
devout souls throughout the years who would wrap themselves
in the wonder of the prayer shawl and *daven* without food or
drink into the failing light—*daven* with such fervour that—if
you listened carefully, you could make out the distant sound
of the Chariot nearing. "Listen. Can you hear it?" some of the
older men would ask as they glanced up from their tattered
prayer books, their lips trembling, their eyes filled with longing.
"He's coming. He's coming."

Hopefully, the time was fast on our heels when God's female indwelling would be savoured and the glory of woman
too would sound from every nook and cranny of this ancient

house. But even as things were, what a *mitzvah* it was to stand in its presence once again!

"You ready?" asked Mom.

"Ready," I answered.

I had forgotten that this was the turn of the year, but was instantly reminded, for it was all around us—in the faces, the voices, the very prayer books; and in the blink of an eye, we were ushered into that privileged time that returns and returns again. Even as we entered through those stately mahogany doors, we were greeted by sounds older than memory—the haunting tones of the *Avinu Malkeynu*, which bring your soul to its knees. "This I know, this I understand," I whisper to Rose.

Mom opened her purse, handed me a *babushka*. Quickly, I slipped it on. Wishing a Shana Tova to the other late-comers, we approached a table to our left, where Rose picked up one of the two remaining *mahzors*. Our heads covered, in single file, the three of us made our way up the winding staircase, then took our place in the women's gallery. We stood along side the other women, the history of our people on our shoulders, and effortlessly, the words came flowing out of us. "*Avinu Malkey-ey-ey-nu*," (our father, our king), we chanted again and again, every syllable of every word, a yearning, a reaching, a plea for compassion. "*Eemaynu malk'taynu*" (our mother, our queen), I whispered from somewhere deep in my soul.

I peered down from the gallery, but could make out only parts of the lower level. A blur of prayer shawls. Old-timers, middle-aged men, young lads grasping their *mahzors* with avid fingers, a cantor whom I knew not at the *bima*, Rabbi Zalman next to him, the Ark of the covenant in his grateful arms. No sign of Dad.

And now we were sitting, and the harrowing tale of Avraham and Yitschak filled the room. Sacrifice, was that the crux of it?, I wondered. Or was there something still deeper—something on which sacrifice stands? Oh, but what does a person do on the Day of Remembrance when she cannot remember?

Now exactly how this happened I could not say, but even as I was lamenting the destruction of memory, something in me rebelled. No, I won't let the shock doctors rob me of the moment, I found myself asserting. I took a deep breath, determined to let this sacred time of year wrap me in its compassionate arms, touch me with its healing fingers. And something akin to these words began streaming through my head: *For sins against Ruthie, against Mom, against Dad, against Rose, for lapses I recall and lapses I may never remember, I plead for forgiveness. Have compassion on me, on Ruthie, on Gerald, on the soul of the Jewish people, on all your weeping children. Of poison, pestilence and hunger, rid us. Of oppressors who grind us into the dust, rid us. Bring forth a year anew. Hear our voice. Hear our...*

Suddenly, from the corner of my eye, I spot a patch of blue. I turn, and there is Dad, feet from the *bima*, his tallis draped over his shoulders, the *shofar* in his hands.

And now the cantor is chanting the prayer over the shofar. And now Dad steps forward. High up into the gallery lifts his eyes. He lights upon his wife and his daughter Rose, and nods. He does not see me. Does not see me.

And now he is raising that ancient instrument to his lips. And now he takes a deep breath. And now is the first note sailing through the gallery. One straight three-second blast. Next comes the one-second notes, followed by the staccato: Awaken, awaken from your slumber, they call out.

And now Dad lowers the shofar. And a murmur goes through the crowded synagogue. I look about. Some people's eyes are aglow at the *mitzvah*. With others, there is a touch of sadness. And many, so many have turned to their neighbour, a wistful expression on their faces. "Is there not one more?" the woman in black next to me asks.

I glance back at the *bima* to find Dad's eyes meeting mine. Steadily. Plaintively. Tears begin trickling down his face. He stops to wipe them away. Then to my delight, he does something curiously out of keeping with the solemnity of the occasion—he looks directly at me and winks. Then he takes a deep breath and once again lifts the shofar to his lips. Instantly, a hush descends on the worshippers. And a single bold note issues forth. And the man holds onto that note longer, longer, longer as oppressor after oppressor returns to dust and the weary old year into nothingness sinks.

"Dad, Shana Tova to you too," I murmur.

My father was the third and final member of my immediate family to welcome me home. To say that he was jubilant would be a gross understatement. Hey, had he his druthers, a national holiday would have been proclaimed. Once we were back at the Inkster house, he insisted on my living there and could not stop hugging me. It was soon apparent that he had nothing to overcome to take me back into his heart, for I'd never been out of it.

Dad's age was far more apparent than Mom's. The full head of springy hair that had once sent his *yarmulke* tumbling was now sparse, although he continued to straighten his *yarmulke* out of force of habit. His face, his trunk, his arms were thinner. And he now made his way carefully, favouring his left side. His back, right?

Because of that bad back, Dad had retired three years ago, shortly after turning sixty-four. As I came to understand it, he spent his days playing with his grandchildren, feeding the birds, helping out at schul, campaigning for the NDP. Oh yes, and according to Mom, getting under foot every second of the day.

Now at first anyway, Dad did not have the same pressing need as the rest of us to tease out the details of that fateful day—which suited me fine, for I was sufficiently confused by the differences between Mom's and Rose's accounts. "Enough that *they're* making you *meshugah*," asserted Dad. "*I'll* just sit." And sit he did in his favourite living room chair as Rose and Mom scrambled to fill in detail after detail. Though he did roll his eyes when Rose asked Mom, "You sure I accused Nomi of betraying the family?"—my only clear indication that Mom's version of events just might be more accurate. In the end, though, he had a point or two of his own to make.

"So the three of you are idiots. What else is new?" he exclaimed, plunking his feet up on the ottoman. "But for future reference, let me tell you geniuses something. If my choice is between gaining an anti-Semite or losing a daughter, guess what. I'll take the anti-Semite. Now Naomi," he added, stretching out his arms, "how 'bout giving your old dad another hug?"

"Mr. Innocent over here!" objected Mom. "Looks to the women to take care of everything, then blames us when we get it wrong. As for *your* hubby..." she goes on, turning toward me.

"Hold on," I urged. "Earl and I acted like jerks, sure, but from the sound of what everyone's telling me, you weren't totally fair to him either."

Now had I uttered such words during any other season, likely as not, a brouhaha would have broken out. But special are the Days of Awe. Starting with Rosh Hashanah and ending with Yom Kippur—it is a time when Jews everywhere are called upon to reflect, to repent, to right what is wrong. Not that the rest of us were believers like Dad, but if you live a Jewish life faithfully enough, it is as if you believed.

"Okay, I'll give you this," said Dad, whipping out a cigar and leaning back in his chair. "I was so upset about the rest of his *meshugas*, I was kinda luring him into a trap when I asked about the Middle East. Naomi, sorry about that. And if you're ever on speaking terms with him again, well, tell him I regret that."

"Fine! Fine! We're all *farshtunkeners*, and the anti-Semite's a prince among princes," countered Mom sarcastically, throwing up her hands. "Okay, okay.... I have something too. Just could be he had a point about my always dismissing him as uncouth—which incidentally, we all know he is."

And so our discussion went. Not that any of us came within

a country mile of broaching the issue of how a feud mentality came to infect this family or the personal cost to me. Hey, we were gutsy—not stupid. And judiciously limiting our scope to what could be handled, we were doing well. But then we began speaking of my plans and we banged into the proverbial brick wall precisely where we might have anticipated it.

"If Naomi's not a doctor," asked Dad, "what's she making medical decisions for? Now if she's a doctor, please tell me. Far be it from me to strip my own child of her M.D."

It was two p.m. that same afternoon. Dad still in his prayer shawl, we were sitting around the kitchen table polishing off a late lunch of eggs and gefilte fish. And for the last half hour, the three of us had been trying in vain to bring Dad to at least tolerate the idea of me tapering off the drugs.

"Moshe, you think either of us are a hundred per cent comfortable with this?" asked Mom. "But she's made up her mind; and better here than at Rose's with kids around."

"But how can she do this against medical advice?"

"How can you ask that?" demanded Mom, waving her arms in the air. "*Schmuck!* Look at her! Listen to her. And you know, Moshe, the pills drive her crazy."

Dad coated his gefilte fish with horseradish, then took a bite. "If the doc said she needs them, then she needs them. Anyway, woman," he added, glancing mischievously at his wife, "*you* drive *me* crazy, and I don't get rid of you."

Mom rolled her eyes, then looked at Dad pointedly. She reminded him that the medical profession had a long history of blunders. "Take bloodletting," she said.

"Long time ago," he answered.

She reminded him that the doctor who ordered the drugs was the same idiot doctor that had ordered the electroshock. "So what do I know from electroshock?" he shot back. "Maybe it was necessary."

Seeing Mom strike out, once again Rose stepped up to the

plate, assured him that I would be proceeding slowly, carefully. But Dad continued to shake his head.

Having already shot my bolt, I could think of nothing to add. Suddenly, however, Shabbes came to mind.

"Hey, Dad," I ask, "member what you used to say about Shabbes? That it's built on time, so can never be destroyed."

A big smile comes to my father's face. "Great that you remember that, Naomi."

I reach over, touch his hand. "Look, I don't wanna upset you, but it's not true. "Electroshock," I add, "it annihilates time—even Shabbes."

Instantly, he turns pale. "But sweetheart, how?"

"There are years of my life I can't remember. All that time, it's wiped out. Like it never was. Now Dad, after my second year at U. of M., just how many times you figure I joined you for Shabbes?"

Dad scrunches up his forehead, stops to consider. "Well, at least a hundred, maybe two hundred."

"The thing is, I have no memory of a single one. Each and every one—annihilated! Caput."

"They invented a machine that destroys Shabbes?"

I nod.

"But I thought ... Ida, you know about this?" he asks, turning to Mom.

"Yeh. Sorry, Moshe."

A cloud comes across my father's face. He rises, begins pacing back and forth. "But what they're doing, it violates everything sacred," he insists. "C'mon. They should be stopped."

Delighted by the turnabout, I too got up from the table, plied Dad with kisses. Then taking in that he was okay, I did something I'd been aching to do since arriving home—sought out my old bedroom.

The room was exactly as I remembered it. The same small cot. The same olive green blinds. Bone tired, I stretched out on the bed. Now something about knowing that I would actually be sleeping here tonight emboldened me. "Tomorrow," I mumbled to myself, letting my eyelids drop. "I'll begin the withdrawal tomorrow."

Half an hour later, while Mom did the dishes and Dad was upstairs checking a passage in his prayer book, Rose and I were hovering over the kitchen table, splitting a week's worth of my new pills into quarters. Correction: I watched. Being the one and only family member sure of hand, Rose did the actual cutting.

"Hey, Ro, this cutting edge talent of yours, it could come in handy," I jested. "I mean if accountancy goes out of vogue, you could always land a job as a *mohel*."

"Sure. Sure. Just what every woman wants," she replied, not losing a beat. "A new penis a day, and a tailor-made one at that."

As I stood in that kitchen taking in the blurred image of Rose pressing a knife against a pill, I had what might be called a "St. Pukes' moment." Am I truly going off the meds? I asked myself. And this wondrous homecoming, did any of it really happen? Now questions of this ilk had come before. Nor were they about to stop. It was at this juncture, however, that I discovered something. A trick, as it were. Even if it's a dream, I told myself, even if I awake in the shock line—broken and alone—let it be a glorious dream, a dream worth grieving. Then I shook off the fear, refocused on the task at hand.

Now I had been so preoccupied with the meds, the fact of it being Rosh Hashanah had again slipped into Never-Never Land. Thankfully, not for long.

"So, we doing *tashlich* or what?" asked Dad, returning to the kitchen suddenly.

"Now?" asked Mom, turning to face him.

"No, after I'm ten feet under! Of course now!"

Mom eyed me, and her face melted. "But Moshe, see how exhausted Naomi is.... Maybe we shouldn't."

I looked about, saw faces rapt in anticipation. "Let's do it," I said. And after the mandatory reassurances, the matter was settled.

As Mom and Dad readied themselves, I wracked my brain. What was *tashlich*? Part of Rosh Hashanah, wasn't it? Something to do with water—water and sacrifice. But there was something more basic. I could feel it.

"Hurry, girls," insisted Mom.

Rose quickly finished splitting the pills. As she was returning the pieces to the bottle, she looked up, saw Mom glancing anxiously at her watch. Getting the point, Rose nodded, then screwed the cap back on, leaving several pieces on the table. I stared at the remnants and without exactly knowing why, pocketed them.

"Hurry up, you two. Dad's in the car waiting," Mom called out several minutes later, turning around to look at us.

Rose and I immediately slipped on our sweaters and made our way out of the house. Now curiously, Rose hesitated as she stepped off the bottom stair. Even as she hit the sidewalk, she glanced over at the flowerbed next to the veranda. Awash with lush chrysanthemums, it was—some white as lilies, some purple as aged wine.

"Your favourite flower," I observed.

Rose nodded. Taking her time, she drew my attention to one of the purple chrysanthemums—the largest I had ever seen. Then she knelt down, began tugging on it, teasing it out ever so gently, taking that extra care not to miss a rootlet.

Mom watched from the car window but did not interfere. Rose must still be doing the gardening, I realized. But why is she unearthing a living plant, and one that she has obviously taken pains to nurture?

"You girls coming?" shouts Mom the second that the task is complete, "or should we take out an ad in *The Winnipeg Free Press* for a couple of new daughters?"

We had an exhilarating drive north, in typical Cohan fashion, us backseat drivers periodically chiming in, "Let's pass this one." We continued on well past the city limits, watched open wheat fields give way to dense woodland. "Think this is it," said Dad, eventually slowing down. We pulled up on a small patch of gravel just off one of the country roads. Exiting the car, we followed a well-worn path which took us to a rapidly flowing stream, the water shimmering in the bright rays of the sun. We passed a pimply young lad with a high-powered fly rod, saw his line go sizzling into the water. We passed an older man, a simple pole in his hand, a pail of wriggling worms at his side. Then, arriving at an isolated stretch, Dad said, "Is good," and we all stopped.

All eyes on him, Dad lowered his head and recited the *tashlich* prayer, and I recalled that passage from Micah where we are instructed to cast our sins into the river. Then he removed his prayer shawl, leaned forward, and extended one of its fringes over the edge of the stream. *Oy!* That blessed garment, is he gonna drop it?, I wondered. No, he was just shaking it— sending infinitesimal specks of dust wafting into the air. And now Mom steps forward. She removes a scattering of bread crumbs from her pocket and sure enough, she sprinkles them into the water. And inevitably going the way of all flesh, they wither. They vanish.

And now is Rose gazing—and with oh such tenderness—at that lush chrysanthemum pressed to her bosom. She brings it to her lips, kisses it as ardently as one might a lover about to depart for battle. Instantly guessing its fate, I shudder, open my mouth to protest. But ere I can so much as utter a word, into the stream, also, it is cast.

The dust, the bread are one thing; this vulnerable fellow being, another. Struggling with a dilemma as old as humankind, we can none of us take our eyes off it. Buoyed up by the current, off into the distance it is whisked. Further. Further. "Water's the stuff of life," we whisper to one another. "Maybe it'll survive." Though from the look on Rose's face, it is clear that she is fully aware that she has placed it in harm's way.

Sacrifice, yes, I realize. Atonement, yes. But something else too. A letting go. And it is then that I do it. I reach into my pocket. Even as those pills brush against my finger tips, legions of questions come swirling through my mind: Will I get through the withdrawal safely? Will any of my memory ever return? Have I lost Ruthie for good? And what in the world can I make of what's been made of me? Then I turn off these weary old questions like you would a tap, knowing that they will return soon enough. Grateful at having my family back, I raise my eyes, behold them as they stand there etched against the quiet all-knowing prairie sky, looking so resplendent, so beautiful. Then I gather together each of the pills, lift my hand out of my pocket, reach as far back as my arm can stretch and farther. And with a snap, into the current I fling them.

14. NAOMI

MINIMALLY, IT WAS A STROKE of good luck arriving during the holy season. Not that other times lacked possibility. And not that the gentle embrace of the holidays could spare me, or indeed any of us, the turbulence ahead.

The Days of Awe came and went—something to tap into on those nippy prairie nights but which could not linger, could only return and return again. Family stayed, and knowing me as only family could, they kept finding ways to reach in, to grab hold of my hand. Let there be no mistake about it, however. It was a "rough go" for some time, Mercifully, not right away, though. And there were moments so tender that...

It was day two of the Days of Awe, and the first rays of light were peeking through the triple-paned windows. The rest of the household ostensibly fast asleep, decked out in an old pair of Dad's pj's, I was hunched over the kitchen table, three bottles of pills in front of me, a cup of coffee in hand, a cigarette dribbling out of my mouth. Excited at the prospect of beginning the withdrawal, I butted out my ciggy and began eyeing the fluphenazine with fierce determination when unexpectedly, into the room sauntered Mom. She was clad in Dad's terry robe (dad's casuals looked fabulous on this family) and she was surprisingly alert, as if she'd been up for hours.

"Up early, baby," she observed. "Hope you slept okay. You'd like some toast, yeh?"

"Slept just fine, and sure."

Mom popped the bread in the toaster, poured herself a cup coffee. No sooner did she spot the pills than a curious look came over her. "You aren't by any chance squeamish about seeing people get needles?" she asked.

"Oh, I'd say I'm pretty used to that. Why?"

"I think I'm actually going to enjoy this," she stated mysteriously. Then she disappeared, returning minutes later with a syringe and bottle of insulin.

"Ida, what's going on down there?" we could hear Dad yell down at us.

"None of your beeswax," she retorted. "The Cohan women are having a party, and—nothing personal—but you aren't invited."

Offering no further explanation, she inserted the syringe into the insulin. Upon withdrawing it, she instantly began flicking away at it. "Those good-for-nothing air bubbles, they'll be the death of me yet," she murmured more to herself than me. Once she was content with the look of the fluid, she hoisted up her nightgown, baring a sizeable stretch of thigh. Now as even her casual acquaintances knew, Ida Cohan was a woman reticent about her body. Even hugging her own children was a stretch. So there was something touching about being with her at such a moment. "Mom, glad the two of us can do this," I assured her.

She nodded, inserted the needle, then peered up at me with a timid smile. "So," she asked, "you taking the pills on your own or you waiting for Cardinal Richelieu to rise from the grave and do it for you?"

I immediately complied.

"Okay, time for our treat," she announced, heading for the toaster.

I lit another cigarette. "So Mom," I asked, the smoke slowly drifting out my nostrils, "what's the deal with air bubbles?"

"What's wrong with you anyway?" she spat out. "Feh! No one wants to hear about things like that."

"Don't know a whole lot of psych patients, do you? *Of course* I wanna hear."

Mom looked at me at first guardedly, eventually semi-conspiratorially. Tentatively, she began to elaborate. Before long, we were leaning forward in our chairs, eagerly swapping tales about symptoms. "And you think I can make it through a night without having to *pish* at least twice?" she asked, her eyes wide.

"Seriously," I pointed out, "my mouth's so dry, I couldn't spit if my life depended on it."

And so began a new morning ritual. Of all our times together, I could swear that these were the moments that Mom and I most cherished—when we could let down our hair, and *cvetch* to our hearts' content.

Being on three-quarter dose was neither as exhilarating nor as scary as I'd anticipated. I coped, even played tag with my nephew, and I slept like a charm. On day five, Rose suggested tackling the next level. Half also appeared to go well. I was distinctly more alert, and the world that greeted me was less of a blur. And so it is that I took the next step. Again, at first, I seemed fine. But, when I rose the following morning, I was feverish.

All that day, my eyes watered, my nose ran. So I crawled into bed early. In the early hours, I awoke with a start, gasping for air. I switched on the light, turned to peek out the window. What's happened to the blinds? And what in God's name are those green tigers doing here? Seconds later, I heard myself yelling, "Mom, help me."

My parents came running, Dad in his long-johns, Mom in her nightgown.

"Get that tiger off me," I screeched. Dad took one look at me and suggested calling Dr. Allen. Now I must have started screaming again. Or maybe I was just whimpering, for I could hear Mom plain as day.

"Whatchya mean call Dr. Allen?" the woman asks, glaring at her husband. "She said this would be hard, so it's hard. Like we're suddenly fans of 'easy?'" Then she sits down on the corner of my bed, peers into my eyes. "Naomi," she urges, "just an idea, but maybe you should stop screaming?"

I try to pull myself into her world. "Stop screaming? Why, Mom?"

"Why? Why?" she stammers. "Well ... because of the *goyim*, that's why."

"The *goyim*?"

"This nice young English couple—the Mauncoat-Carters— they moved in next door, and for me and Dad, a little scream- ing—so what else is new?—but best we shouldn't alarm the *goyim*."

I found myself chuckling despite myself. Now I did calm down, but the flu-like sensations grew steadily worse. So next morning, I did the sensible thing—returned to the previous level. The identical problem, however, arose next time I tried to cut back. "If this's too hard on you guys, I can always go to a hotel," I offered.

"You launching a new career as a bellhop?" snapped Mom. "No? Then sit your *tokhes* down and stay put."

And so it is that with help from everyone, I persevered. One morning, I awoke, and gone was the headache, the sweats. Thrilled, I rushed to the phone, told Rose, and in celebration that evening, the entire clan trekked over to Kelekis for burgers and fries. Five more days, I held that level. Then I did the un- thinkable. I went off the fluphenazine entirely, did the Jewish equivalent of a "hail Mary"—don't even ask—and waited for full-blown schizophrenia to set in—which, surprisingly, it did not.

Now after a particularly restless night, one morning I awoke to a bitter taste in my mouth. I dragged myself to the john, grabbed the toothpaste. As I was brushing my teeth, my eyes lit on the mirror, and I caught sight of something most unexpected. A passably normal face—not a hint of a twitch anywhere.

"Hallelujah!" I cheered.

"Naomi, you saying what I think you're saying?" Mom called up excitedly.

Now with a change this titanic, it can take a person a while to appreciate the full extent of it, especially in light of the after-effects. Then too, at times, our loved ones pick up what we do not.

It was early afternoon, and the family was relaxing around the dining room table. I cleared the dishes and returned to find Mom squinting away at a newspaper. "*Oy* are my eyes sore!" she exclaimed. "I could swear they make the print small on purpose. So read for me, baby," she asked, handing me the paper and pointing.

"But I can't even make out normal-sized lettering," I reminded her. "Maybe Dad…"

Dad leaned back in his chair, grimaced. "What? Your mother works her fingers to the bone to make you a beautiful lunch and you can't even look at a newspaper for her?"

Reminding myself that it would do no harm to go through the motions, I took hold of the paper. "Wi … Winni … Winnipeg Blue Bombers…" I stammered. Astonished, I looked up at my parents. They smiled encouragingly. Unable to believe my eyes, I looked back at the paper. There it was—lettering crisp as bills fresh off the press. My heart racing, I proceeded to read every word, every syllable of the article aloud.

I was walking on air, I was so happy. I kissed my parents. I bundled up, ventured into the great outdoors, and like an infant fresh from the womb, I drank in sight after sight. I happened upon a quaint little tobacco shop, made out the sign "Fall In" over the door, managed the gap without tripping. I bought a day old copy of *The New York Times*, leaned against the counter, read an entire article on the Watergate scandal.

Such a *mechayeh*! The printed word, the visual world itself, I had it back.

The next couple of days, fortune continued to smile on us. Mom sold a property on Burrows—ergo, the bills in arrears could be paid in full. And the day after that, three boxes of my clothes arrived.

"Know what I think? The *farshtunkener*'s actually letting you go!" exclaimed Mom.

And sensing that she was right, at long last, I allowed my mind to turn to Ruthie.

You see, I had vowed never again to expose her to a mother on drugs, nor to involve her in a marital row—and the primary obstacles gone, this could be our moment. Calling Gerald, surely that was the next step. Now Ger, it was fortuitous that I rang you when I did. In retrospect, though, would that we had connected earlier!

From the very first day I'd laid eyes on that man, I knew that he was always but a whisker away from danger. People accept a certain amount of difference—hell, the Brits even consider it part of their national heritage—but go too far, have the wrong type, and you risk being skinned alive. Some folks respond to the breach in the established order with murderous rage. Being heart-felt humanitarians, others are more inclined to cure you of your true nature. Either way, you're up shit's creek without a paddle. Now mostly, Gerald could pass. And mostly, folks warmed to him. However, like Miu, I worried, and the phone call that day was hardly reassuring.

"Ger," I said, "great to hear your voice too, but I can tell something's wrong. Give."

In the vaguest possible terms, Gerald acknowledged that he had been involved in "an incident." Then he changed the subject entirely.

"Nomi," he gushed, "Les boy has started paying attention in school and damned if that little tyke didn't receive a gold star on his last assignment!"

"Not surprised," I observed. "Les always was brilliant. And Ger, how's Ruthie? I wanna know everything. Actually, the main reason I called is..."

"Maybe you should ask her yourself," Ger replied. "Love, she's being asking to speak to you and rest assured, Earl is onside." Then he did something that took my breath away—actually put my daughter on the phone.

This was it—the shot that I had been waiting for. "Baby, this is Mommy all the way from Winnipeg. Winnipeg, that's where Winnie the Pooh comes from," I began. There was a deafening silence on the other end.

After several abortive attempts, Gerald returned to the phone. "Just give it time, love," he said. "We'll try again next week."

"Absolutely, but Ger, about that incident."

"Nothing to worry about," he insisted.

During the week that followed, I did indeed worry about Gerald. To be honest, however, I so looked forward to the next kick at the can with my daughter that I spent little time reflecting on anything else.

Come the big day, I sat down at the kitchen table, made my voice as gentle as possible. I asked Ruthie about Les. About her doll. About her Dad. *Bupkes, bupkes,* and *bupkes.*

"Now Ruthie, you don't have to say anything if you don't wanna," I eventually ventured, "but bet there's something you *wanna* tell me, isn't there, sweetie?"

A long silence followed.

"I hate Glenda," she suddenly declared. "She *did so* push me—cross my heart and hope to die."

Exactly what had happened, I wasn't sure, but whoever the dastardly Glenda was, I could have kissed her. And so began those little chats of ours. About Winnie, about this fireman's helmet that I was to buy her for Christmas.

"Fireman's helmet?" I asked.

"Yeah, and it needs to be red and real real real hard."

"How come, sweetie?"

"So, you can't get…can't get…"

"Can't get a booboo on your head. That it, sweetie?"

"Uh huh."

"You know, pumpkin, sometimes things happen, and they never happen again. No more booboos on the head in this family. Okay?"

"Um, so Mommy, can I have a toy gun like Les's? It's black, and it goes bang."

The little girl whom I was getting to know anew was clearly en route to becoming a tomboy. What was also clear, she was still spooked. She continued to freeze the first few minutes of a call, and once she yelled, "I hate you," and slammed down the receiver. Nonetheless, when asked if she wanted to speak with me, she generally said yes. A beginning. A definite beginning. Of course, only time would tell how this fraught relationship of ours would unfold. As for her father, eventually, I'd have to talk with the man also—I knew that—owed him a thank-you even, but I was in no hurry on that score.

Now Gerald never did explain what he meant by "incident," and from all indications, last thing he wanted was another person on his case. So I stopped pushing. Ger, be assured that I'd not make that mistake again. Not that the ever present threat to you did not linger in my mind. And not that there was any dearth of reminders of the special jeopardy in which all of God's first born find themselves.

You see, despite our heartfelt conviction that we were better than Torontonians, as I was coming to realize, Winnipeg had its share of bigotry. Sometimes it was against the new "minorities" who now made up the lion's share of Winnipeg's immigrants. That said, walk down the streets of our fair city, and it was pretty clear who was principally getting it in the kisser—Canada's First Nations. And hey, not just in the south-end, but to my dismay, in the north-end itself. While thankfully, my folks did not fall into this trap, oh so many long-time residents had a fixed image of the north-end, and that image was decidedly not Aboriginal. "C'mon," our neighbour Estelle would *cvetch*, "I believe in rights for everyone, but Aberdeen—*vey iz mir*— can you even recognize it any more?" They looked back with nostalgia to "the good old days of the north-end"—the days of the Schwartzes, the Panofskys, and they viewed the change in make-up as a kind of tragedy.

Now to be clear, this was still a few years before the Indigenous presence in Winnipeg swelled to numbers that made it famous throughout the world. But many had come. Fleeing communities where they could not eke out a living, they arrived in the big city, hoping for a better life. They took what meagre shelter they could in ramshackle dwellings along Redwood. They lost jobs for turning up what Europeans deemed late, if they were hired at all. And the remarks that you would hear from people who should have known better!

"That really was exciting!" I exclaimed. "Glad you dragged me out."

It was a nippy day at the start of winter. Still wasted from the withdrawal, I had been sticking close to the house. Rose adamant that it would be good for me to get out, the two of us had just done something long overdue—taken in a basketball game together. We were now heading north on Main, our coats wrapped tightly around us, snow gusting up into our eyes.

"So Rose," I said, "that special shot of what's-her-face's— quite something!"

"Her name is Evans, and it sure is," Rose exclaimed. "The hook shot, it's her tour de force. My guess is that had she been around during the great era of the Edmonton Grads, they'd have snapped her up in a heart beat. And notice how convincingly she fakes a shot before going for the hook. How she manages that is…Oh Nomi, look," Rose suddenly said, her eyes peering into the distance. "You remember Morton."

I wiped my glasses, then focused. Not five yards away stood two men chatting—one balding and in a parka, the other long-haired, with sideburns. Now Morton had been but eighteen with a full head of raven black hair when last I saw him. No question, though, but the prematurely balding man was our Morton.

Eager to reconnect with my childhood buddy, I rushed over. As I neared, I noticed a dark-haired Aboriginal man sitting on the curb a few feet from him, his legs spread out, his head drooping, a bottle of beer in his hands. He had gentle eyes, was wearing an old army jacket. No scarf, despite the weather. Now I was about to greet Morton when he turned to the man with sideburns and exchanged knowing looks.

"Typical," Morton sneered, gesturing toward the Aboriginal man. "About all his kind ever does, eh, Ed?"

"Damn straight," agreed Ed.

"And *those* people…" Morton started to say. Then he noticed the two of us, and his eyes lit up. While he greeted Rose, he positively gushed over me. "Naomi, son of a gun! After all these years!" he exclaimed. "Gained a pound or two, I see. Oh," he added, a smirk spreading across his face, "guess a gent's not supposed to say junk like that to a lady. I hope I haven't offended."

I caught Rose's eye, and she nodded.

"Morton, listen, it's not me you've offended," I told him. "It's the entire Aboriginal community."

"Starting with this man over here," added Rose.

"But the man's drunk as a skunk," objected Morton. "Wouldn't know what we were saying anyway."

"Not so sure of that, and not the point," I answered.

Morton shrugged. "Whatever," he said. "Look, great to bump into you,"—and in seconds, he was gone.

I looked at Rose pointedly. Then I lowered my eyes only to

find the Aboriginal man peering up at me intently.

"Friend of yours?" he asked.

Horrified that he had indeed heard, I sat down on the curb next to him. "Um, really sorry about that, Mr...."

"Name's René," he stated, taking a swig of beer. "Live on Redwood, eh?"

I took out a cigarette, lit up, offered him one. "Naomi, Inkster Boulevard."

"Yeah, yeah. Got a cousin on Inkster. Good place. 'Preciate what you said back there. The Creator, he gave you a good heart, Naomi."

Before long Rose joined us on the curb. Now how we got onto the topic of U. of M. I'm not sure, but René started describing a malicious parody of Aboriginal life that had appeared in a campus newspaper a few years back. "Some of our people," he said, "they raised a stink and the university took note. Usually, though, they could care less, eh?"

As René was talking, the wind picked up. He started to shiver. I removed my scarf. "Please take this," I urged.

He nodded, pulled the scarf around his neck. Then he fished through his pockets and handed me a limestone. "For you," he said. Suddenly, he spotted something—I never did figure out what. Seconds later, he was eyeing the two of us suspiciously.

"René, something wrong?" I asked.

"No offence, Naomi, but mind your own Indian business," he muttered. Then he brushed the snow from his jeans and without another word, staggered off.

Needing to wrap our minds around this unnerving turn of events, instinctively, Rose and I headed for familiar territory, and for hours we hung out at Kelekis, mulling it all over.

"Not sure we'll ever know what made him freak, but you can sure understand the man's distrust," I observed.

As I lay in bed that evening, I thought of René. I thought of the land of the mighty Red River in the days before the white man. And for first time in a long while—too long—I thought of Jack, his trusty radio at his side.

"Hey kiddo, wanna smoke?" I imagined Jack asking. I imagined telling him that I'd made it off the meds and him giving me a pat on the back and warmly exclaiming, "A real turning point—atta girl!" Then I imagined him overhearing Morton's diatribe and turning up the radio just a tad louder.

As I appreciated more with every passing day, making it off the meds *really was* a turning point. Critical aspects of my life improved. I did not slur my words. And better able to function, little by little, I started piecing together bits of a life. I landed part-time work in the typist pool at Manulife. And taking to heart Rose's advice about keeping up on current events, on days when I had the energy I began venturing forth to the old Salter St. library where I would browse through the Winnipeg and Toronto newspapers, delighted that I could read. And read I would—one article after another. I even began contemplating returning to school and beginning a Masters.

What can I say? While I had made substantial progress, I still had blinders on. The thing about blinders, however, is that they tend to slip off when you least expect it.

It was a typical morning toward the tail end of a typical week. I was sitting at my regular table in the library, browsing, as was my wont. The library was relatively deserted—just a solitary figure crouching in the reference section. Ten sections from six different newspapers were scattered about the table. Having skimmed through several articles in *The Winnipeg Free Press* and taken due note of the Schreyer government's latest achievements, I adjusted my glasses and was about to reach for the *Toronto Star* when it struck me that I was sitting on a gold mine. So why restrict myself to newspapers?

Excited at the prospect of expanding my repertoire, I headed to the back of the room, slipped into the stacks. I returned with a book on Milton's *Paradise Lost*. Now as I was struggling with a paragraph on the relevance of Puritanism, I felt myself fading out. Seconds later, I faded back in. While that was a common enough occurrence, I was strangely uneasy. As I turned the page, I realized why. I was on page 24, and while I had a vague recollection of flipping pages, I had almost no recall of the material I had just read. Keeping my cool, I started over. Now to be clear, I did not zone out again, and with every fibre of my being I focused intently on the text before me. Nonetheless, something about the logic evaded me. How come I can manage newspapers and not this?, I asked myself. And suddenly it hit me. With the paper, the content was straight-forward, the pieces short. Of course, there was always the possibility that I simply needed a break.

Opting for the latter explanation—or rather, deciding to put it to the test—I exited the library, took a leisurely stroll down Church St, stopped at a confectionary, had a bite to eat. Half an hour later, more determined than ever, I re-entered the library, this time picked up a book at random, by chance, a fifth-grade math text. Should be a snap, I assured myself. After all, grade five significantly predates the gap in my memory. Metaphorically crossing my fingers, I went straight to the heart of the matter, flipped to a page with test questions, started at the beginning: What is $(5x5) \times 10$? I sat there and stared blankly.

Perspiration trickling down my brow, I sought out an arithmetic text for an earlier grade. Now to my relief, I aced the additions, and I took the first subtraction question in my stride. Then I came across one that utterly flummoxed me: 92 minus 69.

Needing to get some sense of the magnitude of the problem, I grabbed my coat and rushed home. A sense of foreboding beginning to close in on me, I slowly made my way into the living room and approached the piano. Now I had been itching to play it since moving back, but somehow did not dare. However, I had already started drawing back the proverbial curtain, and I was not about to stop.

My heart in a flutter. I sat down, put my fingers to the ivory, plunked out *Twinkle Twinkle Little Star*. My performance, it was competent enough, but if I was being perfectly honest with myself—and it was time to be, wasn't it?—it lacked something—a certain bounce. Next I tried a modest but spirited adult piece, whose name eludes me. Again competent, but woefully uninspired. A bit like ordering sexy lingerie and receiving serviceable underwear. Then mustering up my courage, I took a go at the one piece that had always been my heart's delight—*Moonlight Sonata*. This was the clincher. The very notes were wrong, and nothing I could do would make them come out right. Speaking of scaring the *goyim*, for two long hours I sat on that bench, one discordant screech after another flying from my fingertips.

"Damnation!" I thundered, bringing my fist down on the keys.

Alarm in their eyes, Mom and Dad came rushing into the room. "Something you need help with, Naomi?" Dad asked.

I looked at my parents; I looked at myself looking at my parents. Through my eyes, they were less vibrant than they should be—and their voices, they lacked texture, as it were. Then it hit me like a thunderbolt. Awful though it was, the blur created by the meds had been masking a far larger problem. And all this time I'd been telling myself that once I was drug-free, I…

"Naomi…" Mom began.

"Not now," I insisted.

Knowing that I could ill afford to lose the thread—not after following it this far—I rushed upstairs, stormed into my bedroom, began pacing back and forth. Okay, okay, I said to myself. Whatever extra confusion the meds created, that's over. Time to face facts. Whole skills are gone—skills I'd had since teenaged years and earlier. I can't follow the logic of a simple scholarly text. Can't do elementary arithmetic. Can't play the piano. Get confused on a regular basis. Forget what's said from one minute to the next. And my lost memories, not one has returned. No, not a one. And it would be sheer folly continuing to pretend that they will. There's something else too. I thought back to Rosh Hashanah, to time hanging out with the family. There were moments when the old intensity broke forth—in the presence of ritual, when I flew into a rage, occasionally, even in quiet times with Rose, but except for those fleeting moments, I was no longer fully alive, was I? No wonder Ruthie has such trouble relating to me.

"Damn Dr. Higgins!" I roared. "Damn Earl! Damn the two of them to hell and back!"

Two weeks had passed, and still I was in a rage. I would slam doors with little or no provocation. The thought that this could have happened to me—that an establishment which calls itself a hospital could have done this, that a husband entrusted with his wife's welfare could have done this—it was too much. And now there was no wiggle room, nothing to wait for, no way to qualify. The final verdict was in. I was damaged profoundly. Irreparably. And were I in a position to yank out the cohonies of everyone responsible, I would surely have done so. As it was, alas, only my poor parents were around.

Now Dad kept his distance but otherwise seemed fine. Mom, however, seemed livid with me. It was as if my rage were a personal affront to her.

"And she just keeps flying off the handle," Mom was complaining.

All the way from my room, I could hear their voices. "I heard that," I shouted accusatorily. Then realizing that the woman had a perfect right to say what she wished in her own house, I called out, "Sorry."

"Never mind with the 'sorry.' Get your *tokhes* down here," insisted Mom. "Something I need to say to you."

As I entered the kitchen, Mom was hovering over the counter dicing vegetables, while Rose sat quietly at the table.

"Realize I've been in a foul mood lately," I acknowledged.

"My apologies, but let's get this over with, okay? Cause I'm really not up to company."

Putting aside the kitchen knife, Mom muttered something about family not being company. She looked away, then gradually focused in on me. "No point mincing words. I know why you're *broigez* with me. You think none of this would have happened were it not for what you call 'my feuds.' Wish I could say you're wrong, but I can't."

I glanced at Rose, confused.

"The day you left," Rose explained, "you muttered, 'you and your feuds.'"

Never had it occurred to me that Mom would think such a thing. "Oh Mom," I gushed, instantly calming down, "whatever I said that day, let it go. And really, it's not you I'm pissed with."

Tears began streaming down Mom's face.

"Listen to me," I urged, holding her eyes, "we all fucked up, but none of us did this. Please, Mom, don't put this on yourself."

She smiled awkwardly—her way of acknowledging. And the two of us sat down.

"You know," she observed, "I never thought I'd turn into my own mother, but I guess I did. Your *bubbeh*, she was always on the warpath because of some suspected insult to her husband—all of it such trivial stuff, you couldn't imagine. And before you knew it, half the relatives already we weren't talking to."

"So she's the reason..." began Rose.

"Yes.... But still, immediate family really do have to come first, yeh?" Mom hastily added. "And with men like your father who..."

At this, once again Mrs. Fenster came to mind. "Mom, I know I'm pressing my luck here," I said, "but can I ask you about something else from way back when?"

"So who's stopping you?"

"Now I know that Mrs. Fenster hurt Dad's feelings," I began, "but it was *bupkes*. He'd have been over it in a week—two tops. Why did you make a federal case of it?"

She sat pensively, her hand on her chin. "Afraid this isn't going to make your day, but know what?" she eventually said, her eyebrow arched. "I can't remember."

Rose giggled. Mom glared at her momentarily, but then a grin broke out on her face. The three of us exchanged looks and started to crack up, and for a moment there, my anger was gone. Then I could feel it building up again. "Gotta go," I announced abruptly. "Just not fit company right now." Mom nodded, and I rushed upstairs, threw myself on my bed.

For what seemed like an eternity, I lay there in a blind rage. "How dare they!" I shrieked repeatedly. Then suddenly, something broke. I was not raging any more. I was wailing at the loss of everything that I was or could have been. Now I must have been making more noise than I realized, for before long I could hear Rose outside my door calling my name.

"All right to come in," I whimpered, "but for the love of God, don't fuckin' tell me it's gonna be okay."

Rose cracked open the door, sat down in the doorway, but said nothing—just lent her presence. I continued to sob, only vaguely aware of her, my entire body wracked with convulsions. After a long long while, I could hear movement, then I felt a kiss on my forehead. I reached for my sister's hand, brought it to my lips.

"Nomi, okay if I sit down?"

"Uh huh. And don't worry. I'm through biting everyone's head off. Doesn't taste that great anyway."

Slowly, Rose nuzzled in next to me and gazed into my eyes. "You know, I love you more than I love anyone," she swore. "Always have. Always will."

I nodded.

"Like, I have my own family, right? Great kids, a hubby that I adore. But put it this way: If I didn't have either, so help me, Nomi, I would never let you out of my sight."

"Seems to me I remember a time you didn't," I stated, breaking into a grin, "but you had this idiot sister who was forever running from you. But c'mon, Rose," I teased. "'Fess up. Look at yourself now. Accomplished. Desirable and desired. You really telling me that you could limit yourself to a life of chasing after me?"

She paused. "Well," she said with a suggestive smirk, "maybe if my sister was my brother or like maybe if you grew a penis…"

We both laughed. Once again I caught a glimpse of a woman truly comfortable with her body and everything about it. Then I started to feel the next wave of grief sweeping over me, and I saw Rose's eyes grow concerned again.

"It's okay, Ro," I assured her. "Go home to your husband and kids. I'm just going through what I hafta go through, right?"

"Sure?" she asked.

"Sure? You gotta be kidding!" I answered.

15. NAOMI

1974-1976

OVER THE NEXT YEAR and a half I enjoyed many a Shabbes with my folks—felt my pulse quicken as my father greeted the Shabbes queen. I welcomed in Chanukah at the home of my sister for the very first time, to my delight, saw the faces of my niece and nephew glisten as the dreidel spun before their awe-struck eyes. Oh so often, Rose and I sat inches from one another, listening to each other breathe, picking up on each other's sounds. And with bated breath, I awaited my weekly call with Gerald and Ruthie, savouring every moment as if it would never come again. The blinkers having fallen from my eyes, mostly though, I was locked into a solitary journey in search of the old me, in preparation for the new me through horizons as broad as the prairie sky, through spaces as tight as the eye of a needle. Others could drift in and out, yes? Others could lend a hand. However, with the exception of Rose—and even then only for moments—accompany me, they could not.

Turning those lost years into a full-scale research project, I began by unearthing the names and numbers of classmates that I'd been close to, even contacted several. Only to two did I breathe a word about ECT, for the instant redefinitions of who I was, I did not need. I played it by ear, sharing selectively, cutting awkward lines of questioning off at the pass. Getting used to dealing with tricky situations, this was good practice. And hanging with these old buddies, I discovered many a curious thing about myself. "High holidays with you, what a gas!" exclaimed my friend Joe. "'Member 1965?"

"Remind me," I prodded.

"You know, toking up outside the schul. *High* holidays, right?" he added with a grin.

Once a bit of a pothead, I ticked off in the checkbox in my mind.

I also kept my ear pricked for references to favourite films so that I could watch them anew. Additionally, I conducted an extensive investigation into what I was likely to have read. Now the reading thereby occasioned was tough slogging, at times overwhelming. The trick was not to measure my progress by what would once have been.

Even as I was relearning, brick by brick, I was laying the foundations for a new way of being. Getting into the habit of keeping thorough records, this was essential. If I spoke with Rose—anyone—I'd minute it. If I picked up a book, I would never just read. There beside me would be my trusty index cards. After a couple of paragraphs, I would stop to summarize. At the end of a text, I typically walked away with thirty, forty cards. "My portable intellect," I called it. It even became a running gag in the Cohan family.

"*Oy!* Such terrible news!" Mom would groan. "Naomi's been in a car crash, they had to amputate both legs, and she can't find her portable intellect."

"Why that's horrific!" Rose would exclaim.

"Yeh," Mom would answer. "A real shame about her legs too."

Dad put a somewhat different spin on things. "All these notes, sweetheart," he would say, lifting his feet onto the ottoman, "clearly, you've the makings of a fine Talmudic scholar. You ever consider...?"

Most precarious of all, of course, was the inner journey. I would creep up on myself, as it were, peek through mental doors just barely ajar. Not to see what no longer existed, for sadly, nothing would come of nothing. To take in what lingered and did not linger—the phantom images, the orphaned thoughts that had somehow found dry land and survived the deluge. Enshrouded in mystery, for years now, they had been whispering to me from the threshold of the abyss, almost tangible. Bringing them home—that was the challenge.

Now at first, I drew a blank. Then the path ahead started to clarify.

Closer and closer squeaked the killing machine. Onto my temples, it latched. And fireworks lit up the noonday sky. And the rivers, the streams, the lofty mountains, the very air turned red. Red as the sands of an irate planet. Red as a battlefield drenched in blood. "We've done it. We've breached the barrier," announced a triumphant voice. Even as the voice trailed off, a bittersweet odour filled the air, and an eerie calm set in. Then into the temple of my soul advanced the marauding army, muskets pointing, bugle blaring.

"Take no prisoners," ordered the commanding officer.

Quaking at the menacing sight of the armed invaders, a lone toddler in frayed overalls darted into the woods and hid under the branches of a sycamore tree. As the din of the battle grew louder, the frightened waif wrapped her arms around the trunk, shut her eyes and held on for dear life. When she opened them again, a bullet was shattering her skull. Horrified, I drew close, peered into the luckless infant's eyes and saw that she was me.

And now I grow dizzy. And now I am laid out on a cold grey slab, the smell of death in my nostrils, the pain of the ages echoing through my brain.

I awoke with a start. Just a nightmare, I assured myself, mopping my brow. I reached for the clock. Three-fourteen. I closed my eyes, but for the life of me, couldn't get back to sleep. Something ephemeral, something almost subterranean was clattering away at the base of my skull. With a dread so poignant that I could taste it, I started to climb out of bed, intent on distracting myself. Then it dawned on me. Could this be the break I've been waiting for? I rubbed my eyes, flicked on the light, grabbed a stack of index cards, sat down on the edge of the bed, waited.

This flicker of memory, what is it? I ask. As if a hammer were striking from deep within my skull. "*Pound. Pound. Pound,*" I write. There's something else here, isn't there? Something about Adonoi. I take a deep breath, try to still my racing heart. "*Adonoi,*" I write, "*Mary Mother of God, Buddha, Ishtar, Inanna, Allah, anyone with ears that receive and a heart that quickens, make it stop.*" I pause, light a cigarette, lay in readiness. Another sliver of memory struggles its way into consciousness. And so the process began.

Days later, other fearful words followed. About a chill on my temple. About a sheet bunching up my feet. About a silent scream so shrill that it filled the universe. Nothing extensive. Precious little when you consider the stretch of time in question. No question, though, what was staring me in the face—ECT memories, lone survivors, bold swimmers who had swum their little hearts out and somehow made it to dry land.

Even as I was recording these memories, I pursued complementary lines of inquiry. I pumped Gerald for information. More importantly, with the aid of an attorney, I got hold of my hospital record. Now that medical masterpiece, that was a whole different kettle of fish. In all fairness, however, it was likewise instructive, and in more ways than one.

The term "unladylike" appeared five times—no sexism there, right? The term "inappropriate," twenty-seven times. Seems us loonies have a singular talent for it. What was especially revealing, even the most mundane biographical detail ended up sounding like a disease—including something as innocuous as wearing glasses. I kid you not. Quote: "This be-spectacled patient has limited affect," wrote someone called "A. R." (See Naomi Smith, St. Patrick-St. Andrew's, p. 16 line 12.)

"Be-spectacled, eh?" observed Mom wryly. "Hope it's not catchy."

"Yeah," I quipped, "and good thing that they didn't notice I'm also be-trousered, be-fingered, and be-cigaretted."

Now at one point I became so incensed that such a caricature passed as official truth—that this is what our institutions do—that I angrily flung the document into a waste bin. Keenly aware of what was at stake, ten minutes later I fished it out, sat down on the edge of my bed, and started combing the record for hard facts—dates, types of treatment, concrete actions. Next I tried to link the clinical record with my phantom words. Initially, I came up short. Then thankfully, I thought of Rose.

"So Rose," I noted as we hunched over the kitchen table the following day, "you said you had your worst migraine on July 12. On July 12, I had ECT. Fits. Now Ro, this may sound totally bananas, but any of these passages resonate with the worst migraine ever?"

Acting as if she'd been asked a perfectly normal question—and that was her way—Rose picked up one index card, stared at it, picked up another. "Like, most of these thoughts just aren't mine, but Nomi, see this," she said, pointing to the line 'I am a totally blank wall.' "I do remember feeling like that once, and I know approximately when."

And so it is, bit by bit, my shock history was reassembled.

Critical though all the components were, not surprisingly, most of my time was spent getting the snatches of memory down in black-and-white. At first, I concentrated on the handful surrounding the administration of ECT. Eventually, I focused in on the stretch between coming to in the corridor and going off meds. Soon I had literally thousands of cards. Fine to initially use cards, I realized, but for this to provide yeoman's service in the taxing years to come, I needed greater order. Also a form that would allow new material to be added readily. Hence, a system of binders materialized.

I began with a single black binder. Before long, there were so many binders that I was having trouble keeping track. So I transferred all the material in the last black binder into a red binder and continued on. My own system of colour coding, yes?

Now throughout this period, frequently, I called to mind the *tashlich*. The trick was not just retrieving, it was letting go. And let go, I did. Of memory as we know it, years of my life, passions. I even accepted that at best I'd end up a filmmaker of passing interest only—strictly amateur at that.

Of course, when something's particularly dear to our heart, it's easy to trick oneself, yes? Thankfully, my folks saw it—saw it loud and clear.

It was a good day to shoot. The drizzle having let up, the grass was sparkling in the noonday sun. My eyes keen, my grip firm, I was crouched on the sidewalk directly in front of our house, my movie camera in hand, a folded-up script peeking out of my back pocket. Intent on my mission, I aimed the camera at the boulevard, slowly began advancing toward it. Shortly thereafter, I zoomed in on those breathtaking tulips that for days now had been blossoming with whimsical abandon at the entrance to Mrs. Goldman's porch. If I could but capture the beauty!, I marvelled, moving in for the close-up. If I could make visible the dance!

The film rapidly used up, I rushed home, descended the basement stairs where a simple makeshift setup awaited—a projector on a wobbly table, a standard-sized screen on the wall. Leaning forward, I threaded the projector. With great apprehension, I turned it on. And what appeared? A series of lifeless panning shots, a hodgepodge of grass and tulips—no rhyme or reason to it.

Albeit disappointed, intending to get right back on that horse, I jotted down several pointers, then quickly reloaded the camera. Mounting the stairs, I arrived in the kitchen to find Mom home early, her cartwheel hat on, a huge smile on her face.

"You look like the cat that ate the canary," I mused. "Must have made a sale."

"Sure did. You know the old Ostry house on Landsdowne? Got $25,000 for it."

Now as I was congratulating Mom, her eyes fell on the movie camera. "I see you're still slugging away, yeh?," she observed, sitting down across from me. Then a concerned look came over her. "You know, Naomi," she observed, "it's been months now. If it didn't make you miserable, I'd say, 'what's the harm?'" Then she caught my eye, and her face melted. "Oh baby, film—this is what you've lived for since you were just a little *pisher*. It's awful—really awful," she murmured, "but you *do* know it isn't working, yeh?"

I looked at her, looked away, then nodded. And that evening when the family trundled over to Kelekis to celebrate the sale, I did what I had to—left the camera behind.

A few times over the next several days I considered trying a still camera. But why would that be any different? Eventually, I picked up several balls of yarn from the market and began knitting my daughter a scarf. As I sat on the couch trying to remember whether to knit stitch or purl stitch, now and then Dad would pass by, stop and stare at me. His eyes would narrow as if he were trying to figure out something. Yet he would say nothing.

"Damn it, Nomi, purl stitch," I muttered to myself. Two weeks had passed. During that time, my otherwise accomplished sister had let our mother butt into her personal business on four separate occasions, had even let Mom inveigle her into reading a treatise on the virtues of monogamy. "Let her walk all over you, why don't you?" Sam had exclaimed. My knitting needles in hand, I was in the living room, leaning back on the couch, now staring in disbelief at the lop-sided scarf on my lap, now wondering what it would take for Ro to stand up to Mom. I had just started to unravel a particularly problematic section when in waltzed Dad. I figured that he was here to watch me again—not my idea of sterling entertainment, but what the hell?—but no, something had to be up, for there was a meticulously wrapped package under his arm.

"So my Otto Preminger," he said, "your mother tells me things aren't going so hot."

I nodded. "Actually Dad, if you're referring to my not-so-budding film career, I let it go a few weeks back, but I'm fine. Honest."

"You know what I would feel in your place? That God never closes one door but he slams another. But what can we expect? A God at our beck and call?"

I shrugged. "Incidentally, you old softie, whatchya got there?"

"What? A man can't pick up a little something for his own daughter?"

Demonstrably pleased with himself, he proceeded to hand me the package, settle into his favourite chair, plunk his feet onto the ottoman, then sit there beaming.

"Not my birthday," I pointed out, already beginning to tug excitedly at the wrapping. "Not Chanukah. So Dad, what is this?"

"Let's just say another door," he answered.

As the wrapping peeled off that present, I could see it coming— a Leika still camera, not unlike the one he'd picked up for me decades ago, but with more bells and whistles. How did he know?

"Dad, it's wonderful," I gushed, touched and more than a little apprehensive. "And if I screw this up too, you know, that doesn't stop it from being wonderful."

He straightened his *yarmulke*, smiled knowingly. "If you make mistakes, is that so terrible? You know what mistakes are? God's way of providing guidance."

I must have been receiving a whole lot of divine guidance— for to say that my first pictures were bad would be a gross understatement. An unmitigated disaster, they were—out of focus, tops of heads lopped off! The thing is, though, unlike with arithmetic or film, to my surprise, with a modicum of work, they improved dramatically. Partly, I suspect, because I'd been taking still pictures forever. Partly because of the relative simplicity. I didn't have to keep track of a long drawn-out operation. One shot is one shot, yes? The thing was to trust my instinct, break a rule or two, wait till the time was ripe.

I began with a subject that I knew like the back of my hand. "*Oy!* Not this again," exclaimed Rose. "All right—you old rotter— but do you ever owe me!"

Over the next few weeks, I took several rolls of Rose, also one of her partner, Lisa. And while there were four or five duds per roll, the rest were minimally passable.

Now it was around this time that Sam began begging for pictures of the kids. "C'mon, sister-in-law-woman," he insisted. "You've got an eye for it. And we're family."

"Okay, but so it won't be a total loss, let's combine it with a trip to the zoo," I suggested. "Be a treat for the kids."

The trip was a hoot for all three of us. Larry made a face at a monkey. I clicked the shutter. A single peanut in her hand, Dana timidly reached into the elephants' cage. Click. I examined the photos a few days later. A Cartier-Bresson, I wasn't, but I would have to admit, there was a certain something there. An unusual use of light. A slight off-centre touch that seemed to work. I just needed practice. And practice, I did.

Now one day, I was examining an image that I had captured of a panting German Shepherd, the unmistakable look of doggie bliss on his face, and something of singular importance dawned on me. My relationship with the camera, it was hardly just technical. The camera, it was my other eye. Almost—dare I think it?—an ECT-free eye. Subtler, more penetrating, it was letting me see what my naked eye could not—providing texture, vibrancy, nuance. And what hidden worlds it sought to uncover!

The camera as a way of unveiling our neighbourhood, this particularly spoke to me. Significantly, unlike in early years, I was not drawn to any of the famous north-end sites. The way of life, the telling gesture—this was my passion.

I happened upon an old woman blowing on her whitened fingers tips as she stood at a bus stop on Salter. I aimed, I shot. Nothing particular in mind, I lingered outside a dingy little pawn shop on Selkirk, waited patiently as customers ambled in and out. In drifted an athletic man wearing a sheepskin jacket and earmuffs. In went a mother and child, both in duffle coats. Suddenly, three young men in parkas appeared, the youngest pulling a toboggan. While the youth with the toboggan waited on the sidewalk, into the shop filed the other two, determined looks on their faces. Some time later the men made their way out carrying a large television set, their arms straining under the load. A small crowd gathered as they began lowering that baby onto the toboggan. I raised my camera. Instinctively, I stepped back so as to include the amazement on the faces of the children. I stood in readiness as the young men bent at the knees—further, further. I saw their breath turn to steam in the frigid air. I saw one corner of the television touch the toboggan. I saw the jaw of one of the children drop. I clicked.

Now one afternoon, as I was crouching outside of Gunns Bakery adjusting the aperture, I was approached by an old bridge partner of Mom's—the indefatigable Mrs. Federman. "Your mother's been showing me some of your photos," she observed. "So you willing to be the official photographer at my grandson's bar mitzvah or what?" Now if you knew Mrs. Federman, you would know that "what" was not an option, though argue with the woman, I did.

"Really not good enough yet," I pointed out.

"Is nothing," she assured me. "Just a small family affair."

One hundred and twenty-four people attended that small family affair. In the fullness of time, twenty-eight became clients. Soon I began picking up jobs as well from Rittberg Realty.

The time came when I was able to cut back to once a week on my typist job, actually set up as a photographer. I charged for most of my services. Did First Nations and feminist events for free. A way to give something back, yes?

Of course, I differed in key respects from other photographers. I had to toss a higher percentage of my photos, and I relied on my sister to do the books. Nonetheless, in its own inimitable way, it was working. Continuing to make it mine—that was the ticket.

I was sitting at the kitchen table, a stack of my finest photographs before me. Placing one after another, I was testing out different arrangements, with an eye to a possible exhibit. And that's when it hit me. I was no longer Naomi Smith—mental patient. For however long it lasted, I was Naomi Cohan—photographer.

Eager to celebrate, I slipped on my coat. Then I slung a sweater over my shoulder and headed south, humming to myself as I made my way through the snow-lined streets. I stopped to offer the sweater to Danny—a homeless teenager who hung out at College and Main. I bought a hotdog from the legendary street vendor Arty the Farty—I kid you not, a close personal friend of Schmuel the Fool, sworn enemy of Hecky Schmecki, and cousin twice removed of Foyer the Lawyer—and with a gusto that I'd not experienced in ages, I proceeded to devour it in three bites. I located a confectionary, where I purchased four different types of sugar-free candy for Mom. Next, I dropped in at that *heimish,* old hangout—North-Winnipeg Smokes, *kibitzed* with the owners, who knew from everyone's business, swapped Emma Goldman stories, picked up wine-tipped cigars for Dad. Then I flagged down a cab, got off in the market area, where I found a panda bear for Ruthie, a pants suit for Rose, a silk shirt for Sam, a wickedly provocative Marlene Dietrich poster for Gerald. "Dietrich in a top hat and tux—*oy,* I don't mind telling you, if I were twenty years younger, I wouldn't be adverse to *schtupping* her myself!" confided seventy-year-old Mrs. Weiss, glancing at her husband suggestively.

When I arrived home, my folks were at the dining room table. Bent over a cribbage board, they were needling each other mercilessly, each angling to throw the other off their game. A bottle of insulin was sitting in front of Mom, a used syringe next to it.

"How come another shot today? You okay?" I asked Mom.

"Happens some time. Not to worry. So whatchya got there?"

I immediately handed everyone their presents, watched their faces light up. Then I eyed the two intently. "Look," I said, "something I need to tell you. I'm gonna be able to manage. You know, have a real life despite everything."

Tears in his eyes, Dad rushed over, plied me with kisses.

Mom let out a huge sigh of relief. "I've been waiting to hear you say that," she exclaimed. "So, when you going to sue for custody?"

"C'mon Mom," I reminded her, "you know that's not in the cards."

"So I want to bring my daughter and granddaughter together—the crime of the century! Shoot me."

As I retired that night, Mom's dreams for Ruthie and me lingered in my mind. No, I was not about to sign onto Mom's agenda. Clearly, Ruthie belonged with her father. About one thing, however, Mom was undeniably right: I had to find a way to become a larger part of my daughter's life. Visiting Toronto, that was something I just could not face. But Ruthie and Earl, could they not visit Winnipeg—perhaps stay at my folks?

Next day I passed the idea by Gerald. "Can see that," he said, "but love, you really have to talk to Earl." I passed the idea by Mom. Not only was she agreeable, she immediately began planning where to take her granddaughter.

"And of course, if we accidentally lose your "ex" during one of our excursions, what's the harm?" teased Mom.

That evening, I plunked myself in front of the phone with every intention of dialing Earl. As I lifted the receiver, however, that year of unbridled horror began swirling through my head. I saw Naomi Smith searching up and down Palmerston, not a clue how to find her home. I saw Earl grimacing and sticking pills under her nose. And like the swallows in the still of March, it all came rushing back. My heart pounding, I laid down the receiver and walked away.

And so another month passed, interesting in the way life is, however, with no real movement on the Ruthie front. Maybe because I wasn't ready. Maybe because no one quite was.

Then came a moment that was to test the mettle of each and every one of us.

Pound. Pound. Pound. It was early morning, and that infernal banging would not stop. Not able to get my bearings, I pulled the covers over my head, praying that the orderly, Nurse Ann—whoever it was—would take the hint and make themselves scarce.

"Naomi," a voice called out.

"I don't want it. I don't want it," I shrieked.

"It's okay, baby—nothing like that," I could hear Mom clucking. "It's Mom, yeh? But you really do need to get up."

"Mom?"

"Sweetie, Earl's on the phone."

"At this hour?"

"Oh *bubeleh*, he says it's an emergency."

16. NAOMI

TERRIFIED THAT SOMETHING had happened to Ruthie, I pulled on my jeans and tore down the stairs, only vaguely aware that I was about to speak with the very man whom I had been fleeing for over two years. I entered the hall, grabbed the phone while Mom followed at a distance, peering at me nervously.

"Earl, it's Nomi. For the love of God, what's happened to her?"

A stillness set in—thick as the dust on the keys of an idle piano.

"Earl, tell me."

"Her?" he finally answered. "Sorry, Missus. Should've been clear. It's not Ruthie."

I breathed a sigh of relief, called out to Mom that Ruthie was fine. Then suddenly, I knew. "It's Gerald, isn't it? Oh Earl, is he ... is he...?"

"No. He's alive, but it's not good, and Miu's nowhere to be found." Shaken to the quick, he proceeded to stammer out that there had been some sort of attack, that he'd arrived home to find Ger flaked out on the porch, drifting in and out of consciousness. "Nomi," he cried, "the man's hurt—hurt bad."

I took a deep breath, knowing full well where my next words would propel me. "I'll be on the next plane to Toronto," I told him.

"Was hoping you'd say dat. If there were anyone else, I..."

Then his voice grew thin and he added, "but Missus, you really can do this? Can handle travelling alone and...?"

There it was—that infantilization that whisked the ground out from under a person—and I had to deal with it—and better now than later.

"Look, no one's asked me a question like that in a long time. Let's just assume we're all adults here and try to pull together for Ger's sake, okay? So which hospital?"

"No hospital, Missus. We're at my place."

"But why...?"

"Christ, Nomi! You know perfectly well why. Now, sorry to be draggin' you into this. And if you want out..."

I got an image of Gerald, naked and vulnerable, the astounded eyes of nurses and doctors overwhelming him, even their seemingly benign curiosity a violation. "I love him too. And I'm in," I announced.

Seconds later, I was explaining to Mom, giving her the names and number of clients to call. Then the two of us rushed upstairs to pull together a few changes of clothes.

"Just be careful," she urged. "Don't let that *meshugener* talk you into anything."

Now I assured her that I would only be staying until Gerald was back on his feet and we'd come to some kind of understanding about Ruthie. Nonetheless, she continued to look at me uneasily. Then we both fell silent, as if worried that words would betray us.

"You'll call every day, yeh?" she finally asked, reaching over and touching my cheek. "Now Naomi, I'm not saying it's wrong to go, but I'll tell you something. When people get thrown together, nothing remains simple. *Bupkes*."

I nodded, quickly zipped up my overnight bag, furious with myself for having let Gerald blow off all discussion of the earlier incident. "Mom," I uttered, taking her hand in mine, "all that love you and Dad've been lavishing on me, that's why I'm able to do this." She smiled, gave me a kiss on the cheek, though it was clear that she was secretly praying that I'd change my mind.

Half way down the stairs, I turned around. "One other thing…" I started to say.

"Yeh-yeh, call Rose, tell her what's cooking. Like I couldn't figure that one out!"

Minutes later, Mom's warning echoing in my ears, I was out the front door, en route to the very house which I had moved mountains to escape, about to face the man who but yesterday I could not bring myself to speak to. Ger, while I have no regrets, be assured that no one but you or Ruthie could have induced me to come.

I stepped onto the porch of the Palmerston house—a visitor and not a visitor. Quickly, I glanced around. The solitary pine by the fence showed little sign of life—hopefully, not a harbinger of things to come. I held my breath, rang the doorbell, praying that Gerald was holding his own. After what seemed like an eternity, I heard movement in the hall. Then abruptly, the door sprang open, and there he was—the man of my nightmares—his plaid shirt on, his hair unkempt, his face worn. Oh my! This exhausted *shtick* of a human being, he was a far cry from the boogeyman that I had been dreading. It was clear that he was apprehensive, and I knew that we would have to talk. At the moment, all I wanted was to see my poor abused friend.

Earl invited me in, gave me a peck on the cheek, said the fever was down.

"And the children, how they taking it?" I asked.

"I've told them he's sick. So of course, they're upset."

Suddenly he shook his head. "Damn it, Nomi!" he exclaimed. "While I'm grateful to you for coming, this is not how I imagined the two of us hooking up again."

"Oh Earl, I'm so sorry for what you're going through, and me being here like this, it must be strange for you, for me also, but eventually the two of us will talk—promise."

Earl nodded. "Brace yourself," he warned. "Oh and Nomi," he added, "we're still in the dark about what happened. See what you can coax out of him, okay?"

Then to my surprise, he led the way to the basement. Utterly transformed from the unfinished cellar of two years ago, oak-panelled it was, a fridge, stove and counter toward the window, two rooms off the dining area, bright florescent lighting overhead. Now barely had we descended the last stair when a piteous groan shot through the space.

"My God, Earl, where is he?" I cried.

We took the door to our left, entered a bed-sitting room complete with lounge chair and curtains. Belying the cheerful décor, there stretched out on a bed was a mercilessly ravaged being, unrecognizable were it not for the flannel pajamas. Ger's face was badly cut—its contours all but obliterated. And there was an unnatural tightness to his jaw.

Trying not to wake him, I tiptoed to his side. I knelt down, gently pulled back the blanket. His abdomen had been bandaged and blood was seeping through. As Earl begins to comment, suddenly Gerald's eyes flicker. Then he opens them with a start, peers desperately about.

"Gerald, it's Nomi," I murmur. "Fella, you're safe; and Earl and I and are both here."

"Nomi," he utters through a tightly held jaw.

"Sorry to put you through this, but there's something I need to look at," I eventually say. "Sweetie, if it hurts to talk, don't. Just nod or shake your head."

He nods. Then with great care, I part his lips. Wire. Clearly his jaw has been wired shut. So he *has* received professional medical attention somewhere along the line.

Now as I release my hold, he tries to communicate. To his obvious consternation, however, his words are so garbled that neither of us can make them out. I place an index card on a book, extend it toward him, deposit a pen in his hand. Shaking from the effort, he scribbles down several barely legible words, then peers up expectantly. "Had to leave hospital. Appointment Dr. Hunt Dec. 3. Remove wire," it reads.

"We understand," I assure him. "Now sweetheart, that's over a month away. Right now, let's just focus on getting you better. Now if you can remember where Miu is, we'll contact her. Otherwise, we'll..."

Again Gerald begins fumbling with the pen. We steady his hand. "Called Miu right after attack," he writes. "Said couldn't go through this again."

"She disappeared a few times before," whispers Earl. "I doubt she'd have taken off had she an inkling how serious it was. Probably be back."

Whereupon Gerald begins to whimper.

"Oh Ger," I say, holding his eyes, "I wish things weren't so awful. But listen, wherever she is, Miu loves you. And Earl and I, we're sticking right by your side."

He nods. Seconds later, he begins coughing, and terror shoots through his eyes. I act quickly to support his jaw. Again, he grows calm. I take his hand in mine, moved at the sudden realization how tiny it is—rather like a child's. Almost contentedly, he murmurs my name. Then back surges the horror, and he starts to howl with such ferocity that Earl and I fear that he'll harm himself.

My heart breaking, I catch Earl's eye. "Sorry if what I am about to do embarrasses you," I murmur. Then I strip off my shirt and crawl into bed next to Gerald, placing his head on my bosom.

And calm goes his breathing. And ever so slowly, he drifts to sleep.

Whatever had befallen Gerald—and aside from the obvious, we could only guess—it had left him in a terrible predicament. The very fact of being alive seemed to fill him with dread. And every time the terror came upon him, up would shoot his temperature.

The gravity of the situation upon us, and intent on doing what we could, the next several hours, Earl and I spelled each other off, always ensuring that at least one of us was by Gerald's side. We placed a cot next to his bed so that Earl could catch some shut-eye. With bated breath, we cleaned the wounds, wound fresh bandages around him, all the while reminding him who we were, that we would never hurt him. We gave him aspirin. Blending and adding water so that it could be sucked in through a straw, we fed him liquid vegetables. I began pulling together the ingredients for chicken soup. Earl began calling every Tom, Dick, and Harry that could conceivably shed light on Miu's whereabouts. And briefly, Earl and I talked, though about immediate practicalities only.

He was now chair of the mathematics department, he explained. So there was money enough for us to order in for supper. I shouldn't worry about the sleeping arrangements—we'd take turns catnapping next to Gerald and using the master bedroom. And yes, Les and Ruthie knew that I'd be here when they returned from school.

Now Ger would cringe at the slightest sound, and he kept staring anxiously at the door, as if anticipating an intruder. Inevitably, sooner or later, he would pass out. And moved to tears, Earl and I would struggle to make sense of the gut-wrenching scene that we had just witnessed.

"You know what I think?" Earl conjectured. "Just follow me here. He was in a place he considered safe—maybe a familiar butch hangout—so let down his guard. Then a vile s.o.b.—a homophobe, whatever—suddenly barges in."

Now all our suppositions had a ring of plausibility, but something didn't quite add up. The depth of terror. The extent of the injury. That almost claustrophobic look as if the walls were closing in. And over time, I got the strangest feeling that we would never know the whole story, for this was one of those occasions where knowing—indeed, even speculating—was an affront to dignity.

Be that as it may, to our relief, Gerald gradually accepted that in this one room, anyway, he was safe. While he'd inevitably startle upon opening his eyes, he would soon recognize us and begin breathing more easily. By late afternoon, additionally, his temperature was treading lower. And for a moment, a calm set in. The arrival of the children, however, signalled hurricane season. It was also my next reminder that I was hardly a stranger in this house.

"Where's Momma Gerald? I wanna see him. I wanna see him," yelled Les.

"Me too," declared Ruthie. "And you said Mommy was gonna be here."

"Yeah," shouted Les. "Liar, liar, pants on fire. Hang'em up from a telephone wire."

All the way from the basement, you could hear them. Eventually, an exhausted Earl crawled downstairs and collapsed on the cot.

"You've been up all night. I'll talk to them," I offered.

When I arrived in the kitchen, there were the two children, white as a sheet, looking considerably older than I remembered.

The second that he laid eyes on me, Les lit up, came running into my arms. Hiding behind her bangs, meanwhile, Ruthie peeked at me uneasily. Then her chin began to tremble, and she asked, "Mommy?"

I nodded. She stood there, uncertain. Holding one arm around Les, I extended the other toward her. She started to back away, then stopped. And to my relief, eventually, into my arms also she came.

After we all had a long hug, we hit the living room, snuggled together on the couch. "Listen, kids," I told them, "I know you're upset, but we need to pull together now, yes? You know, like the crew of the Star Ship Enterprise. Now Momma Gerald is sick—too sick for you to see right now—but he's doing better and it won't be long before..."

"He's dying, isn't he?" insisted Les, tears rushing to his eyes.

"Is that what you've been thinking? Oh sweetie, no. Honest."

He looked at me with suspicion. "Liar, liar, pants on..." he started up again.

"Sha," I urged, raising my finger to my lips. "Les, you're a bright boy. Now think. Would Daddy Earl have sent you to school if Momma Gerald were dying?"

Les's forehead scrunched up as he considered the proposition. "No," he conceded.

"What about Momma Miu? Is she dying too?" inquired Ruthie.

"No one's dying. And Momma Miu's just away. You know, sometimes adults have to get away."

"Like you?" asked Ruthie, her eyes open wide.

"Not exactly, pumpkin, but somewhat. Hey? You want a for-sure, don't you?"

"Uh huh."

"Sometimes, you know, adults only have a few for-sures. Anyway, kids, this I can tell you for sure. No one's dying. Momma Miu's away for a bit. And Momma Gerald, he's sick right now. And you know what someone needs when they're sick? A whole lot of sleep," I suggested, lowering my voice to a hush. "And how can we help them sleep?"

"By being very, very quiet?" Ruthie whispered in my ear.

"By being very, very quiet," I whispered back.

Now Les seemed to have accepted that Ger was going to recover, and unlike Ruthie, he was not remotely worried about Miu. "She takes off all the time," he explained—informative in its own right. And seemingly at ease, to my surprise, he shifted into a different gear entirely. He specified which of his classmates had the largest muscles. Then came a humdinger. "Psst, Nomi," he whispered, his hand cupping his mouth, a mischievous glint in his eye, "can I ask you something?"

"Why do I get the feeling that I should say no?" I quipped.

"If I wash my cock real real clean, will you suck it?"

"Oh Les, that's gross."

"C'mon, Nomi. You're s'pposed to say 'no.' Darn! Now I have to start over. Okay, here goes: If I wash my cock real real clean, will you suck it?"

"No," I screamed.

An impish grin spreads across Les's face. "So what are you anyway?" he whispered. "A *dirty cock* sucker?"

I groaned, despite my best effort not to. "Very funny. Look. Jokes like that, they're not something women appreciate. Bet Momma Gerald doesn't like them either."

Les looked away and went silent.

"It's okay, Les. We all screw up when we're upset. Anyway, make you a deal. No more dirty jokes, and you can tell four clean ones."

"*Five* clean ones," countered Les, looking up at me again. "Deal?"

"Deal."

Now Les never did crack any more jokes that day—just kept glancing nervously in the direction of the basement. Nor could he bring himself to eat supper. Nor could either child understand why they couldn't at least bid goodnight to Gerald. "Not fair," Les insisted. And as I was tucking in Ruthie, she started to cry.

"Oh pumpkin, Ger-Ger really is getting better," I assured her.

Ruthie remained closed-lipped for several minutes. Just stared at the wall. Then she whirled around, eyed me suspiciously, and out it came. "You gonna be here when I get up?" she asked.

"That's a for-sure."

"But then you'll go away and be gone for a million years."

"It's been hard for you, baby, hasn't it?"

"If I had a little girl, I wouldn't leave her for a million years."

I knelt down, gave her a kiss on the cheek. "And if you had a little girl," I asked, "what special things would you do for her?"

"Well, I'd brush her hair—oh, and I'd be sure to bake her favourite cake."

And what sort of cake would that be?"

"Chocolate-chocolate, all gooey."

That night as I lay on the cot next to Gerald, mopping his brow, trying to allay his fears, I wrote myself several notes including, "bake gooey chocolate cake." Would that the rest of her wish list were so simple, but now that the ice had been broken, surely Earl and I could figure out something. She was *our kid*, and clearly, we had to.

Over the next several weeks, Gerald continued to gather strength. Soon he was able to sit up, make it to the washroom and back. To an appreciable degree, his confidence returned. Nonetheless, he kept his own counsel, despite our frequent requests for information—*any* information. It was not just that fear had nested deep in his soul. The man seemed humiliated.

There was something else too. While it became noticeably easier for him to talk, he was loath to do so. Occasionally, he would murmur the odd word—call out my name, Miu's name. Mostly, however, he retreated into a bubble of silence—not like someone afraid to speak, more like a person who had made a decision. And again and again he would turn his face to the wall—just stare at it blankly.

The silence, did it comfort Ger? Would it gobble him up if he lingered too long?

Only about Miu did he ever inquire and even at that, only in a guarded way utterly uncharacteristic of the man we knew. At approximately seven p.m. each day as we brought him his supper, he would hand us a note reading, "Any word?" Now for a long while, we hadn't a thing to report. By the end of the second week, however, Earl had unearthed two salient facts. One: that Miu had headed north to mull things over. Two: and this we found particularly promising—she was expected back at work in a few months' time. Now we were hoping that the news would lift Gerald's spirits. When we told him, however, he merely nodded, then closed his eyes.

What particularly worried us, even the children held little interest for him. And consistently, he declined to see them. "Gerald, the kids really miss you," Earl would state. "Okay if they come say hello?" And Ger would just lie there and shake his head. So we kept telling them that it was not yet time.

By the beginning of the third week, the kids were chomping at the bit. "I wanna see Momma Gerald, I wanna see Momma Gerald," hollered Les.

"Please, Ger," we implored him, "let them come down if only for a minute." To our growing frustration, however, again with that shake of the head.

"Had fuckin' enough of this. We're letting them visit," swore Earl one day, throwing up his hands. "Case closed."

"The hell we are!" I shot back. "The man's depressed for God's sake. Forcing things on people—that your answer for everything?"

Now clearly, this issue had the potential of becoming a major bone of contention between Earl and me. Nor had I the foggiest idea what to do if he acted on his words.

What a gorgeous day it was! I peered out the kitchen window, saw the regal sun spreading its resplendent robes everywhere. Dying to cut loose and drink in the brilliance, I slipped on my green leather jacket, zipped up Ruthie's and Les's coats, took a stroll with the kids. With Les thankfully providing a running commentary on our whereabouts, we veered north-east and happened upon a pocketed-sized park called "St. Albans". Clearly a dog-owner's delight, for a half dozen mutts were romping about. Ruthie bent down to pet a puppy. Then at the kids' behest, we stopped to play Simon Says.

"Don't like this game any more," Ruthie soon announced, upset at finding herself eliminated. "Why can't we ever play 'I'm Thinking?'"

Les willing, the three of us sat down on one of the benches, started the new game. "I'm thinking of someone just feet away who has four legs," Les stated. Ruthie quickly guessed that it was the puppy, and then it was her turn. "Okay," she said, observing me coyly, "I'm thinking of someone just feet away who wears a green jacket and ... and who I hate."

At this, Les eyed my jacket. "Millions of people that could be," he immediately said.

I assured Les that everything was okay, asked if he could give Ruthie and me some alone-time, and after he had beetled off, I looked at my daughter. "You know, pumpkin," I said, "it's okay to hate me."

Instantly, Ruthie's eyes began to tear. "You aren't gonna go away forever and ever just cause I hate you, are you?"

"Sure not. And if you have something you're finding it hard to say, don't worry. Whatever it is, it won't send me away forever and ever."

"I wanna see Ger-Ger, I wanna see Ger-Ger," she screamed.

And I would have to confess, just for a moment, Earl's solution was sounding good.

Now we sent the kids to play at a neighbour's for the rest of the day. However, in the fading hours of the afternoon as I lay in bed reading, there came a gentle tap at the door. I opened it, expecting to see Ruthie. To my surprise, it was Les, his chin quivering.

"Oh Les dear, what is it?" I asked.

"Nomi, someone hurt my daddy, didn't they?"

There it was—the folly of secrets. I knelt down, put my hand on the poor boy's shoulder, and looked him in the eye. "Sweetie, yeah," I said.

Another day with no solution. Another fight with Earl. I started pulling together the ingredients for Gerald's supper and switched on the blender, wondering if there were anything that we could say to Ger that would release us all from this stranglehold. I poured the liquid into a glass, inserted a straw, crept downstairs.

Gerald was sitting upright in bed, a note in his left hand. He had clearly made an effort, for his hair was combed and the unmistakable odour of Old Spice wafted through the room. "Well how about that? Hi there, handsome," I said, passing him the glass.

Ger nodded, took one sip, then as expected, handed me the note. My muscles clenched as I peered down at it, for how I had come to dread that question! To my astonishment, on the index card were the words: "Ready to see kids."

"Gerald," I exclaimed, looking into his eyes, "this is great. Really great! So you aren't lost in there? You *do* know what you're doing?"

"Yes and no," he wrote.

Now part of me was itching to find out more. Last thing any of us could afford, however, was to let the moment pass. So I kissed him on the forehead, then rushed upstairs to find Earl.

"Ger-Ger isn't talking right now," Earl explained to the kids, "but he hears everything. So you can tell him what you like—about school, whatever."

Earl and I both held our breath as we ushered the kids down those stairs. We opened the door. Ruthie took one look at Gerald and went flying into his arms. "Ger-Ger, I'll make you better," she cried out.

At that precise moment a glint entered Les's eye. Defying everyone's notion of decorum, he made a fist, brought his arm back, then his hand advancing in slow motion, pretended to thump Gerald on the snout. Now for a second there, Gerald looked aghast. So did Earl. Then Ger's face relaxed. And for the first time in ages, the beginnings of a smile began to play around his lips.

With the new dispensation, life in the Smith household took an abrupt turn. Earl and I stopped bickering. The kids looked happier. And although Gerald's disposition could hardly be described as sunny, his eyes would light up the second that he heard the pitter-patter of little feet on the stairs.

Earl and I noticed the difference, came to an executive decision, and soon the basement bedroom became a veritable drawing room, a silent Gerald holding court. We hauled out the desk, squeezed in a couple more chairs, and Gerald would point to indicate who had the floor. Now mostly, Gerald called the shots. Nonetheless, he kept ending up a captive audience for all of Les's jokes. Also for a series of photographs henceforth known as the "Gerald Collection".

Actually, the Gerald Collection opened up a brand new vista for me and the kids, for they took an avid interest in how their favourite person was portrayed. We'd sit together, scrutinize the photos. "Like this one best," Ruthie would say, pointing to a picture of Gerald winking at the children. Also, we would decide as a family what to shoot next.

"Okay, everyone," I said, adjusting the reflectors, "so yesterday we did Gerald Sipping Through Straw. What's your pleasure today?"

"HOW ABOUT GERALD KICKING PHOTOGRAPHER'S BUTT?" Gerald scribbled in big black letters.

And to Ger's obvious delight, with the aid of a second camera, we acceded to his request.

Now much as Ruth delighted in these sessions, once the photo shoot came to an end, she would invariably scamper to her father's side. Ger would notice, exchange looks with me—his own quiet way of conveying solidarity, yes?

By the end of week four, Gerald was puttering about, and for all intents and purposes, the situation was stable. Of course, no sooner did my folks get wind of this development than they began pressing me to return forthwith. And in truth, I was tempted. How I longed to see everyone! But as I was forced to acknowledge, how right Mom was about nothing being simple! Here were two children who were mine in a way that Larry and Dana could never be. What complicated matters further, Earl and I had not yet talked. Nor was I keen on leaving before Gerald's wires came out. What if this were his moment to re-enter the world of speech?

Now while I touched on all these factors when speaking with my family, perhaps predictably, they dismissed everything else as peripheral and focused on Earl and Ruthie.

"So what you waiting for?" asked Mom. "The return of the *Moshiah*? You need to talk to Earl? Then talk to the *momser*. Though know what I'd do? Grab Ruth and run."

"My best guess?" asked Rose. "That you have feelings for the guy after all. Anyway, just in case, something you should know. In third year university, you discovered that you don't like the missionary position."

"Now you tell me!" I giggled.

Of course, intriguing though this revelation was—and yeah, I promised myself to pump Rose for more info—Rose was far from the mark. I harboured no such feelings for Earl. Nor did I feel frightened by him, apprehensive at the sight of him—any of that. In fact, I hardly had any feelings for him at all.

Surprising to me, but as I was soon to discover, not exactly surprising to Earl.

"How's she cutting?" asked Earl, tentatively entering the living room.

"Just like a knife," I answered.

I was sitting on the couch, browsing through the newspaper. Alone as it happened, for earlier, Gerald and the kids had bundled up and taken off to Christie Pits.

Earl handed me a cup of coffee, lowered himself into one of the burgundy chairs, eyed me intently. "So can we have that talk now?" he asked. "No chance of being interrupted. Told the whole pack of them that no one's welcome back for at least an hour. Even bolted the front door for good measure."

"Child-proof and Gerald-proof too," I joked. "Not at all

shabby. Any chance we could keep it locked for a day or two?"

"Think I could use a whole month," he quipped.

I laughed, laid down the newspaper, then took a deep breath, aware that the inevitable could be postponed no longer.

Clearly contrite, Earl began with care, even humility. "Missus," he stated point blank, "this is awkward for us both, but let me just say something here. I owes you an apology. I should never have signed for the electroshock. Nor should I have forced medication on you. It was wrong, pure and simple."

"Earl, thank you for that," I answered.

"I could trot out a thousand and a half excuses," he continued, his eyes sharp, "but I'm a Newfie, for Chrissake, and we knows better than to trust authorities. Nomi, just when did I turn into a gormless mainlander?"

"Boy! Are you asking the wrong person!"

Earl chuckled. "I guess so, but I have another question that maybe you *can* answer. Nomi, are you, well, after hating me?"

I hesitated, but the truth, that was all that either of us could afford. I reached for a cigarette, lit it, let the smoke trickle out my nostrils. "I get the feeling you want me to say that it's water under the bridge. I can't. Let me tell you something, Earl. Gerald once assured me you're a real good guy. He's right. I've seen it. But I have to make my way through life with a compromised brain. Some days, I can barely recollect my own name, and hey, nothing personal, but on days like that I hate your guts."

Earl nodded.

"Now the time was when I was pissed with you nonstop, and mostly, I've let that go. But can I let it go altogether? Maybe a better person could. I can't. I'm not sure you'd even want me to. 'Cause when I'm not pissed at you, I don't feel much of anything. A certain warmth, of course, but that's about it. Um, I've shocked you, haven't I?"

"Actually, no. Now I kind of know the answer to this next question, but I don't ask it, I won't be able to live with myself, is all. Any chance the two of us reconciling?"

"Earl, I understand that Nomi Smith loved you, but the thing is, *I* don't. Sorry. Don't think I ever wanna be anyone's wife again, but certainly not...well..."

"Fair enough," he stated. Then he leaned forward, put his hands on his knees, and looked at me thoughtfully. And that's when he asked the question that set the world spinning. "One more thing," he said. "Would you consider moving back?"

"But ... but after what I said, why would you even...?"

"Not as my wife. As Ruthie's mother. I know the two of you miss each other. And yet we both know she needs to live here. Think of it, Missus. This could solve the problem. You'd have your own space. And we could takes turns with Ruthie, sort of like we have with Gerald."

The renovations immediately leapt to mind. So that's why he'd done it. I took a puff of the cigarette, another puff. "The basement suite, that where you're thinking I'd live?"

"The house. I'd take over the basement, probably add an extension off the upstairs kitchen for a study. We'd have two different rooms for Ruthie, two different kitchens—one in each of our sections. See as little or as much of each other as suited us, right?"

"I can see you've been planning this for some time, but the thing is, I can't give up Winnipeg. Built a life there. Have family I love, a sister I should never have..."

"Family?" he protested. "What the blazes is your own daughter if not family?"

I looked at him straight on, nodded. "Earl, I know. I know. And all this time you've been raising her by yourself, clearly been a fabulous father, and you deserve something better than a half-assed explanation. Let me tell you one more thing, though. You know how people who are okay are anchored in themselves?"

"Nomi, I don't want to hear any more. I..."

"My internal anchor," I persisted, "it's broken. My Winnipeg family, they're my anchor, and without them, I'm adrift."

At this, a far-away look came over Earl. "Got it," he answered at long last.

"But I *would* like more contact with the kids—both of them," I added. "How'd you feel about regular visits? Me visiting the kids, the kids coming out west to visit me?"

"Les too? Christ, I..." he began to say. Then he stopped himself. "Yeah, the little guy would like that," he mused. "Visits with the two of them, fair enough. Nomi, I'm trying here. What's best for everyone, that's what I want."

"I can see that," I answered, touched by his good will, "and I wish I could see my way clear to suggest something more substantial, but let's just go with visits, well, unless..."

Earl's brow raised. "Unless?"

"You'll think this is crazy."

"Try me."

"What if we found a middle ground? I live in Winnipeg part of the year, in Toronto the rest. Same general split of the house. Now I'm not saying this is a go. I'd hafta mull it over, talk to the folks, but whatchya think?"

We had arrived at a surreal moment. The very lights seemed to flicker. Nonetheless, Earl eagerly declared himself willing. As we started tossing around the idea, I too began warming to it. Now in retrospect, a sign at the entry to the premises stating, "Grownups Thinking. Come back in a week" might have come in handy around now. Be that as it may, soon—only too soon—everyone was banging at the door calling out, "Let us in."

"Think we should?" I asked, gesturing toward the entrance, a twinkle in my eye.

Earl grinned. He ostentatiously approached the front door, started to unbolt it. Then he made an abrupt turn and fetched another round of coffee. Only once we were half way through that next cup did he actually unlatch the door.

"Hey, you guys forget you have children?" sniped Les, throwing his jacket on the couch. "Bet *I* know what *you* were doing."

"Les, what were they doing?" asked Ruthie.

And back into the busyness we were dragged.

As I crawled into bed that night, I found myself actively grappling with the idea. Ruthie and I could be a real mother and daughter. And where is it written that a person can't live in two cities? Maybe even maintain a photography practice in both? As for Earl, perhaps with the marriage caput, we could actually pull off being friends of sorts. Gone would be the servicing—sexual and otherwise—those roles that leave a woman in a perpetual one-day position. And Ger is living proof that Earl makes a first rate ex-husband. In fact, downright excels at it. Now if only he would stop calling me "Missus!"

I awoke still flirting with the idea. A possibility—a distinct possibility. Earl and I talked further. Then I solicited Rose's advice.

"A big step, Nomi. Take your time," she advised.

I phoned Mom.

"What do you mean 'dual residence?'" she shrieked. "You forget what happened last time you shacked up with that *farstunkener*? I'm against it, hear? One hundred and one per cent against!"

As I retired that evening, I could not get Mom off my mind. Ignoring her wishes was a nonstarter. But might she not come around?

Three long days we waited, and not an inch did the woman budge. But neither did she stop speaking to me. Not exactly a ringing endorsement, but not hopeless either.

"Give her time," suggested Earl. "Meanwhile, let's talk to the kids."

"Okay, but carefully," I cautioned.

Next day, after passing the idea by Gerald, we did indeed broach the topic with the kids, though tentatively. To be clear, we apprised them of *both* possibilities—living here part time on one hand, frequent visits on the other. While both excited them, perhaps predictably, they greatly preferred having me in Toronto. And so it was that the pressure for dual residence started to mount.

"Talked to a buddy at work," said Earl over the lunch. "He and his missus did something similar. Definitely doable. So Nomi, let's just…"

"Can I paint one of my rooms blue, one green?" interceded Ruthie. "Can I? Can I?"

Now later that afternoon Earl stopped me in the hall, said the kids really wanted this. "So Missus, we're doing this, right?" he asked. And without intending to commit myself, I found myself answering, "probably"—to this day, I'm not sure why.

How like a celebration was supper next evening! Earl and I whipped up a feast—lobster, dumplings, Jiggs Dinner. Once everyone was seated, Earl lowered his head, brought his hands together in mock prayer just as he had that evening in that restaurant so long ago.

"Holy Mary full of grace/Keep your son outta my face," he chanted.

"Outta my face, outta my face," chimed in Les.

"And may we set up Nomi's quarters post haste," added Earl, winking at his son.

Throughout supper, half joking, half serious, Earl kept referring to our tentative plans as the dawning of a new era. "Can't keep us Smiths down for long," he declared. And as we wolfed down dessert, his eyes alight, he led the family in song, beginning with Tickle Cove Pond, everyone stamping their feet in unison and joining in the chorus.

Now while Ruthie joined in only a couple of the songs, she was ostensibly enjoying herself. As Earl and I started in on the dishes, however, she began peering at me anxiously.

"Something wrong, pumpkin?" I asked.

She shook her head.

Half an hour later as Les and I were going toe-to-toe in a hotly contested game of cribbage, Ruthie approached. For several seconds she remained silent—just stood staring. "Mommy, you promised you'd wash my hair just as soon as supper's over," she suddenly screamed, turning and stomping off. "You promised. You promised."As I was lathering up her hair that evening, I wondered how this little girl would fare in the long run with a mother who could not be counted on to remember. How other Torontonians would react. And that's when it hit me—what if I was making a mistake?

It is a wind-swept afternoon, and the entire Cohan clan is afloat on a tiny iceberg, in the midst of a vast ocean. Our finest Shabbes clothes on, we are huddled together for warmth. Out of nowhere appears a shofar. As Dad lifts it to his lips, I tiptoe off in search of shelter. Spotting a lone bed on the horizon, I make my way over to it and lay down, Suddenly, I am surrounded by doctors, all of them taking notes.

In the distance, a familiar voice calls out, the words barely audible over the blast of the shofar. I leap from the bed, turn about, catch sight of Mom stretching out her arms. "Baby, come back," she beseeches. "Kinechora, come while there's still time." I begin inching toward her. Suddenly, the iceberg begins to break apart. Relentlessly, the crack spreads, leaving me on one side, my family on the other. My floater is starting to pull away. I rush to the edge, hoping to make the jump. Too late. I fumble with my glasses—straining for one last look at my loved ones. Then my eyes lower, and I take it in. There carved in the ice in front of them is the word "reality."

I awake with a start. "Dear God, I'm losing touch with reality," I exclaim.

I was beside myself a good part of that night, aching for my family and spooked to the bone by the eerie closeness of St. Pukes. What made me think that I could live here?, I asked. Now at first I felt like a failure. As I lay there, however, little by little, I got in touch with one undeniable fact—I really had made progress. I had merely gotten ahead of myself. And what

I needed to do—needed to do quickly, admittedly—was get back to ground zero.

Come morning, I phoned home. Then I talked to everyone in the house, being especially careful with Ruthie. "Pumpkin, I'll be back in exactly a week," I promised. "You know how you can tell a week's almost up?" I asked, reaching for her little finger. "Let's say each day Mommy is away is one of your fingers. When you get to *this* little hinky-pinky here," I said, giving it a shake, "we're almost home-free."

"You're never coming back ever ever, are you?" Ruthie exclaimed.

After breakfast, Earl and I closeted ourselves in his study and talked. "But, woman," he pointed out, yesterday you seemed almost certain."

"I know, I know. But I'm just not sure I can live here. Can't even think about it right now. I told you my family was my anchor. Well, I need my anchor."

"Christ! How do I even know you'll be back in a week?"

"I said I'll be back. Either you believe me or you don't. But Earl, if *you* don't believe me, how can *our daughter*?"

Twenty-four hours later, with tensions once again rising, I was on my way home. Hours after that, I opened the door of the Inkster Blvd house, took one look at my father, his *tallis* draped over his shoulders, and instantly, I could feel my heart settle.

"Dad," I throw out, "you're a level-headed fella. So tell me, how did you manage to get such a screw-up for a daughter?"

"*Nu?* What can I say?" he answers, opening his arms wide. "When a guy's lucky, he's lucky."

17. NAOMI

DECISIONS THAT CHART a course for our lives, these are not easy to make—nor should they be, not if we are to take the business of living seriously—and bottom line, there were three things which I could not sacrifice—Ruthie, my sanity, being my mother's daughter. Now initially, I focused on trying to bring Mom around. Meanwhile, Mom was wrestling with her own demons. While she was secretly relieved to have me here, so terrified was she at the prospect of "the *meshugener hunt*" again gaining control of her daughter that whenever the topic of Toronto arose, she would literally seethe with rage. And on whom but her daughter could she visit that rage? And so we treaded water—getting along tolerably well as long as we avoided the verboten topic, coming perilously close to World War Three otherwise.

"So what did you expect?" asked Mom, throwing up her hands in frustration. "That after falling for one of his lines again, we'd throw you a 'welcome home' parade?"

Two days had passed. A gift to be here despite the bickering. Now I had hoped to see Rose straight away—*schmooze*, enlist her support—but she'd had previous commitments. Finally, however, we'd finagled some alone-time. And with it came a most revealing glimpse into my sister's world.

We were sitting on her living room divan sipping tea. Thankfully, Rose did not seem to resent the mentoring role that she'd inherited, though something was clearly eating at her for she had been fidgeting for the past hour. She refilled our cups, then eyed me intently. "Hold on," she insisted. "A reality check, okay? Didn't you do everything right? Get yourself to safety? Give people twenty four hours to get used to the idea? Nomi," she added, you didn't go crazy. Just got scared, is all. Lots of scary stuff here too, and you'll have to decide if it's worth it."

"I get that," I answered. "Here's where I'm really stuck— what do I do about Mom?"

At this, a sadness came over Rose. "You know, Nomi," she said, "you might want to count your blessings. I'll tell you something—like, you're the only one she gets quite that pissed with."

"Kinda miss the upside here," I retort half joking. Then I see the anguish in her eyes. "You're serious, aren't you?"

"Sure am. You know why *I* never get under Mom's skin? The woman doesn't take me seriously. Curious thing about these last two years—she's rarely lost her temper with you. It's because she's been seeing you as damaged. Well, damaged and all, you're back in the canary's seat. So Nomi Brenda Cohan, put that in your pipe and smoke it."

"I didn't realize," I said. "Ro, um, this impasse between me and Mom, maybe it's not something you want to weigh in on."

Rose waved her hand dismissively. "Don't be silly. Anyway, I know you. You're not remotely through considering this, and you won't be okay if Mom's not on board."

"Ro?"

"Yeah."

"If Mom doesn't realize what a powerhouse you are, she's a blithering idiot.... Really do love you."

"Sure, sure," she quipped, "but will you still respect me in the morning?"

Striking while the iron was hot—progressively, Rose's default mode—she immediately phoned Mom, and before long the four of us were sitting in my folks' living room, servings of cake and strudel before us. Now Rose and I repeatedly implored Mom to look at the situation from my point of view, but Mom just kept shaking her head.

"Why are we even talking about this?" Mom suddenly shouted, throwing her hands in the air. "The man holds you hostage and you think he's a nice little *boytshik* you can play house with! Do something this *meshugah*, maybe you *do* belong in a nuthouse."

Now who knows what would have happened had Mom made her point more judiciously—but this below-the-belt attack demonstrably piqued Rose's ire.

"Damn it, Mom, you can't talk to Nomi that way," she exclaimed. "For God's sake!"

Astonishment flashed across mom's Mom's face. Her eyes wide, she stared at Rose. Then to everyone's surprise, she acknowledged that just maybe she had misspoke.

"No 'maybe' about it," Rose plowed on. "As for the rest of it, I'll grant you Nomi's better off here, but you keep kidding yourself that she can gain custody. Being in Toronto—that's the only way she'll see much of her daughter. Oh Mom, be honest," she added. "If it were your daughter, wouldn't you...?"

Despite her initial shock—and even now she was having a hard time computing that *Rose* was speaking back to her—a plaintiveness had settled over Mom. Moments later, she looked at me straight on, nodded—and Rose and I breathed a sigh of relief. Then a wily look entered our father's eye, and we were quickly disabused of any illusion that the rest was a cakewalk.

"Shouldn't kids learn about their heritage?" he asked. He proceeded to rhyme off a litany of Jewish holidays—including ones not celebrated since the Stone Age—then suggest that Ruthie join us for them. "Now she's born of a Jewish mother and so's a hundred per cent Jewish, but I'm a reasonable man," he went on, plunking his feet on the ottoman. "Let's say the child's half Jewish. So let her come for half of the holidays."

Of course, Dad was milking the situation for all it was worth. Nonetheless, to a degree, he had point.

"If it's Earl you're worried about, try introducing it as a possibility only," suggested Rose.

A couple of hours later when I called the Palmerston house, I did indeed take advantage of the occasion to introduce the thorny question of the holidays. "Expose an innocent child to that religious mumbo-jumbo—in a pig's eye!" Earl swore. Nonetheless, something in his tone suggested he was not totally ruling it out. A surprise, yes? But nothing compared to the one that followed. As I hung up the phone, I turned. Mom was standing in the hallway, observing me keenly, clearly had been listening in for some time.

"Baby, even an ex-marriage is a matter of give-and-take," she observed, catching my eye. "Try asking for *one* holiday."

"One?"

"One."

"Mom, which?" I ask, moved that despite everything, the woman was eager to help.

"What else? The one that makes us a people, yeh?"

Later that evening, as darkness gathered us up in her comforting arms, in the quiet of my room, I pondered Mom's words. And as slumber beckoned, I pictured the flow of generations, that piece of eternity that we owe our children. And there and then I vowed to make Pesach with her Jewish family a live possibility in my daughter's life. Ironic, perhaps, but all those years, Ruthie—that's why.

The tension having lifted, the next few days, I had a ball—schmoozing with Mom over coffee, roving up and down Salter, camera in hand. When I was not with Mom or out and about, I was upstairs leafing through the binders. Too heavy to *schlep* back and forth, I realized, but at least they existed, and their sheer being-in-the-world, this was a treasure.

Time ticked by quickly. And before we knew it, there was but one day left in my Winnipeg retreat. That evening, Mom and I did something we'd not done in years—kicked up our heels and took in a movie together.

Twenty-four hours later I stepped back into the Palmerston house. Speaking of challenges, I arrived to an eerily patient ex-husband, a Les who was regaling all and sundry with smutty jokes, a daughter who was shocked to see me, and a Gerald who had demonstrably missed his doctor's appointment. "See, pumpkin, Mommy kept her promise;" I pointed out, eagerly reaching for my little one's hand. "Ger, I'm rebooking now. And Les, put a sock in it," I said.

Curious, those subterranean processes of ours. We like to think that we arrive where we do by step-by-step logic, but how often this is not so!

That first night back I dreamt that it was my thirty-second birthday, and my best friend Dr. Higgins and I were sitting on the steps of St. Pukes, jovially tossing back cocktails. "Mrs. Smith, have I got a present for you!" he jubilantly exclaimed. Whereupon, a ten-foot high shock machine came barrelling through the wall. I awoke in a cold sweat. Just as soon as I'd got my bearings, I thought of Ruthie—what that little girl was feeling, what every little girl has a right to take for granted. Then in my mind's eye, I get an image of Jack, his cigarette dangling from his lips. "Easy there, kiddo," he advised. "It's like locating your room at St. Pukes, right? Just need to find your own way."

"But Jack, does it always have to be so hard?" I asked.

Now I knew that this was a child's question. Something about asking it, however, allowed me to let it go. Shortly afterward, as was my wont, I started to replay my dream. As I arrived at the end, I was struck by the inanity of a ten-foot high shock machine, and I started to laugh. And at that moment, strange though this may seem, the path ahead started to become clear.

The following day, I embarked on a personal odyssey. To pull off dual residence, I would have to find my photographer's legs in this city. And what is not unrelated, I'd have to be able to navigate Toronto solo. I recalled that glorious adventure with Ger years ago. And so it is that with my camera slung over my shoulder, I took a jaunt over to Kensington Market. I positioned myself outside two different cheese emporiums, took close-ups of Italians, Portuguese, Jews exiting the premises, little bundles in their hands, that satisfied look that people get when they've tasted just a sliver of everything. I squatted down in the middle of Baldwin, screwed in my wide-angle lens, captured shops on both sides, chickens strutting about in cages, produce spilling over into the street. Rising and changing lenses again, I ventured into shop after shop—waiting for that special moment. Not the big aha. The surprise of the ordinary that makes your eyes glisten and leaves you grateful for being alive.

At a fruit stand, an old woman in a *babushka* was thumping a watermelon while her little granddaughter looked on in awe. Click. At one of the vintage clothing stores, a young man was trying on a pair of scarlet knickerbockers several sizes too large, his hand holding onto the waistband, a sheepish grin on his face. Click. Four doors down, an incredulous Jewish shopkeeper was peering into an open milk carton while a feisty young Portuguese woman stood there, her hands on her hips. I waited until the shopkeeper lowered his glasses and peered over them, then shot. Down Baldwin I went. Down Kensington. Along Augusta, where a group of street musicians dressed in orange and black had struck up a tune. The rhythms of that remarkable market, I let them guide my hand, tutor my heart. Camera in hand, some day I would take in the wonders of Chinatown, of Yorkville, of St. Lawrence Market. However, every city that the locals adore has one special spot where God lingers just that extra moment. In Winnipeg, it is the north-end. In Paris, the Latin Quarter. And surely in Toronto, it is Kensington.

For over three hours, I lingered, I shot. Now and again, people stopped to chat with me. Several put in orders for photos. Now whether it was instinct or not, I could not say, but shortly after jotting down the name and address of the tenth such person—one Miriam Himmelfarb—I found myself drifting out of the market and bearing east. For a while, I hadn't a clue where I was going or why. Still perplexed, I neared Spadina, crossed the street. And there it was—the place of the devastation—all twelve storeys of it.

At the sight of that cement monstrosity, I started to quake, and for a second, I considered retreating. No, that's not what artists do, I reminded myself. Steadying myself, I approached the front door, sat down on the steps, waited, watched. Like an archer of old, his bow drawn, I bided my time, knowing that nothing could be rushed.

Patient after patient stood on the steps, made their way about the grounds. I was disappointed that I knew none of them. I was relieved that I knew none of them. Out the front door shuffled a young woman in jeans, her hands shaking, slobber dribbling out of her mouth. Had I once looked like that? A middle-aged man was standing on a stair, seemingly oblivious to the conspicuous dampness at his crotch, the puddle at his foot. I spoke to a handful of patients, gave money, offered cigarettes. However, out of respect, I took no pictures. Nor did I want to intrude on family or friends. And so it is that I continued to wait, no idea what I was looking for but confident that I would recognize it.

Suddenly, toward the front door strutted three professionals. One was transparently a doctor. While I caught only the odd word, he appeared to be expounding on a condition called "hysterical personality disorder." His very tone signalled contempt. But more than that, that self-important look—I recognized it, recognized it instantly. Bingo.

I waited until they were feet from the door, aimed the camera, then shot. I quickly advanced the frame, took a second shot, a third, a fourth. The look, I had captured it. I'd also made a most edifying discovery. As a photographer, the boys in white did not scare me, for the tables were turned. *They* were not looking at *me*. I was looking at them.

Even today, as I think back on it, I am struck by the rush of freedom. Remarkable the power of a camera. While hardly foolproof, beats the hell outa Prozac, eh?

Now I did not as yet realize how this discovery would play out in the years to come. One thing, however, I knew. The mere presence of St. Pukes was not going to ruin my life. Nor need it cast a pall on the decision at hand.

Exhilarated, I rushed home, entered the living room with a renewed confidence. "You okay with me putting up a photographer's sign in the front window?" I asked Earl.

"You aren't by any chance telling us...?"

"Well, put it this way: What photographer would advertise in a city where she wasn't intending to live at least part of the year?"

Les looked at his father, saw his face break into a broad smile.

"Yeah, thought you guys were doing it," piped up Les.

"Mister, you wants your mouth washed out with soap, just keep it up," warned Earl.

That evening, Ruthie and I talked. And over the next week, the phone lines between Toronto and Winnipeg were on overdrive, for almost instantly, high-level negotiations ensued. "So of course you'll be in Winnipeg over the high holidays and Pesach," stipulated Dad. "What kind of Yid isn't home for Pesach and the high holidays? Maybe my little Ruthie too?"

"Christ, woman! Christmas with the kids is a no-brainer," objected Earl.

"The anti-Semite gets Christmas, we get Chanukah," Mom rejoined.

"Do try to work in *our birthday*," pleaded Rose.

It quickly became apparent that no one could get everything they wanted. So I took the obvious next step—stopped all further input, sat with the muddle. Two day later, I had my itinerary.

So far so good. I was treading the path that was mine to tread. Which brought me to the final item on the to-do list.

The official explanation of Gerald's wires still being in was that he had lost track of the doctor's appointment. A blatant fabrication. Be that as it may, Gerald clearly needed to be getting on with his life.

As the day of the rebooked procedure rolled round, I consulted Gerald, then raised the issue with the whole family, and we committed ourselves to going the extra mile. According to my index cards, what we decided was: 1) a cab would transport Ger to and from the doctor's; 2) we'd stipulate a woman driver; 3) I'd accompany him; and 4) we'd celebrate later that day with Earl whipping up a feast and Ger reading us a Newfie story.

A reasonable sounding plan—but, as my Dad always said, man plans; God laughs.

"Just remember—I'll be right here waiting," I assured Gerald. We were in a cramped waiting area, and Gerald's name had just been called. He paused long enough to catch my eye, then calmly followed the nurse down the hall.

The wait felt endless. Eventually, a door creaked open and Gerald appeared in the distance, an elderly doctor with spectacles at his side. As he drew close, you could tell that his jaw was considerably more relaxed. Promising.

I immediately rose to greet them. "So Ger, is...?" I began.

Barely had these words escaped my lips than to my utter surprise, Ger handed me a note. "Operation a success," it read. Now for a fleeting moment, the meaning of the act eluded me. Then suddenly, I knew.

My heart sinking, I placed my hand on his shoulder. "Ger, that's great," I murmured, "but old friend, we were all kinda hoping..."

Sadness in his eyes, Gerald shook his head; and for all intents and purposes, the discussion was at an end.

Sobered by the depth of his pain, humbled by the awareness that we had all of us misread him so—me as much as anyone—I apologized profusely, then spirited Ger out of the area. No sooner had we stepped off the elevator than he threw his arms around me, held me long and hard.

"Ger, I love you," I said, peering deeply into his eyes. "Everyone does, and so help me, everyone will stick by you. Now when we get home, you'll be facing one confused and pissed-off family, but fella, they'll get over it. Sweetie, you know that, yeah? Hey, how about we grab ourselves a coffee first, give you a chance to catch your breath?"

The next few days were brutal, for none of us was prepared for this. The kids threatened to stop speaking also. Ever the diplomat, Earl swore a blue streak. But the fact remained, the man was in far more trouble than we had let ourselves realize. Of course, under the circumstances, it made sense for him to stay on in the Palmerston house. But what in God's name was happening?

Now one night, I stood in the middle of the bedroom trying to recall something Gerald had once said about grief, hoping it would light our way. Probably in one of the binders, I muttered. I sighed, realizing anew how much I relied on them.

The conundrum of the binders weighing upon me, minutes later I climbed into bed fully clothed and shut my eyes. When next I opened them, to my surprise, there were my binders, sitting on a shelf. I reached for one. Into thin air, it vanished. I reached for another. Gone. I awoke with a start.

There were a number of things of which my sister Rose was

certain—the dearness of her family, the primacy of the physi-
cal world, the importance of living a life of integrity. After all
that we had been through, however, on one issue she declared
herself a hundred and one per cent clear. Never again would
she feud with me. Also, she would pay careful attention to
what she called "those slight episodes"—those minor bouts
of confusion that snuck up on her now and then, made her
late for a meeting, pilfered a minute or two from her head.

"Nomi—she's like the other side of my hand. Something
happens on *this* side," Rose would explain to Sam, pointing
to the back of her hand, "think this other side knows nothing
about it?" And so when that disorienting image of *disappearing
binders* started flashing through her head, she made a point
of dialing me.

"Nomi, the binders, you're lost without them, aren't you?"
she asked.

"Kinda," I answered, "though if they were here in Toronto, I'd miss them the second I set foot in Winnipeg. So don't
worry about..."

"I'll tell you something. In some ways, I'm as lost *without
you* as you are *without the binders*. And like, I hardly saw you
when you were last here. Let me see what I can work out....
Twin prerogative," she quickly added, skilfully cutting all
possible objections off at the pass.

Adamant, Rose proceeded to discuss the situation with Lisa.
"How about us killing two birds with one stone?" suggested
Lisa. So, after a week of arm-twisting, the details of which I
never could keep straight, the two of them set off for Toronto
in Rose's old chevy.

A roof rack on top of the car, they arrived here loaded down
with everything but the kitchen sink. I kid you not—a toy
walky-talky set for Les and Ruthie, the full set of my binders,
two suitcases crammed with my clothes, ledgers for my Toronto business, an album filled with childhood pictures, also,
photographs of humpback whales.

"Humpback whales?" I asked, incredulously.

"Dad's peace offering for Earl," Rose clarified.

Lapping up one another's presence, that first night, Rose and I stayed up till all hours, talking about every little thing. Next morning, Rose and Lisa set off by themselves to take in the sights of the big city—the Science Centre, the Planetarium, Allan Gardens. Meanwhile I lugged the binders to the bedroom, began pouring over them. Nothing that I came across even remotely illuminated Gerald's plight. Nonetheless, what a relief to have them at my fingertips again!

That night, the three of us took in a production of *Jesus Christ Superstar*, each of us promising on pain of death not to breathe a word about this to Dad. And first thing after breakfast the next day, everyone—Gerald excepted—hit St. Lawrence Market where we picked up a night table for Lisa's mother, a mahogany bookcase for me, treats for the kids. By early afternoon we had set up the bookcase along the southern wall of the master bedroom, and begun arranging the binders on the bottom shelf.

"You know, Rose," I observed, as the last of the binders slipped into place, "great to have these here, but it doesn't exactly solve the problem of which place to keep them."

To my delight, Rose proceeded to explain that she'd duplicated the entire set—same colour scheme. "Here's the *shtick*," she explained. "Say you add a page. You mark it 'P' to remind yourself to photocopy it, take the copies with you when you change cities."

Of course, I was well aware that I would have to build in extra steps if this system were to work. Nonetheless, it was reassuring to have the beginnings of a method. Even more reassuring to be receiving yet another reminder that Rose could still find her way into my head—as she so obviously had.

Now later that afternoon, once again Rose and I grabbed some alone time—sat down on the bed together, *schmoozed*. We began by speaking of Mom, Rose agreeing to drop in on her for morning coffee every so often.

"Hey, Ro," I said, lighting a cigarette, "the thing about Mom never respecting you enough to give you hell, it hadn't dawned on me till you said it. Never even saw her blowing her stack at me as a sign of respect. Just saw myself as the one picked on."

"Can understand that. You *were* too."

"Anyway, Ro, tell me, now that you've got her attention, is it better in some way?"

Seemingly ignoring me, she reached for the family album, began flipping though it. "Interesting you should ask," she said, suddenly looking up. "You know how they say 'beware what you wish for cause you just might get it?' Well, they're right. Believe me—I no longer envy what you had....But like, that doesn't mean I couldn't have used more respect growing up."

"Gotchya."

"Know one of the downsides of growing up your identical twin? And yes, there are others. Not just for Mom, but for a number of people—it's like you were the original, me the copy. Pretty close. Hard to tell us apart. But not quite up to snuff."

"Sounds brutal. You know," I added, "that's never how I felt about you."

"You don't have to tell *me* that," she pointed out, "but it still was what it was."

At this, we exchanged looks. Then I fetched refreshments, and before long, buns and steaming *café au lait* in hand, we were propped up on the bed, leafing through the photo album. We pored over a picture of Rose age eleven planting tulips. "See that shadowy figure over there? That's Mom watching me from the window," Rose explained. We looked at one of me and Leo Pinsky dressed to the nines for our high school graduation.

"Remember how Dad used to refer to your boyfriends?" Rose asked.

"Yeah. 'So who is it this time?' he'd say. 'Peak, beak, blimp, or shrimp?'"

We both cracked up.

"Graduation night, that was your first time, wasn't it?" she asked.

"Second time." And that's when I remembered. "Rose, speaking of sex, didn't you say something about my not liking the missionary position?"

Rose eyed me curiously, took a sip of coffee. "So you *are* interested in Earl."

"Fuck no, you *dumkopf*! But here's the thing. Those years with Earl, I felt no desire, *bupkes*. But without the meds, I can feel again, and maybe some day, with somebody..."

Rose smiled sympathetically. "Sorry. Didn't quite understand about the meds and sex. Now Nomi, I know this is the kind of thing that embarrasses you, but you, well, want to know what you like, don't you?"

"Call me a cockeyed optimist, but I think that just might make sex a tad more enjoyable."

"Your legs over the guy's shoulders," she specified. Without a hint of discomfort, she proceeded to describe a few other positions that I might consider, and I was again reminded of the difference between us.

"Oh and Nomi," she added, "one other sisterly tip. If you've no partner and you're not partial to vibrators—which I recall you aren't—you might want to try a cucumber."

I could feel my jaw drop. "A what?" I asked, staring at the woman in disbelief. "C'mon, Rose. You're not telling me that I've actually..."

"No, no. Sorry. Not you. Me. Works well, is all. And like, I don't waste it either. Just chop it up afterward, toss it in the salad, or whatever else I'm whipping up."

I reached over, grabbed a cigarette. "And the salad part, Sam doesn't mind?"

"Oh, the Samster would blow a gasket if he knew. You know husbands."

At this, we both smiled. Now charmed though I was by Rose's

candour, I found myself wracking my brain trying to recall if I'd ever eaten a salad at her place. I couldn't exactly ask her at this point. Oh well, I told myself. Adds whole new meaning to cooking with love. And before long we were flipping through the album again.

"See how I'm looking at you in this one?" I went on, pointing to a picture of the two of us feeding the birds. "It's 'cause you'd inadvertently gotten crumbs on old man Schwartz's yard. And I was thinking, *oy!* Is he ever gonna come after us!"

"Some *farshtunkener*, that guy, eh?" she exclaimed. "Hey, remember the time he threatened to call the police on us?"

Now as we were *schmoozing*, I found myself struck anew by photography's power to draw you down memory lane. And suddenly, Gerald came to mind.

"Rose, hold on a sec," I said.

It was just after dinner. At my request, Earl had picked up one of Gerald's albums. Lisa and Rose had taken Ruthie out for a stroll; and the time was ripe.

Nervous that this will accomplish little more than upset him, with great apprehension, I invite Gerald upstairs, then pull out that album. "Ger," I begin, "what I've done here, it's presumptuous as hell, and if you say no, I won't press. But I'm asking you—no man, begging you—trust me and thumb through this."

I take a deep breath. Gerald starts to shake his head, asserting that control with which we have become so familiar of late. Then he lowers himself onto the chair next to the bed and opens the album. The first few pictures are of him. He looks at one of them, nods. And now his eye drifts to the bottom of the page.

There in soft focus is a picture of Miu holding an infant Les. Tears in his eyes, he sits there staring at it. Then he flips the page. At the bottom left is a shot of Miu grabbing the Panama hat from his head, a look of mischievous delight on her face.

He seems to be avoiding it. He literally eyeballs every other picture. He starts again at the top. Then suddenly, he zeroes in on it, and a sigh issues from his lips.

Gerald's lips begin to quiver and before long he is wailing. For several minutes, he weeps. Then he lifts the hanky from his vest pocket, carefully wipes his face. And that's when he does it. "Well, h ... h ... how..." he utters, almost in a whisper. With great difficulty, he repeats these words. Then he starts to cough.

"Doing just fine, fella," I say.

He hesitates, clears his throat, clears it again. "Well how bout that?" he finally spits out. "Who'd have thunk yours truly had so many tears in him?"

I can feel tears coming to my eyes. "So good to hear your voice!" I exclaim. "Ger, don't worry. We won't press you to talk about anything."

Gerald nods, weeps a while longer. Then he straightens his tie, picks up the album again, points to the picture. "Miu and I, we took that photo on self-timer the day I bought the Panama hat," he explains. His last words trail off, and once again he slips into a coughing jag, and once again he hesitates. His voice clearer, he proceeds to recount how he first broached the issue of gender with Miu.

"Y'know, she really is the love of my life," he murmurs.

"I know, Ger."

"You're feeling critical of her, I can tell," he continues, regarding me keenly. "But Nomi, how would you feel if you had no clue from one day to the next what shape your honey would be returning home in?"

"Pretty damn awful, but...Okay, let me think about this."

Gerald catches my eye, smiles. "Incidentally, love, thanks for hanging in with yours truly. Know I've been quite the handful. Um, you weren't sure you'd hear my voice again, were you?"

"Well, I've been hoping, but..."

"Sometimes, just by speaking," he explains, "a guy feels like he's buying into something—everything actually—the current world and all that it inherits. Centuries of bigotry, brute force, violence cosmeticized. Sounds stupid, I know," he adds, shaking his head, "but even this second, even with it just between the two of us, that's how it feels."

I can sense him teetering on the brink and hold my breath.

"Hey," he suddenly asks, "ever tell you that when I was three, I went silent for five whole months?"

"*Oy!* Ger, what happened?"

Gerald shrugs. "Don't remember any of it. Too young. According to my old man, though, they dragged me to doctors. Tried punishing me, bribing me, the whole enchilada, eh? Then one day, they awoke in the middle of the night, and what do they hear but their kid calling out for a drink of water!"

"So maybe 'cause you needed something?"

"Maybe."

"Now why didn't we think of that?" I joked.

"Take it I've been getting your goat?"

"Honestly, Ger?" I asked, catching his eye.

"Honestly."

"There's been moments that I've felt like strangling you. But you know something strange? It's been a genuine relief to discover that even you can be a pain!"

In the days that followed Gerald avoided all mention of the assault, but continue to speak, he did. And in short order, he and Les moved back to their own apartment. Naturally, we were all delighted. Though would it last?— that was the question.

"*Brrrng*," went the door bell. I had just poured the coffee; and Rose, Lisa, and I were sitting around the kitchen table trying our damnedest to figure out what it would take for the NDP to pull off a victory in Tory-blue Ontario. I opened the door, and there was Gerald, looking absolutely magnificent—a new double-breasted overcoat on, loaded down with bag after bag of croissants, buns, donuts.

"I can see you've been busy," I observed, smiling ear-to-ear.

"Why that I have, love," Gerald answered. "I'm afraid I mislaid my baking pan for a while there," he added, a shit-eating grin on his face.

He removed his galoshes, placed the goodies on the kitchen table, and took a seat. "Been a tad inhospitable, I fear," he said, gazing at Lisa. "So how about you and me making up for lost time? Name's Gerald," he went on, tipping his hat. "And Lisa, I understand you're doing your Masters in Anthropology at U. of M."

For the next half hour, he plied Lisa with questions, displaying a surprising knowledge of anthropology in the process. Then he inquired about my binders.

"Go ahead and show him. Don't worry about us," urged Lisa.

Now while I had assumed that Gerald was simply interested in checking out my new memory system, as we mounted the stairs, he pointedly referred to "documentation," and the second that we entered the bedroom, he crouched down, scrutinized each and every binder as if forging a mental map. Then he reached over, removed Black Binder Number Three. Making himself comfortable on the chair, he proceeded to read that binder word by word, every so often a tear trickling down his cheek.

At one point, his eyes intense, he read an entire passage aloud: "*Count backward from ten, and you'll be fine.*" *Ten. Nine. Eight. Oh my God! Can't move a muscle. No way to breathe.*

"Hell!" he exclaimed, looking up at long last. "I thought I understood, but I didn't. Nomi girl, promise me something. Don't let the fuckers get away with this."

I nodded, though I was unclear what he thought I could do. After all, horrific though it was, what had happened was perfectly legal. "Ger, this's personal for you, isn't it?" I asked, catching his eye. "You know, 'cause of not being able to do anything about…"

"Nomi, really, it's not that. There's something here—something too awful to ignore. So love, don't forget about this. Promise me."

"Promise," I said.

The next few days, so much was afoot in the respective Smith households that it was hard to believe that the ever busy earth had not turned on its axis a few extra times. Having noticed the superabundance of typos, and feeling a veritable drive to take charge, Gerald set about retyping Black Binder Three. The following day, he called into work, and without batting an eye, he announced that he would be returning in a week's time. And later that very day Earl received notification that his article "The Humpback Whale as Fisherman" had been accepted in the journal *Animal Behavior*.

"But Dad," protested Les, upon hearing the title, "even us kids know that whales aren't fishermen. Next you'll be telling us they wear boots and cast nets."

"Lester, my son, you'd be surprised," Earl remarked enigmatically.

That evening, family and guests trotted over to Country Style to celebrate. That's a cozy Hungarian restaurant on Bloor West where the lighting is dim and such rare delicacies as cherry soup grace the menu. We ordered two Transylvanian platters, and how the children's eyes popped when they beheld those culinary delights! Over a foot high the platters were, stacked with wiener schnitzel, Parisian schnitzel, cabbage rolls, roast potatoes, onion rings on skewers at the top.

"Next time, can I have a platter all to myself?" asked Les, polishing off his third cabbage roll.

"Sure, laddio," quipped Earl. "Can have your own bottle of Pepto-Bismol too."

That night, once again a bleary-eyed Rose and I stayed up late. Sometimes talking. More often just looking at one another and wishing that the moment would never end.

"Ro, I..." I began.

"Shh. I know," she said.

One and a half days later, at six a.m. sharp, Rose and Lisa packed up the car and set off for Winnipeg, intent on making Sault Ste. Marie by nightfall.

"I'll do this again," Rose assured me. "Toronto—pretty interesting place, well, for a city out east....Oh my sweet Nomi, please take care of yourself," she urged, folding me in her arms.

With a heavy heart, I stood on the sidewalk and watched as the car disappeared down the street. Now it was a block away. Now a mere dot in the distance. Now nothing more than a lingering thought on a hazy winter morn.

It was hard seeing my sister go, but I was heartened by the realization that I would be back in Winnipeg shortly. Also by the enduring sense that while I could no longer hold her in my sinews as once I had, somehow she was holding me in hers.

After breakfast that day, Gerald turned up. And again he immersed himself in Black Binder Three. I stood there watching, unsure what to make of the curious scene unfolding before me. Occasionally, his eyes would narrow. Then he'd flip back to a former page as if checking some fact, some image. Obviously, the man was not just reading. He was trying to figure out something. But what?

That afternoon Ruthie brought home an assignment with a gold star on it, came flying through the front door squealing, "Daddy, look. Daddy. Daddy. Daddy. Daddy." And up went the photographer's sign in the bay window.

END OF BOOK TWO OF NAOMI'S MEMOIR

AN ALTOGETHER DIFFERENT TIME

DAY OF THE EXHIBIT, JANUARY 7, 2008

"IT SUCKS—UTTERLY SUCKS," she stated point blank. "Like totally bites the big one." It was three p.m. on a nippy Toronto afternoon, and the engines of "progress" were barrelling full speed ahead. In city hall, the mayor's tailored young assistants were roving the corridors, working malleable councillors for votes. And on Bay St. even normally temperate brokers were beyond exuberant, going "long" on materials, financials, and technology as if the current bull market would never end.

To the north, where movers and shakers seldom ventured, stood a small innocuous government building called "The Office of the Child Advocate," and albeit to far less fanfare, here too, wheels were spinning. For two long hours, officials and youth had been seated about the round mahogany table in Conference Room A. Their faces earnest, the youth were adamant. Whether they were in mental health facilities, in care, or in conflict with the law, they were on those stupid meds. And something had to be done about it.

"Mr. Milner, they just drug us up, y'know," continued Keisha, a tall Jamaican girl of thirteen. Me, my friend Jessica, Louise, like the least little thing happens, they start pumping the 'crazy pills' into us."

"We're not saying they're not good for anything," Allen added, "but how come no one ever asks what *we* want?"

The Chief Advocate—Don Milner—nodded. Milner was a

left-leaning liberal who had made small but incremental changes since becoming chief advocate some five years ago. More was now focused on systemic advocacy—"systemic advocacy arising from the priorities of the children," he typically made a point of stipulating.

The meeting having come to an end, Milner quickly summarized, then thanked everyone. "Same time next week," he suggested, eyeing his day-timer.

Seated slightly back from the table sat Ruth Radcliff—the newest member of the advocacy team. Milner glanced over at Radcliff, partly to check that she could make it, partly because there was something about Radcliff that compelled you to look her way. Radcliff nodded in turn, inserted the appointment into her Blackberry. She proceeded to slip each of the youth a couple of subway tokens. Then she made her way to her office, sat down at her desk, let her eye wander over the document in front of her.

A handsome woman in early middle age, counsellor Radcliff had such a commanding presence that when she entered a room, the whole world seemed to hold its breath. With her penetrating blue eyes and short, cropped hair, she looked like a warrior about to do battle. Today, she was wearing a tailored tweed pants suit with matching vest, a single pearl earring dangling from her left lobe. Now she often wore tweed, and given her appearance, choice of friends, and brand of activism, she was frequently mistaken for a dyke—a mistake that rather tickled her, for she was passionate about queer rights, as was her husband Bruce. "We come by it naturally," he once suggested with a sly smile.

Radcliff was something of an enigma in the world of law—a crackerjack lawyer who produced tons of quality work yet who somehow managed to protect her private time with her family. She and her family lived on Pape—Toronto's Greek neighbourhood. Her daughter Laara was a tomboy; her son Don, a feminist who wished that he could campaign for Hillary

Clinton; her husband Bruce a loving laid-back man.

Now Ruth had a zest for advocacy and an impressive track record, and so had been a catch for the Office, though she was even more thrilled to be here than they were to have her. Coming to the aid of children, that had long been her passion. And nothing was quite so rewarding as fighting for the rights of racialized youth. Nonetheless, this deepening concentration on psychiatry was beginning to worry her. Not that she was unaware of the draconian power of psychiatry. But what if their actions culminated in disturbed adolescents being deprived of urgently needed treatment? Hardly the most appropriate sentiment for an advocate, she realized—not that she had or ever would let it interfere—but she had been around the block a few times and had seen a thing or two.

As she settled in at her desk, she glanced at her watch. Three o'clock. If she was going to make it to the exhibit, she would have to leave shortly. Her eyes returned to the material on her desk. Beside the legal papers lay yesterday's copy of the *Toronto Star*, opened at the arts section. Reluctantly, she picked up the newspaper, once again eyed that write-up. "Masterful," wrote the reviewer. "Naomi Cohan searches the world with her empathic eye, always finds just the right treasure to set before us, and the space devoted to the homeless artists is a rare delight. Mark the latest exhibit of Toronto's own roving camera queen a 'do-not-miss.'"

Ruth grimaced, then angrily flung the newspaper onto the floor. Since her mother's inexplicable rise in popularity in the early nineties, it never ceased to amaze Ruth what people would say about "the roving camera queen." Not that she begrudged her mother the good fortune exactly. Since the birth of her first child eleven years ago, she'd seen first-hand how hard parenting was, so had softened toward her mother—obviously, she noted, glancing down at the newspaper, not quite as much as she had imagined. Be that as it may, even her son could tell that she still resented the woman.

As was her wont whenever the unsettling subject of her mother arose, Ruth reached back into childhood: The interminable waiting. Arriving home with her best friend Nora to discover no dinner, no mother even, for her mom had forgotten everything—including inviting Nora over. Those looks that she'd invariably met—"as if I were a mere interruption," she had told her husband. "Or this niggling problem Mom couldn't wrap her mind around. As for parental neglect, don't ask." In all fairness, not that everything was her mother's fault. Anyone could see that the woman had a bone fide disability. Perhaps if she had received proper treatment.

At the thought of treatment, Ruth grimaced. Although it was shrouded in mystery, the entire family knew that her mother had received psychiatric treatment back when. Medication. Also, wasn't there talk of ECT? And maybe instead of helping her, that was why she acted as she did. But empathic? Only someone who'd never laid eyes on the woman could call her empathic! As for adding her name to that document....

The document on the counsellor's mind was the very one that she had been eyeing but minutes ago—Naomi's power-of-attorney-for-personal-care. For the umpteenth time, Ruth reached over, picked it up. She stared at the tick next to "jointly and severally," saw her aunt Rose listed. Significantly, no other name appeared, even though "jointly and severally" implied a minimum of *two* attorneys. And in that curious contradiction lay a microcosm of the dilemma between mother and daughter. Naomi kept inviting something from her daughter. Ruth kept declining.

This was the dynamic. Ruth herself saw it, even regretted it, but was stymied. "You think if you gives your ma an inch, she'll take a mile. Dead wrong," her father had assured her. But that wasn't it. As she was well aware, at most her mother would take another couple of inches. It's that every solitary inch, pained her to the core.

In this case, she'd already given the inch—acceded to her

father's request to give her mother's documents a quick once-over. But add her name, she could not, even though Gerald had pleaded, "C'mon, Ruth girl. Your Aunt Rose's way over in Winnipeg." Even though her father had exclaimed, "Christ, Ruthie! You're a lawyer, and we're after talking about your own flesh-and-blood." All reasonable points, Ruth conceded in the safety of her own mind. But...and here, as usual, she came to a full stop.

She put aside the document, shook her head. Why was she so angry? Her mother's inconvenient lapses hardly held a candle to the gut-wrenching parenting she came across daily. She hadn't screamed at her day in, day out. Hadn't attacked her. Or had she? Always, always that question. So stark. So uncompromising.

Abruptly bringing herself back to the pressing matter at hand, Ruth cleared her throat, reached onto the floor, picked up the review, and nodded, despite herself. Then once again, she glanced at her watch. Not since she was a child had she attended any of her mother's exhibits. She had simply made excuses like at Pesach—don't get her started on that one. But heartless, she was not. And we were talking her mother here. And this exhibit was special, and this was the last day.

While Ruth advanced toward the coat rack, in the myriad of Cohan-Smith households between Winnipeg and Ottawa others were likewise going about their day. For the last hour an elated Naomi had been presiding over the art exhibit. "Naomi," one of the homeless artists was exclaiming, "this man's been gawking at my sunset photo for over ten minutes now. And his comments—almost makes me feel like a real artist!"

"But Glenda," Naomi pointed out, "you *are* a real artist." Naomi smiled to herself. Yes, her homeless protégés had learned their craft well and were taking Parkdale by storm.

Having recently won the Wykoffe Award for Photo-activism,

at the ripe old age of sixty-four, Naomi was on a roll. Daily, she was on the phone with antipoverty groups. The press courted her. And she could not count the number of community centres launching programs modelled on her "Photographing Our Lives" Project—some even following her cue in forsaking digital, in other words, *really* teaching the art.

Although she continued to struggle—having to take notes voraciously—Naomi seldom thought about shock. As she told her friend Miriam, she was grateful it had finally been abolished and what's done, is done. Nonetheless, every so often when she was least expecting it—after an exhilarating day at the race track, after a cozy evening of old movies and cocoa—she would shut her eyes and find herself back in that corridor.

Her high spots? Traipsing through north-end Winnipeg, camera in hand. Ruth graduating top of her class. *Schmoozing* with Rose. Her regrets? Losing sight of Jack. Even now not being able to pull off being the mother for whom Ruthie yearned. The quiet awareness of those pieces of her that were gone.

"Jesus, Mary, and Joseph—another typo!" As Naomi presided over the exhibit, Earl was in his study swearing a blue streak and correcting those interminable errors familiar to all who write. An accomplished author in his mid-seventies, he was working on his third book. Having come to a financial arrangement with Nomi that allowed her to turn the Palmerston house into a home studio, he lived in North York with his third wife Thien—a writer also. His high spot? Watching Ruth make minced meat of witnesses in the courtroom. His biggest regret: Never having ascended the academic ladder.

Even as Earl was proofreading, miles away, Les was leaning into a lectern, glancing at his notes, while doing his damnedest to deliver a passably interesting lecture on criminology. A student in the front row, meanwhile, was snoring. "If all the world were drowning," Les suddenly announced, "and I about to die, I'd stand upon my lecture notes because they are so dry." The class roared.

A well-liked prof at Carleton University whose evaluations were nonetheless borderline, Les was in the middle of a gruelling tenure review. He lived in the Ottawa valley with his wife Gina and son Mike. His high spots? Cycling. Taking part in amateur standup on those increasingly rare occasions when it fit into his busy academic schedule. His biggest regret? That he had ended up living his father Earl's dream.

"Okay," continued Les, looking up at his students again, "let's rock."

"*Rockabeegaboogee bee*," blared the radio. Having taken early retirement four years ago, Rose was at home babysitting her grandchildren while listening to what the kids called "the old fogie station." She and Sam still dwelt on Polson, though over the last decade, she had spent far more time in Toronto than anyone would have predicted. As she aged, being away from Nomi was getting progressively harder. Go figure. Sam would grumble about these absences, but he knew that there was nothing to be done. "I love you with a passion," she would tell him, "and best thing I ever did was marry you, but Nomi and me, we were together in the beginning…. Now come here, mister. Your favourite wife wants to ravish you."

Her high spots: Alone time with Nomi. That look of un-adulterated bliss which would come over Sam when she blew on the nape of his neck. Her regrets: Ever having lost track of Nomi. Resenting her niece so. To this day, having no comeback when her mother would dismiss her with a toss of the hand and her legendary "*feh*."

"*Feh!*" A frail woman in her late eighties, Ida was on her knees, scrubbing a recalcitrant spot on her kitchen floor. "*Feh! Feh!* Who's ever seen such a spot?" she muttered to herself. "But if that stinker thinks it's gonna get the better of me, it has another thing coming." A widow, she had stayed on in the Inkster house even after her death of her beloved Moshe some fifteen years ago. Adamantly, every year she turned down Rose's "invitation" to move in with her. She managed, yeh? Why should she not manage? Was she a cripple on a cross or something? She swept the floor, watched television, injected herself. Now when Naomi was around or Rose's brood came over, with help, she would make Shabbes, though for herself she did not bother. "Who would bother just for themselves?" she would ask her hairdresser Edie. Some mornings as the sun began to rise, she would peer out her back window and half imagine that she could see her darling Moshe puttering about, casting crumbs about the yard.

Her high spots? *Pesach* with the kids. Trips down memory lane. Those glorious months when her daughter Naomi joined her. Now if you asked Ida about regrets, she would look you straight in the eye and insist that she had none. But one thing kept eating away at her. Because of her foolishness, her daughter had lost so much. Oh, others may celebrate Naomi Cohan the photographer. But what did they know of that brilliant sensitive child?

"Child, it's *your* body, and guess what—*your* decision," advised Gerald. Even as Ida scrubbed her floor, Gerald was on his kitchen phone, discussing "the facts of life" with a young trans man. He reluctantly wrapped up, then rushed to the oven, where a piping hot pan of cinnamon swirls awaited. He'd be heading to the exhibit soon and was not about to arrive empty-handed.

As he started easing the buns out of the pan, a note caught his eye. He smiled to himself even before reading it. "Back by seven. Staying forever," it stated. Now notes of this ilk frequently graced the kitchen table in Gerald's abode, and over the years, many a visitor had wondered about them, but few had any inkling of the story behind them:

Back in the seventies, for months Gerald's partner Miu had

been missing. Now one day when his arthritis was acting up, Gerald had been applying heat to his achy hands when the phone rang. "It's me," declared the voice on the other end. Instantly recognizing who it was, the poor man gasped. "Ger," Miu resumed, "I had to get away, make a separate life for myself. But I couldn't do it, couldn't give you up. Please can I come home?

"I know I don't deserve ... I ... I..." she'd stammered.

"Love, just come," he offered. And he was beyond ecstatic when she did. Next morning he awoke with a start. He cast his eyes about. No sign of Miu. He checked every room. Gone! How could he have let himself end up here again? Back and forth, he paced. Then suddenly, the door to the apartment creaked open, and you could hear crumpling sounds—like someone struggling with groceries. Seconds later, Miu entered. She saw the expression on her beloved's face. And from that day forward, whenever she was away unexpectedly, there on the table a note awaited.

Touched that after all these years she still made the effort, Gerald removed the rest of the buns, shed a few tears. As he reached for his handkerchief, he caught sight of his reflection in the kitchen mirror and began to chuckle. Not bad for an old geezer. And why as a trans man, he was rather in vogue these days, he noted, tipping his hat and smiling to himself. Not that he did not continue to be hassled now and then. But sure as shit is a cat, the trans revolution, it was finally happening.

In his seventies, Gerald was as dapperly dressed as ever—always a vest, a Panama hat, cuff links. Having retired six years ago, on most days he could be found hanging out at the 519 Community Centre, where he ran groups for folk struggling with gender identity. "The bigots out there make you feel like a freak?" he would ask. "Listen. You and me, we have a long and glorious history. We come from kings, queens, spirits, and gods."

His high spot? Seeing this new generation of trans kids reach for the sky. His regret: After all these years, still not being able to face what befell him that terrible day when the ground came out from under—suddenly. Decisively.

The Parkdale Gallery at Dundas and Dufferin was a favourite among Toronto politicos. The location was to die for—smack in the middle of the action. What added to its popularity, while it had seen better days, hence the generous rates, the space was palatial—large rooms, sculptured ceilings, even an opulent foyer complete with low hanging chandelier.

The event now in progress had attracted folk from far and wide—an Ottawa politician, a prominent Peterborough artist, a contingent from most every shelter in the GTA—and it was decidedly upbeat. Visitors were immediately greeted by a huge sign that proclaimed, "Welcome. The Margin is the Centre, the Centre, the Margin." And they quickly found themselves in a brightly lit room, which opened onto a smaller room at back. Photographs of different sizes and shapes were arranged along the walls—and while the homeless motif dominated, queer, disabled, racialized, trans all found a niche. Hence the diversity among the spectators.

It was now four p.m., and a good seventy people were milling about—examining photos, commenting, munching on nibblies. Among them was Ruth, who had arrived but recently and was making her way through the main room. Now unlike most of the other patrons, she was speaking to no one. Nor was she in any hurry to encounter the artist.

Having just come across a picture which worried her, ever the lawyer, she was struggling with a tricky ethical question— whether all of the subjects were capable of giving consent—when to her surprise, on the west wall, she caught sight of a portrait of a demonstrably capable person, moreover, one whom she knew well. Oh my! There in her pristine glory was Gerald's old friend Annie. In the picture, Annie was mounting the top stair of the Dovercourt post office, her signature trousers with red suspenders on, an apron over the trousers, a cigar butting out of her mouth, a letter in hand. Next to this portrait was a companion piece. Standing on the sidewalk in front of the post office, her lips playfully extended, Annie was kissing a young black woman in a wheelchair, while a gaunt white man looked on, his eyes popping out of his head. Under the two pictures in mauve lettering was the text: "My name's Annie, my friend is Ethel. We are gender queer and we live, love, and mail letters like everyone else."

So Mom has balls after all, conceded Ruth. Or was that clit? Pleased, she resumed her promenade, stopping now and then to get a better look. As Ruth was taking in an overhead shot of a man lying face-down on a backless bench, a small crowd began gathering in front of a huge photograph to her right. "I was there," insisted a stout woman in blue jeans. "And let me tell you. Naomi was with us when them assholes came a-banging on our windows." Curious, Ruth drew closer, eyed the picture carefully. In the foreground looming large was a caravan of dumpsters and bulldozers. In the background, the obvious destination—a handful of tiny ramshackle cabins. Toward the edge stood a number of distraught beings, some holding onto each other weeping, one being restrained by police, a few shaking their fists. "We are not a blight," read the caption.

Not bad, but a tad overstated, thought Ruth. Then she stepped into the second room, and there it was—the much-touted exhibit of the homeless folk. Well aware that she was now poised to bump into her mother, Ruth began methodically taking in the display. She saw what she expected to see—pictures of bag-ladies with overloaded shopping carts. She saw what she did not expect—a shot of a blank wall with the words "Two lovers—Dave and Yoko—once slept here."

Suddenly hearing her mother's voice, Ruth turned around. In the centre of the room stood two small tables where reproductions from the homeless artist display were being sold. A smock draped over her shoulders, Naomi was seated at the furthest one, chatting away with a middle-aged Indigenous woman. There was no avoiding it. The look on her mother's face was decidedly warm. Why does she never look at me like that?, Ruth wondered, though even at the moment of asking, she found the question pathetic.

Stalling, Ruth approached the safer of the tables—even convicted felons get to check out the scenery when en route to the gallows, she assured herself—then she began examining the postcards. She glanced up just in time to see the woman of the hour stepping her way.

"Sweetheart, are you ever a sight for sore eyes! So glad you've come," said Naomi, putting her hand on the table. "Enjoying the exhibit?"

"Yeah, it's, well, good," stammered Ruth. "Congratulations."

"Maybe you'd like to meet some of the artists? Possibly join us for coffee later?"

Here it was—that extra inch that never failed to set her teeth on edge. "Look, Mom, I really have to go. I'm glad I came, though. We'll talk later, okay?"

While she could read the disappointment in Naomi's eye, Ruth said goodbye, paid for the postcards, and began to leave. She took a few steps, then stopped. Should she go back? Buying time, she slipped into the washroom, splashed water on her face. When she stepped into the gallery again, in the distance, she could hear Naomi asking someone, "In your work with residential school survivors, you ever come across a Jack Carpman?" Not having a clue what this was about and not keen on finding out, she returned to the first room, began making a beeline for the door. Just as she was about to enter the foyer, however, for no apparent reason, she turned to her left. Sweet Jesus! Adorned by neither frame nor caption, looking almost like an afterthought, was a photograph so simple, so at-the-bone that it took her breath away.

It was an outdoor shot. On a sidewalk lay a figure curled up in a fetal position. You could make out only a vague shape, for a tattered blanket was draped over the person. Nonetheless, two parts of the body were visible—the edge of a foot, part of an arm and hand. Disturbingly raw-looking, the hand was clasping a small teddy bear. A child, guessed Ruth. She looked again. While she couldn't be certain, the length of the body seemed to suggest otherwise. Could this be an adult—a fragile adult holding onto the only thing of significance left? Perhaps a teddy bear from childhood? Or perhaps this teddy once belonged to the luckless person's child.

As Ruth stood there, moved by the vulnerability, held by a sadness that she could not name, she thought of her own children. Then to her surprise, her eyes welled up with tears. She recalled the *Star* write-up—"Naomi Cohan searches the world with her empathic eye." Not able to bear it, she all but ran out of the room. She approached the table in the foyer, picked up her coat, then made her way down the stairs. However, just as she was on the verge of pulling off a clean escape, Gerald approached.

"Love, good that you came," said Gerald, tipping his hat. "Um, Ruth girl, something wrong?"

Ruth hesitated. "Ger," she finally said, "you may find this question strange, but my mom, did she ever assault me? I realize that she's your best friend, but if you know, please tell me."

Gerald's eyes grew concerned. "My! Well, not that I'm aware of. And honestly, love, just can't see it. Hey, wanna go for coffee, tell yours truly what this is about?"

"It's okay. Honestly, just a feeling."

"You know, Ruthie, you might consider having a sit-down with your mom and..."

"A sit-down! Excuse my language, but the woman doesn't give a flying fuck about me!"

"Can't agree with you there," asserted Gerald. "Look, I don't what that this assault stuff is all about, but this, I know. Your mom loves you. Kinda think you know that too. Think about it. Why else would she of all people spend half her life in Toronto?"

An uneasy look came over Ruthie. Slowly, she shook her head. "Not necessarily for my sake and not good enough," she said. "Being physically present, that can't be the sum total of parental responsibility. Um, strange thing about today, though, Ger. A couple of these photos, I'd have felt proud to have taken. Now you'd think that'd thrill me, but it doesn't."

"Not so strange. All your life, you thought it was your dad you took after. Well..."

"Oh Ger, don't say it," Ruth urged. "I'm nothing, nothing, nothing like that woman."

Two hours later, Ruth was sitting in the living room of her condo, a Sloe Gin Fizz in hand, slowly, methodically, trying to untangle the perennial knot in her head.

"A problem?" asked her husband Bruce, hesitantly entering through the archway.

"Not a thing," she answered, "well, unless you count being attacked as a child. That or not being sure about anything."

NAOMI'S MEMOIR

BOOK THREE

2
0
0
8

2
0
0
9

ETC.

18. NAOMI

*E*XCEPT FOR A *solitary figure, the treatment room was empty. Outside, rats were scurrying about—big beady-eyed rats, known to nibble on people's toes. Inside, the paint on the walls was flaking, the floor was bare, and in lieu of furniture stood deep steel tubs. Hidden within the recesses of one such tub lay a middle-aged woman, sweat trickling down her brow. Only her head could be seen, for a thick canvas covered her body, trapping her in—arms and all. "This is bedevilment," she suddenly shrieked, her eyes darting about. "Have mercy on a God-fearing woman and let me out!" An-other hour passed, and another. And still she lay, her face red, her eyes drained.* (The Interventionist Years: Hydrotherapy Session, Toronto Hospital for the Insane, 1928)

Not bad for an aging artist, I noted, chuckling away to myself. And outstanding for a group which had taken up photography but three months ago. I exited the streetcar at Lansdowne, riding a high. I dropped in at a local Afghan supermarket, began inspecting the fruit. This was for a totally new group of homeless folk—one I'd just started working with, and hell, I wouldn't do it—wouldn't settle for that blemished produce customarily bestowed on disenfranchised populations—the kind that announce to the besieged and weary, "This is all you're worth! Bite me." I exited the shop with a basket of shiny Macintoshes, lush grapes, bananas with nary a spot on them.

Then I wended my way to the Dufferin Community Centre. My Toronto workplace, sporadic though the work was, yes? The DCC, as we call it, it is that rambling red building near Dufferin and Queen—the one with the garish purple roof and tinted windows. Open 24/7, it has been home to many a progressive program, serving people with addictions, ex-inmates, refugees. Decades ago, psych survivors formed the bulk of the clientele, though now it is that larger though not unrelated population clumsily known as "the homeless". Now I cannot say that the Centre's programming in this area has made a difference that could be measured, but hey, it has provided tools—helped people stripped to the bone organize, fight back. And my colleagues and I, we were a modest part of that.

I pick up my story here because there are moments in the flux of every life that are destined to be markers—and for me, 2008 was one. Imagine, if you will, thirty-two years having passed, a Canada famous not for social justice but for people freezing to death on the streets of our cities. So what else can a person do but fight back? I was now sixty-four years old, thinner, grey as a hoot owl, settled so to speak, mind you—and I kid you not—still *schlepping* between cities. Thanks to the modern miracle of dual residence, both my Winnipeg and my Toronto family had remained an integral part of my life, yes? And in their own way, everyone was doing well.

Of course, the world had grown older, and us along with it. The oldest surviving member of my family, my mother was nearing ninety. Astute as ever, she still kept up the Inkster Blvd house, even attended community meetings. "What? You'd rather I do *bupkes* and die of boredom?" she would ask. Well on her way to becoming family matriarch—and how it suited her—Rose was a grandmother six times over. "Little Ruthie" was now a grown woman, with children and a career of her own. And Ger had become a highly respected figure in Toronto's increasingly vocal trans community.

Now my life had not been what I dreamt of in my salad days

when I reached for the stars. Nor had I established the relationship that I wanted with my daughter or even found Jack. But hey, I had accomplished something of what I had set out to do that day so long ago when first I hung the photography sign in the bay window. I had helped raise a child—seen her turn into an unapologetic woman who held her head high, who claimed her place in the world as a matter of right. I had maintained a happening photography practice in cities thousands of miles apart. I was blessed with two impressively anarchistic grandchildren with dreams of their own. I had zealously protected my relationship with Rose, my mother, Gerald. I had seen my beloved father pass away peacefully in his own bed, knowing that both his daughters were keeping a watchful eye on the home front. And all the while the camera was never far from sight—letting me see, putting food on the table, unlocking the mysteries of life, allowing me to function as an activist.

Oh I had remained, as Rose described it, "a kick-ass shit-disturber" all right. Of course, I couldn't make political movies. Nonetheless, in my own way, I told half decent stories—ones that cried out for change and which the public intuitively understood. Now until the early 1990s, I had divided my time between several different causes. I had stood up with the striking miners in northern Manitoba. Initially pulled in by the Quaker genius for being *in* the world and not *of* it, I'd also become involved in prison abolition. Eventually, though, in the antipoverty movement, I had found a more focal way to contribute. I had also found sisters and brothers whose presence warmed my heart. In a blinkered universe— which is surely the grounds on which we mortals pitch our tent—linking up with others who also know that safety is an illusion and who make no bones about it, what a relief it can be! Like a window opening in an airless room. And so yes, you might say that the years had been good. As for the last few days—fucking awesome!

Some homeless artists and I—the rat pack as Toronto's art

community was calling us—we had pulled off a remarkable exhibit. And why, everyone and their sister had turned up. Even Ruth. As I climbed the stairs of the community centre, I wondered how Ruth was dealing with her inevitable regret at having come. You see, when she made overtures toward me, sooner or later, she invariably regretted it. Now the impasse between the two of us—that was an old story. She had grown into an exceptional woman. A capable mother. As a lawyer, what a force to reckon with—snooping around in obscure nooks and crannies, coming up with arguments of such consequence that the presiding judge himself would be left scratching his head. "How can there be security of the person when the medications undermine the person?" she had argued just last month. But oh how our personal history gnawed at her! Now I had kept hoping that as she aged, for her own peace of mind, she would come to take the bad with the good—but the idea of doing so seemed almost repugnant to her. Not that deep down I couldn't relate.

Feeling for my daughter, then doing what I had to—letting it go—I brushed the snow off my coat, entered the building. The second that I set foot in the lobby, Haesun the receptionist, together with a coterie of well-wishers bestirred themselves, rushed over to congratulate me. "Naomi for Prime Minister," shouted Glenda, our resident kidder. "And Glenda for Governor-General," I returned playfully. Then I sequestered myself in the closet-sized office at the back.

While the exhibit was a much needed shot in the arm, getting back to my day job, if I might so call it, was like arriving home after a long absence. Eagerly settling back into my regular routines, I returned the backlog of phone calls. I lunched with the program coordinator Chris, discussed grant applications. Then I tackled the basement meeting room—pulled out the cameras, arranged the chairs. Last and most important was setting up the table at the back, the fruit in the centre, a tempting array of munchies surrounding it.

This was only the second meeting of the new group. What if no one showed?, I inevitably asked. Then the miracle at the very core of this work started to happen. Despite having little reason to trust, slowly but surely, our people began trickling in—first Elizabeth in her baggy jeans, then Jeremiah in a tattered shirt. Before long, coffee in hand, ten of us were sitting in a circle, and the room was alive with talk, a healthy suspicion in many an eye.

"Can you go over the different camera thingamajigs again?" asked Elizabeth, seemingly the most enthusiastic of the novices.

"Absolutely. Right after check-in," I answered.

And after several false starts, we were in the thick of things—some pushing for techniques, some jockeying for position, some content just to be momentarily out of the cold. And oh so many with that delightfully sassy look in their eye that announced that if you didn't like who they were, why you could eat shit.

"So, Naomi," piped up six and a half foot Ned, rising and hoisting up his shirt. "See these sores on my back? Well, they fuckin' hurt. Everywhere I bed down, the cops are on my case. Days I don't eat. Got a bed bug itch. Had a shelter staff yell at me."

"You got a point?" pressed stout Jeremiah. "Or you treating us to another gripe fest?"

"Yeah, big shot, I got a point. My point is... My, um, my point..."

Jeremiah snickered, ostentatiously rolled his eyes.

"No laughing at people. C'mon, Jeremiah—your guideline," I reminded him.

At this, Ned whirled about, glowered at Jeremiah. "No, shithead, keep right on laughing," he threw out. "In fact, may you laugh so hard your anus turns inside out."

Jeremiah scrunched up his eyes, I suspect in an attempt to visualize, and the snickering came to an abrupt halt.

Now Ned had never expressed himself quite so graphically

before, so his words came as a surprise. Savouring the effect, an unmistakable smile of vindication on his lips, he sat back down. "Okay then," he continued, "my point, right? Our lives are hard, and seems like instead of helping us, they're waging war against us. So why should any of us give a rat's ass about depth of field?"

"Maybe because in a war, you need ammunition," I ventured.

"Praise the Lord and pass the ammunition," sang Leonard, waving his hands about as if conducting an orchestra and grinning mischievously. "Praise to the…"

"So we learn about that junk and just go out and shoot?" asked Ned.

"Not exactly. We begin with you. The sores. The cops. The bedbugs. These are things that get in your way, yes? So how about we take it from there?" I walked over to the flip chart, jotted down "cops," "bedbugs," "rude workers." "So," I asked, "you guys game for generating a larger list of things that get in your way?"

"Fuck, yeah," exclaimed Elizabeth, whereupon, diplomat extraordinaire that she was, she proceeded to rhyme off half the centre staff, in many a case, with good reason.

Now one man stomped off cursing half way through—"bum wipe," he dubbed the evolving list—and understandably, Ned kept inquiring about digital. Nonetheless, we largely stayed on task.

When the group dispersed an hour later, a few lingered, a middle-aged woman with activist smarts suggesting ways to mobilize against tasers. Another woman who had outlived three husbands and who was, as she put it, nobody's fool, pointedly opining, "The larger the copper's weapon, the smaller his pea-shooter, don't ya' think?"

All and all, I was cautiously optimistic. Against all odds, ten of the original fourteen had returned; and every last one had contributed. Humbled, I sat down, started making copious notes. Now I was struggling to fill a gap in my memory when I looked up to discover that Ned of all people had returned—an engaging, almost a flirtatious look in his eye.

"Why, hello, again. You lose something?" I asked.

"Young lady, I just might have at that," he answered enigmatically. Blatantly pleased with himself, he immediately took a seat, then began unbuttoning his coat as if settling in for a long stay.

"*Young* lady?" I observed, bemused. "You know I'm twice your age."

"There needs no ghost come from the grave to tell us this."

I sat there stunned. Why if I was not mistaken, he was quoting from *Hamlet*. "You've studied Shakespeare?" I asked.

"That against your fuckin' ground rules too?" he fenced. Instantly regretting his tone, he apologized. He proceeded to point out that a liberal arts background was hardly the exclusive domain of the housed. "Being habitually sold short," he added with a knowing look, "that's another item for our list, wouldn't you say?"

"You betchya," I answered, "and incidentally, I too apologize."

"Anyway, to answer your question, yeah, I once had a very different life. But that's not what I'm here to talk about. Naomi, listen. You have ammunition. My brothers and sisters are dying out there, and frankly, ammunition—that's what I'm after."

We caught each other's eye, smiled. And for the next couple of hours the two of us sat side by side, tackling the ABC's of photography. Oh yes, the man had the necessary fire in the belly all right.

Riding a high, shortly after Ned departed, I took camera in hand and began prowling the streets of Parkdale. That evening I took many a shot of the new galleries that had sprung up along Queen West. Mostly, though—and this was my heart's delight—I chronicled the ebb and flow of the populations that I'd come to adore. The hypnotic shuffle of the drifter, the no-nonsense gaze of the seasoned sex worker, the camaraderie of the crack-heads as they leaned against a dumpster and passed around some blow.

It was with renewed vigour that I turned in that night. Such were the victories—what my world looked like on a good day. All things considered, a kind of triumph yes? Nonetheless, without realizing it, or what is perhaps more accurate, realizing *and not realizing*, over the years, I had lost something—and no, not simply what had been stolen from me. Strange how we can go for decades, our eyes front and centre, attending to the immediacy of what is thrust in our path. All well and good—arguably, necessary. We are the stuff of our history, however, and sooner or later a person has to take stock.

And so it was to prove.

The Centre, it was abuzz with the news. Contrary to the predictions of the pundits, and much to the delight of devotees like my grandson, first lady and presidential hopeful Hillary Clinton had pulled off a narrow but stunning victory over one Barack Obama in the New Hampshire primary. And on the Republican side, senator John McCain had edged out governor and business darling Mitt Romney with a five per cent margin.

"Bloody hell!" exclaimed young Zack—an ardent follower of Aryans Forever. "To think the good old U.S. of A's gonna be run by a dame, a nigger, or a gimp!"

Feet from the speaker stood seventy-year-old Ayanna—a long time member of the Black Action Defence Committee. A shrewd look in her eye, the wily senior bided her time as the cocky youth bombarded us with one offensive remark after another. "Bro, I'm totally with you," Ayanna eventually observed, "but you know something? According to a recent study, there's a correlation between using the 'n' word and your Johnson shrinking. A real shame," she added nonchalantly, seeing the poor devil turn pale, "but apparently, young man, use it often, and you can lose an entire inch."

Not long after this masterful piece of footwork, Ned turned up, a bounce in his step. The second that he set foot in my office, the reason for his excitement became abundantly clear. He had gotten his hands on a Leica—and to good effect. In short order, he had pulled out a stack of photographs and the two of us were seated side by side, scrutinizing them methodically.

"This shadowy part—highly effective," I mused, gazing with admiration at a compelling shot of a teenager reaching into a dumpster.

"To be frank, I'm not sure how I pulled that off," he acknowledged sheepishly.

His confession opening up the way, we quickly launched into another lesson. And when he took off two hours later, there was a smile of determination on his face. Alone once again, I picked up where I had left off the other day, reviewing the list of obstacles. I immediately inserted the phrase "being sold short." Half an hour later, I was leaning back in my chair, trying to conjure up an image that would do justice to an obstacle identified by Elizabeth when a spate of shouting pierced the air—not angry exactly, but desperate, like the howls of a tormented animal. To my relief, it quickly petered out, but seconds later, it started up again.

"Need help over there?" I eventually called out, poking my head out the door.

White as a sheet, Elsa, the assistant coordinator, tiptoed up to me. Periodically glancing uneasily in the direction of the lobby, she proceeded to whisper, "There is a schizophrenic in reception who is really out of it. Being disruptive and he's scaring Glenda's kids. So like, if he won't leave, we might have to involve the police. Now Naomi, I know you don't..."

"No way," I insisted. "Now I suspect he's famished."

I check the cupboard. One Hershey bar. I pick it up, begin advancing toward reception, wondering what poor soul has wandered in out of the cold, frustrated how easy it is even for so-called "progressive" workers to cop out.

Suddenly, a single word comes flying through the air—"shit!"
Oy! I'd have recognized that voice anywhere. But after all these
years, that he'd just turn up! My heart in my mouth, I quicken
my pace. I pass by Glenda's two little boys, who are tugging
at their mother nervously. With barely a nod, I pass a young
woman in tears. Then I come to a full stop. Surreal though it
feels, there he is on the edge of the sectional, shivering. His
parka is grimy, his face wrinkled. No radio in sight, but yes,
yes, lest there be any doubt, a hand-rolled cigarette is dangling
from his chapped lips. Saliva is making its way down the cigarette, as he sits there muttering. For a moment I hesitate. Then
I draw nearer, kneel down in front of him.

"Hey there, Jack," I murmur.

He continues mumbling to himself, seemingly oblivious to
the fact that he has been addressed.

Repeatedly, I call out to him, but to no avail. In the background, people who do not know him from Adam are whispering, one wondering if he is violent, another taking it upon
herself to pronounce him "totally out of touch." And now
our executive director is entering the room, an all-too-handy
cell phone pressed to his ear. A time when a person needs to
know with a certainty whose side she's on. Whose side she
has to be on!

"Indomitable Jackman," I call out.

Suddenly Jack whirls about and gazes at me bewildered. Then
his eyes narrow. "Shit!" he exclaims. "Now I'm *seeing* things!"

"Believe me, Jack, I'm no hallucination."

"Oh really?" he asks, a familiar glint in his eye. "Prove it."

"C'mon. Only a hallucination would fall for that one."

He pauses as if uncertain. "Kiddo?" he asks at long last.

"Uh huh."

Little by little, a smile breaks through his leathery face. "Well
how about that! Naomi, sorry about the confusion. Someone
swiped my radio a few weeks back and I'm just not myself."

"Don't worry, Jack. We'll get you another."

Realizing that I am serious, he nods. Then he lets out a deep sigh. And in seconds, he is sobbing, tears streaming down his cheeks, mucous bubbling out from his nostrils. Suddenly, the cigarette drops from his lips. While Elsa rushes to stomp it out, I cast about for a Kleenex. Then I recall the day in that corridor so many years ago when this very man appeared from out of nowhere, gallantly reached for my hand. Instinctively, I slip my hand inside my T-shirt, bring my shirt-covered fingers toward him.

"Hey, old friend, blow," I say.

Jack hesitates. Then he leans into me, surrenders to the moment.

And so it is that in the twilight of our existence—his, mine— once again Jack Carpman enters my life. Abruptly. Irrevocably. And once again, without so much as a warning, the world was to change.

Oh Jack, would that you had found me sooner!

19. NAOMI

*A*s THE SCORCHING SUN *bore down on them, on the grounds of a sprawling hospital, a scattering of naked men and women—twenty in all—were being herded toward a low-lying building in the distance. As the group neared its destination, a young man in a doctor's uniform made his way over, offered what sounded like reassurance. "But why can't we just shower in our own ward?" a woman asked. Even as this query escaped her lips, the large metal door creaked open, and along with her companions, she was ushered in. Once the door was securely shut, the doctor drew closer. He peered in through a peep hole. For several minutes, he watched, and as he looked, almost imperceptibly, the expression on his face shifted from alarm to stony calm.*

Not an hour later the doctor was sitting pensively behind a desk, a stack of twenty certificates in front of him. He looked at the top one long and hard, as if trying to settle on something fitting. Then he picked up his pen. "Cause of death, septicimia," he wrote. (T4: The Annihilation of the Mental Patients, Germany, circa 1939)

You ever notice how it is seldom just one thing that shifts? We go about our affairs for long stretches at a time more or less without a hitch, when suddenly in all corners of existence, most everything comes to a head—as if unbeknownst to us, a lever had been triggered. Perhaps our choices catching up with us. Though at times I suspect that the universe has its own rhythms, moods, inclinations. Be that as it may, what was happening on other fronts was beyond my ken. Even as Jack and I stepped through my front door, however, already I was aware that I had been moved more profoundly than I had been for years. Exactly what was going on for Jack is not for me to know. This much, however, was clear. Life had kicked the stuffing out of him, then kicked some more. And still, he was doing his damnedest to be the *mentsh* I remembered.

"Fact is," stated Jack, leaning back in his chair, a toothpick bobbing up and down between his lips, "I've been on the streets since the days of the Harris Tories. For a while I shacked up in this cardboard hut under the Bathurst St. Bridge. But guess you know what became of those huts, eh? Anyway, after our so-called progressive mayor screwed us over royally, I started bedding down under the Gardiner Expressway onramp."

I blinked my eyes, still barely able to take in that the man was actually here. "And on nights when it gets too cold?" I ask.

"Well, if I absolutely have to, I get myself to a shelter. Not my thing, though."

Jack having agreed to let me feed him, grease dripping from our fingers, the two of us were hunkered down at my kitchen table, polishing off the remains of a roast chicken dinner, and at long last, I was finding out what had befallen the man. He spoke of crack nightmares that would send him into a panic. Of the good old days when he and his buddies would cozy up to the fire, the stars like a blanket comforting them.

At one point, he had attempted to return to his people. "Kiddo, a person has to at least try," he clarified—but you could tell from the embarrassment in his eyes that he could not reconnect. Over the years he had also landed the odd job—as a carpenter's assistant, as a deckhand. Sooner or later, however, the voices would catch up to him. Now while the tough row he had hoed was etched in the lines on his face—no question, the old Jack, he was in there. He would crack jokes and cite chapter and verse of land claims, but every so often a deflated expression would steal over him and he would stare at the wall.

"I'm sorry about this," he noted at one point. "Well, you know, about the way I get. Anyway, I need you to know that I'm not unaware. Shit!" he exclaimed, shaking his head. That sounds wimpy even to me. Okay if we pretend I didn't say that?"

I smiled conspiratorially, then gently laid my hand on his.

"So the consummate asshole, you sure he's not going to turn up?" he suddenly checked.

"No way. Incidentally, he's not that bad," I hastened to point out, "though you may be happy to learn that the consummate asshole and I are divorced."

Jack refilled his plate, slipped the toothpick into his shirt pocket, began working his way through an extra crispy drumstick. "Can't say I'm sad about that," he responded. "Nope. You asked why I stayed away. In a word—him."

"Gimme a break. We're talking 35 years here—longer than most marriages last."

"True," he returned, "but a person lets things go long enough, it gets almost impossible to pick them up again."

Now I was keenly aware that once Earl was out of the picture, I could have done a whole lot more to find Jack. Intent on sparing us both useless recriminations, however, Jack was having none of this. He reached over fondly, removed a strand of hair from my eyes. "Naomi, I'm here *now*," he pointed out. Then he changed the topic entirely, and before long we were chewing over old times. One reminiscence tripping over another, we spoke of Nurse Ann. Of tonguing. Of that old nursery rhyme that he'd culled forth to help me find my room.

"Can I ask you something?" I eventually queried, my eyes fixed on his. "Why did you do it—help me so?"

He took a sip of his coffee, folded his arms, knit his brow. "I saw it, right? Saw person after person zombified. Saw them take you apart too—bolt by bolt, screw by fuckin' screw. Horrible, right? But do you know what really got to me?"

"Seeing me in the corridor that day?"

"Yes, but not the day you imagine. You see, while *your* memory begins there—and I always respected that—not so for *mine*." He went on to divulge that there was a time he had lost his way. "Fact is, I'd given up on life…. Oh yes, I had," he persisted. "Basically, I'd settled for an existence of trivial acts of rebellion and basking in the applause of other inmates. What is it they call that? Has the word 'pond' in it."

"Being a big fish in a small pond?'"

"A big Aboriginal fish in a small white pond at that," he observed with a wry smile. "Then something changed. Not overnight, 'cause for the longest while you weren't on my radar. Then I opened my eyes, right? Watching you, kiddo, it was like a breath of fresh air, eh? Day after day, those piss-ass officials would zap you, and day after day, you'd struggle back, do everything in your power to hold onto even a sliver of awareness. And how I rooted for you! Anyhow, one day after hours of you lying there seemingly blotto, you called out, 'Tiger, tiger burning bright, in the forest of the night.' The staff, they thought you were seeing things, but I know poetry when I hear it. And I said to myself: Nope. Not gonna let them destroy this one. And that's when I determined to be your friend. A good decision all around, even one that gave me something of a new lease on life. Not that there was squat I could do about the damage. Shit!"

"Oh Jack, you did plenty," I answered, catching his eye. "In Judaism, we've a name for the kindness you showed. Call it a *mitzvah*, a blessing, yes? So thank you."

Jack instantly went quiet, got a far-away look as if lost in thought. Seconds later he began speaking about how people "in hell holes" help one another out. "Hell holes—that's exactly what they are too," he suddenly muttered. "Give me the street any day of the week."

He observed me cautiously, saw that I understood—or was it that I *still* understood? Then he fished the tobacco and rolling papers from his pocket, plunked his elbows on the table, and set about his art. Despite a slight tremour in his left hand, his hands and eyes still worked skilfully together like a clever seamstress, like a photographer on the prowl.

"Hey," I asked, "'member the way everyone used to *ooh* and *ahh* as the perfect cigarette emerged from your finger tips?"

Jack gave the cigarette a few extra twists, grinned. "Yeah. Brad, Bob. Oh and that Bob, wasn't he something! He was around during your time, right?"

"Not sure."

He caught my eye. "Naomi, I really think he was. Chinese chap. Glasses. On the short side. Always on the phone talking to his 'stockbroker.'"

"Oh yeah. Any idea what became of him?"

"As it happens, I do. Became a fuckin' billionaire."

"C'mon. You don't mean…"

"Honest. I'm not shittin' ya'. After all this time, it turns out the man wasn't delusional. He really was talking to his stockbroker—and to good purpose too."

"And those ingenious St. Patrick's doctors," I quipped, "they couldn't cure him of this deplorable non-delusional state?"

"Apparently not," said Jack, breaking into a grin. "It seems non-delusional personality disorder is a tough nut to crack."

At this, we both laughed.

Now he brought up Brad and Emily, also patients that I did not know from Adam, though presumably, I once had. However, as he proceeded to trot out fellow travellers that I was confident neither of us had been remotely close to, I started to get an eerie sense that something besides my memory was amiss.

A sense of dread descending upon me, I caught his eye. "Jack, I can't help but notice that you've left someone out," I hazarded.

Seemingly ignoring me, he pulled out his pouch, began rolling another cigarette.

"Jack?" I tried again.

"I didn't want to upset you," he answered, his eyes glued to the cigarette. "The thing is, the woman, well, Zelda killed herself five, six years ago."

"My God!" I exclaimed. "What was it, Jack? The pain of losing her child?"

He looked up, but said nothing. Now I was about to probe further, but the phone rang. For six rings, I ignored it. Come the seventh, I forced myself to rise. "I've a very old mother," I explained, "and well, you just never know."

To my surprise, it was Ruth. While insisting there was no emergency, she wanted to head straight over and talk, though luckily, she settled for breakfast tomorrow. When I returned, Jack was leaning back in his chair, puffing away on that perfect cigarette. And there on the table in front of him lay a second cigarette—also perfect. With that gallant flourish so typical of him, he extended it toward me, and for the first time in our history, leastways, as far as I recollect, I accepted.

"You know, you were right about my being a smoker," I observe, lighting up.

He catches my eye, nods. Then once again, he falls silent.

"Can see you don't wanna tell me," I finally observe, "but Jack, I loved her too."

At this, his face melts. "Okay, Naomi. The long and short? They zapped her. Now one shock into the second series, she begged them to stop, asked me to get in touch with a lawyer and everything, but the thing is, they had her signature, right?"

"And the suicide?"

"In the middle of her second series, the stupid buggers up and gave her a day pass. Twelve hours later she turned up dead on the floor of a public steam bath, a suicide note in hand."

I shake my head in dismay, and in whispers, we speak of the Zelda we knew and loved—the generosity of her heart, her uncomplicated wisdom—and tears in our eyes, as if it were yesterday, we lament the senselessness of this tragedy. Then little by little, we slide into the one topic that but an hour ago, I'd have given my eye teeth to steer clear of.

"Naomi, remember what you said that day we came upon the shock lineup?" Jack asks. "'They're human beings! In the name of everything holy, how can they do that to them?'"

"You remember my *exact* words?"

"You see, they knocked my socks off because as far as I could make out, most shock victims don't put it together for years. And here you were just six months later..."

"I think I did go back and forth on it," I counter.

"Still."

Leaning back in his chair, he takes an extra long drag on his cigarette, lets the smoke trickle out his nostrils. And that's when he says it. "You know, kiddo, I always thought you'd be the one to throw down the gauntlet, force them to end that abomination once and for all, but I guess we all..."

I stare at him. "Force them to what? Jack, I'm confused. Back up. Just when did you say Zelda was shocked?"

"Six years ago, well, give or take..."

"So shock wasn't abolished in the eighties?"

Jack looks at me astonished. "Oh Naomi," he murmurs, his face softening, "you really are out of touch."

"So it would seem," I utter more to myself than him. "Enlighten me."

"It never stopped. It never decreased. It never got better. But shit! You know how they spin things. Even when it comes to naming. What's that handle they used to have for it? Still trot it out today as if it's, well, current, and actually means something."

I suddenly feel sick to my stomach, but I am determined not to flinch. "Modified," I spit out, returning his gaze.

The next couple of hours are something of a blur, though according to my records, Jack and I subwayed to the Dufferin Mall, picked him up a radio, a new pair of boots. Then at his behest, we stopped off at a local gym, watched youth sparring. Upon exiting, we stood on the sidewalk, and as the wind whistled about our ears, we chuckled at what old relics we'd become.

"You think *you've* got it bad forgetting the odd word?" I quipped. "What with ECT and age, *I'm* lucky I can find the nose on my face.... Hey, this is my nose, isn't it?" I asked, playfully grabbing at his.

"And this is my mouth, isn't it?" Jack rejoined, to my surprise, kissing me.

As Jack pulled back, we paused for a moment, looked at one another tenderly. Then we let it go, I suspect, neither of us wanting to alarm the other. Now it was bitter cold by this point—hardly a night where even a young man should be out braving the elements—never mind an old-timer in his seventies. So I urged him to return home with me, stay until the weather let up or at least until morning.

He considered for a moment, then shook his head. "Naomi," he said, his voice earnest, "You think I'm fit company, you think I'm the indomitable Jackman, but..."

"Honestly, I..."

"Listen. A guy gets kicked from pillar to post, sooner or later, a demon grows inside of him. No shit! Fact is, you've no idea what I can be like, what I'm capable of doing, and trust me, it's better that way."

"Oh Jack, I won't pretend that nothing that you could do would ever throw me. But you know what? I'd get over it—a person does. And even if it's far more serious than I'm imagining, the two of us, we'll work it out. Now if you need to take off right now—I get that. And if you need to keep me at arm's length, I get that too. But Jack Carpman, you're loved—loved precisely as you are. So don't you dare disappear on me again."

At this, gratitude and confusion vied for dominion in Jack's face. Suddenly, he clenched his fists, first one, then the other, not angrily—more like a person trying to get a grip. "Honestly gotta go now," he finally squeezes out. "But kiddo," he added, catching my eye, "see you at the Centre a week this Thursday at five."

Now he started to thank me. In mid-sentence, however, he turned the radio up high, and without another word, walked away.

A lump in my throat, I stood on the sidewalk, unable to budge until he had totally disappeared from view. "Oh God, please watch over him," I whispered into the merciless night air. And the second that I arrived home, I burst into tears. I wept for Jack. I wept for Zelda. I wept for generations yet unborn. I wept for folk everywhere, whatever the place, time, circumstance who'd been brutally sliced to ribbons by the system. As evening drew on, I crept upstairs, began pacing back and forth. Suddenly, I came to a standstill and stood there staring at the bedroom walls.

Now I had looked at these walls day after day for decades, but not like this. It was as if I were seeing them through a stranger's eyes. Why index cards filled with notes were taped everywhere—above the bed, over the dresser. "*Remember to pick up the dry cleaning*," read one. "*Edna's husband's name is James*," read another. Not exactly sure where I was going to go with this, I picked up the camera. Methodically, I began photographing much as I would were it someone else's living history. A long shot of each wall. The lens screwed in backward, macroshots of individual cards.

As I stopped for a smoke, the binders caught my eye. More history—and in more ways than one. You see, from the thick accumulation of dust on top, you could tell at a glance that one of them hadn't been touched in years. I picked up the camera again, aimed, zoomed in. Then one by one, I removed the binders, photographed titles, passages here and there, avoiding that one binder only.

Eventually, with trembling fingers, I reached for the neglected binder, forced myself to open it. Transparently, a record of my descent into electroshock hell, it was as chilling as ever, but if I thought that its secrets were about to be wrested from it, I was quickly disabused, for it was also as enigmatic as ever. I sat down, closed my eyes, let the decades wash over me. "There's something here," Gerald had insisted. "So love, don't forget about this. Promise me." I had reneged on that promise, hadn't I? Avoidance. A very complicated avoidance. I recalled the 1980s' exposés by Ontario Coalition to Stop Electroshock. Pictures of demonstrations on City TV. Pronouncements by the Ministry that suggested that they were actually going to do something. Then clear as if it had been yesterday, a scene from distant yesteryear flashed through my head.

It was right after the great escape. Us Cohan women were at a Middle Eastern restaurant. Having divulged how her friend had fared post-ECT, Mom had asked if it was like that for me. Then she had looked at me nonplussed. "But how could that be?" she protested. "This is 1974. What happened to Linda, that was back in the fifties when they knew from nothing." So she too had thought it had been abolished, phased out, magically transformed, *epes*. If something offends us to the very core of our being, then we stop hearing about it, do we instinctively define it as a horror of the past? And the bureaucrats, the establishment, do they count on this?

I was onto something. I could taste it—read it in my quickening pulse. I wanted to pull at the thread, see what else would unravel, but suddenly Ruth's phone call leapt to mind. Agitated about something or other—possibly me—she was coming over first thing tomorrow, and if I stayed up any later, I'd be totally useless to her. So I laid down Black Binder Number Three—for such it was—and crawled into bed.

Pulled out of a deep sleep by the sound of ringing, I reached for the phone. Even before I answered, I could sense that it was another problem, that this was simply going to be one of those seasons where you can't catch a break. Sure enough.

It was Rose letting me know that they had to take Mom to hospital.

Now she assured me that for the time being, everything was under control. "But Nomi," she added, "listen. Despite what Mom thinks, it's just not going to work her living by herself."

There it was. What with the ever growing needs of an aging parent, for years Rose had been pressing me to move back permanently. Not a bad idea. And it would allow the two of us more time together—a prospect we both welcomed. If only Ruth and I could first come to a better place! Now I was about to suggest a tentative game plan when Jack came to mind.

"Let me think about this," I answered.

"Don't think too long," cautioned Rose. "Oh and one other thing. I received the weirdest call from Ruth. Brace yourself. While she apologized for how far-fetched this sounded, you know what she asked? Whether you were ever into ritual abuse."

"Sure! In my spare time when I'm not plotting the downfall of western civilization. Rose, you've gotta be joking!"

I laid down the receiver and tried to concentrate on Mom. Inevitably, however, Ruth assumed centre stage in the theatre of my brain. Ritual abuse! Where on earth was she getting that from?

With great reluctance, I made my way back to the binders, searched volume after volume for any mention of it. Nothing. I smiled wryly at the thought of what a loss I'd be at over breakfast tomorrow. Then for the second time, I turned in. And for the second time I closed my eyes and drifted off.

I dreamed that I was in a boxing ring at Maple Leaf Gardens. Barefoot and pregnant— but give me some credit, demonstrably not in the kitchen—I was performing before a audience of a thousand people, facing 50,000 opponents, with no advanced notice, no boxing gloves on, and without having received a single lesson.

Strange how innocent we appear in dreams. In the real world, as I was to be reminded, nothing is that simple.

"Mom, believe me, I'm trying to be unfair—scratch that; I mean fair—but the truth of the matter is, you weren't there for me," said Ruth.

It was eight a.m., and Ruth in her emerald pants suit, me in my housecoat, for the last hour the two of us had been sitting across from each other at the kitchen table, barely pecking at the breakfast in front of us. Now given Rose's timely revelation, I had expected to be accused of strangling babies in their cradles, but alas, it was the same totally reasonable complaints that Ruth'd had all her life, and the unvarnished truth was, I was sick of it.

"I'm sorry, Ruth," I answered. "You deserved better. I wasn't always very feeling. I was away more than any other mother on the block. I'd embarrass you in front of your friends. And so yes, guilty as charged."

"No need to be flippant about it. Do you have any idea what it was like growing up with you as my mom?"

I straightened my housecoat, realized that I had indeed been flippant. "Probably not," I acknowledged, "but I did what I could. And look at you. Brilliant lawyer. Two kids of your own. Don't you think it's time you gave up hating your mother?"

Ruth glared at me, then to my surprise, nodded. "I know. I know," she uttered. "What in Christ's name is wrong with me?"

"You..." I began.

"Mom," she exclaimed, vaguely bemused, "surely you're not about to answer that. I mean even you must know that..."

"Rhetorical question, gotchya...but know something?" I persisted. "My own life's rather a muddle right now. So how about we cut to the chase? I'll start. Your Aunt Rose called last night."

"She told you what I asked? Damn! She promised not to."

"Oh, Ruth, she's my twin sister, so can't exactly help it. Anyway, something you should know. Your *bubbeh*'s had another episode, and while there's nothing final, I may end up living there full time. So the two of us, we really can't afford to be..."

At this, Ruth visibly bristled. "Apply a bit of pressure, why don't you? Fuck you!"

"Shh," I urged, putting my hand to my lips. "Just let all this go. I'm your mother even if the world's most imperfect one, and I'm honestly on your side. So tell me what's really going on."

Now Ruth's anger quickly dissipated, and it looked as though she were collecting her thoughts when all of a sudden, the colour drained from her face.

"My God, Ruthie, what?" I asked.

Ashen, but somehow looking every inch a lawyer, Ruth rose from her chair. "Okay, I think I know how to do this," she murmured mysteriously.

Offering no further explanation, she led the way into the living room, and after motioning me to stay, she stepped into the dining room, then turned around, her eyes urgent.

"Sorry about the rigamarole," she said, "but I suspect it will help. Okay, at risk of sounding melodramatic, let me just say that I have this memory."

"A memory? Okay, baby, I'm listening."

A long silence followed. Then in a voice ever so thin, she murmured a solitary word—"blood."

I could feel my heart sink. "Oh Ruthie, you remember that day?" I exclaimed.

She glanced at me nervously. "So something really *did* happen?"

And with these words, with this frighteningly simple question, a death-like pallor settled over the house—as if every nook and cranny knew what was there for us to know—that the chickens had come home to roost.

"Sweetheart, I'm so sorry," I murmured. "Maybe if you could say what you remember...?"

Ruth opened her mouth as if about to speak. Then she looked

away. "There was an issue over crayons," she suddenly stated, her tone measured. "I think maybe someone broke one, though that, I haven't a fix on it, but this part I recall clearly: I was here in the dining room—that, I'm sure of—and I heard a crash, maybe a few crashes—I couldn't swear to the number. Then there you were—blood on your face, your hands, your clothes. Over and over you called my name, what seemed like a crazed expression on your face. Now I was trying to make myself as small as I could, hoping that if I could just get small enough, you wouldn't be able to see me. But suddenly, your eye was on me. Then you actually started staggering toward me. Oh Mom," wailed Ruth, turning toward me, her face white, tears trickling down her cheek. "I can see it. You were getting closer and closer."

"Sweetheart, I..."

Ruth shook her head, took the time to collect herself. "Look, I was an infant and so undeniably your responsibility. Nonetheless, I'd never come after you for damages—promise," she adds. "After having lived with you all those years, you think that I am not aware that there were extenuating circumstances? So tell me because I *need* to know, *have a right* to know. What in Christ's name did you do to me?"

I take a deep breath, peer into my daughter's eyes. "Child, listen," I urge. "What you saw, it was real, and it is something that should never ever have happened, but this, I can assure you. I was coming to comfort you—not attack you. No one—absolutely no one—laid a hand on you."

"Comfort me?" asks Ruth aghast.

"I handled it dismally. And later, I thought you had forgotten it. Totally stupid of me, and I'm so sorry that my little girl had to suffer from my stupidity."

"But Mom, where did the blood come from?"

As I start to explain, slowly, Ruth inches her way back into the living room, the entire time her eye fixed on the mirror. For a moment, she lingers on one section of the mirror only.

Suddenly, she whirls about, her eyes riveted on my forehead. She begins to shake her head, then just stands there, staring in astonishment. "So you really didn't attack me?"

At Ruth's instigation, we returned to the kitchen, and for the next several hours the two of us talked. She spoke of laying awake night after night praying that I would not peek in on her. I explained about the meds, about shock, about finding myself in an alien world. And again and again, she shook her head in dismay. "But how could Dad of all people have done that?" she asked. "Oh Ruthie, he simply did what thousands of husbands do," I answered.

"Look, Mom," she eventually said, her face worn, "this doesn't make everything hunky-dory between us, but if you're wondering if I believe you, I do. You're a lawyer long enough, you know when someone's fudging the facts. You aren't."

How I ached to throw my arms around my daughter, but I knew better. I urged her to talk to Earl, to Gerald, or both. Then tentatively, I reached across the table, touched her cheek. For a second there, she looked soothed. Then her muscles tensed.

"Mom, I no longer want to hurt you," she offered, "but please don't.... Oh and don't take it personally if I'm out of touch for a while."

Whatever Ruth was feeling—and she wasn't one to take others into her confidence—in the days that followed she carried on with her professional life as adeptly as ever. In fact, I was later to learn, she successfully argued a groundbreaking case that very afternoon.

Be that as it may, just as she had forecast, she made a point of avoiding me although there were signs that she was stepping through our treacherous family history in her own way, for Earl phoned complaining, "Know what your daughter is after calling me? A sexist prick." Also for the first time in ages, my grandson turned up, as delightfully pro-feminist as ever.

"Hey Grandma, no sweat if you've other things to do," Don said, "but Mom suggested that I pop over and we take in a movie. You up for *Antonia's Line?*"

Unsure of my read on anything, and not able to bear the silence, eventually I called Gerald. He had little information, and to my chagrin, he too appeared to be livid with Earl. "I understand about the meds, but look, *he* didn't scare the b'Jezzus out of her," I pointed out. "Me, I did it! And where does she go with all this? Think she can just click on 'my-mom's-a-manic.com?'"

After the talk with Gerald, I paced the hall for hours, searching for answers. Now while it hardly put my mind at ease—nor should it—a call to Rose brought a temporary calm. Also a much needed reminder of the other revelations of the past few days.

"My poor niece!" exclaimed Rose, "but knowing—finally knowing—this has to be a good thing."

"Ro, Ruth can't be overjoyed with me right now, and if she needs you to, well, side with her, please try."

There was a flicker of hesitation. "In my own way, I'll be there for her," she finally responded.

"When Ruth rags on me, you really can't stand it, can you?"

"Now there's the understatement of the century! Um, Nomi? Something I need to ask. Your heart-to-heart with Ruthie, it has to be bringing back those terrible years."

"Sister mine, you don't know the half of it," I respond.

20. NAOMI

JANUARY 2008

Even as the middle-aged woman nodded, a wizened old man stepped forward, his gait faltering, his eyes keen. He peered up into the heavens. He looked down, his eyes gently caressing the pebbles at his foot. "We understand who we are," he announced with great dignity. And we stood there breathless, held by the moment. And I could swear that you could hear the universe go still. —Quoted from Brown Binder Number Six

IN THOSE DREAMY old days in our white stucco house on Inkster Blvd, at times when it turned so cold that us children were reluctant to set foot outdoors, his blue on blue *tallis* draped over his shoulders, my father would stir the cocoa, then sink into his living room chair, plunk his feet up on the ottoman, and tell us that for everything there is a season, a time for every purpose, yeah, every purpose under the sun. And right, he was. There is a time to sow, a time to reap. A time to sally forth. A time to sit patiently and listen for that murmuring heartbeat of the universe that makes itself heard in the quiet hours. This was a time for readiness. I could sense it. Also a time to reflect, and reflect I did.

The various revelations of the last few days, I turned them over, turned them over again. I saw my own shortcomings, my mistakes. Inevitably, though, and every bit as powerfully, yet again, I found myself face-to-face with the horror that was

St. Pukes. To think of what it had unleashed! Jack reduced to abject poverty. Generations of people struck down by a killer treatment that the medical profession flagrantly misrepresented. My daughter, my own child, who was but an innocent bystander, she too was a casualty of new, improved, safe, and effective electroconvulsive therapy, wasn't she? Earl also, despite the role he'd played. And then there was Zelda, struck down by that treatment just as surely as if she'd expired on the table. I could not erase the past, I realized, not even my own part in it. Just maybe, however, I could bring past and present together to change the future. And so it was that after a brief hiatus, once again I picked up the camera.

If every journey begins with a single step, just as crucially, it is reinvented and given shape by the second step, the third, the fourth. And then there are paths cut off so abruptly that it makes a person rage, then weep, then live to rage anew.

I'd just spent two exhilarating days shooting, and after grabbing a quick breakfast, I eagerly launched into a third. "Love, don't forget to come up for air," jested Gerald. Eventually running out of film, I slung a knapsack over my shoulder and trekked over to Parkdale Camera for fresh supplies,.

"Twenty-six rolls!" exclaimed Mr. Turay Junior as he tallied up the amount on his cash register. "Another big project—and still sticking with film, huh? Rest assured," he chuckled, "you've just made one sentimental Black capitalist plenty happy."

"Reason enough," I responded.

Buoyed up by my mission, I exited the premises with a bounce in my step for the first time in days. Now as I made my way down the crowded street, not two yards up ahead, I spotted a large-nosed feisty old street peddler selling gloves. "Ladies, gents, and anyone not an idiot," the old pro barked, holding up his ware, "one hundred percent fleeced-lined gloves and at such ludicrous prices, I'm virtually giving them away." Now I smiled at him and was seriously considering picking up a pair for Jack when something caught the corner of my eye. I turned. What I beheld made my blood go cold, my hair stand on end.

Sprawled out in the alcove just in front of the T.D. bank was a figure covered with newspapers—judging by the shoes, a man. Hardly an unfamiliar sight, but he was far too still for my liking. Suddenly, I was seized by an apprehension—almost a certainty—that it was Jack. An irrational sentiment, and I knew it, so started to walk away. What does it matter who it is?, I asked, instantly turning back. With great trepidation, my heart in my mouth, I drew close. I crouched down, peeled back layer upon layer of newspaper. To my relief, the man was breathing, and he was decidedly not Jack. Why had I scared myself so? Then I took in the puckered skin, bluish lips. "Someone call an ambulance, someone get blankets, anything," I called out, quickly removing my coat.

A small crowd gathered as the ambulance pulled up and people were still shaking their heads in dismay as it sped off.

"You'd think the authorities would do something," commented the portly woman who had dialed 911. "I mean, people like that, shouldn't they be in a mental hospital where they can be looked after properly?" she continued.

I thanked her for her help, then walked off heart-sick. "Oh Jack, how could I have left you out in the cold?" I murmured.

I had just received a rude awakening, and I immediately started doing what I could for Jack. I cleared the odds and ends from my basement apartment in the hope that I could prevail on him to move in. With the space totally separate, might we not find a way around whatever shamed him so? I proceeded to stock up on what felt like a life's supply of his favourite tobacco—regardless of where he ended up hanging his hat, surely that couldn't hurt. I gathered together forms for Old Age Security. And itching to hear his voice again, to know that he was safe, to know that he was warm, I began counting off the days.

Finally, Thursday arrived. When five o'clock rolled around, I, poked my head into the DCC lobby. No sign of Jack. Aware how hard it is for homeless people to turn up at all—never mind on time—I took a seat directly across from the reception desk and waited patiently. Eventually, I called it a day.

Immediately upon arriving home, I rushed upstairs to check my answering machine. A call from Rose, clarifying that Mom was back from hospital. Nothing from Jack. Next morning, reminding myself that he had managed for decades without any help from me—thank you very much—then facing the unavoidable fact that reconnecting with me could have simply proved just too painful—I proceeded to jot down a few more notes about the mirror incident in the hope that they would some day serve Ruth. Then I phoned Mom.

"Hey Mom," I said, "good that you're home. Sorry about not calling sooner. You made yourself breakfast yet?"

"You think I need a reminder?" she instantly shot back. "Of course I made myself breakfast! What do you and your sister think I am? A greener just off the boat?"

After the two of us had *kibitzed* to our heart's content and I'd satisfied myself that she really had eaten, I sat down at my kitchen table, opened the *Toronto Star*. I read the latest on the Karlheinz Schreiber affair. I skimmed the editorial, checked out the Op Ed piece. Then a headline inches from the bottom of page four caught my eye—"First Homeless Death of the Year." I held my breath, brought the paper closer. "This can't be!" I shrieked.

We look upon the pain of others with horror, sometimes heartfelt compassion. Yet never in a million years can we imagine it happening to us. Then willy-nilly, something happens that strikes so close to home that it makes your head spin. And we wonder how we did not know.

Jack Carpman was dead. The very words sounded like an obscenity. Yet there in the casket the luckless man lay, and here the rest of us were. It was a cold day for a burial, and every mourner to a person looked weighed down by the senselessness. Then almost imperceptibly, something in the very air shifted. There came a gentle murmur. Then a wizened old man with long white hair stepped forward.

His eyes alert with the wisdom of the ages, the elder lifted his head proudly. "We understand who we are," he announced with great dignity, "and we know where we came from." And I swear that you could feel the universe go still.

Later, we gathered at Jack's cousin Vern's for a smudge. The sweetgrass, smouldering in an abalone shell, it quieted our minds, chastened our hearts. Knowing what Jack would have wanted, realizing that I needed it too, I proceeded to invite everyone to my place for dinner. We ate, we drank, we burned sweetgrass. And sitting in the living room amid photographs of homeless folk, we passed around an eagle feather and spoke of that dear sweet man.

Nothing that was happening diminished our sense of the tragedy. Nor did it remotely temper our anger. Nonetheless, as we sat there exchanging stories, one truth stood out: Wherever he went, Jack Carpman had touched people's hearts.

"The guy I knew, tell you one thing, he always shared his grub even though he had nothing, less than nothing," stated Ned. "That was our Jacko for you."

"My name is Emily," declared a woman who I'd noticed earlier, "and Jack showed me that not all men are the same."

Emily from St. Pukes! And just look at her—so confident, so poised!

When I retreated to the kitchen to tackle the dishes a short while later, Emily followed. Both of us caught up in the privacy of our own grief, for a while we tended to the dishes without a word, though now and then she glanced at me almost furtively.

. "I see you remember me," she said at long last, her voice hushed. "There's something I always wanted to tell you. I don't know how to say this, so I'll just say it straight, okay? You were special to Jack, and not only as a friend. I know he's unlikely to have said anything, and I figured you might want to know."

"He told you?" I asked, acutely aware that this wasn't Jack's way.

"Sort of. Like, there was this day I was particularly upset about the sperm. You remember how I used to be, Naomi?"

"Well, I have a few memories, yes."

She observed me thoughtfully. And after settling into drying again, she spoke at length about how Jack comforted her, had even answered questions of an intimate nature.

"And I'll tell you what he said at one point," Emily continued. "'While I've days where I can be a regular s.o.b.—not that part of me. All it want to do is crawl inside one particular woman and die.' Anyway, I go, 'You mean Naomi, don't you?' And well..."

"He didn't answer, did he?" I quickly interjected. "Emily, I appreciate what you're trying to do here, but..."

"But Naomi," she insisted, her eyes suggestive, "a woman knows."

I felt a flicker of anger. Then calling to mind the unique circumstances under which the three of us met, I instantly softened and reached for her hand.

Knowing that in our own inimitable ways, together we had done Jack proud, that night I was able to catch some shuteye, although twice I awoke shrieking his name. I dedicated the following day to mulling over Jack's life.

I imagined Jack in early childhood, a bright eager little boy, all eyes, romping through the woods, sitting at the feet of elders, ferreting out the secrets of mother earth. I imagined him a lad of thirteen, his attention divided between the racist words of a white schoolmaster and gazing desperately out the window. For some time, the images came hard and fast. By mid-afternoon, they faded, and without intending it, I slipped into revisiting our relationship.

What was personally compelling about our relationship was not just the largesse of the man—notable in its own right—and not just our history, it was what made this history what it was—our ability, our drive to touch the place of vulnerability in one another. We recognized each other and reached out. There was something else too—that quality which Emily had picked up on, then trivialized. A physicality—albeit Jack and I had seldom touched. In fact, were I being perfectly honest with myself, when it came to truly embodied connection, there was Rose, then Jack, then no one. The realization brought tears to my eyes. The absence, I could actually taste it. As the day receded, the intensity of the feeling lightened. Partly because it had to. Partly because Jack would have wished it. Partly because there is a poetry, indeed a sublimity to the solitary existence which only us singles comprehend.

The loss of Jack and all that he symbolized lingering in my heart, I felt saddened, yet strangely centred as I turned in that night.

Next day, I virtually dodged a bullet. It began with a call from an old ally. A handful of antipoverty groups were tossing around ideas for a conference, and could I lend a hand? Thrilled to discover that homelessness would be front and centre, I offered to assist with the finances. I opened my mouth, about to commit myself to a leadership role. Then my eye caught Black Binder Number Three. Not so fast, I cautioned myself.

Later that day, just before dimming the lights, I picked up the phone to call Rose. With little to hold me in Toronto, I was intending to announce that I'd be imminently closing up shop. Now I dialed the area code all right. Then I stopped dead in my tracks.

Minutes later, without exactly knowing why, I again lifted the receiver. This time, I called Ger, asked if he knew that people were still being given ECT.

"That I did, love," he answered.

"Interesting," I observed, "cause somehow I didn't. Me,

who's routinely around psych survivors. Incidentally, years ago, I made you a promise. I never kept it."

"I know. Figured it was just too painful for you to think about it, right?"

As I lay down the phone, it dawned on me how comparatively easy it had been for me to focus my activism exclusively on homelessness. Suddenly, I got an image of Jack stretched out under the onramp, his body blue, his radio lying useless at his side. Not that homelessness isn't critically important, I reminded myself.

Rising at the crack of dawn, the following day, I lit two *yarhzeit* candles, one for Jack, one for Zelda. I put in a call to Rose, told her how much I loved her. I wrote Ruth an obscenely long letter in the hope that someday it would feel right to give it to her. Then I sat at the table and stared into the flames, mulling it all over—my sister, Mom, Jack, Zelda, my daughter. My life. My life.

It felt agonous, it felt gratifying to be taking stock. The curse and reward of being human, yes?

Two days later, I picked up the phone again and decisively took the plunge.

"Ger," I said, "if Ruthie's okay with it, I'm gonna close down here, make Winnipeg my home, but not just yet."

"What big news!" he exclaimed. "You'll visit us often, eh? Do some Toronto exhibits?"

"Absolutely. Oh, and believe it or not, the Winnipeg bit, that's not the main reason I called."

"My! So what's cooking?"

"Ger, I'm ready to move on electroshock—like really move—and I could use your help."

"Love, thought you'd never ask."

21. NAOMI

JANUARY 30–APRIL 11, 2008

> *It had been a long day of testimony, even for city hall,*
> *and from every indication, the marathon event was in*
> *its final stretch. Several reporters had begun folding*
> *up their equipment. The attractive woman with the*
> *salt-and-pepper hair who had just spoken was at this*
> *very moment stepping away from the podium, her*
> *long floral dress swishing as she moved, Suddenly,*
> *she whirled about, urgency in her eyes. "I just can't*
> *leave it like this," she announced, leaning into the*
> *microphone. "Not as a woman, not as a mother."*
> *And to a person, everyone in the bleachers sucked*
> *in their breath.*
> —Quoted from Brown Binder Number Six

IF ONCE UPON A TIME, I needed to put the relentless saga of
ECT behind me—and surely I did—what I needed to do now
is wield it as a weapon. And so it is that at the unlikely age
of sixty-four, once again this embattled old warhorse embarked
on a long and complicated project. This time, however, as an
activist and this time I was not remotely alone.

Now we all have privileged moments. By this, I do not mean
grand old times, though hey, I am all for that. At the risk of
sounding new age—something closer to transcendence. While
most of us would be hard pressed to define it, we tend to recognize such times when they come upon us, yes? Our heart

beats faster. We feel driven by purpose. And even the mundane is infused with meaning. Such a time was this. Now a large variety of folk can be credited with making this breakthrough possible, and I hope to make as many of you as I can visible. For me personally, however, it began eons ago, with a man called "Jack," a woman called "Zelda," And then there was that loyal old chap in the Panama hat—and Earl, bless you for ushering him into my life.

It was like being transported back in time. Just as he had decades ago, for a long while Gerald sat in my room, puffing on his pipe, leafing through Black Binder Three. "Count backward from ten and you'll be fine," he kept muttering. "Ten, nine, eight.…" You had to be touched by his perseverance, by the sheer fact that the man continued to care. At the same time, I was itching to get down to brass tacks, and if that binder had anything to offer, surely one of us would have stumbled on it light years ago.

"Hey there, detective Gerald," I finally said, laying my hand on his shoulder.

"Got it," he noted, with a sheepish grin. "Detective Gerald laying a big fat egg."

Now I assured him that I dearly wished this binder had proven to be the gold mine he'd always imagined, and he nodded good-naturedly, though from the look in his eyes, it was clear it would be a cold day in hell before he would ever let this preoccupation go. Be that as it may, a team player at heart—and that Ger always was—he promptly returned the binder to the bookcase, then led the way to the living room. The two of us proceeded to chart out what was ostensibly a more promising course. We decided that if we were to address electroshock successfully, we had to first learn something about it. A novel approach, yes? And as Ger and I agreed, one that we could wholeheartedly recommend to the professionals. Like, it couldn't hurt.

Being an accomplished researcher, Gerald took the lead. His initial homework was checking out ECT references on Google. Now as Gerald was sorting out the different types, I started to break the news to the family, starting with Ruth.

"Ruth," I began, "that move to Winnipeg that I mentioned earlier, well it's firmed up and it's looking fairly imminent. "Baby," I added, "I need to know your mind on this."

"Fair enough. Look," Ruth responded, "we don't see all that much of each other when we're in the same city. So what's the difference? That sounds horrid, doesn't it? Anyway, I've always known that's where your heart was. So yes, it's fine. Um, I really mean it," she added, her voice softening.

I thanked her for understanding, took a deep breath, then let the cat out of the bag—that I was coming out as a shock survivor, and I was coming out swinging.

A long silence followed. "Never in a million years would I have imagined you doing something like that," she exclaimed at long last. "Mom, this is great—really great."

Heartened, I immediately contacted the rest of the family. Everyone quickly came on side—well, everyone except Earl, who worried this would complicate his relationship with his daughter. Then I proceeded to give notice at work.

Now throughout this period, I continued to slug away on the new photograph series. And bit by bit, I let my nearest and dearest know about it. Rose was uneasy. Nonetheless, she understood their potential power, and at my behest, arranged for a Winnipeg showing. Gerald, meanwhile, sniffed out possible Toronto venues, but I was reluctant to finalize anything here yet. You see, the city of Toronto was ground zero; this was where the battle would be lost or won—so to speak—and critical as the photos were, they hardly sufficed. As Ger and I agreed, if we were to deliver any kind of blow to the Canadian shock industry—and no less was our mission—we had to be more strategic. What was also blatantly clear, we had to know this area inside out.

Sensitive to the problems that a full scale research project would present—and to this day, Rose retained a felt sense of my impairment—upon getting wind of what was involved, Ro talked to the family. As long as we were both back for Pesach, they could spare her, they agreed. "Sis, I'm coming, and that's final," she stated before I had so much as asked. "Nomi, you think it's just generosity?" she added emphatically. "I need— like *viscerally need*—to be a part of this."

Whereupon, she flew to Toronto. Rank amateurs though we were, in no time flat the three of us had transformed ourselves into an investigatory team that was to die for and before long we had unearthed many a salient fact.

It seems that ECT was invented in fascist Italy in 1938—the inspiration, hogs en route to the slaughter rendered docile by an electrical cattle prod. No shit! And wonder of wonders, the very first human recipient was none other than a homeless man, an experimental subject, apparently, who had been dragged kicking and screaming from the street. Now in the fifties modifications were introduced—hence the standard reference to *modified* electroshock, to *new and improved* electroshock. To our surprise, however, it turned out that the modification had *bupkes* to do with the brain. It was for the protection of body parts that could easily be fractured. Moreover, it was hardly new.

"Just read this," said Rose handing me a book by Dr. Peter Breggin. "Nomi, even back in your day, the overwhelming history of ECT's the history of *new, improved* ECT."

An anomaly, yes? And hardly the last we were to encounter. Strange. While it was the devastation of human life that fuelled our passion, so alarmed were we by the contradictions in what was passing as science that for the longest while, here the momentum lay.

It was a blustering day, and the loose-fitting panes in the old bay window were rattling like there was no tomorrow. Sipping cocoa and snuggling up on the couch, Rose and I were settling into a cozy evening of television-watching when Ger turned up unexpectedly, his pinstriped suit on, a magazine tucked under his arm.

"What's up?" I asked.

He plunked himself down in the burgundy chair opposite us. "Well, my fella conspirators," he explained, brandishing the magazine, "I've dug up something you just might find interesting. Shock survivor testimony delivered before the Board of Health."

He proceeded to read us several passages. And how they resonated with me!—our first indication of a possible new direction.

"Sis," suggested Rose, "perhaps we should focus exclusively on testimony."

"In time, I can see that, but not yet. Minimally, we need to wrap our minds around the party line if we're to debunk it. You guys have been doing most of the reading," I added, glancing at Gerald, then Rose. "So, tell me—cause I'll be damned if I get it—officially, how does ECT work?"

Even as the words escaped my lips, you could see from the look on Rose's face that there was no straightforward answer.

Rose took a sip of her coffee. "The strangest thing. The authorities all say they don't know how it works. They simply assert *that* it works.

I look at her curiously.

"A far cry from scientific, I agree," she asserts, "though the modus operandi, it's clear. Like the treatment essentially consists of delivering sufficient electricity to the brain to produce a grand mal seizure."

"Grand mal seizure!" I exclaim. "And no one disputes that?"

"Well, Nomi, it's more than a claim. It's the stated purpose."

"People, correct me if I'm off-base here, but don't doctors treating epilepsy do everything in their power to *prevent* grand mal seizures?"

Rose and Gerald look at each other stunned, then back at me. "We're onto something here, aren't we?" asks Rose, a glint in her eye.

And so it is that we waded further and further into the professional literature—all of it important, all of it carving out a foundation on which to stand. However, as many a researcher before us has discovered, in the final analysis, there is only one type of inquiry that the world holds its breath for—the one which brings you face-to-face with yourself. And that's when the real drama begins.

And so it was to prove.

"Time for us to get down to it," announced Gerald. It was eight p.m. Having just polished off enough shepherd's pie to feed an army, the three of us had turned the kitchen table into Operation Central—piles of books and computer printouts strewn about us.

Gerald cleared his throat and peered over the impressive stack of books in front of him. He had assumed responsibility for the safety and effectiveness studies, and for six whole days now he'd been postponing this meeting, insisting that he needed more time.

Suddenly he shot us one of his famous grins. He proceeded to rhyme off study after study that established brain damage. Then he began quoting extensively from a 2006 effectiveness study by Colin Ross.

"And current whatchamacallit—empirical studies?" I queried, the excitement beginning to mount.

At this, Gerald positively beamed. "Latest major empirical study—Sackeim, 2007," he asserted. "By far, the largest study in shock history. All outcomes what they call statistically significant. Now the report, it's convoluted as a constipated Jesuit after a ten day bender," he went on, rolling his eyes, "but the long and the short? Cognitive impairment. Substantial memory loss, and this for every single type of electroshock."

"But Ger, you sure?" Rose checked.

"Sure as shit is a cat. But hey, see for yourself," he offered, handing us each a copy.

While Gerald attended to the dishes, Rose and I took the copies to the living room, fastidiously poured over them. While the term "brain damage" was not directly used—a no-no to actually mention it, we later learned—all the markers appeared to be there. Moreover, we saw proof positive of something that I had long suspected—that women are impacted more adversely than men. In the process, we came upon a seemingly innocuous measure called "AMI-SF" scores. Now initially, we ignored it, assuming it was probably unimportant. Finally, however, we put it together. What was being measured was nothing less than inability to recall details of your own life. Again, statistically significant for every type of shock, again that alarming gender difference.

"Well?" asked Gerald when we rejoined him in the kitchen.

"This calls for a celebration," proclaimed Rose. Whereupon, she swung open the fridge, whipped out a bottle of wine, and soon the three of us were *kibitzing* and clinking glasses, Gerald even regaling us with some vintage Newfoundland jokes. A treat, for Gerald was an accomplished teller.

As laughter rang through the halls of that aged house, we slipped into the preoccupation of oldsters everywhere—swapping tales about our grandkids. Now an hour and a half into the *schmooze* fest, I was about to suggest that we call it a night when it struck me almost as an afterthought that Rose had still to report.

"Naomi Brenda Cohan, you're a God-damned slave-driver, you know that?" Rose shot back, "but if it'll get you off my case—fine!"

Now she had been researching the procedure itself, so started walking us through it. She began by providing details on the "prepping" protocol. "So then a cuff is wrapped around the patient's arm to monitor blood pressure," she continued. "Next comes the anaesthetic, then the muscle relaxant."

"Muscle relaxant?" I asked.

Rose nodded. "Precisely. Remember, Nomi, it's so no one will break their back. Anyway, Simon Legree," she went on, "like the lungs are a muscle, and so naturally after the muscle relaxant takes effect, the patient can't breathe on their own, and so an oxygen mask is slipped on. Now, after that—and get this—a rubber gag..."

Even as she speaks, a stifling sensation seizes me. As if a giant block of ice were pressing on my lungs. I lay down my cigarette and am about to open a window when a light goes on in Gerald's eyes. Suddenly, the pen drops from his hand. "Hold your horses, there. Rose girl, what did you just say?" he asks, staring at her.

"A rubber gag is..." Rose repeats.

"Before that."

"The bit about the muscle relaxant?"

"Yup."

"Well, they administer a muscle relaxant, and so all of the muscles stop."

"And the lungs are a muscle.... The lungs are a muscle," Gerald mutters to himself.

"Gerald?" Rose asks.

"Give me a sec, folks," he answers. "Something the two of you need to hear."

Without another word, Ger lays down his pipe and darts upstairs. When he returns, he is holding none other than Black Binder Three. Apologizing for where we are heading, he sits down and proceeds to open it at the very page where he'd placed a stick-it all those years ago. I brace myself, sensing the inevitability. "'*Stop fighting us,*'" he reads. "'*There's nothing to be scared of. Count backward from ten, and you'll be fine.*'"

"*Ten. Nine. Eight,*" I continue, almost in a trance. "*Oh my God! Can't move a muscle. No way to breathe. How could they not know?*"

Rose's eyes dart between the two of us, uncertain where to settle. "So Ger, you saying...?" she begins to ask.

Eyeing me ever more keenly and pausing suggestively after every phrase, Gerald repeats the entire passage by heart. Then I hear the binder close, and for what seems like an eternity, the three of us sit there frozen.

"They forgot the oxygen?" Rose murmurs as if from far away.

Now I start to nod, but to my surprise, again Gerald is shaking his head.

"Nope, that's not it. Can't be, Nomi girl, or you'd be dead—dead as doorknob. Think. How did you hear them? How did you know you couldn't breathe? That you couldn't move a muscle?"

"Well, I... *Gotenyu!* No anaesthetic!" I exclaim. "*Oy! Oy!*"

"Easy there, love. Now I'm kind of thinking, yup," answers Gerald, picking his words carefully, "but something still doesn't add up. You see, if they had skipped the anaesthetic, why in Sam Hill would they suggest counting backward from ten?"

Now I'm disappointed, but I'm forced to admit that Ger has a point. Strangely, however, no sooner do I concede that point than the suffocating sensation returns. But why?

Seemingly wrestling with her own demons, Rose's forehead furls. For the longest while she appears lost in thought. "Nomi," she finally observes, "when we were kids, for months after our tonsils were removed, whenever I was upset, you'd wrap your arms around me and urge me to count backward from ten. Remember?"

"Vaguely, Ro, but what's that hafta do with the price of tea in China?"

"Possibly nothing, but like, maybe a whole lot. Sweetie, I hate to ask this, but how would you feel about trying to find out?"

As Rose reaches for my hand, I can tell by the look in her eye the gist of what she's suggesting, even something of the magnitude. If I go along, something tells me, I will never be the same. My instinct is to run. At the ripe old age of sixty-four, who in their right mind would knowingly open such an obvious can of worms? Then again, what if it could shed light on even one of the imponderables that have been dogging us for years? I instinctively turn to Gerald. His shoulders raised, the man looks terrified. Who knows what this may be dredging up for him? Now he is calming down. He's waiting, isn't he? Waiting to see what'll happen. Praying for all our sakes that I am making the right decision, I cast a wistful look at Rose. Then I shut my eyes.

I imagine myself in a lonely stretch of corridor. I can feel my back pressed against a stretcher. I conjure up a shrill voice urging, "Naomi, count." No! Not any of it's right.

"It's no use," I protest, opening my eyes and shaking my head.

"Sweetie, it's okay," coos Rose. "Really, it was just an idea."

I glance at Gerald, see that he's hanging in. Then I take a deep breath and turn to my sister.

"You're doing this, aren't you?" she asks, once again clasping my hand in hers.

Even as her palm presses into mine, my eyelids drop. Faintly, in the background I can make out Rose urging me to imagine myself in my twenties. Then her voice trails into nothingness—and whole decades begin to peel away—slip, slip, slip through my fingers. And I am in a free fall. Into darkness, I descend. Into suffocation. And now I am squeezing through the ever-tightening eye of a needle. And now I am back there.

Trapped, I am in a cubbyhole of a room, the walls closing in. Other hapless souls must be nearby for I can hear piteous groans in the distance. Possibly, I am strapped into a stretcher, for I am flat on my back and for the life of me, I can't budge. I see a blinding light overhead. A band that feels metallic, it is encasing my head. Bodies are hovering over me—taking my pulse, adjusting my neck. One of them peers into my eyes. Another is inserting a rubbery object into my mouth, manipulating my body as if I were a lifeless doll. And now a woman with all the trappings of a nurse is ordering me to calm down. Dear God, what will these Philistines do to me if I don't?

"Nomi," a familiar voice breaks in, "a staff member's urging you not to fight them."

"Ro?"

"Ger and I, we're right here. Nomi, who's encouraging you not to fight?"

"Um, a nurse."

"Doing just great, sis. Now someone's suggesting counting."

I listen, and except for an ominous shuffling sound—possibly the nurse puttering about—the silence is deafening. "Now?" asks a man with a gravelly voice. And with that single word, a dread comes over me.

I'm gonna die, I'm gonna fucking die, and not an easy death. Death by fire. Death by drowning. Death by lightning sword. Maybe if I start counting, before I know it, it'll all be over. Count, Nomi. Count. Count backward from ten, and you'll be just fine.... Son of a bitch!

Struggling to reenter the present, I open my eyes. I can tell that I am in the kitchen and that Rose is smiling at me. "You knew?" I ask.

"Just a guess."

I look my sister in the eye, recall that she'd her own experience of those treatments. "Oh Ro," I murmur, "it wasn't totally a guess, was it?"

She reaches over, gently touches my cheek, then shakes her head.

"No one *spoke* those words. I *thought* them," I explain to Gerald. Whereupon, I breathe a sigh of relief. To my dismay, however, again the suffocation strikes.

Pain is ripping through my chest like an angry tornado. My lungs useless, I am being buried alive. And soon I'm gonna disintegrate into a hundred thousand pieces, and not the angels, not the archangels, not God himself will have a prayer of making me whole.

"Nomi, come back," I can hear Rose plead.

I grab the edge of the table, struggle to steady myself. It's useless.

"Breathe, sweetie. Breathe now," she presses, her tone urgent.

The contours of Rose's face, they are beginning to dissolve. And once again her voice is trailing off.

"God damn it, Nomi, breathe," she suddenly shrieks. "*We* have to breathe."

Mercifully, my chest expands. In whooshes the air. One breath. Another. I exchange looks with Rose—and she nods.

"Love, you okay?" asks Gerald, his voice quivering.

"Sorta, Ger, I mean, under the circumstances.... You know, I always suspected something, but not this.... The two of, you're fuckin' geniuses," I choke out seconds later, catching Gerald's eye. "So there *was* no anaesthetic. And that's why I felt it, and even by conventional standards, this has to be..."

At this, fury spreads like wildfire across my sister's face. And she rises.

"Rose, where you going?" I ask.

Rose whirls about, daggers shooting from her eyes. "I'm phoning Ruth," she thunders. "Let's sue the asses off these fuckers!"

If this were a novel or a Hollywood movie, there is no question what would happen next. A court battle would instantly ensue; the judge would pound on his gavel, glower down at the cowering accused, announce that in all his years on the bench, never had he witnessed such a flagrant violation of the public trust. However, as I was reminded as I listened in on the extension that evening, in the real world—and ultimately, no other yardstick matters—there is a pesky little matter known as statute of limitations. And herein lay our first road block.

"I'll check case law," Ruthie offered, "but I doubt there's anything we can do. For sure, failing to anesthetize sounds like incompetence, but even were we to establish by a preponderance of the evidence that this had happened, the statute of limitations…"

"Damn! So how much did we miss it by?" Rose asked.

"Oh, a tiny matter of thirty years."

"Thirty years!" shrieked Rose. "That would've left her only a few years to lay charges. And what survivor could conceivably get their act together quick enough to…?"

"I understand, Auntie Rosey," answered Ruth, "but the law's the law."

We had arrived at a moment of truth. Now initially, Rose and I were crestfallen. We retreated to the living room, spoke of this as a major blow. Gerald joined us, for some time said nothing, just observed keenly.

"Hey there, women," he finally urged, a twinkle in his eye, "the fight's the same. What happened, still happened, eh? And pardon my French, but if you ask yours truly, there's more than one way to skin a cat."

Struck by his level-headedness, Rose and I looked at him, then looked at each other and nodded. And albeit sobered by the experience, back into the fray we ventured.

From now on in, it was full speed ahead. Realizing that we could pull off little alone and the importance of the personal crystal clear, we began rooting about for an activist group to partner with—preferably seasoned. Enter the antipsychiatry organization CAPA—Coalition Against Psychiatric Assault—virtually the only game in town. Upon learning that I was indeed a survivor and that we meant business, the chair met with us, one Inna Adolfsson—a tall Swedish woman, whom Ger and I took an instant shining to.

"Here's the *shtick*," I said. "Highlighting testimony, it's a no-brainer, and if we combine a public hearing with the first exhibit of my collection 'My Life As a Shock Survivor,' I'm pretty sure the media would show."

"They just might at that," mused Inna. "How about coming to a meeting, laying it out to our members?"

As Rose and I snuggled up close that night, she looked at me knowingly. "Nomi, it's getting to be as much about the people as the exposé, isn't it?" she asked.

"So help me, sis, it always was," I answered.

"This's a question of human rights, this's important," insisted the wiry little man in the "Psychiatry Psucks" t-shirt. "Anyway," he added, "I'm ninety-nine per cent certain that we can pull it off."

It was my first CAPA meeting, and what an eye-opener it was! We were in a large seminar room on an upper floor of the legendary Ontario Institute for Studies in Education. Coffee cups and half-eaten donuts were everywhere, and around the white tables—eight in all, arranged in a rectangle—sat people from all walks of life—psychiatric survivors, academics, artists, self-styled anarchists—most in jeans, many arguing, all with a philosophic bent, some rude by conventional standards, the whole lot of them transparently fond of one another.

At one point, the group launched into an animated discussion of logistics—and it yielded a most revealing glimpse into the heart of this transparently vibrant community.

"If we do this—and again I vote yes—we'd have to raise a whole lot of moola first," stated Pete, leaning into the table, his eyes alight. "The point is, it is *essential* to subsidize survivors outside Toronto who haven't the money to travel. Es-sen-tial."

Barely had that clearly principled activist spit out these syllables than the first of several members began voicing their agreement. As others followed, there were nods throughout the room.

"Bottom line," affirmed Pete, his eyes afire. "A high percentage of our brothers and sisters won't be able to get here to testify without a subsidy, and leaving things like that, it's simply unacceptable. Let me repeat," he reiterated, "un-ac-cep-ta-ble."

Now as Pete was winding up, something unexpected happened. In the midst of what felt like a unanimous agreement, a lone figure—a bear of a man with thick bushy eyebrows and a baseball cap, an old timer named "Ari"—lay down his donut and noisily cleared his throat. He proceeded to adjust his hearing aid. Then he stated gently but firmly, "I disagree. What you're suggesting, it's an insult to survivors."

Instantly, all eyes were on Ari.

Now for a moment, it looked as if Pete were going to launch into another defence of subsidies—and woe betide the ignorant clod who disagreed. Biding his time, however, Ari waited for the dust to settle. "It's insulting to assume that survivors are helpless without hand-outs," Ari eventually resumed. "Enough that the general public sees us this way. Old friend," he continued, eyeing Pete with obvious affection, "you think when it's really important, we can't manage on our own? Remember the Madness Conference? Strapped though we were for cash, we hitchhiked, but we got ourselves there."

As Ari concluded, Pete looked away, and Inna grew pensive. And for some time afterward, so quiet was it that you could hear your heart beat.

"How many here agree with Ari?" she asked at long last, demonstrably moved.

There was a moment of hesitation. Then slowly, the oldest woman present raised her hand. Next came Inna's hand. Soon all hands save Pete's were in the air. For several minutes, no one spoke—almost as if words would be indecent. Then Pete caught his friend Ari's eye, and without explanation, he raised his hand as well.

It was one of those thrilling moments. It's not that Ari was right and Pete wrong, for truth to tell, both were right and eventually a solution incorporating both perspectives would be necessary. It is that what had descended upon the room when Ari spoke was the unfettered wisdom of the survivor. How could I have lost sight of a knowing that pure?

An hour later, the meeting ended, still without resolution. As I said my goodbyes, nevertheless, I was walking on air.

Awaiting word, the following day Rose and I visited the CAPA website, where we discovered a curious statistic—two to three times as many women as men are shocked. "Only stands to reason," observed Rose wryly. "Women are more harmed by ECT. So of course, we're singled out for it. Who can question the logic of that?"

Aware that we might have little time later, days of packing followed, with Rose meticulously labelling everything. On the second day, I stumbled across those pouches of tobacco that I'd bought for Jack and I proceeded to distribute them to shelter residents—well, all but one, which I slipped into my pocket at the last minute, unable to part with it. On the third day, I received a most unexpected call from the chair of the Community Centre. How would I feel about them cosponsoring? "But how in the world did you hear about it?" I asked amazed. Half an hour later came word from CAPA. It was a "go."

The date would be Saturday April 12—mere days before Rose and I took off for Winnipeg. Survivors would testify in the morning and early afternoon in the council chambers of City Hall. The photography exhibit and press conference that followed would be at the Parkdale Gallery.

The basic frame quickly agreed to, for the next two months we were snowed with work. I took the lead handling early responses from the press. Ari and Pete took the lead reaching out to survivors. And little by little, Inquiry into Electroshock 2008 became a reality on the political landscape.

Now the enthusiasm was there. The buy-in was there. And we were fixing our wagon to this star no matter what. Nonetheless, while I couldn't quite put my finger on it, as the days progressed, something about the photography collection started to bother me.

For two long hours I had been sitting at my desk, staring uncomprehendingly at the photographs. Something was missing. What? My notes had been photographed. My binders had been photographed, also me at work with my camera—all reliable markers of my post-ECT existence. Instinctively, I glanced at the mirror. Suddenly, I knew what it was—the phantom me, the patient whom I'd never met, the invisible doppelgänger, the other Mrs. Smith. Ah, but how to capture her? No clear thought in mind, yet trusting in the wisdom of the search, I took charcoal in hand and started to sketch.

As it began springing to life under my fingers, the Mrs. Smith figure caught me by surprise. I was using just enough strokes for it to be discernable as a relatively slim young woman, but for sure, there she was cowering in the corner. I was about to add a few lines to suggest a hospital gown, but instead found myself hinting at nakedness. Once the sketch felt right, I started in on a second sketch, a third, a fourth. Each progressive Mrs. Smith was heavier than the one that went before, each progressive Mrs. Smith less articulated so that in the end, the woman disappeared before your eyes.

Once fifteen sketches had emerged, I laid them out in order on the kitchen table. I removed seven of the originals. Then I picked up my camera and began to shoot.

Now one day, Rose and I arranged the entire series along the kitchen walls just to get a sense of it. For a few minutes, we beheld the pieces with all due solemnity. Then the sauciest of grins began to break out on Rose's face.

"Did I ever tell you your art sucks?" she quipped.

"Quiet, or I'll sic one of the zombie sisters on you," I shot back.

"Is it a bird? Is it a bat? No," shrieked Rose, pointing. "It's zombie sister number four."

We both burst out laughing. Then Rose sat down at the kitchen table, observed, "You know, they *are* haunting—wonderfully haunting—but how come naked?"

"What psychiatry does, it's *that* personal. Also there's the gender thing, yes? And hey, nothing says woman like a naked female body, right?"

"Let me just say this: *I'm* comfortable with my body, and I'm not sure *I* could do this, but if you can live with the odd reporter who just won't be able to resist taking a shot below the belt, I say go for it."

Now as I walked away, I realized that the two of us had not been personal like that for eons. Understandable, but not good enough.

It was later that same day. Gerald and Miu were off on their monthly pub crawl and the time was ripe. I had secretly baked two pans of ginger snaps—Rose's favourite—then lured her upstairs on the pretext of having additional photos to show her.

Quickly sizing up the situation, Rose grabbed a handful of cookies, hopped onto the bed, then peered up at me.

"You joining me or do I tell Mom on you?" she quipped, grinning.

For the next several hours, we lay there propped up on pillows, *schmoozing* about everything under the sun. Now at first, we were horsing around. Then the mood turned. Rose missed her old partner Lisa, she confessed. While she still loved basketball—even climaxed at the sight of a masterful shot—"a tad too much detail for you, right?" she opined—a run of the mill game no longer did the trick.

"Ro," I finally hazarded, "you saying that you're having a belated midlife crisis?"

"Not exactly, but there *is* something that I've been keeping from you. Remember how you were always the literature buff, and I just wanted to shoot hoops. Well, it appears that there's more to this identical twin business than either of us realized."

"You've developed an interest in literature?"

"The thing is, I've applied for the M.A. in English at U. of M. Now I know that literature was always your thing," she added, touching my cheek. "So Nomi, I need to hear from you."

This, I had not suspected, and clearly breaking the news had been no easy matter, but lying on that bed, our entire history lying with us, we started to find our way. Nor, as it turned out, were my feelings the major obstacle.

"The fact is," Rose confessed, "for years I've been telling myself that I'm stalling because I'm worried for you—and that's true to a point—but mostly, I fear for myself."

I picked up the last of the ginger snaps. "What the worse thing that can happen? That you'll be accepted and hafta put up with a bunch of eggheads?"

"You know what I really dread? That I'll be fine—fine—but nothing to write home about. And it's not my fellow students that worry me. I won't meet the standard you set, and I won't be the only one who notices. You know," she suddenly added, "right from the outset, Mom'll totally lose it if I enter graduate school. She'll keep thinking that somehow the *meshugah* university screwed up registration and admitted the wrong twin."

"Oh Rose, almost all of your life, you've been your own person. When it comes to literature, you will be too. You just need to find your way. C'mon, remember what it was like when you first took up basketball?"

Rose looked at me, a smile of recognition on her face.

"Tell you something else. I'm not at all sure I was ever the more capable one. I was simply lucky enough to have things come easily. As for Mom's reaction," I observed with a grin, "now if that isn't reason for going, what is? Anyway, my guess is that she'll be so pissed about these latest photos, she'll barely notice anything else."

"You think?"

"Hey, if that doesn't work, I can always announce that I found Jesus."

"Or married Earl all over again," suggested Rose giggling.

"C'mon, I'm your flesh and blood. How much is it to ask?"

"Trust me. You'll hafta settle for Jesus."

Rose caught my eye and nodded. And so it is that after years of hesitation, Rose began asserting her own claim to the world of literature. At the same time, eight new photos were added to my collection, the caption reading "The Other Mrs. Smith."

More securely grounded in one another, Ro and I returned to the task at hand with a vengeance. CAPA likewise moved into high gear—and before long, meetings of the organizing committee were stepped up to twice weekly.

Now bit by bit, the disparate pieces of our enterprise were coming together. As we approached the finish line, nonetheless, a puzzling snag arose. Gerald, of all people, skipped the one and only mandatory meeting—where tasks to be performed on the actual day were being divvyed up. Not an insoluble problem on a practical level, but hardly characteristic of the man.

"Maybe Miu simply needed him," Rose conjectured.

Given who this man was *to us*—to *the entire enterprise*—this was not exactly convincing, as Rose herself had to know. Then came an even more perplexing development.

It was eleven-thirty a.m. the day before the big event, and all of the engines of activism were roaring. Already, Inna and I had held interviews with three reporters—and that wasn't the half of it. While Rose was at the kitchen table assembling the press packages, I was in the living room finishing up my twelfth call of the day with Inna.

Now barely had I laid down the receiver when the phone rang again. Assuming that it was Inna with another last minute detail, I innocently blurted out, "So, stranger?"

An eerie silence followed.

"Sorry. Someone there?" I asked...."Anyone?"

There was a quick clearing of the throat. Then an angry female voice spat out, "You think what you're doing's so great? Big shot, take it from me. It absolutely isn't." And without speaking another word or even allowing a response, she slammed down the phone.

Now I had been a shit-disturber far too long to blow this incident out of proportion. You organize outside the mainstream, you expect a degree of flack. Nonetheless, I found myself fretting about the woman. Could this be a mother who had signed for her daughter to be shocked? Or a survivor who felt that it had saved her life?

That afternoon Les called from Ottawa, advised me to break a leg—good thing we seldom heed such advice, yes?—and that evening, my grandson and two CAPA members coming to lend a hand, nervous but excited, Gerald and I drove to the art gallery, oversaw the mounting of the pictures. "Not bad, if yours truly doesn't say so himself," observed Gerald, stepping back to get a wide-sweeping view. Of course I figured that Gerald was now back in full swing. Just as Don was positioning the last of the photographs, however, Ger drew me aside and confided that he would not be able to make it to either event, though the three of us would celebrate later.

"Love, don't ask. Just trust me," he implored, as I opened my mouth to protest.

I arrived back home too pooped to pucker. Now inevitably, as my head hit the pillow, the phone began ringing off the hook, Three calls from reporters. Then a frantic call from Mom.

"Honest, I don't blame you for what happened back then," I assured her, "and Mom, enough with the worrying. Rose and I have never missed Pesach and never will."

Eventually, Mom settled down, as she invariably did, though what spectres haunted her slumber, I could only guess. Now I took a few more calls, but finally, I closed my eyes. However, once again, "brrnng," went the phone. No way I'm getting that, I swore. But what if it's that irate woman? Hands down, she was the last person in the world that I wished to speak with—for clearly, she'd as soon smack me as look at me—but better now than later. And God only knows what might happen at the hearing if this grievance of hers were allowed to fester.

Beads of perspiration forming on my brow, I picked up the receiver. To my surprise and delight, it was Ruth.

"Okay if I come tomorrow, sit with you and Aunt Rose?" she asked.

"Oh sweetheart, you betchya," I answered.

22. NAOMI

> *"I'm Martha Andrews, and I'm as old as dirt," an-*
> *nounced the elderly woman, her voice steadier than*
> *any of us imagined possible. And the audience hung*
> *on the very sound of her, even as a lover hangs on the*
> *breath of his beloved.*
> —Excerpt from Brown Binder Number Six

I WON'T PRETEND that no mistakes were made, nor that an abiding sorrow wasn't an intricate part of the mix. Nonetheless, something rare took place that day, something that makes one's spirits soar. How often are others afforded even a passing glimpse into the nitty-gritty of lives like ours? And how often do invalidated people get to stand with their peers and staunchly proclaim their truth? For me, for my sisters and brothers, this was a sacred moment, and we gave ourselves to it with a passion. And then there was the pride of having made it happen—happen for everyone, from survivor to onlooker, from the quick to the dead. Now some say that every time a story that has been long hidden emerges from the shadows, the universe comes to know itself. Listen, oh listen, and help make the world whole.

Located in new City Hall not far from the financial district, Toronto council chambers is a huge gallery, dominated by the councillors' seats arranged in ever expanding concentric circles. Microphones are built into the seats. There is a massive bleacher to the side for spectators. Up front is a portable stage, also equipped with a microphone. "Important and functional," screams every square inch of space. But yes, as my family and I agreed as we peeked in that misty April morning, it was exactly right. The thing is, strip people of their humanity, and they need a tangible sign—however illusory—that their grievances have a place in the corridors of power.

Now aside from the ever-diligent civil servants setting up, not another soul had yet put in an appearance. So off for coffee we went. Ruth seemed relatively comfortable as we *schmoozed* in the cafeteria, and I would have to say, I was hopeful. Though could she stand us for long?—that was the question.

"You know, sweetheart," I observed, wiping a crumb from my chin, "very little if anything is going to be from the perspective of family members. It's…"

"It's okay, Mom. I know," she answered.

Now it was not long before those mandatory worries that arise at such times intruded. Would I make a total ass of myself? And what if only CAPA diehards showed?

While Rose and Ruth offered the standard reassurances, we all of us returned to the chambers with some apprehension. When we swung open the door, we could barely believe our eyes. The space was transformed—utterly. A veritable multitude of folk from all walks of life had come—some in suits, some blue jeans, some with rainbow ribbons, several sporting wild and wonderful hats, a couple demonstrably trans. So help me, it was as if the angels on high had let down their hair and colour had entered the universe.

Reporters were roaming about. Dave—the one-armed videographer—and his son Schmuel hummed to themselves as they set up the camera. Old friends greeted one another. And *oy* what a turnout! Although nary a councillor was present, most of the council seats were filled. And a good forty, fifty additional eager souls were hanging out on the bleachers—chatting excitedly to one another.

As my family and I made our way in, we picked up the buzz around us. "It's happening—really happening!" Rose exclaimed.

To one side, a handful of old-timers in khakis were bickering, each insisting that they personally had invented the term "psychiatric inmate." Feet from them, a couple of women were holding each other's hands, offering heartfelt words of encouragement—one, curiously, a physicist. Now as the physicist was speaking, Ari entered the room. Spotting us, he hurried over, embraced my entire family one by one, as if we were long lost friends. A reminder, this was a family in its own right, yes?

Minutes later, I again let my eyes travel around the room. Standing next to the podium, a young housewife in an embroidered apron was brandishing an egg, her hand high over her head. "Let's say this is your brain before ECT," she was stipulating—obviously, a home-grown demonstration of sorts. Now closer by, a crowd was gathering. Curious, the three of us took one look at each other, then advanced toward them.

Periodically lifting a hanky from his pocket and mopping his brow, an elderly man with a scraggly beard and a lazy eye was spinning a yarn. Clearly, he was an old Commie for as we neared, you could hear the term "petite bourgeoisie." The fable was about a time when the parts of the body ruthlessly competed with each other, each eventually going on strike to demonstrate that it and it alone was indispensable.

While a few of us exchanged looks throughout the telling, recalling a somewhat different version, according to his, the anus triumphed. The mighty anus pulled in his muscles, stopped all elimination, and before long, a horrendous plague overtook the community. Legs could not move. Arms lay useless at the side, not even able to reach for food. The overtaxed lung piteously gasped for air. "Piteously," the narrator reiterated. "Like nothing that had ever been witnessed before."

"So to make a long story short," the storyteller continued,

"the time came when the community had to capitulate. The anus, it was agreed, was in a class by itself."

The punch line still a mystery, all eyes were on the old man. A pro, he worked that pause, saying nothing for several seconds, the suspense agonizingly delicious.

"Anyway, comrades, not to belabour a point," he eventually concluded, a mischievous look in his eye, "that's how assholes came to be bosses."

My heart leapt. Something else I had forgotten—what a treasure my people are!

Even as I was delighting in the crafty old teller, a young reporter buttonholed me for an interview. Now the phone call the other day had totally slipped my mind—so caught up was I in the excitement—but as I rose to do the interview I caught sight of a woman glowering at me. The second that the interview ended, I drew closer. Better we come to terms now, I reminded myself, than later with microphones in our hands.

As we started to talk, to my relief, it was quickly evident that she was not my irate caller—just a confused attendee looking for assistance. I listened to her story and offered the odd suggestion, then I took a good long look around.

"Mom, is something wrong?" asked Ruth.

"It would seem not," I answered.

Moments later, Inna signalling that we were about to begin, we promptly took our seats. Inna nodded at Beth—a well-known Black disability activist who would be chairing. Clad in a deep royal blue cloak and walking with a pronounced limp, slowly, Beth made her way over to the lectern at the front. And the room went quiet.

Her eyes ablaze, her grey hair lending that extra dignity, Beth leaned into the lectern, welcomed everyone, declared this a historic occasion. "You are not here to please others—not the professionals, not CAPA," she announced. "This is *your* day. Speak *your* truth."

She finished to thunderous applause. Then again the room

went quiet. And little by little, to my immense pride, my sisters and brothers did it. Mustering up their courage, oldsters, youngsters, women, men began to tell their stories, some from their seats, some stepping up to the mike at front, some visibly self-conscious, some confident, all responding faithfully to the moment.

A tall middle-aged woman in a gabardine suit started the ball rolling. "Okay, here goes," she said, speaking from her seat, "My name is Jane, and I had fifteen bilateral shock treatments. It was just after the birth of my second child. I went to my doctor, I did. I told him I was exhausted, told him I had two little ones at home and couldn't manage. 'Well, lassie,' he said, 'we've a treatment that will fix you up just fine.' Not once did he say that you'll lose your memory. Not once did he say that you'll be condemned to a life of note-taking, but that's what happened—I suspect that many of you here can relate."

You could tell by the sea of nods that a good half the audience could relate. With the stage set, a plethora of testimonials followed. Mostly women testified, woman after woman stating that they had been depressed, or that the doctor thought this would help them be a better wife, or that it was just after the birth of their child, or they had committed the "egregious sin" of loving another woman. Each story was unique, each powerful on its own, but with common threads weaving in and out, together they packed a wallop. The thing is, while you might be able to dismiss one speaker—if you're a total hard-ass, possibly two—who could dismiss everyone?

Now while I knew none of these people, the bond between us felt palpable. Then ever so slightly, the world turned.

A slip of a woman in tattered jeans stepped up to the podium. "They call me Rita," she announced, staring directly at me. I braced myself. That piercing tone, the English accent, it was the voice on the phone the other night!

While she was forty if she was a day, as Rita stood there,

you were seized by an almost irresistible urge either to run away or to leap onto the stage and protect her—you weren't sure which—for with her glaring eyes and diminutive stature, she looked like a raging child. To my astonishment, however, within seconds, an utter calm came over her and she began supplying salient details about her life. She had been a successful conference planner who arranged major international events. She went into a tailspin upon relocating to Toronto. Hospitalized, she had so many meds pumped into her that she was clueless what she was authorizing when they plunked the papers in front of her.

"And then I didn't know anything," she continued. "These other patients, they'd lead me about, show me where the loo was, show me—and there's no way to put this delicately—how to use the loo. And after that—well, not a single other person helped—not even the luminaries of the so-called survivor movement...." At this, she glanced at her watch. Then a fierce determination entered her eyes.

"Okay, fast forward," she suddenly uttered. "Do you know what I do now? Collect disability and hold on for dear life. As for organizing even a pathetically simple event like this, I wouldn't have a prayer. Yet we're all called 'survivors' as if we're magically on equal footing.... Do you get what I'm driving at? Do you?" she asked, her eyes fixed on mine.

Our ability to pull this off—that's what had felt so personal. She had a point. Not that my life was the cakewalk that she assumed, but were I in her shoes, might I not feel the same?

Humbled, I caught Rita's eye, nodded. And ever so slightly, her face softened.

During the break that followed this last piece of testimony, I started to seek Rita out, but the business of the day intruded. As I returned to my seat, a good dozen more people entered, including a very old woman with a cane. Quite something that someone that age had made the effort to come! Would she be speaking?

Now despite the comeuppance—actually, in part because of it—the day so far had been remarkable. Though, who could have been prepared for the testimony to come?

"The day I was admitted, my husband was asked to sign this blank form," said Louisa, eagerly mounting the platform the second that we resumed. "Now you might wonder: who in their right mind would sign such a thing? But they were doctors, so..."

"Big deal—I was a rebellious teen!" asserted Dan, the prematurely balding man who spoke next. "Rebellious teenager—duh! I mean, gimme a break! But you know what really gives me the heebie-jeebies? After I gave the doc the 'fuck-you' sign, I heard the s.o.b. say, 'that's one smart-assed kid—let him feel it.' Anyway, next day they wheel me in. They put a gel on my temples. They put a gag in my mouth. I go to take a breath, and it won't come. I was all of thirteen, right? Now I ask you," he pressed, peering into the crowd, "if that's not child abuse, what is?"

"So failing to anesthetize—not exactly an oversight," I could hear Rose whisper. Taking in the implication, I nodded. Then I glanced at Ruth. She was leaning forward as if about to whisper also but she stopped, for already another horror story was unfolding.

"At first I thought I was—you know, okay," observed Usha. "Of course, it hadn't worked. I was still sad, no? But I figured that I was just one of those unlucky womans who somehow hadn't benefited. At least it hadn't hurt me. But gradually, I am noticing something. I am having these what-do-you-call-them? Spells—How to explain?"

"And so of course, I didn't have a clue what sex was," continued a perky little woman with green hair, "but I'm one adventurous broad. So I soon found out," she added, grinning suggestively. And the audience roared.

Even as the green-haired woman was testifying, another survivor mounted the podium and grabbed the mike. "I've just one thing to say," she announced. "You've heard it from most everyone else. Now hear it from me. Abolish it!" she shrieked. "That's it. That's all I fuckin' have to say." She stepped away from the microphone, and seething with rage, off the podium she stomped.

Now it looked as though the aged woman with the cane was getting ready to speak for she lifted herself up, but it was soon apparent that she was just heading to the washroom. A few more minutes passed with no one else budging, though the odd survivor glanced at the podium as if wondering if they dare.

Then a woman thin as a rake reached out her bony little hand, switched on her mike. She immediately ordered the videographer to turn off his camera, then stipulated the pseudonym Jennifer. "I'm from Windsor and I'm a childhood sexual abuse survivor," she announced, lowering her eyes. "My father," she clarified. "His penis in my mouth—no one can tell me that's not rape. Anyway, when the abuse memories started coming hard and fast, I, um, found not eating helped. It does too in point of fact. Now I admit things got a bit out of hand, but the long and short? They took me to hospital; my husband signed whatever they asked him to; kicking and screaming, I was dragged onto a gurney; and twelve unilateral treatments followed. Now people ask about effects. I could rhyme off a whole laundry list, but in the interests of expediency, I'll settle for just one." And here she looked up at long last, stared into the audience, her eyes frighteningly empty. "I was alive before," she stated. "I'm not alive now."

"Never again should this happen to *anyone*," stipulated Catherine. "Let me be clear about that. Nonetheless, like most everyone else, I keep asking: Why me? All I did was give birth, and look what they made of it! Eight years of my life wiped out. I live on borrowed meaning—my brother's stories, my aunt's recollections. To this day, I can't remember the first four years of my son's life. Now I used to be an actress—considered one of the most promising up-and-coming young stars in Canada. And now? I have this job as a clerk. I transfer figures from one column to another. Nothing very complicated. And really, that's about all I can manage."

Now to all appearances, Catherine's testimony was over, for she had started stepping away from the podium, her long floral dress swishing as she moved. Suddenly, she retraced her steps, leaned into the mike. "I understand that we're only supposed to talk about *our own* shock experience," she explained, "but I just can't leave it like this. Not as a woman, not as a mother. 'Cause if I couldn't protect her then, the very least I can do is stand up for her now." She proceeded to say that once upon a time she had a wonderful and talented daughter, who loved to sing, who even composed, that the last time she herself was in hospital her daughter was admitted for depression, that her daughter was given ECT, that but a week later, her daughter killed herself.

A silence still as death followed Catherine's testimony. *Gotenyu!* Who could conceivably speak after what we had heard? Then it happened. With great care—for the sitting had been hard on her—the elderly woman with the cane rose, started hobbling up to the platform. Slowly, she took it, as folk in the bleachers craned their neck to get a better look. And now she was approaching the microphone. And now she cast her eyes about, nodded as if asserting the correctness of being here. "I'm Martha Andrews and I'm old as dirt," she announced. A wave of gentle laughter rippled through the room. Then the room went so quiet that you could hear your very breath go in and out.

"Okay then," Martha affirmed. Then in an utterly calm voice, almost matter-of-factly, she spoke of being raised to be dutiful, of bringing seven healthy children into the world, of subsequently giving birth to a dead child, of never wanting anything to go in or out of her ever again, of sleeping with her husband anyway because it was expected, of having an additional child because it was expected, of agreeing to ECT to cure some spiritual quandary because it was expected, of somehow raising her family, of no longer even recollecting the nature of the spiritual quandary. "Or anything else much," she added, sardonically.

"And so yes," she went on, leaning into her cane, "I take notes all day long. That's what I have to do to manage. And to think that in this day and age, they're still..." At this, she looks away, then gradually focuses back in on us. "Look, here's the thing," she continues, her eyes keen. "I'm eighty-six years old. Eighty-six. And the other day a dear friend of mine—also a lady in her eighties—was given shock, 'cause apparently that's now the treatment of choice for depressed seniors. And so I have to ask. Is this it? After all our years of service, is this what we have to look forward to?"

Now, as the elderly woman is being helped down from the platform, I see my daughter look at me encouragingly. I glance at the clock. It is now or never. I switch on my microphone. "My name is Naomi Cohan," I announce. "Without question, I am one of the lucky ones for I've been able to have a bone fide career. Also through the years, I've had incredible support from my family. But I too have a story to tell. I tell it for myself. I tell it for all our perished sisters and brothers who can't be here to lay their story next to ours."

Whereupon I look over at Ro, see her eyes beaming. Then I scan the audience, spot Rita, see her nod. Reluctant, but a nod regardless. And like everyone else, amid kin, allies, fellow survivors, I say my piece.

I caught Inna's eye. "Let's do it," I said. The press conference started within minutes of our arrival. And while it hardly gave us the same rush as the hearing, it was anything but disappointing. My photographs surrounding us, fellow survivors quietly cheering us on, Inna and I stood side by side in the middle of that august room and spoke confidently of brain damage, of electroshock as a feminist issue, of using art to body forth this tragedy.

"So would you say creative people are at greater risk of ECT?" asked a square-faced reporter toward the tail end of question period.

"Well, there's Ernest Hemingway," Inna pointed out. "There's Sylvia Plath."

"And Naomi, what do you think?" he asked.

"Perhaps," I answered, "but as my peers here will tell you, the point is, *all* human beings hit rough patches, and all human beings need to be allowed to be creative, whether it be Hemingway or your meddlesome Aunt Minny. One of the great tragedies of shock is that some people are diminished, their creativity sacrificed."

At this, the *tashlich* leapt to mind. "Lemme tell you something," I found myself saying. "there's a ceremony my folks used to perform at Rosh Hashanah. It's about sacrifice, yes? As I think about it now, though, you know what occurs to me? To our detriment, our entire society is built on sacrifice. We have throw-away people, whether it be crazies, people in conflict with the law. But, c'mon, we can do better than that."

"So no throw-away people?" asked Len from the CBC, signalling to his cameraman.

"Precisely."

Three additional follow-up questions came quickly on the heels of that one. Then Inna glanced at her watch. "Hate to do this, but just time for one more question."

"Lynn Adams of the *Toronto Sun*," called out a contralto voice. Seconds later a large woman in a striped pants suit elbowed her way to the front. "My question has two parts, and it's for Naomi. In your testimony, you spoke about not knowing your daughter or husband, also never getting used to being a mother or wife. So, how does your daughter feel about you as a mom? And how does your family feel about you going public?"

Faced with the killer question after all—and just why are those always twofers?—I took a deep breath. "Okay," I began, "the truth is, while we heard today from many shock survivors who no doubt were first-rate parents, I never was. My daughter, absolutely, was cheated. You see, I…"

Now I had been surprised often today, but what happened next literally takes my breath away. Even as I stand there trying to figure out what to say, what to leave out, Ruth intercedes, asserting that she'd like to answer. I nod gratefully, though in all honesty, I can't help but wonder if I'm about to be thrown under the bus. Ruth instantly comes over, stands next to me, faces the reporter.

"I'm Ruth Radcliff—Naomi Cohan's daughter. I was only a few months old the day they pressed that button on the ECT machine, but that's the day I lost my mother," she states definitively. "Our elected officials claim to care about children. Well, maybe they should think about what it means to lose our parents needlessly. It was my mom, of course, who was damaged profoundly—until today, I don't think I quite took in how profoundly—and despite that, she's managed to give to my brother and me in ways I have not always properly appreciated. As for your other question, let me be clear, I've never been more proud of my mom than I am today."

My heart bursting, I look with unmitigated admiration at my daughter. She notices, seems uncomfortable. After sneaking a quick peek at the reporter, she abruptly leans forward, puts her mouth to my ear. "Mom," she whispers, "I meant every word, but when it comes to you, I'm a fuckup. So don't count on me."

"Sweetheart…" I start to answer.

"And her ex-husband's proud of her too," a familiar voice suddenly announces.

I look about. Now when he slipped in, I do not know, but dressed in his good blue suit, Earl is standing at the front of the crowd, a single long-stemmed rose in hand.

"Earl, you didn't hafta, but thank you for this," I respond, tears in my eyes.

"Sometimes," he explains, "it takes a man's children to show him he's being a jerk."

The press conference at an end, I thanked the media for coming. Then arm-in-arm, the three of us took in the exhibit together, Ruth and Earl asking questions, all three of us chortling at the sight of familiar notes miraculously transformed into art. "Remember how Les used to hide the notes?" asked Earl. "Oh and how about the time *this one* appeared in the freezer?" exclaimed Ruth, pointing. As we stopped to take in the Mrs. Smith pictures, a number of psych survivors made their way over, asked one or all of us a question. It felt good to be hanging out with Ruth and Earl, greeting the world together like the family we'd never had the chance of becoming. Not that I had lost sight of what a bonehead mistake it was to marry Earl. Nor that I was ignoring Ruth's warning. But this family, might we have made it, I wondered, had psychiatry not been permitted to intervene? A sad sweet thought—the crowning jewel on a remarkable day.

After we had traversed the gallery twice over, Earl glanced at his watch. "Gotta get home to the Missus," he said. "Um, Nomi," he suddenly added, drawing me aside, "something I need to say here. Gerald is after telling me that your friend Jack passed recently. My apologies for not expressing my condolences sooner." With a vulnerability almost childlike, he went on to confess that he had always been jealous because he knew that Jack was the one I loved.

"Earl," I acknowledge, "to be fair, you had the harder role. I mean, think about it—what if Jack had been stuck being the long-suffering husband and you got to play the heroic stranger who rescued me in the corridor?"

We were clearly in a charmed moment, for despite his dislike of hypotheticals, Earl smiled, a quiet gratitude in his eyes. I leaned forward, kissed him on the cheek. He nodded, then turned to go. Just as he was heading off to fetch his coat, however, he was waylaid by a young reporter asking his opinion of psychiatry. Repeating the question, Earl rolled up his sleeves, grinned like a Cheshire cat, and it was clear that we were in for a treat. "Well, let me just say this," he began. "I'm an islander born and bred. Now one thing us Newfies have in great abundance are humpback whales, and as far as I can make out, shrinks, they're rather like humpback whales."

"Don't quite get it," said the reporter.

"Well," continued Earl, "when a school of herring appears, the whales circle them, blowing bubbles through their blowholes. Now the bubbles, they act like a net, Once all the herring are in a tight little ball, the whales go in for the kill."

Not having the foggiest where this was heading, the reporter shook his head. "But Mr. Smith, what does this have to do with psychiatrists?" he asked.

"The shrinks, they manufacture bubbles of their own."

"And what are those?"

"We're after calling them diagnoses, aren't we? And here's the thing, you blow enough nonsense about, sooner or later you snag most everyone."

At which, Earl left the hapless reporter scratching his head, while a number of survivor onlookers stood there chuckling.

A good hour later, the event drew to a close. The day had been stellar, and we all knew it. CAPA members came over, shook my hand. We thanked each other, vowed to continue the fight. And slowly, the faithful began to depart.

As Ruth left, she made a point of clarifying that she still needed distance from me. "But Mom," she added, catching my eye, "I'm glad I came."

"Me too, sweetie," I murmured.

Now I knew that at this very moment Gerald would be at his place eagerly awaiting Rose and me. And mindful of what he'd so selflessly orchestrated, how I looked forward to the three of us celebrating! Also, nothing could be clearer but that Rose and I needed to talk. All in good time, I assured myself—but not just yet.

Determined, I approached my sister. She took one look at me and knew.

"You want me to call Gerald, tell him we'll be late, don't you?"

I nodded gratefully, gave her a quick embrace, then turned about. You see, I had discovered something about myself. Whatever else I was, I was a psychiatric survivor—indeed, a shock survivor. They felt it too, I realized, eyeing the stalwarts who remained.

Then it happened. From all corners of the room we gathered. What only we knew—what we needed to affirm—something significant had occurred between us.

"Catherine, both as a mom and as a survivor, my heart weeps for you," I offered.

"What you said about routinely getting lost, I've been there," shared Catherine, eyeing me fondly. "And Usha," she hastened to point out, "those spells, I get them too."

"I doubt that the s.o.b.'s will ever give a tinker's damn about anything any of us said, but at least we said it, right?" asserted Dan.

Knowing that words hardly sufficed, Usha reached out her arms. Almost instantly, Catherine followed suit. And so it is that as patrons filed out of a trendy Toronto art gallery, a small band of shock survivors who might well never lay eyes on one another again sealed their bond with a group hug. It felt right. It felt like the only way to part. Still, this fond farewell, it had not included everyone, had it?

Now I had been avoiding her, but I knew in my bones that she was still here.

With a touch of pathos, I watched the others disappear. Then I cast my eyes about. Only a few enthusiasts lingered, but yes, Rita was among them. She was standing in front of the Mrs. Smith series. She was not looking at the pictures. She was looking at me.

Just as I was mustering up the courage to approach, she came over. "If this is your idea of art, a piece of advice—don't give up your day job," she observed caustically, gesturing toward one of the photos. "Incidentally, I've been watching you, and *I'm* not going to be that easy."

"Tell me something I don't know."

Instinctively, we headed to the far corner of the room, then took a seat. Now I started to ask Rita about her life, but she put up her hand, stopped me. "Lady, let's just get this over with, okay?"

Admitting that she was the woman who had called last night, she proceeded to explain that in the weeks leading up to the hearing, she kept thinking that spilling her guts would simply be humiliating, but that she too had gotten something from participating. "Don't you dare ask me what," she cautioned.

"You know," I acknowledged, "you were right about my privilege, but maybe you can benefit from it. Why not let me..."

She grimaced. "Playing Lady Bountiful, are we? Anyway, you're about to blow Toronto. So why would I put an iota of credence in any offer of help from you? Boy are you ever a piece of work!"

"Fair enough, but here's my Winnipeg number," I offered, handing her a card. "If..."

"And pray tell, which of us is that supposed to make feel better?"

Now she reluctantly pocketed the card, and I figured that was the end of it. Just as I was rising to leave, however, she cast me a knowing look. "Naomi," she said, pointedly using my name, "your daughter hates you, doesn't she?"

"Say what?"

"Hates—h-a-t-e-s—you know, as in can't stand, a pronounced aversion to."

This time, the woman really took me by surprise. I wanted to force her to retract, but what was the point? I felt an old ache coming over me, could feel my throat turn dry. "But she's been so supportive today. How...how did you know?"

For a split second, Rita looked apologetic. "That was cruel of me, wasn't it? Something I neglected to mention in my testimony. I'm one high-flying bitch. Always was. Nice to know that at least part of your personality survives electroshock, wouldn't you say?

I chuckled, despite myself.

"Look, lady," she continued, "I'm not saying you're not important to her, but I've been watching her—watching her watching you, actually—and every so often there's a look in her eyes.... I see you know what I mean."

I nodded, then sat back down, took out a cigarette, fiddled with it. I was proud of what we had pulled off today—Ruth as much as anyone—and nothing that had been said nullified that. At the same time, this was its own moment of truth.

As I sat there, I called to mind the good old days, when just like the rest of us, little Ruth would eagerly anticipate Pesach, when she would come rushing up to me and ask, "How many more days, Mommy?" Immediately thereafter, I remembered the time in her teens when she dug in her heels and it became painfully apparent that she would come no more.

Then I looked straight ahead, saw Rita staring at me in that unnerving manner of hers. Of the hundred and fifty odd people who had turned up for the event—and who odder than this duck?—who'd have thunk that we'd be the ones with the most in common? Or was it simply that we were the ones with the luxury to admit it? Whatever, I probably was not seeing the last of the woman. Ergo, definitely, definitely, there was no God.

I recalled something that Ger once said—that I had a soft spot for impossible people—and I vowed to strangle my mother some day soon. Clearly, the prototype, yes? The complication of family buzzing in my head, intuitively, I tried to imagine the families of those who had borne testimony—the ones who had been mentioned, the many more who had received no mention, though willy-nilly, were affected. Then I settled back in my chair, sensing the inevitability.

"Rita, the daughter that can barely bring herself to speak to you, what's her name?" I asked.

"My son's name is Tony," she answered.

23. NAOMI

APRIL 12-16, 2008.

I tell a coherent story   some days.
Some days, every thought is stitched so securely
*   to its neighbour*
Not a living soul could guess that it was   misplaced.
Some days   almost nothing slips through
*   the able fingers of my mind*
Even on a bad day, I generally pass.
One day   I stood in front of my peers and
*   LIKE everyone else, let it all hang out*
As long as I live, I will never   forget that day
I PRAY TO God, I WON'T.
Of course,   passing is   good too.
It gives us   a life
The one and only price
Integrity.
—Excerpt From Grey Binder One, 2009

BEING WITH MY PEERS, warts and all, that was a rare gift—one that was to continue to nourish me in leaner years. Close to my heart, I have held it. And while I kept peeking at Rose, trying to pick up how she was faring, eventually, that evening, Rose, Ger, and I did indeed celebrate. For the longest while, we sat on my balcony, our hearts a blazing hearth. We knew not what tomorrow would bring, and no one was under any illusion that the tide had turned, but hey, this, we knew. While we were not now what we had been in our salad years when we dreamt of moving heaven and earth, a loud clear call we had issued, and the people had come, the people had spoken.

Strange what marks the turnings in one's life journey. For some, it is birthdays, for some, deaths, others, weddings. For me, the first was sitting in a darkened room, peering up at a silver screen. The last, without question, was a very special hearing. It would be critical also, though, to factor in the hearkening of Pesach. As phone calls from Mom multiplied and Pesach loomed, I knew that after all these years, finally I was returning home.

An opportunity. Also, a moment of reckoning, yes?

The next couple of days were fraught, as endings and beginnings typically are. And packing was the least of it. While everyone and their Aunt Kapishkas turned up to bid me farewell, as forecasted, Ruth kept her distance, and I could only pray that the hatred that Rita had read in her eyes would not be the final word on our relationship. However, as I hovered on the brink of departure, of all people, it was the one that I was setting out with who weighed most heavily on my mind. And mirroring each other in this as in so much else, I likewise weighed on hers.

You see, we needed to discuss my testimony and hadn't. And so it sat there between us—what it was and more than what it was. Now by any normal understanding, it fell to me to broach it. However, for the first time since our twenties, we were in a fix that I was clueless how to tackle, so close was it to the core of who we were.

Of course it may well be that once a decade, at the bare minimum, people who care passionately for each other need to take their relationship apart then put it back together. Be that as it may, we danced around the problem, so loath were we to go there.

"Rose, anything on your mind?" I asked just before turning in the day after the hearing.

"Nothing I can't handle. And you?" she fenced.

How is it that it we spend the better part our lives coming to terms with our personal failings, yet typically leave the most critical stone unturned?

As the ever gracious sun shot through the cracked windowpane, bathing the kitchen in splendour, I glanced at the calendar to double check. Just one day to go. Lured further into the kitchen by what felt like an unassailable memory of Hershey bars, I opened the cupboard door above the stove. The top shelves were empty. No munchies in the bottom one either, but tucked away at the very back—its presence, a stark reminder—was the last of the tobacco I had squirreled away for Jack. Feeling that tug at the heart that one feels at such times, I shook my head and abruptly shut the door.

Seconds later, Rose staggered in in overalls, *schlepping* a huge box. "Time to pack the utensils," she announced. We laboured in silence. Just as she was heading to the washroom, however, she stopped, inquired how I was feeling about Ruth, then suggested calling her. "Look, I wouldn't presume to tell you how to relate to your own daughter," she continued, "but..."

I looked at Ro standing there, doing her damnedest to be helpful. And I knew that come hell or high water, we had to bite the bullet. Even if it meant a full-scale blowout.

"It's not Ruth that we need to talk about," I said. "Ro, about the other day..."

"Was wondering if you'd bring that up. You know, sis, I really do get it that you had enough on your plate."

The story of our telepathy, I had not told it, you see. I had stood up at city hall, laid bare the family feud, and it goes without saying, gone into details about memory loss. Not a word had I breathed, however, about the injury that was uniquely ours.

I sat down at the kitchen table, knowing this could take a while. Rose sat also, albeit with a reluctance uncharacteristic of her.

Ostensibly, we were two grown women in our senior years sitting down for an adult-to-adult conversation about a recent development. As we lowered ourselves into our seats, however, nothing could be clearer than that we were a hair's breadth away from unearthing an issue that we'd dared not touch— never mind name—in almost sixty years.

"You've every right to be pissed," I acknowledged, "but as God is my witness, it's not that it isn't important to me. It's that even had I spent the vast majority of the time explaining about us, it would still be the part of the story that no one got—not even my fellow survivors—and Rose, I so needed to connect with them."

At the word "need," Rose turned beet red. "For Pete's sake, it's *me* you're talking to. You think I don't get your needs?" she exclaimed, shaking her head in disbelief.

"Not what I meant." I reached into my pocket for a smoke. "Ro, listen," I urged, "I love you like no other, and last thing I wanna do is hurt you. And naturally, I..."

"You insist on getting into this? Okay, but no holds barred. I need to be visible. That really too much to ask?"

"No," and I apologize. Now in retrospect, I could've handled this with greater sensitivity, "but you've gotta understand, leaving out the twin factor..."

"*Twin factor?* Twin factor! Is that how you think of the two of us?"

"Unfortunate choice of words, but hear me out. It was a last minute decision; and the stakes were high, the deck stacked. Think back, Ro. Remember how people used to gawk at us in childhood? The point is, one word about the mysterious powers of identical twins, and no one would have seen a woman butchered by psychiatry. They wouldn't even have seen two sisters wrenched apart by an indifferent system. At best, they'd have seen a curiosity. You *know* that. So cut me some slack here—please."

Rose considered for a moment and it looked as if she were softening. Seconds later, however, her nostrils began to flare. "So what am I—expendable?" she suddenly tossed out. "Someone you can cast aside whenever the truth of who we are becomes inconvenient? You know something?" she snapped. "You were an asshole growing up and you're an asshole now." At which, she threw her hands in the air, and without another word, stormed out of the room.

Taken by surprise, I leapt up from the table. Agonizing over whether or not to go after her, I had just set foot in the hall when the front door slammed. Now for a moment, I couldn't wrap my mind about what had happened. Then in my mind's eye, I glimpsed seven-year-old Rose, a stunned expression on her face. And suddenly, I knew.

I returned to the kitchen. Seconds later, the front door creaked open. Then a relatively calm, albeit distant Rose re-entered the room. Her manner subdued, Rose joined me at the table. She slowly reached over, gently laid her hand on my shoulder.

"Oh Ro, I really do love you," I murmured.

She got up, plugged in the kettle. Her way, I realized, of pacing herself. Settling back down, she leaned forward, held me with her eyes.

"You're hardly a jerk and I know that you love me," she begins, "and like, maybe with you returning to Winnipeg, it's stirring up old wounds. I don't know. Because honestly, there were moments in childhood that were pure torture. Nomi, you kept obliterating me—and each friggin' time, it was like having my heart ripped out."

"I'm so very sorry. What happened, it was brutal. Now I wish I could say that I didn't know, but despite what I've told myself, of course, I did."

At this, Rose nodded. "Okay, I don't believe in getting mired in the past, but like, sis, minimally, when you need to sideline me, do me the courtesy of warning me. Also if ever you write about your shock experience, the part about us, include it, okay? Now sometimes you genuinely do need to shut me out," she conceded. "I get that."

"You didn't as a child."

"For sure, that's my part in this, but Nomi, we aren't children any longer. There's a pattern here, and it has to stop. Also, there's times when *my* needs have to come first."

"Agreed."

Now I started doing what I could to reassure Rose when a contemplative look came over her—the first indication that there was even more at issue here than met the eye. Then she slipped into sharing how incredibly hard it was for her to challenge me.

"As people go, I'm not exactly gun-shy," she pointed out, "but knowing that I am adding to your *tsores*, even if only a smidgeon, you can't imagine how that feels. I mean, you're my sister, my injured sister, and so how could I conceivably? So mostly, I don't. But pulling my punches, that hasn't exactly worked either, has it?"

"Listen, Rose, you never have to hamstring yourself like that—I'm not that fragile."

She looks at me and smiles. "You aren't, are you?" she muses. "One other thing," she adds. "Lately, there's been a role for me in your life—fellow researcher, activist, *epes*. For years now, my role in Winnipeg has been far less clear. Naomi Brenda Cohan, don't you dare let me become peripheral."

Understanding her point only too well, I nodded.

Then she poured us both a spot of tea and in a voice almost childlike, began commenting on how deeply she misses her "older sister."

"Older sister?" I query.

"C'mon. You know exactly what I mean ... Nomi," she continues, a vulnerability coming over her, "forgive the *chutzpah*—and after giving you grief all day, it *is chutzpah*—but could you be my older sister again—I mean, just for the night?"

Touched, I reached for her hand, assured that her old buddy was there for her. And before long, we were cuddled up on the couch, *schmoozing* about the bad old days.

A resting place, yes? And it felt good to both of us. That said, the work of leaving was hardly done.

"Ger, not for a second could I have survived Toronto without you," I said. "You know that, right?"

It was mere hours before the big departure. And there were boxes everywhere. Surrounded on all sides, Gerald and I were on the porch, grabbing those last moments of alone time that people parting from one another sorely need.

"Something for you, love," he stated, reaching into his pocket. "A memento." And for the second time in our history, the man handed me a pen, once again, a silver beauty. "I see you remember," he added with a tender smile.

I immediately threw my arms around him, held him long and hard. Then the two of us fell into reflecting on our history together. And all the while at the back of our minds lurked the shadow.

Over thirty years ago, that was. And while who knows what he whispered to Miu in the middle of the night, in all this time, not a word about the assault had he breathed to the rest of us.

Finally, throwing caution to the wind, I said, "Ger, I'm just gonna say one thing, then let it go. All these years, you've been convinced that you're fated to pass your days in fear. And maybe on some level, you are, but that you're doomed to remain frozen in that moment—forgive me—but I somehow doubt it. And that doubt, Ger, politically fucked though it is—that's *my* parting gift."

A nervous smile playing at the corner of his lips, Gerald nodded. And for a moment, we stood in silence, struggling with something that defied words.

"You know, Ger," I quipped affectionately, "I think we should mass-produce you. I mean, in all fairness, don't you think that every Canadian family should have their own trans man to keep them from going kerflooey?"

His eyes twinkling, Gerald tipped his hat. "Can't argue with that, love. Hey, when a woman's right, a woman's right."

Letting go of what could clearly be broached no further, the two of us proceeded to sort through last minute details—including getting copies of our shock material to Rita.

"A new friend?" he queried.

"Don't ask. Oh, one other thing. In one of the dresser drawers—can't recall which—you'll find a letter to Ruth. It's about that day. If the time comes when you think it'll help her, could you do me a favour and give it to her?"

Obliging as always, Gerald quickly agreed. Whereupon we rejoined Rose.

Together, the three of us packed up the personal items in the washroom. Then we opened the bedroom door, and sure enough, there were the binders smack in the middle of the floor precisely where we had left them.

Now Gerald grabbed one of the garbage bags from off the bed, but he stopped himself just as he was about to toss out Black Binder Three. Eyeing that dilapidated old notebook almost with affection, he carefully placed it back on the floor.

"Best we leave them a day or two in case you change your mind," he suggested. "Incidentally," he went on, "either of you fair damsels see the piece in yesterday's *Star*?"

Without further ado, he reached into his back pocket, whipped out a photocopy of the bottom half of page fourteen. There plain as day was an entire column devoted to our event. "Psychiatrist As Humpback Whale" read the headline.

"Figures," exclaimed Rose, tossing back her head and laughing. "The crazies, the broads, and the trans delightfuls do all the hard work and at the last minute, in waltzes the straight-as-an-arrow male and snaffles the headline!"

Gerald winked at Rose. Then he rolled up his sleeves, and we continued our toils. Though soon, only too soon, amid hugs and tears, he departed.

"Incidentally, love," he threw out as he exited the house, "I do think she'll show. Oh and Nomi," he added, "about what you were saying before, I love you too."

Not long after Gerald left, the doorbell rang.

"Expecting someone?" asked Rose, her face brightening.

"It seems we are," I answered.

As I held my breath, not daring to anticipate, briefcase in hand, looking every inch the attorney, Ruth popped her head in. "I'll bet you thought I wasn't coming," she said, nimbly hoisting herself up top of the largest packing crate, "and no slight intended, but to be perfectly honest," she immediately added, "I almost didn't." Tears in my eyes, I welcomed her. And for the next short while, draped over this or that, the three of us sat in that train wreck of a living room, saying our goodbyes. Needing to keep things light, Ruth steered us toward safe topics—her daughter's braces, the Winnipeg weather. Then came an about-turn.

"Mom," she inquired, seemingly out of the blue, "so how do you feel about leaping into Pesach so soon after arriving?"

An unusual, even a gutsy question, I couldn't help thinking, given our history. After all, as Mom would put it, it hardly took an Einstein to see that her rejection of Pesach was personal.

"Thoughtful of you to ask," I offered. "And yes, it's quick for sure, but I'm pretty sure we can pull it off." "Ruth, you wouldn't by any chance consider joining us this year?" Rose suddenly suggested. "You know, this could be your *bubbeh*'s last Pesach," she added pointedly.

"Oh Aunt Rosie!" Ruth exclaims. "You know I've always loathed that holiday. Promised Land—give me a break! Oh no you don't, Mom," she insists, turning toward me. "Don't you dare tell me how it's all a metaphor. Okay-okay-okay.

Change of topic. You know those binders of yours—could I have my own copy?"

Perplexed, I stared at her. "Well, there *is* an extra set. In fact, as coincidence will have it, you could even pick it up now. But sweetheart, what gives?"

"It's just that they could come in handy if we ever charged the hospital, is all."

"But Ruthie, the statute of limitations ... um, I thought..."

"Yes, it's highly unlikely, but best I hold onto them. Also, there's this other thing. Actually, it's nothing," she states, abruptly reversing herself. "The two of you, just have a good Pesach, okay?"

Whereupon Ruth kisses us both quickly, asserting that she needs to "beetle over" to the law library. Now Rose starts to ask the obvious question. Even as the opening words slip from her lips, however, a marked impatience comes over Ruth, and before Rose can so much as spit it out, Ruth is on her way. As we hear the front door close, Rose eyes me quizzically.

"Sis," I explain, "I know it's not your idea of family, but we're not exactly the family she'd have chosen and she's doing the best she can. As for those legal references, for the time being anyway, let's not even try to figure them out. Oh Ro," I add, "I understand, I really do, but if you're taking it personally, do consider: When she looks at you, don't you know who she sees?"

At this, Rose eyes me sympathetically. Then inexplicably, a look of vague bemusement comes over her.

"What?" I ask.

"Nothing, really," she answers, barely able to keep a straight face. "It's just that I suddenly realized what Mom would call this."

"And what would that be?" I press, my eyes already lighting up in anticipation.

"One more fact about identical twins they neglected to include in the how-to manual."

We take one look at each other and crack up. Minutes later, Rose gives me a peck on the forehead. Then she glances at her watch, then eyes me meaningfully.

"Ro, just give me a sec here," I urge.

Excited to be going home at long last, and clear what I have to do, I walk through every room of this house where I've lived these many years, bidding each a final farewell. The photo lab. The study where once my tiny daughter slept. The gallery where once.... Ah, well, I remind myself, it's not the end of the world if I don't remember.

I linger for a moment in the kitchen. With a tenderness so sweet that it catches me unaware, I smile wistfully at the thought of the one task outstanding. Then I open the cupboard door above the stove and reach for the sole remaining item—that pouch of tobacco that I have not been able to part with. As I behold it, questions flood my mind—not sensible questions, those twilight queries that slip past our inner censor, surprising us, tutoring us: Are the voices gone now? Is he warm at last? Is he on his way?

"Oh Jack, tarry not," I whisper. "Go, go, go toward the stars."

24. NAOMI

On this, the morning of the first seder, Mom and I place each of the symbolic foods in the gold-lined seder plate. Yes, the shankbone, here, the horseradish there. Each morsel in its own place. Each with its own story, each part of a larger story. With sundown tonight comes another telling. To make it ours, that is the task before us. Blessings on all who gather in this house to enlarge on the telling.—Memo to self, April, 2008.

I AM ENDING the last book of this my memoir with Pesach because holidays have served me faithfully as markers over the years, and hey, a holiday is as good a place to end as any. Now to be clear, I am not superstitious. Strictly speaking, I am not even a believer. The thing about holidays, however, is that they create opportunities, openings to do what you might not otherwise do, say what you might not otherwise say, and better they should happen and prove ephemeral than not see the light of day.

Now the older I grow, the more inclined am I to believe that the very concept of beginnings and endings is arbitrary. Possibly, a subtle form of human hubris. Minimally, an optical illusion. Be that as it may, from the second that we stepped off that plane, you could sense that there would be a grace to this Pesach, and I like to think that in their quiet moments, even the least enthusiastic of our visitors felt it.

With Pesach looming larger with every passing minute, the homecoming was every bit as rushed as we had anticipated. Except for that first night back, Rose had little time to spend with Sam. There was no time to unpack, no time to catch Mom up on the details of the hearing, not even time to drive ourselves *meshuger* wondering about Ruthie—just time enough to make like *balebostes*. And how absolutely wonderful that felt!

Early, the night before Pesach, Rose drew me aside. Without cracking a smile, she proceeded to inform me that she and her hubby were engaged in a strictly scientific experiment to discover how long an older couple could screw without resorting to Viagra.

"My God, Ro," I exclaimed, "break that illustrious record and I'll be able to say that I knew you back when!"

Rose laughed. No sooner had the merriment slipped from her lips, however, than a serious look came over her.

We caught each other's eyes, both aware that a critical part of our new resolve was meeting its first test, that this simply was one of those moments when her needs had to have priority.

"Sorry about there still being a shitload of work to do. You mind?" she asked.

"Go for it," I urged. "I'll hold down the fort until the seder."

Now while Pesach dominated my waking thoughts, in the wee hours of the following morning, I discovered that other preoccupations had been lurking just beneath the surface, for I was visited by a most telling dream: My binders were accidentally dumped into the Red Sea. Forthwith, in full regalia, the tribes of Israel and the entire Egyptian army swooped down from the sky and started squabbling over property rights. In the snap of a finger, the Middle East's quintessential patriarchs Moses and Pharaoh were sitting crossed-legged on the sand, their quills poised. Just as they were on the verge of signing what would appear to be a historic agreement, clad in white wigs and armed with legal briefs, Ruth turned up, along with a lanky adolescent who was the spitting image of Dan, the two of them insisting that the binders were the exclusive property of shock survivors. "Also, there's this other thing," murmurs Ruth, slithering down onto Moses's lap and drawing her fingers suggestively through his beard.

I awoke with a start, but it was not the shock of the erotic imagery that was grabbing me. Ruthie's mysterious words were clinging tenaciously to my brain—like day-old gum to the bottom of a sneaker. I bolted upright, switched on the light. Why did they sound so familiar? And that's when I realized. They were the precise words that she had uttered just before rushing out of the Palmerston house. At the time, she had been suggesting that my binders might come in handy. Then she'd shaken her head, taken everything back. I lay there as baffled as the other day, but this time, it was not so easy to let it go.

I recalled Dan's testimony. A child survivor, he too had been shocked without anesthetic—and Ruth had noticed. Was it something he had said? And was this the urgent matter that had drawn her to the law library so precipitously?

"Lazybones, get your *tokhes* down here," Mom's voice suddenly cried out.

I jotted down my suspicions, dressed, then hurried to the kitchen.

"Still can't believe you're back. May you have a good and *kosher* Pesach," Mom exclaimed the second that she laid eyes on me. "Baby, you know why we Jews wish each other a 'kosher Pesach?'" she asked. "'Cause with all the dietary laws, with this and with that, getting through it without tripping up—the head rabbi should be so lucky! But like in life, what does it hurt to wish people the best?"

With rapt admiration, I beheld my mother standing there. This tiny old woman whom Rose and I called mother, her skin had wrinkled, her face was spotted—but that same live intelligence danced in her eyes.

"Mom, you don't know how good it is to be with you," I

said, my heart instantly lightening. "Know why? 'Cause more than anyone else, you know who you are."

"What? I should mistake myself for somebody else?" She opened the fridge door, whisked out the celery, then turned about and eyed me inquisitively. "You know, Naomi," she pointed out, "I wasn't born this way. *Kinechora*, I have a few years on you and your sister, and when you get to my age, you simply know a thing or two."

And so it was to prove.

It was three p.m., and "all was quiet on the western front." There was a magnificent bird browning in the oven; and already, Mom's white candles lay in readiness. Nonetheless, I could stand it no longer. Obsessive though I knew it was, I was itching to find out what Ruth was up to. Now I was about to call her when the phone rang.

"Naomi, sorry to bother you. I realize you're deep in preparation," said Rose, "but I haven't been able to stop wondering about Ruth's references the other day. In fact, I had the strangest dream about Ruth and the binders."

I quickly explained that she was picking up on my dreams again. Then I asked her if she had given any further thought to the mysterious way in which Ruth had left.

"Yes, but nothing helpful," stated Rose. "Tell you what I find really perplexing. Why was she so reluctant to say anything?"

The call, alas, ended with no further clarity—so I did indeed dial Ruth. Bruce answered. We exchanged a handful of pleasantries, the whole while Bruce sounding uncharacteristically tense. Then I asked to speak to my daughter.

Bruce cleared his throat, then audibly hesitated.

"I ... I see," I stammered. "Look, I'm obviously placing you in an awkward position. Just tell her I called."

Stunned, I laid down the phone. Never had it dawned on me that Ruth wouldn't be home to me. And today of all days! Now for a split second, I thought of catching a flight to Toronto, even—I kid you not—of moving back, but that crazy, I wasn't. While part of me ached for my child, it was clear where my home was. And whether Ruthie ever visited or not, indeed even if she turned down every solitary call, I would treasure this day just as I had treasured all the Pesachs that had come before. And with the occasional trip to Toronto—to see loved ones, to march proudly with CAPA on Mother's Day—I would live out the rest of my years in one city only—the one I adored.

At the thought of Winnipeg, I made my way over to the window, slowly drew back the curtain. There was the boulevard, stretching for miles, as far as the eye could see, the grass confident in itself, neither inviting you in, nor pushing you away. And to my delight, as my eyes drank in its quiet dignity—the seemingly endless stretch of green, the unapologetically blue sky—my soul stirred with the humbling sense of the expansiveness of nature. And a deep calm came over me. Oh yes, even in the city where a mere echo of its majesty shines forth, there is a peacefulness about the prairies that only its creatures comprehend.

Jack's people, they understand the sanctity of place, yes? As do our child selves. However, it was as if I were discovering it for the first time. This precious terrain—rich as it was austere—this was my ultimate anchor. This, my spirit guide.

"Mom, I'll be back in a bit," I announce, making a grab for my camera. "I've some photos to take. Then I'm off for a walk."

"Daughter, welcome home," she answers.

Now as I walked out that door, I recall thinking how good it was that I was settling into myself before the gathering of the clan.

One of these tenuous feelings you'd be at a loss to explain, yes?

"C'mon, you old battle-axe, you," said Sam, turning to Mom. "You know we can't start until you do." The preparations as complete as they would ever be, *yontif* was finally upon us. Dressed in our finest, the *yarmulkes* ranging from traditional black to dewy purple, four generations of excited Jews were squeezed into the dining room, Sam at the head. On the table before us lay crystal wines glasses, long white candles in candlesticks polished so you could see your own reflection. And a big grin on his face, Sam was *kibitzing* with Mom. Suddenly, Mom cleared her throat. And the *kibitzing* came to an abrupt stop.

Keenly aware that she just might be doing this for the last time—and God forbid she be taken from us any time soon—clad in burgundy and looking every inch the matriarch, Mom rose to light the candles—now one, now the other. And now was Sam opening his *Haggadah*. He pointed to the matzo, announced, "This is the bread of affliction that our ancestors ate in the land of Egypt. Let all who are hungry come and eat."

As in previous years, Sam paused frequently to pose questions—transparently, the fun part. He asked why we were the chosen people. And why had God hardened Pharaoh's heart? Then came a query that none of us had heard before. Pointing to the egg on the seder plate, Sam eyed each of the scholars in the family. "A question for the eggheads," he specified. "Why did I crack the shell?" Several hopeless replies followed. "The real reason?" he responded at long last. "*Nu?* So the egg won't roll away."

And we all laughed. A moment of Pesach humour, yes?

"Which bring us to Rabbi Akiba," he went on. "Why…" he began. Then he stopped dead in his tracks. Strangely, someone was knocking on the front door.

Straightaway, his entire demeanour altered. He stared in the direction of the hall and glowered. "What ignoramus would interrupt Jews at Pesach?" he muttered. "Ah well, if we ignore them, maybe they'll just…"

Now while we'd all been under the impression that Mom had been nodding off for eyes were shut, clearly not, for she instantly opened them and shook her head.

"What? You after the coveted Nudnik of the Year Award or something?" she exclaimed. "A news bulletin for you, Buster

Brown. Anyone who takes the trouble to *schlep* over is welcome in this house, yeh? And *especially* on Pesach."

Being the one most readily able to extricate herself, Rose immediately got up and made her way to the front door. Seconds later, she called out for me. Now in retrospect, had I had my wits about me these last few days, perhaps I could have guessed. Be that as it may, I approached half expecting to see the prophet Elijah or some other figure straight out of the heady world of the *Haggadah*. What seemed every bit as curious at the time, dressed to the nines stood Ruth and Gerald, Ger looking strangely apologetic.

"*Gut yontif*," I uttered, excitedly embracing them. "Boy! Did you guys ever have me bamboozled! All this time I had no idea you'd actually decided to..."

While Ruth returned my embrace, she speedily extricated herself. "That's not it," she quickly pointed out. "Mom, there's something I have to tell you. I just figured it out yesterday, and it somehow felt right to tell you today because..." And here, she caught sight of the *Mogen Dovid* dangling from my neck. "Christ! Maybe not," she stammered, as if suddenly taking in the awkwardness. "Look, Ger and I can go a friend's place tonight, and we'll come back tomorrow morning, and..."

Even as Ruth was speaking, Rose threw up her hands. "Sure, sure," she exclaimed sarcastically, "bring us half way to orgasm, then leave us in the dark. Look, Ruth," she continued, "your timing sucks, and what you don't know about Jews and Pesach, your mom and I could write a book on, but don't be an idiot. I'll ask Sam to hold off on the reading for a few minutes. Then you're going to tell us what this is about."

Now while the rest of the family remained seated, even continued discussing symbols, the seder was officially on hold. For indeed, stay our visitors did. However, Rose and Ruth had gotten off on the wrong foot, and the tension continued to mount. Ruth proceeded to mutter something under her breath, and to everyone's dismay, Rose almost responded. Then there the four of us were huddled in the living room—just feet from the main action—Ruth in Dad's old chair, our very presence, a disruption.

"Let's keep it down," urged Rose, her voice almost at a whisper, "but tell me, because I'm dying to know. What's so important you had to interrupt a seder?"

"Okay, it's still a long shot," Ruth began. "Here's the thing, though. I've been at the law library plowing through old volumes of the *Royal Statutes of Ontario*, and I've found a whole new way to go after the hospital."

"*Oy!* Scratch what I said before," Rose urged. "I've become an intolerant bitch in my old age. An honoured family tradition, in case you haven't noticed."

"Really?" observed Ruth. "I'd have thought the honoured family tradition was the quote *twins* ganging up on everyone else, breaking other people's confidences, and..."

"Damn!" protested Rose, "I was just..."

"Both of you—enough already," I insisted. "Ruthie, you've come a long way to tell us something. Please tell us."

Now the situation did not look at all promising for Ruth was shaking her head. Suddenly, however, Rose's face softened—dramatically. Ruth noticed and started to relax. Then the two of them caught each other's eye, nodded. And so it was that with a quasi-toothless urchin periodically popping her head in and with Sam doing his damnedest to keep everyone else engaged, a proposition of sorts was set before us.

"Okay, Mom, you know how Dad signed for the ECT?" began Ruth, her eyes earnest. "How most of the women testifying only received ECT because others signed? Well, except for kids, what happened to those treated before '78, it wasn't legal. You see, until '78, there was no Ontario statute allowing adults deemed incompetent to be given treatment."

"None?"

"None.... Presumably, an oversight."

Astounded, I reached into my pocket, withdrew a cigarette,

in the process took in an adorable sight. The urchin with the missing tooth, her eyes alight, she was standing in the doorway, two entire boxes of chocolate-covered matzos in tow, grinning mischievously at me. I winked at her, motioned for her to beetle back to the table. "But he signed this bone fide form that..." I started to point out.

Ruth nodded. "Oh the hospitals gave relatives—read husbands—forms to sign all right. A transparent attempt to cover their ass. Nonetheless, *ipso facto*, no law authorizing it means that people were treated without consent."

"And Ruthie, treatment without consent, how is that viewed?" asked Rose.

"Just follow me here. *Legally*, it constitutes assault."

Thrilled, Rose and I broke into a broad grin. Then we took one look at Gerald; and instantly, we knew. "Dare I ask? Again a five-year statute of limitations?" I queried.

Gerald nods, and the room goes quiet. Now Rose and I are demonstrably disappointed. To our surprise, however, Ruth states that both an assault and a negligence charge just could fly.

At this, she plops her feet onto the ottoman, and a familiar glint enters her eye—that glint we had all seen in the court room. "You see," she resumes, "the clock doesn't start ticking when the offence happens. It starts ticking when you first learn of it."

"But we've known of the electroshock all along," I point out.

"Exactly what I was telling myself, but here's the thing: You didn't know that there was negligence until a couple of months ago, right? And you didn't know that there was an assault until when?"

I ostentatiously glance at my watch. "Oh I'd say forty seconds ago max.... Clever," I observe, looking up again. "So how come you called it a long shot?"

"Pragmatics. We win and it would open up a floodgate of suits, and what judge would want to be responsible for that? Still, if we land the right one—Pearlson, say—you never know. So, Mom, you game?"

Strange. Even while savouring the moment, I was not kidding myself. I knew that Ruth wouldn't have cautioned me for nothing—ergo, our chances of prevailing were slim at best.

"So what's with the hesitation?" a familiar voice unexpectedly intervenes. "You were never one to shy away from a struggle." I look over. Mom is hovering in the doorway, obviously been there for some time. She hobbles into the room, explains that she's been deputized to bring us back to the seder, and that we'd better return soon—but then again, what do men know from timing? Then she kisses her granddaughter and launches into a vivid account of what she calls my "legendary resistance efforts in childhood."

"You serious? She actually spat on the counter?" Ruth asks, a bemused look on her face.

"Ruthie," I affirm, "what you've done here, it's wonderful, and long shot or not, if you're up for it, I'm up for it."

At this, there are congratulations all around. Now ostensibly Ruth has accomplished her mission, but something in her eyes suggests that she is reluctant to call it a night. Nonetheless, she gets up, whispers she'll let us get back to our service. Ergo, it is now or never.

"You guys have come all this way," I point out. "Sure you won't join us?"

Gerald immediately accepts, but Ruthie shakes her head. "Nothing personal," she shoots back, "but I'm no fan of the Promised Land. More to the point, I'm hardly a Jew."

"But Ruth," states Rose, "it..."

I wince, sensing the mistake.

"Jesus H. Christ!" Ruth blurts out, her voice somehow getting away from her. "Spare me the God damn Pesach spiel. I just came to pass on the information. Last thing I need or want is..."

You can hear gasps coming from the dining room.

Mom watches keenly. And her forehead furls. I recall the stories about Earl and exchange looks with Rose, terrified that history is about to repeat itself.

"Mom, honestly, she didn't mean..." Rose and I both hasten to point out.

"Sure! Sure!" exclaims Mom, throwing her hands on her hips and looking Ruth straight in the eye. "The only way you could pass on this information was by hopping on a plane and crashing a seder. And I'm the queen of Sheba! Look, your talking too loud, I could care less about, and by all means, identify how you wish, but obviously, young lady, whether you're a Jew, a Christian, a Moslem, a Rastafarian, an atheist, or a duck, you wanted to be at this seder, yeh? And we want you. So shut up, and get your *tokhes* in there.... Gerald," she says, suddenly focusing in on him.

Charmed despite himself—and in truth, he hadn't a chance— Gerald rises, tips his hat.

"Rude of us to ignore you. What's a seder without guests, yeh? And what better guest than you? What? Think I don't know what a friend you've been to this family?" At which, she hooks her arm under his, and the two of them step into the dining room.

Now we none of us expected this—and obviously, we had just been disabused of any illusion that the mantle of authority had passed to the next generation—be that as it may, clearly, the die was cast. Sensing that there was no more to be said, and yet wanting to show her support, Rose walked over to Ruth, planted a kiss on her cheek. And without further ado, she rejoined the seder.

Alone at last, Ruth and I looked at one another and smiled. She had just been finessed, and we both knew it. Now exactly how much she had or hadn't consciously intended, I wouldn't presume to know. Nor was I about to ask. Nonetheless, here we were again—mother and child—the Pesach dinner before us, our kin at our side.

"You honestly don't hafta," I said, smiling at my daughter. "In fact, if you don't wanna, you don't have to do any of it. Enough that you've laid the groundwork."

"About the seder, I'm not sure," she answered. "As for the rest, I am in. But Mom, I need to be clear. I haven't stopped resenting you. I suspect I never will. Oh, I know it's not right. It doesn't even make sense at this point, but I've tried, and I can't change it."

"I can live with that if you can. Lemme tell you something, though. I too struggle with ambivalence—not about you, though I can imagine it seeming that way—about what I feel, what I want more generally. Part of the legacy of shock, yes? So I've had to come up with other ways of knowing. You know what I see when I think of what you've done these last weeks?"

Ruth raised her eyebrow. "Someone who's flip-flopped all over the place, I wager."

"Someone who spoke out at the exhibit, someone who's been doing a ton of research, someone who's here after all these years and has yet to march out that door. And Ruth," I added, "it's up to you—and we'll love you regardless—but we all of us hope you don't."

Whereupon, Ruth and I caught each other's eye, not like mother and daughter exactly—more like one adult with another.

"So Ruthie?" I asked, getting up myself.

"You know, I really was trying to keep my voice down. Incidentally, was Grandma always so shy about expressing her opinion?" she quipped, a sheepish grin on her face.

"You thinking of rejoining this family? Count on it!"

Ruthie hesitated for a moment, then nodded. And so it is that after a twenty-three year boycott, once again my daughter graced the seder table at the Inkster Boulevard house. Not perfect, I agree. No long-term security here. But hey, and as every parent worth their salt knows, you take what you can get.

Whatever that seder was for Ruth—and no question, it was a stretch—the unabated torture that she appeared to fear, it was not. While she was uneasy, as the evening drew on and long forgotten memories surfaced, progressively, she entered into the spirit of the holiday. Dipping for each of the plagues. Eating the sandwich of *charoseth* and bitter herbs. Mostly though, she enjoyed the songs. And like everyone else, she pounded the table when we came to the *Chad Gadya*.

As I sat there feasting my eyes on her, the terrible fate of Catherine and *her* daughter came to mind. To think that could have been us! And in that fleeting instant, as this brilliant young attorney lifted her voice with her kin, a most harrowing truth dawned on me—from the very beginning, the two of us had dodged a bullet. I glanced over at Gerald, moved by his part in our story. Then I looked back at my daughter, took a deep breath. Oh yes, we had something to be thankful for. Even if my God could never be her God, even if my people could never fully be her people. Even if where I dwelt, there she could not tarry.

"Good that we devote so much of the seder to song, yeh?" announced Mom suddenly, smiling at Ruth. "Baby, you know what living to my age teaches you? In life, you sing or you cry, but better you should sing."

At first we stuck to traditional Pesach songs, but soon a broad array of ditties swept over the room, expanding our vision, lifting our hearts. "There once was a Union Maid," belted out Gerald. "Give us bread but give us roses," squeaked Mom.

Now what inspired Rose to choose this one, she never did tell us, but at one point she looked at me and said, "Hey, sis, bet you remember this one." And from her lips issued my old Peretz School anthem.

"You remember my anthem!" I exclaimed. "Why I haven't..." I stopped in mid-sentence for a most curious expression had flashed across my daughter's face.

"You know, Aunty Rosey, I know that one," she observed, turning toward her. "An old song of my dad's."

Now four separate individuals—including the child with the missing tooth—immediately pointed out that the song was Yiddish, but the information did nothing but perplex Ruth.

"Ruthie, whenever did you hear your father sing it?" I finally asked.

She started to respond; then a cloud of confusion settled over her. "Actually, Mom when I think about," she acknowledged, "all I remember is resenting you for singing it because it was, well, Daddy's song."

I instinctively turned toward Gerald.

"Nomi," he said, "not sure this'll help, but I do recall something." He proceeded to state that initially, I sang that song to Ruthie nightly and with her inconsolable after I was hospitalized, there was always the possibility that Earl had tried singing it.

Ruth and I looked at each other, a kinder, gentler sorrow in our hearts. Clearly, there would be no end to the job of untangling the threads in which we had become hopelessly entwined. And who knows if we would ever arrive at a place where we were even remotely comfortable with each other? Possibly not. But at least we had begun doing what we could. And we were doing it together.

At Mom's instigation, the singing started up again, though somewhere in the middle of the second song Rose motioned to Sam. Then the two of them slipped away, and for several minutes you could hear whispering from the kitchen.

"Niece," said Sam, upon returning, "think we could prevail on you to come to the second seder?"

"No offence, but pass," Ruth retorted.

"Being a reasonable uncle and a perfect gentleman, I'll spare you the God damn Pesach spiel," he tossed off grinning, "but how about if your mom leads it? Don't quote me on this, but rumour has it your mom over there could mastermind a seder that would knock your socks off."

Ruth hesitates, then turns toward me—not eager exactly, but interested.

"Sam," I exclaim, "generous of you, but for tomorrow, how about just assigning me a few of the rituals? With my brain as it is, it takes me forever to figure out anything new."

Rose shakes her head. "Overruled," she declares. "Nomi, don't worry. We'll help. Won't we, everyone? Come on, let's hear it from the peanut gallery."

Touched by the largesse, and not wanting to disappoint my daughter, I agree. And then it is that I glance down at Mom's *Haggadah*. It is open at the *ma nish'tana*—the question with which the telling begins. Realizing what that had to mean—that for the last four hours Mom has not been keeping up—I feel a tug at my heart, for there's no denying it, she really is getting old, as I fear, we all of us must. Then I find myself drawing the *Haggadah* closer and staring at the words: *What makes this night different from all other nights?* So what *is* the message of those slaves of old? What *really* makes the exodus different than the vast stretches of time before and after? I flip to an earlier page in the *Haggadah*. Oh yes, I murmur. And the different strands of my life start coming together.

"A practical matter," I state, looking up again. "Do we have another table, maybe one we can extend into the living room?"

"I'm pretty sure there's one in the garage," answers Sam. "So what's up?"

"I've some shelters and drop-ins to visit. Also, some people to invite."

"How come?"

"Sam, at the beginning of the seder, there's a crucial invitation," I pointed out, "and if I'm conducting the service, I need to honour it, is all."

Even as I am teasing out this thought, a light goes on in my grandnephew Avram's eye.

"*I* know. *I* know," he yells, bobbing up and down. "*Let all who are hungry come and eat*...Um, that's right, isn't it?"

"Sure is, Avram. Now year after year, we repeat these words, yes? But we don't heed them. As I read it, the liberation is not just for us. Everyone is to be fed, everyone included, but especially people trod under by the system."

Suddenly, a far-away look comes over Mom, then a hint of a smile. "*Oy!* Good thing your *meshugener* father's not here, 'cause know what he'd do? Open the windows, proclaim that the sparrows are hungry, invite those little *pishers* to join us too."

"That a yes?" I ask.

"Why not?" she answers. "Just no sparrows."

At the thought of sparrows hopping all over the dining room table, the younger children instantly begin to giggle.

"Can we let in the birdies? Can we?" asks seven-year old Josh.

"I wanna sing *Chad Gadya* again, I wanna sing *Chad Gadya* again," chimes in little Ella, already beginning to thump on the table.

"But the seder's over, *bubeleh*," Rose explains, "and I really don't think your poor tired old grandpa wants to…"

Sam looks at his granddaughter, winks. "*D'abin aba bi'trei zuzei*," he begins to sing, a glint in his eye.

And for a moment, however brief—and how we all wish such moments would linger—the unique tribulations of modern day families receded, and back in the world of the *Haggadah* we found ourselves.

Pesach '08 vanished in the blink of an eye, and it was soon replaced by other moments—some good, some bad. Within thirty-six hours, Ruth and Gerald were on a flight back to Toronto, no clear sense on anyone's part whether she was considering returning next year. We had not even dipped into the sleepy month of May when a young woman known to several of us was sexually assaulted near Powers and Sutherland. And since then, we have been visited by another flood—1997 excepted—the worst in over a century, wreaking havoc as far north as the Pas and sending hundreds of distraught Manitobans fleeing their homes. Lest I forget, to the relief of an appreciative city, during that onslaught, a standup homeless man saved a local teenager from drowning. Oh don't get me wrong. On a personal level, something had shifted, and I'm grateful for that. Life goes on, however, and life is never straight forward.

Strange. As I look back on that seder, indeed, as I look back on most any of the cherished moments in my life, something of a paradox strikes me. We cannot live for these moments, can we? It is by an act of grace that they visit us at all. Without them, however, like delicate fruit in the scorch of a brutal summer, we would surely wither and die.

Now a long long time ago, when I was a little imp no older than Ella herself, one sunny afternoon my old chum Mrs. Fenster and I were sitting side-by-side on the rickety stairs leading up to her house. She was barefoot as usual, her toes wiggling unapologetically, her whole body glistening with perspiration. I had been *cvetching* about receiving no invite to my best friend's birthday. At first, Mrs. Fenster responded by plying me with cookies. Then she placed her hand on my shoulder, eyed me earnestly and said, "Let me tell you something, sweetie pie. As much as you laugh in life, that much will you cry, and as much as you cry, you will laugh."

Now I started to laugh, convinced that she had made a joke—the kind grownups make that no one except other grownups get. To my chagrin, however, she was not even cracking a smile. And so feeling utterly foolish, I started to tear.

"You see what I'm driving at, little one?" she persisted, her gaze riveting. "In life, you laugh and you cry."

It has taken me six long decades, but finally I know what she meant.

END OF BOOK THREE

NAOMI'S AFTERWORD

IT HAS BEEN A YEAR and a half since Pesach 2008. The case of Cohan vs. St-Patrick St. Andrew's has yet to hit the docket. Already, though, the alternative press is all over it. Just how many people were treated illegally? they demand to know. Even Rita has become involved. With help from CAPA, she has been using the coverage to mobilize Ontario psych survivors. Meanwhile, Rose and I are trying to spark an anti-shock campaign here in Manitoba. Now we are not kidding ourselves. We are well aware that the deck is stacked against us. And indeed, even with all our ammunition, at times, it is as if we had naught. Despite the excitement over my exhibits, the mainstream media has shown no interest in the legal issues. Nor has any media so much as once reported on what the ECT research actually proves. As for the psychiatric establishment, while we may yet get them by the short and curlies and force a reckoning—and do watch for us here—so far, it is business as usual. Whenever our spirits begin to flag, however, we think of that eighty-six-year-old woman who dragged herself to city hall, threw out the challenge, "After all our years of service, is that what we have to look forward to?" A sobering question when you consider that we will all grow old, yes? And a touchstone that keeps us on track.

The mission aside, the move has worked for my family and me. While I can no longer tune into Rose as once I did—something which occasionally has both of us tearing our hair—just like in early childhood, once again the two of us find ourselves cleaving to each other. Now after almost a lifetime of me needing more space, you'd think that we would run into trouble being in the same city nonstop, and maybe we yet will. So far, though, we have both just been drawn closer. Strange. It is as if something deep within were yearning to come full circle. *Nu?* It would seem that the two of us are again those joined-at-the-hip four-year olds, except this time, I am the more vulnerable twin, Rose the twin rushing to her sibling's defense.

Now I arrived back home none too soon from the vantage point of Mom, for within weeks, she began to decline speedily. It is as if she'd been holding on until she was confident that her family was ready. What with diabetes and heart irregularities, she is frequently in hospital at this point and at best, has another year. Trouper that she is, she still reaches for life, though, butts into her great grandchildren's affairs at every conceivable opportunity, announces on a regular basis, "Think I'm gonna kick off? Do yourself a favour. Don't hold your breath."

As for the rest of our motley crew, Gerald has been researching the role of cross-dressing in poor people's movements. Ruth recently received a City of Toronto award for advancing the cause of youth in care. Earl has begun drafting an article called "Psychiatrists and Humpback Whales: A Comparative Study." Like he's really going to get that one published! Well, maybe in the journal *Retired Teachers Losing Their Marbles Quarterly*. And after a decade of monogamy, Rose has taken up with an old flame.

"At your age!" exclaimed Mom all but *plotzing* upon learning of it. "So what's next? *Shtupping* the Eiffel Tower?"

Now I wish that I could report that Ruth and I have become fast friends. As the two of us acknowledged to one another just last week, however, a deep chasm separates us, and while we can narrow it, as we surely have, make it disappear, we cannot. Still, there are moments that we live for, like when we catch each other's eye and know that we are mother and daughter despite everything. How far this fragile relationship of ours will progress only time will tell, but this much is clear—we are not letting go of the struggle for one another—not now, not ever. Nor will either of us hold our peace should ever another family member come within a country mile of a psychiatrist.

A final development worthy of mention is this writing project, and for this too, I can thank Ruth. You see, in June of last year yet again Ruthie was seized with doubt about that day. Could I have attacked her after all? Could I? Sensing that the time was ripe, Gerald handed her that letter. When next Ruth phoned, she said, "Okay, so you have an idiot for a daughter, but Mom, write. Write about everything. Do it for whoever—yourself, me, others at risk of shock. Just do it." And so it is that yet again, I began rifling through those binders, poking about in the corners of my mind. And little by little, this memoir materialized.

Now they say that a human being is a story in progress—one that gains its full shape and meaning only after the entire course is run. What a shame that autobiography cannot be written post mortem, eh? Hey, don't get me wrong. Not that I'm in any rush.

They also say that the moment of integrity comes in a human life when you can cast your eye with a type of satisfaction over everything that you have been, when you can smile inwardly, knowing that that ineffable thing called "you" makes sense, that your life has unfolded precisely as it had to. Now here truly is the curse of electroshock, for much as I want to, I can neither achieve such an overview nor affirm wholeheartedly that which I do know. The unvarnished truth is, I am a person profoundly interrupted and nothing about that is settling. And I urge you not to minimize that for capable though I am, I am also fumbling about in the dark—an infant wondering what has happened to the light. The shock machines are still whirring, moreover, and the boys in white are still lying. And so "attention must be paid." Bottom line: You cannot rob people of memory—of where they have been and who they are—and think that they can transcend what's been made of them. We are our brain cells; we are our past. Erase that, and as surely as night follows day, you erase us. Hardly a comforting storyline, I realize, but the business of living, including the covenant between us, it leaves no room for fairytales.

This, however, I can say. The older I get, the more I catch glimpses of something that at least strikes me as uniquely me in both my personal triumphs and—truth to tell—my personal failures. And while what befell me in the relentless years will never be something that I can take in my stride, I have taken up the battles placed at my door, claimed them as my own. Yes. And even in the bleakest stretches of my journey, I have met remarkable souls who have lit up the path of courage, unveiled the goodness of the human heart, made me reach for our hidden tomorrows. Oh and moments there are too deep for tears when I know that I am a child of the universe still.

You who have been reading this memoir, who have done me the kindness of accompanying me on this oft fraught journey, I leave you with one of those moments. We have come a long way, you and me, through the seemingly endless St. Pukes' corridors, through the quicksand of my mind. Accept this as a token of my gratitude. And know that the door on the white stucco house on Inkster Boulevard is open, and you are always welcome—most welcome—at our table.

What a buzz was at the seder table! If this night was different from all other nights, this seder was different from all other seders. I, a woman, was at the head. An orange—a Jewish feminist symbol—had found its way onto the seder plate. And interspersed with family sat a vast array of adults new to our midst—four of them Jewish, one a white Christian, one an older Aboriginal man in vest and jeans. Three homeless youth were to my left. And straddling the child's and the adult's table sat fourteen-year-old Reeva—a gutsy gum-chewing sex worker whom I had come across squatting on a sidewalk grate mere hours ago. When asked about Pesach, she'd said, "Don't think I'm a Yid exactly, but hell, someone in the family must've bin somethin' cause my old lady used to light these candles every Friday; and ma'am, long as I don't hafta fellatio some weirdo, like I could use a meal, a place to crash." Her breasts threatening to pop out of her perilously low-cut top, Reeva was still chewing gum, blowing the odd bubble. Not kosher for Pesach, but would God really mind?

Now I had just arrived at that critical part of the service where, according to *our Haggadah* anyway, the leader says, "as Jews, let us celebrate the seder." "As Jews," I began, intending something more inclusive and confident in my design. Suddenly, without warning, like a thief in the night, that moment of stillness steals upon me. I struggle against it, but there is no way in God's creation to stop it. When I fade back in, I find myself in a universe which has shifted—as if the world and everything in it has surreptitiously reconstituted itself in my absence—subtly, decisively. A chair not quite where it was previously. A spoon pointing in the wrong direction. Eyes that are looking at me curiously. All telltale signs of a centre which has slipped away from itself—like when waking from a coma to discover a terrible truth. Why now of all times?, I protest. Then I notice something—the seder plate is still in my hand; and to all appearances, the people are still here.

I lean back, take in the gathering, and before long, a calm settles over me. Somehow, together, it occurs to me, we can pull it off. Not always, of course, but tonight.

"As Jews," I resume, "as Aboriginals," I add, "as trans warriors ... as ... as..."

"As children," Avram unexpectedly volunteers.

I smile at him gratefully. "As children," I repeat. "Anyone else?"

There is a moment of uncertainty. Then a look of fierce determination ripples from one corner of the room to the other. And that's when it happens: One by one, kin and stranger alike begin offering up some aspect of their identity, each declaration a gift in its own right.

"As women," Ruth affirms.

"As disability activists," states the Aboriginal man.

"As queers," asserts Lisa, glancing shyly at Rose.

"As hoes," Reeva announces, "and like, if any of youz feminists have a problem with that, you can suck my dick. I mean can mind your own beeswax," she self-corrects. Then she blows a giant bubble and lets it pop.

"As the most *meshugah* Pesach-goers that ever was," pipes up Mom, beaming.

A pregnant pause follows. Then the shyest of our home-less guests, Lev begins tapping his fingers on the table, while angling his face up just high enough to catch my eye. After several seconds, his chin begins to quiver, his eyes well up with tears. Without uttering a word, one of his buddies rises from the table and stands next to him. Again Lev drums his fingers. Then little by little, his head begins to lift.

"B-b-beggin' your pardon, N-N-Naomi, as ... um, regular stiffs with brudders and sistas like everyone else," he states, to the surprise of all.

I nod warmly. Demonstrably pleased with himself, Lev nods back. Then Lev's buddy lifts Lev's hand up high as if designating a winner, while the entire table cheers.

"You know," I acknowledge moments later, "I can't rattle off everything by myself. So people, where are we?"

With great exuberance and the odd humorous stumble, Ger-ald proceeds to call out all the identities in the correct order, together the whole lot of us punctuating each designation with a thump on the table.

"As regular stiffs with brothers and sisters like everyone else," Gerald ends, grinning and gesturing toward me.

"As psychiatric survivors," I continue, my voice rising into the climax, "as people un-housed, as fellow travellers on this our shared planet—let us celebrate the seder."

That evening, each of us basking in the humanity of our fellows, from relative to honoured guest, we did indeed celebrate. We philosophized, we sang, we joked until our throats grew hoarse from laughter and stars seemed to drop from the sky. In the process, nothing happened of the magnitude of the Red Sea parting. We were blessed with our own private miracle, nonetheless—one that many of us remember from childhood, one that visited me *in extremis,* one that I pray that I be allowed to partake in for the remainder of these my declining years—we touched one another's hearts.

As we cut our paths in this difficult and oft treacherous world, may we all of us continue to find ways to be with one another. Life, it is a lonely venture otherwise. It may even be that fellowship along the way is the whole point of the journey, whether the fellows in question be loved ones, the stranger at our gate, or all our relations. Strip away the trappings of civilization, and what, after all, are any of us but weary travellers whose reward at the end of the day is the sight of a friendly campfire, the smell of coffee brewing? There's the mystery of it—the beauty and the sadness too. Whatever our lot in life, deep down, we need one another's warmth, breathing, stories. And we depend on the generosity of strangers for refuge from the storm. Moreover, as the passing of Jack reminds me, we are here but a short while, yes?

And the rest is silence.

END OF NAOMI'S MEMOIR

GLOSSARY OF YIDDISH AND HEBREW TERMS

aroisgevofeneh gelt	money thrown out the window
bimah	reader's stand at the synagogue
babushka	head kerchief
balebosteh	good homemaker
broiges	to be angry with
boytshik	boy
bubeleh	sweetie, term of endearment
bupkes	nothing
Chad Gadya	the last song sung at Passover
chametz	leaven/food not allowed during Passover
charoseth	a symbolic food that sits on the seder plate
chaverim	friends
chutzpah	nerve/over-entitlement
cvetch	complain
daven	form of praying involving standing and swaying
dreidel	tiny top
epes	something/nothing
farstunkener	scoundrel/a good-for-nothing
feh	term conveying disgust
gevalt	woe is me/warding off evil eye expression
Gotenyu!	Oh my God!

Goyim	non-Jews
gut yontif	happy holidays
haggadah	text read at Passover service
havdalah	a ceremony marking the end of Sabbath
heimish	homelike
iz gut	it's good
kibitz	joke around
kinderlekh	darling children
kinechora	expression used to ward off evil eye
kishkes	intestines area/gut
klutz	awkward or stupid person
linker	leftist with connotation of Communist
mahzor	prayer book
ma nish'tana	question asked at Passover, also indicates rarity
marsh	march
mechayeh	wonderful thing
mentsch	literally "man": connotation: terrific person
meshuga/meshugas/ meshugener	crazy/craziness/crazy person
meshugener hunt	mad dog
mitzvah	blessing, wonderful thing
Mogen Dovid	Star of David
mohel	figure who performs circumcisions
momser	bastard
Moshiah	messiah
nash	eat
niggun	song
nu?	now?/well?/so?
nudnik	nuisance, idiot

Pesach	Passover
pish/pisher	pee/one who pees (someone young)
plotz	faint
Rosh Hashanah	day one of the high holidays (Jewish New Year)
schlemiel	jerk
schlep	carry/drag oneself/haul
schmata	clothing
schmooze	talk
schmuck/shmuck	pejorative term for someone
schtup	have sexual intercourse with/ screw
seder	the Passover dinner/service
sha	quieten down
shikseh	impolite term for a woman who is not Jewish
shofar	ram's horn
shtick	routine/ piece/ point
tallis	prayer shawl
tashlich	New Year's ceremony involving water
tokhes	rear end
tsoures	troubles
vey iz mir	literally "woe is me"
yarhzeit	anniversary of death/candles celebrating it
Yom Kippur	Day of Attonement
yontif	holiday
zeyde	grandfather

ACKNOWLEDGEMENTS

This novel is a work of fiction, with Naomi herself fictional. As I wanted the primary experience—the electroshock experience—understood from the inside, I chose to narrate primarily in the first person, with the first person narrator herself a shock survivor. To put myself in the head of a survivor who has been profoundly damaged, to struggle along with her as she strives to narrate a story, much of which she cannot remember, to accept the inevitable dead ends, was at once exciting, frustrating, and humbling. Both what strengths and what weaknesses this novel has, I suspect, largely stem from that initial gambit.

There is no such animal as St. Pukes. While for reasons of verisimilitude, I located it in a geographic area identified with both survivors and the institution of psychiatry, geography aside, any resemblance to any *particular* psychiatric institution in real life is coincidental. This notwithstanding, I have attempted to keep faith with larger truths, especially with respect to psychiatry in general and electroshock in particular—areas, I would add, which are part of my expertise as a scholar.

I owe an enormous debt to the many people and organizations that have helped make this novel possible: Inanna Publications; my editor Luciana Ricciutelli; my ever helpful readers Margôt Smith and Sandra Carpenter-Davis; Ontario Institute for Studies in Education for granting me study leave; finally, and most importantly, the veritable army of electroshock survivors who have tutored me over the years (Sam Grower,

Wendy Funk, Sue Clark-Wittenburg, Carla McKague, Mel Starkman, Shirley Johnson, Dorothy Kent, Sheila Gilhooly, Hugh Tapping, Leonard Roy Frank; and most particularly, Connie Neil, whose ongoing testimony throughout the 1980s and 1990s ripped the blinkers from my eyes). Thank you also fellow shock researcher Don Weitz. You are the giants who paved the way.

For consulting on trans life, especially trans life in Toronto in the 1970s, I thank transactivists Rupert Raj and Hershel Russell. For alerting me to a possible anomaly in early mental health law, thank-you, Carla McKague. For information on the treatment of broken jaws in the 1970s, I thank the knowledgeable dentists at the Bloor Dental Clinic.

The statistics and the research on ECT quoted in the novel are accurate. The full Sackeim reference is: Harold Sackeim, Joan Prudic, Rice Fuller *et al.* (2007). The cognitive effects of electroconvulsive therapy in community settings, *Neuropsychopharmacology*, 32, 244-254. The full reference for the Ross article is: Colin Ross (2006). The sham electroshock literature, *Ethical Human Psychology and Psychiatry*, 8, 17-28. The relevant Peter Breggin references are *Toxic psychiatry* (1991); *Brain-disabling treatments in psychiatry* (1997); and Electroshock: Scientific, ethical, and political issues, *International Journal of Risk and Safety in Medicine*, 1998, 11, 5-40.

The activist group CAPA is not fictional, though the CAPA characters and the scenes involving them are. Ontario Coalition to Stop Electroshock, similarly, was a real group. By the same token, *Phoenix Rising* is a real magazine, published in the 1980s, and it included the electroshock testimony attributed to it. And while the 2008 hearing is fictional, aspects of real stories and echoes of real testimony are woven in and out. Correspondingly, albeit poetic license comes into play in the italicized historical scenes in book three, they are firmly anchored in fact—hydrotherapy was standard practice in psychiatry and psychiatrists were pivotal to the murder of the "mental patients" in Nazi Germany. Real life establishments which figure in the novel include: the Ponderosa, Kelekis, Country Style, little Egypt, Peretz School, the Winnipeg Film Society, Toronto City Hall, and the Brown Derby—the last, a trans-friendly pub in the 1970s. An effort was made to depict both Toronto's Kensington Market and the legendary north-end Winnipeg as they existed in the historical periods covered. In 1974 and 2009, the Red River did indeed flood, and the details on these floods and on earlier ones are accurate, although the Citizen's Review Committee is fictional.

While like all of the characters in the novel, Ruth is fictional, the well-kept secret that she unearthed is true. Until 1977, there indeed was no Ontario statute allowing people deemed incompetent to be treated. Nonetheless, many people who would have been considered incompetent were given electroshock in the years and decades prior. Ruth is likewise correct about the five-year statue of limitations. Whether or not the artful maneuver by which Ruth hopes to circumvent the statute of limitations would work in a real courtroom, I leave for real lawyers to consider. The fact remains, however, that a real medico-legal void existed in this province, with people—overwhelmingly women—administered ECT anyway.

For reasons of aesthetic balance, I abbreviated the length of time that it would typically take for a shock survivor to get back on their feet. For reasons of clarity—an ongoing struggle in a work of this sort—I made Naomi more functional in the first few Toronto chapters than would have been likely. Correspondingly, despite her daily struggle, Naomi ended up with a considerably broader life than is typical. The intent was to illuminate by a central story that is hardly one of the worst and to let the range of complementary stories shed that extra light.

A final word, as Naomi had been a budding Blake scholar, a number of the quotations in this novel are from William Blake; and like other quotations in this novel, they constitute fair use/fair dealing. The *Phoenix Rising* quotation is from

Phoenix Rising, April 1984, p. 20A. The Peretz school anthem of which we hear a few words, is indeed what was sung in Peretz school at that time. Naomi also quotes from a famous twentieth century play but does not credit it because she does not recall the source. To credit it now, when she states in quotation marks, "Attention must be paid," she is quoting from Arthur Miller's *Death of a Salesman*. The rhyme recited by Rose is called "Vintery Mintery Cutery Corn." It is an old nursery rhyme which is part of oral tradition, though only the last lines are popularly known, no doubt as a result of their use by Ken Kesey in *One Flew Over the Cuckoo's Nest* or the 1975 film based on it. And the line with which the novel ends is from Shakespeare.

Photo: Marko Kovacevic

Bonnie Burstow is a professor at the University of Toronto; she is a prolific author, an activist, and one of the world's leading antipsychiatry theorists. Published books include: *Psychiatry and the Business of Madness*; *Radical Feminist Therapy*; and the novel *The House on Lippincott*. She lives and works in Toronto.